About the Authors

USA TODAY be  penned more than She's married to active girls, and found on Twitter, julesbennett.com three outlets with each release and loves to hear from readers!

In a testosterone filled home (a husband, five boys between ages fourteen and eighteen, and one squeaky boy guinea pig), it's hard to imagine not going insane. The trick is to escape. So in her charming Southern world filled with politics, football, and after school snacks, **Carolyn Hector** utilizes her knack for spinning every plausible situation into a romance story. Find out what she is up to on Twitter @WriteOnCarolyn or find her on Facebook.

Bella Bucannon lives in a quiet northern suburb of Adelaide with her soul-mate husband, who loves and supports her in any endeavour. She enjoys walking, dining out and travelling. Bus tours or cruising with days at sea to relax, plot and write are top of her list. Apart from romance, she also writes very short stories and poems for a local writing group. Bella believes joining RWA and SARA early in her writing journey was a major factor in her achievements.

Irresistible Bachelors

Irresistible Bachelors:
The Ultimate Temptation

JULES BENNETT

CAROLYN HECTOR

BELLA BUCANNON

MILLS & BOON

First Published in Great Britain 2022
by Mills & Boon, an imprint of HarperCollins*Publishers* Ltd,
1 London Bridge Street, London, SE1 9GF

www.harpercollins.co.uk

HarperCollins*Publishers*
1st Floor, Watermarque Building,
Ringsend Road, Dublin 4, Ireland

IRRESISTIBLE BACHELORS: THE ULTIMATE TEMPTATION ©
2022 Harlequin Books S.A.

Snowbound with a Billionaire © 2014 Jules Bennett
Tempting the Beauty Queen © 2018 Carolyn Hall
Unlocking the Millionaire's Heart © 2018 Harriet Nichola Jarvis

ISBN: 978-0-263-30409-1

MIX
Paper from
responsible sources
FSC® C007454

This book is produced from independently certified FSC™ paper
to ensure responsible forest management.

For more information visit: www.harpercollins.co.uk/green

Printed and Bound in Spain using 100% Renewable electricity at
CPI Black Print, Barcelona

SNOWBOUND WITH A BILLIONAIRE

JULES BENNETT

This book is for Allison, who is so much more than my niece – you're my friend, my sounding board and my kids' role model. Every day you continue to inspire me. Even through all of life's obstacles, you rise above and I'm blessed to have you in my life.

One

Max Ford maneuvered his rental car carefully through the slushy streets. Granted this old, dirty snow lining the thoroughfares was nothing new to Lenox, Massachusetts, for the month of February, but it was quite a jump from the palm-draped avenues he was used to back in L.A.

He hadn't been back to Lenox in years and hadn't driven in snow in even longer, but, as he eased off the gas, he realized he'd missed doing this. Shooting a scene for a movie in the snow wasn't the same as spending time off enjoying the pristine white surroundings. Besides, usually when he would shoot a winter locale, it was with man-made snow and not the God-given kind.

Since Max had grown up here, Lenox would always hold a special place in his heart. The population may be small, but the bank accounts of the residents were anything but. The sprawling estates had stood for decades; some were main residences, others second homes.

The two narrow lanes wound through town, and, just as Max rounded the last turn, he spotted a car off the side of the road, its back end sticking up out of a ditch. The flashers were on, and the back door opened. The afternoon sun shone through the car windows, revealing a woman—

bundled up with a stocking cap over her head and a scarf wrapped around her neck and mouth—stepping out.

Instinct told him to slam on his brakes, but he was born and raised on the East Coast and knew better.

Carefully easing his car off the road just ahead of the wreck, Max left the engine running as he stepped out into the frigid temperatures. Damn, that biting cold was something he hadn't missed.

Since he'd come straight from L.A., he didn't exactly have the proper shoes to be trudging in the snow, but there was no way he would leave a woman stranded on the side of the road. Granted he was only a mile from his destination and could've called someone, but that wasn't the type of man he was raised to be.

"Ma'am," he called as he drew closer. "Are you all right?"

He wondered if she'd hear him over the howling wind, but when she froze at his voice, he assumed she'd realized she wasn't alone.

The woman in a long, puffy gray coat turned. All Max could see was her eyes, but he'd know them anywhere. Those bright emerald-green eyes could pierce a man's heart...and once upon a time, they had penetrated his.

"Raine?"

Her eyes widened as she reached up with a gloved hand to shove her scarf down below her chin. "Max, what are you doing here?"

It was too damn cold to be having a discussion about anything other than her current predicament, so he asked again, "Are you all right?"

She glanced over her shoulder, then back at him. "I'm fine, but the car is stuck."

"I can give you a lift," he offered. "Where are you going?"

"Um...I can call a friend."

Max nearly laughed. Were they really going to argue about this? It was freezing, he hadn't seen her in…too many years to count, and he really wanted to get to his mother, who was recovering from surgery.

"Seriously, just get in the car and I can take you anywhere," he said. "Grab your stuff and let's go."

Raine hesitated, holding his gaze as if she were contemplating waiting in the snow for another ride instead of coming with him. Granted they hadn't left things on the best of terms…. No, they had actually left their relationship on very good, very intimate terms. It was after he'd left that something had happened. And he had no clue what that something was because the last time he'd seen her, they'd been in love with plans for a future together.

Still to this day, thinking back on that time in his life left his heart aching.

But now was *not* the time to consider such things. Raine needed to get in, because who knows how long she'd been out here in the freezing cold, and she needed to call a wrecker.

"All right," she conceded. "I have to get a few things first."

She turned into the backseat and seconds later she faced him again, this time with a…baby carrier?

Whoa! He totally wasn't expecting her to have a baby in tow. Not that he'd planned on running into her like this at all, but still…

"Can you hold this?" she asked. "I need to get the base out and strap it into your car."

Base? He had no clue what a *base* was considering the only thing he knew about babies is that he used to be one. Max reached for the handle of the carrier and was surprised how heavy this contraption was. He didn't see the baby for the large blanket-looking thing with a zipper going up the middle. He supposed that was smart, seeing as how the wind was wicked cold right now, and keeping the baby as warm as possible was the best idea.

In all honesty, the idea of Raine with a baby was what really threw him. She was probably married, because a woman like Raine wouldn't settle for a child without having the husband first. And that thought right there kicked him in the gut. Even after all this time, the mental image of her with another man seemed incomprehensible. He had to chalk it up to the fact he'd had no closure on their relationship, because he refused to admit, after years of living apart, that he still had feelings for this emerald-eyed beauty.

She lifted some gray plastic bucket thing from the backseat and started toward his car. He assumed that was his cue to follow.

Max held the handle with both hands since there was no way in hell he'd take a chance dropping what he assumed to be a sleeping baby. Not a peep was made from beneath the zipper. Surely the child was okay after that accident. Her car was barely off the road but enough that the front end was kissing the snow-covered ditch.

Once Raine had the base in, Max carefully handed over the carrier. With a quick click, she had the baby in the warm car and had closed the door.

"I have to get the diaper bag and this gift I was delivering," she stated. "Go ahead and get in…I'll be right back."

"I'll get your bag." He stepped in front of her as she tried to pass him. "It's too cold and you've been out here longer than me. Is everything in the front seat?"

She nodded and looked so damn cute with snowflakes dangling on her lashes, her face void of makeup…just like he'd remembered.

Not waiting for her to protest, Max turned back to her car, cursing the entire way. Cute? He was now thinking she was cute? What was he…five? So they shared a past. A very intimate, very intense past, but in his defense, he hadn't seen her in nearly fifteen years. Of course old feelings were going to crop up, but that didn't mean they had to control his state of mind—or his common sense.

He jerked on her car door's handle and reached in, grabbing the pink diaper bag and a small floral gift bag. Who the hell delivered a gift when the roads were quickly becoming a sheet of ice? With a baby to boot?

Max slid back behind the wheel of his rental, cranked the heat as high as it would go and eased back out onto the road.

"Where am I taking you?" he asked.

"Um...I was on my way to see your mother."

Max jerked in his seat. "My mother?"

Raine barely looked his way before she focused her eyes back on the road, a place he should keep his.

"I swear I had no idea you were coming in today," she quickly told him. "I mean, I knew you were coming, but I didn't know exactly when that would be. If you'd rather I not go...I can come another time."

She was going to see his mother? Things certainly had changed since the last time he'd been in Lenox with Raine and his parents. The way he and Raine had fought to be together, defying both sets of their parents...and it all was for naught.

He cast a quick glance her way, noticed how she kept toying with the threads fraying off the hem of her coat, her eyes either staying in her lap or staring out the window. Why was she so nervous? Was it him? Was she mentally replaying every moment they'd spent together, just like he was? Was she remembering that last night they'd made love, and the promises they'd made to each other? Promises that he had fully intended to keep, not knowing she'd never hold up her end of the deal. Is that what had her so on edge?

"Why are you visiting my mother?"

Raine's soft laugh filled the car. "A lot has changed since you were in Lenox, Max."

Apparently…and since she had pointedly dodged his question, he assumed that was code for "none of your business." And she was right. Whatever she was doing *was* none of his concern. Once upon a time they knew every single detail about one another, but that chapter had closed. They were all but strangers at this point. Could this last mile be any longer? Thank God the drive was in sight.

"I didn't know you had a baby," he said, trying to ease the thick tension, but once the words were out, he realized he sounded like an idiot. "I mean, I assumed you had a life. I just never… So, how many kids do you have?"

"Just Abby. She's three months old."

"Do you need to call your husband?"

Way to go. Smooth, real smooth. Could I be any less subtle?

"No," Raine replied. "I'll call my friend when we get to your mother's house. He can come pick me up."

He? She was calling a male friend and not her husband.

Max mentally shook his head and scolded himself. Still this was none of his business.

He turned into the long, narrow drive. Straight ahead sat his childhood home, now his parents' second home, where his mother was waiting inside recovering from surgery. She would soon begin radiation treatments in town. Thankfully the doctors discovered the lump very early, and chemo wasn't needed.

Max had no clue how she'd look, but he knew he needed to be strong, and being thrown off by seeing Raine couldn't hinder his plans. His mother had to take top priority right now…. God knows his dad wouldn't man up in this situation.

The sprawling two-story colonial-style home always dominated the flat acreage surrounded by tall evergreens. Max loved growing up here and had been fortunate to have been adopted by Thomas and Elise Ford. He never knew his biological parents, and, even though he'd rarely seen eye to eye with his father, he knew there were much worse scenarios he could've entered into as an orphaned baby.

Max pulled in front of the house and killed the engine. "Why don't I take your diaper bag and gift?" he offered. "I'm not comfortable with that carrier…unless you can't maneuver it in the snow."

Raine glanced over at him and laughed. "I've been doing just fine for a few months now, Max. Longer than that before Abby came along."

She got out and closed the door. Her quick jab wasn't lost on him, but he had no idea why she was bitter. She was the one who'd dissed him when he'd gone to L.A. Destroyed any hope of sharing his life with her. And in his rage, after realizing she didn't want him, he had nearly got himself killed.

When he stepped from the vehicle, he noticed she was getting the carrier out, and also had the gift tote and her diaper bag dangling from her arm. Apparently this Raine was a bit more independent and stubborn than the old Raine. Who was he to argue?

He followed her up the steps, careful to stay close in case she slipped. By the time they reached the wide porch, they were stomping the snow off their feet. Max moved forward and opened the door for her, gesturing her in ahead of him.

If she was going to insist on carrying everything even though he'd offered, the least he could do is get the door and be somewhat gentlemanly.

The grand foyer looked exactly the same as when he had left home at eighteen. There was never a need for him to return to this home, because, as soon as he'd left for L.A., his parents had hightailed it to Boston.

His father had always loved the Boston area and thought it would make good business sense to branch out his pubs by starting a second in a larger city. Now his father had a chain of restaurants, and Max still wanted no part of the family business.

The wide, curvaceous staircase dominated the expansive entryway, allowing visitors to see all the way up to the second-floor balcony that ran the width of the entryway. A vast chandelier suspended down from the ceiling of the second floor, the lights casting a kaleidoscope of colors onto the pale marble flooring.

Raine was just unzipping the blanket mechanism covering the carrier when his mother came into the foyer. Max didn't know what to expect when they finally came face-to-face after her major, life-altering surgery, but relief quickly settled in when Elise Ford rushed forward and launched her petite little frame into his arms.

"Max," she said, looking up at him with beautiful blue eyes. "I'm so glad you're here. I hate to pull you away from your work, though."

He was careful how he returned her embrace, knowing the left side of her body was tender from surgery.

"I would drop anything for you, Mom. Besides, I don't start another movie for a couple of months, so I'm all yours." He smiled down at her, soaking in the fact that his mother had been diagnosed with breast cancer, but, had not only fought it, she'd beaten the odds and won. "I can't believe how great you look."

She laughed, swatting his chest. "What were you expecting? I'm sore, and I definitely have my moments where I'm feeling run-down and tired, but today is a good day. Not only is my son home, he brought a beautiful girl and a baby with him."

Max turned to see Raine directly behind him, cradling a swaddled, sleeping baby. While his eyes were drawn to Raine, his curiosity made him look down at the child, wondering what life his ex was leading now. Apparently she'd gotten all she'd wanted out of life: husband, baby, probably that farm of her grandmother's she'd always loved.

"Oh…" Elise moved past Max and sighed. "Look how precious she is. Nothing sweeter than a sleeping baby."

How were babies always instant magnets for women? What exactly was the draw? Baby powder? Slobber? What?

As Max watched the maternal love that settled into Raine's eyes, the softness of her features, the tender smile, he couldn't help but be jealous of this baby.

Perhaps that thread of jealousy stemmed from his lack of being that loved at such a young age…but he didn't think so. Max knew his jealousy had sparked because he once had that same unconditional love from Raine…until she'd broken his heart. So why was he upset? Had he seriously not learned his lesson the first time he got entangled with this woman?

"May I hold her?" his mother asked.

"Are you sure you're up to it?" Raine replied. "I don't want you to hurt yourself."

Elegant as always, his mother waved a hand through the air and smiled. "I'm perfectly fine to hold a little baby. My surgery was two weeks ago. Take your coat off and stay a while, anyway. It's too cold to be out on a day like this."

Raine handed over the baby and made work of removing her coat. Max should've done the same, but he was too busy watching Raine shed her scarf and gloves. When she pulled the crocheted purple hat off her head, she ran a hand over her auburn curls, as if she could tame them. He missed seeing that hair. He remembered running his fingers through it and feeling its silky softness. Truth was, he didn't know he'd longed for such minute things about her at all until just now.

"I need to call my friend to come get me," Raine told his mother. "My car is in a ditch about a mile away."

Elise gasped. "Oh, honey. Are you all right?"

Raine nodded. "I'm fine. Abby's fine. Just scared me, but I was getting ready to call someone when Max pulled up."

His mother turned to him. "Good timing."

Wasn't it just? Fate hated him. He was positive of that. Otherwise he wouldn't be here in his childhood home, with his high school sweetheart and his mother, who had not exactly fought to keep them apart but had expressed her opinion that their teenage relationship wasn't the best move.

Max didn't know what had happened between these two women over the years, but apparently his mother and Raine had made some sort of truce. Hell, he really had no clue what was going on. Even in the times he'd visited his parents in Boston, his mother hadn't mentioned Raine after his first few visits.

Max pulled off his coat, hung it by the door then crossed to Raine. The last thing he wanted to do was get close enough to smell her sweet floral scent or, God forbid, touch her. But, being the gentleman his mother had raised him to be, Max reached for her bag and helped her out of her ratty coat.

"Oh, thanks," she said, not quite meeting his eyes. "If you'll excuse me, I'll make that call."

Raine slipped to the other room, pulling her cell from her pocket. Max turned to his mother who was making some silly faces and equally goofy noises for the baby.

"What on earth is going on?" he asked in a strained whisper.

Elise glanced over and smiled. "I'm holding a baby and visiting with my son."

"You know what I mean, Mom. Why is Raine so welcomed here now, and why are you holding her baby like she's your very own grandchild or something?"

Okay, poor, poor choice of words there, but he was damn confused.

"Raine called me and asked if she could drop something

off," his mother explained. "Of course, I knew she had had a baby, and I've visited with Raine several times over the years when your father and I would come back to Lenox. Trust me when I say, Raine isn't the girl she used to be."

But he liked the girl she used to be. Liked her so much he'd intended on marrying her, making a life with her.

"So you and she are what? Chummy now?"

Raine stepped back into the room and reached for the baby. "Thanks for holding her."

"Oh, it's not hardship holding something so precious," his mother said. "Did you get in touch with your friend, dear?"

"He wasn't home."

Max rested his hands on his hips. Fate absolutely hated him. He'd been home ten minutes, and already he felt as if he was being pushed back into his past, forced to face feelings he simply wasn't ready for.

And before he could think better of it, he opened his mouth. "I can run you home if you want to call a tow truck to pull your car out."

Raine's eyes locked onto his. "Oh, that's okay. I'll call someone else. First I want to give Elise a gift."

"A gift?" his mother asked, clasping her hands together. "Oh, if it's some of that honey lavender lotion, I'm going to just kiss you."

What the hell was happening here? At one time his mother and Raine were at opposite ends of the spectrum, and he was being pulled in both directions. Now he had just entered a whole new world where the two women were clearly the best of friends.

"I knew that scent was your favorite," Raine said, holding up the floral gift bag in one hand and securing the baby against her shoulder with the other. "And I thought you deserved to be pampered."

His mother took the bag, shifted the bright pink tissue

paper and peeked inside. "Oh, the big bottles. Thank you so much, Raine. Let me just go get my purse."

"Oh, no," Raine said, shaking her head. "These are on me. I had planned on bringing you some food as well, but Abby was up all night fussing, and I didn't get to make anything today, because we napped."

Max couldn't take all this in. The baby, the odd bond his mother and his ex seemed to have, and the fact they were totally comfortable ignoring him. He'd been in Hollywood for years, the industry and media swarming him everywhere he went. Yet, here in his childhood home, he was suddenly an outsider.

"Oh, darling," Elise said with a smile. "Don't push yourself. I know you're busy. And now that Max is here, he's more than capable in the kitchen. Besides, I believe my home-care nurse prepared some meals for me before she left."

Max was thankful his mother had hired a nurse and that she'd been able to stay until he could arrive. Apparently his father was once again a no-show in the family when he was needed most.

"Raine," he chimed in. "I'll take you home when you're ready."

Her eyes drifted back to him, and she sighed. "Fine. I need to get Abby home anyway and feed her. I hadn't planned on staying gone long, and I walked out the door with the diaper bag but left the bottle on the counter. And the roads are getting worse."

"Darling," his mother said, placing her hand on Raine's arm. "Please don't feel like you have to do anything for me. Max and I will get along just fine. Visit all you like and bring this precious baby but don't bother with anything else."

Raine's smile was soft, almost innocent as her green

eyes twinkled. "Elise, you're one of my best customers. I'm happy to help."

"You take care of this baby and your other customers first," his mother chided. "I'm seriously feeling good. My radiation treatments start in two weeks, and Max can do whatever I need."

The old Raine would've done anything for anyone. She'd always put others first. Max was glad to see she was just as selfless, just as caring. And it warmed him even more to know that, after everything Max's parents had done to keep him and Raine apart, she could put all that aside and forge a special relationship with his mother.

Raine hugged Elise and strapped the baby back in the carrier. Once they were all bundled up again, he carefully escorted her to the car. He kept a hand hovering near her arm, careful not to touch, but it was there in case she slipped.

The baby started to fuss a little as Raine locked the seat into place, but she unzipped the cover and replaced the pacifier. Instant silence. How did she know exactly what to do? The whole concept of consoling a baby was totally lost on him. Thankfully his social scene the past decade hadn't revolved around children. Some people were natural nurturers, like his mother and Raine. Others, like his father, were not. And even though they weren't biologically related, Max had somehow inherited the not-so-caring trait.

As he pulled out of the drive, he glanced over at Raine. All that gorgeous red hair tumbled from her hat and down her back.

"Where do you live?" he asked, assuming she'd moved out of her parents' home.

"My grandmother's farm."

Max smiled. Raine's grandmother was a woman like no other, and it didn't surprise him that Raine had moved into the historic farmhouse. More than likely she had it overrun with goats, chickens, horses and a giant garden. That had always been her dream.

They used to laugh about it, because Raine had always tried to figure out how she could get all of that in L.A. But she'd assured him that she was willing to try, because she loved him more than this old farmhouse.

Perhaps that was what held her back, kept her distanced from him when he left, and compelled her to ignore his phone calls and letters.

Max passed the spot where her car was still stuck in the ditch. "You going to call a tow truck before it gets dark?"

"I'll call when I get home," she told him.

"Do you want to talk about this?"

She glanced his way. "*This* meaning what? Because if you're referring to the past, then no. If you're referring to the freezing temps, sure."

A muscle worked in his cheek. "Always running from uncomfortable topics," he muttered.

"Running?" she asked, her voice rising. "I've never run from anything in my life. I'd choose better words next time. Or is it too hard when someone hasn't written them for you?"

Max sighed, turning onto her street. The car slid a bit on the icy patch, but he eased the wheel in the opposite direction and righted the vehicle.

Raine was in a mood. Welcome to the club because, now that the initial shock of seeing her again had passed, he could feel all those old memories stirring up inside of him.

"I don't want this to be uncomfortable for either of us," Max said. "It's apparent that you and my mother are…closer than you used to be. But I'll be here for a few months, and so you and I are going to see each other."

Raine turned and faced the front again, her hands twisting in her lap. "The past is dead to me, Max. I have different priorities now, and I don't have the time—or the inclination—to dredge up old memories of that teenage lust we shared."

Ouch. Lust? He'd been head over heels for her, but, with her declaration, there was no way in hell he'd admit that now. She had made her feelings about that time very clear, and he wouldn't beat that dead horse.

Max turned onto her drive and barely suppressed a gasp. The old white sprawling two-story home had definitely seen better days. The stained roof needed to be replaced, paint had chipped off several of the window trims, the porch that stretched the length of the home was a bit saggy on one end, and, from the looks of things, no one had shoveled the snow off the walk.

"Just pull around to the back," she said.

Keeping his mouth shut about the obvious needs of her home, Max eased the car around to the side where a very small path had been cleared from the garage to the back door. The red handle from the shovel stuck up out of the snow, where she'd obviously left it for future use.

"Thanks for the ride."

As Raine jumped out, Max did, too. He opened the back door as she came around, and in seconds she'd unfastened the carrier. Max reached for it before she could grab the baby.

"Let me have her, and you can remove that base," Max told her.

Because it was cold and she knew way more about that contraption than he did, Max started toward the cleared path, watching his steps carefully because he wouldn't dare drop this baby.

Raine came up behind him with her keys and the base. He let her pass to unlock the door, but she blocked the entryway. After easing in, and setting down the base and her purse, she turned back to take the carrier.

"Thanks for the lift home."

Her eyes darted away from his, to the baby, to the snow swirling around them, anywhere but on him.

"Do I make you nervous?" he asked gruffly.

Now she did meet his gaze. "No. You make me remember, and that's worse."

He stepped closer, near enough to see those gold flecks in her bright eyes. "Is remembering so bad?"

"For me it is, maybe not for you." She shifted, holding the carrier between them as if to use the baby as a shield. "I'm not the same person I used to be."

"You're still just as beautiful."

Raine rolled her eyes. "Surely you don't think during the brief time you're home that you can just pick up where you left off?"

"Not at all." But damn if some of those old feelings weren't right there at the surface. "We're both different people, Raine, but you're still stunning. Is it wrong of me to say so?"

"It's wrong of you to be watching my mouth when I talk," she said.

Max grinned. "Just doing a little remembering of my own."

Raine gasped, and Max couldn't suppress his laughter.

"I'll let you get inside," he said. "It's too cold to be out here with that baby."

Just as she started to turn, he called her name.

"What?" she asked on a sigh.

"See you tomorrow."

He walked back to his car without waiting on her to sputter a response or narrow her eyes at him. There wasn't a doubt in his mind she wanted to be left alone, but he just couldn't. Raine had an underlying vulnerability, and like a fool, he couldn't ignore the fact they shared a past and he wanted to know what happened after he left.

Even after all these years apart, all the blockbuster films, all the starlets on his arm and all the lavish parties, Max never felt so at ease, so…comfortable as he did with Raine. He honestly had no clue their past could come back at warp speed and take control over his emotions.

These next few months may be spent caring for his mother, but he sure as hell was going to have an interesting time with the beautifully sexy Raine Monroe.

Two

Raine all but sank against the door. Her heart was so far up in her throat she thought she was going to be sick.

The irony was not lost on her that, when Max had left years ago, she'd been so ready to be his wife and the mother to his children; yet, when he returned, she actually had a child.

But too many years had passed between. A lifetime, really. She'd lived through hell and was still clawing her way out. Her bank account was laughable, and her father was trying to play matchmaker with one of his minions.

Added to that, there was some sort of holdup with Abby's adoption. Raine never could get a straight answer from her lawyer, who was equally frustrated at the untimely manner of the judge. Everything should've been finalized by now.

Other than all of that, her life was great.

Or it was until Max Ford had found her at a humiliating time when she'd wrecked her car thanks to a patch of black ice.

Raine shivered against the memories and the chill that had followed her inside. The Weather Channel update was calling for more snow, and this was just the start of several days. They hadn't officially called it a blizzard, but they were talking in feet and not inches.

She'd have to go check on her chickens and her goats before it got too bad. Worry gnawed away at her, despite the fact that they were each in their own barn, and they had all the necessities an animal could need to endure rough elements. They even had a small built-in hatch to come outside, if they so chose. She loved owning such disciplined, albeit sometimes overly friendly, animals.

At least if she was snowbound, she could finish working on the new lotions for the Farmer's Market next month. Raine was so excited that spring was right around the corner. Each day brought her closer to her favorite time of year, when she could sell all her goods at the market, meet new customers and chat with old ones.

Her finances always dipped in the winter, and she had to really watch her budget. Spring and summer were much more prosperous. Hopefully by next winter her online store would be even more popular, and she would feel more comfortable with her bank account.

Raine had gotten such great starts of cherry tomatoes, lettuce, kale, a variety of peppers and a few types of beans. Indoor winter gardening was quite different, but she had no choice except to take the extra effort to make these plants thrive inside. This was her livelihood and all that was between her and begging her parents for that money they'd taken away when she had refused to live by their haughty standards.

The vegetables were almost ready for the market next month, so all she needed to concentrate on now was making her soaps and lotions to prepare nice, cheerful gift baskets.

But first she had to get Abby sleeping through the night.

Mercy sakes, she had a whole new level of respect for single parents. This all-important job was most definitely not for wimps. But she wouldn't have it any other way. She loved this baby, and her heart had ached nearly a year ago when her cousin, Jill, had come to her and said she was considering an abortion.

Raine couldn't let Jill feel trapped into a decision she wasn't ready to make, especially since Raine had once been in Jill's shoes. Living as a teen with parents who had higher expectations had certainly taken its toll. Of course, their circumstances weren't exactly the same. Jill was in college and just not ready for a baby, whereas Raine had been fresh out of high school and had just had her whole world torn apart. When Raine had discovered her pregnancy, Max had just recently left, and she'd felt so alone. Her parents had been less than supportive, so there was no way Raine would let Jill go through this without a friend and family member to lean on.

When Raine had mentioned adoption, Jill warmed to the idea. And when Raine had offered to be the one to take guardianship, Jill had wept with relief and delight that her baby could live in a loving home.

The scenario seemed so simple looking back now, but for months there were tears and prayers, moments of panic and indecision, hours of contemplation and ultimately pure happiness. After the birth, Jill had returned to school and settled back into her life. She kept in touch with Raine, but said she'd keep her distance for a while so Raine and Abby could bond.

Raine knew absolutely nothing would replace the baby she'd lost years ago. But she loved Abby with every fiber of her being. There was nothing Raine wouldn't do for Abby, no sacrifice she wouldn't make.

Which meant she would do whatever it took to ensure that the little girl's future was secure. But that was easier said than done, since Abby's adoption was still in limbo. All the legal paperwork had been put into place long before Jill ever delivered, so what could possibly be amiss here?

Frustration threatened to consume Raine, but she focused on the here and now. The adoption would go through…eventually. She wouldn't allow any other outcome.

Raine bent down, unzipped the cover over the carrier and unfastened Abby from her seat. Her sweet little bundle was still napping. Raine had always heard the advice "Nap when your baby is napping," but she'd never get anything done if that's how she lived her life.

And who could nap now? Max Ford, Hollywood icon and most eligible bachelor, was back in town. He couldn't get out of Lenox fast enough when he'd turned eighteen, and the tire tracks were still smokin' after he'd landed his first role. Everything had fallen into place with his life-long goals.

She recalled hearing that he'd been in a severe motorcycle accident not long after he'd gone to L.A., and at that moment, Raine had ached to be by his side. But she quickly realized that, if he'd truly wanted her with him, he'd have sent for her as promised.

And if she'd thought hell was when he had left and didn't contact her, it was the entire year after that which had scarred her for life.

Bitterness threatened to bubble up. He'd gotten all he'd ever wanted—without so much as a wave goodbye. But when she looked to the sleeping baby in her arms, how could she be upset that her life had turned out to be less than what she'd expected?

If she'd gone to L.A. when he did, she wouldn't be here now…and being there for Jill and raising Abby as her own was the most important task of her life.

Kissing Abby on the forehead, Raine walked through the old house and headed upstairs. Once she laid the baby down, she could call the tow truck. Hopefully her car was drivable when it was on all four tires again, because if there was any damage, there was no way she could pay for it.

But even if there was damage under the hood, she'd think of something. She'd been doing a lot of praying since Abby had come into her life. Every decision made wasn't just for Raine anymore. Life may have been easier before, but it sure had been empty. Now she was filled with such a sense of joy and purpose, and it was due in large part to this precious little girl. As she lay Abby down in her crib, she made sure to place a very thin blanket over her legs to keep her warm. Raine tiptoed out of the room and went into her bedroom to call a tow truck.

But all she got was the receptionist who indicated all the drivers were out on calls from all over the county, and they'd put her on the list. Which was fine with her. She wasn't going anywhere tonight anyway, and her car was off the road, so unless another driver went off the road and slammed into it, all was well.

Raine put on a kettle of water to boil. She may be the only person left living under the age of sixty who still used a tea kettle and boiled water the old-fashioned way. She knew she was old-fashioned in pretty much everything, which was probably why she had no man in her life. But in all honesty, Raine didn't mind being labeled as "weird" or "hippie" or her absolute favorite, "tree hugger."

So she liked to use her own herbs, grow her own veggies, and make organic lotions, soaps and other feminine products. Did that really make her stand out so much? All this processed stuff was killing people, and she wanted better for her life, her baby.

Which was just one more area where her parents thought Raine was being difficult. They simply didn't understand Raine's need to grow organic and make a little more effort in being healthy.

Her parents were more concerned about driving the

flashiest cars, keeping up country-club appearances and being on the right board of commissioners at said country clubs.

Maybe men were just thrown off by Abby. Some men weren't all that comfortable around children.

Like Max Ford. She hadn't missed those wide, terrified eyes when he'd first caught a glimpse of the carrier. Oh, he'd been the perfect gentleman and had helped her, but she knew men like him, who, at the first sight of spit up or a smelly diaper, would turn tail and run.

Not that Max needed any reason to run. He'd had a life planned with her; yet he still had found something more appealing, and instead of facing her, he had avoided her.

The man was used to winning awards, filming epic movies and smiling that knee-weakening grin for the cameras.

The tea kettle's shrill whistle cut through her thoughts. Why did he have to come back here? Why did she have to run into him right after she had driven her car into a ditch? And why on earth was she allowing past emotions—and unsettled feelings—to ruin her evening? Lord knows she had other things that she needed to focus on.

Just as she grabbed her favorite flavor of tea from the crock on the counter, her cell rang. Raine pulled the phone from her pocket and resisted the urge to groan…as she did each time she saw the number pop up on her screen.

"Good evening, Mother."

"Loraine, I'm calling to let you know the luncheon I had planned for tomorrow has been postponed."

Raine didn't sigh, didn't roll her eyes—okay, in her head she did—but she refrained from physically doing so, because she knew the gesture would come through in her tone.

She found her favorite mug for drinking tea. A tacky one with a hot, hunky man draped around it. When filled with hot liquid, his clothes disappeared. Who needed a traditional tea cup and saucer?

And if her mother forced her hand at this ridiculous luncheon, the mug might make an appearance.

"Mother, I hadn't planned on coming, remember?"

"Oh, darling, of course you'll be here. I mean, really. When are you going to stop being so stubborn?"

Raine opened the small cabinet above her stove and pulled out the bottle of whiskey she kept on hand for emergencies. And talking with her mother was most definitely an emergency.

"Let's not go through this again, Mother," she pleaded as she poured a dab of liquor into her hot tea. "We've agreed to disagree. You don't like my social life. I don't like yours."

"You don't have a social life, Raine!" her mother exclaimed. "I don't understand why you won't get out a little more, get a job, go back to college for heaven's sake. Let someone else adopt that baby. It's not too late to back out."

Not even an option. No way was anyone else going to adopt Abby. Raine never dreamed the adoption process would take this long, but even if it took ten years, she wasn't letting go of this beloved child.

She'd already lost one baby and was blessed enough to have been given a second chance at motherhood. Abby was a precious bundle that tucked so perfectly into Raine's life.

"Mom, I have to go check on Abby."

"If you're so insistent on keeping her, the least you could do is let me see her," her mother said with a huff.

That was a worry Raine had wrestled with, and one that had kept her up many nights. Raine had always heard the saying "It took a village to raise a child," but she just wasn't sure she could allow her mother's influences to trickle down to Abby.

"You've seen her, Mom," Raine said defensively, then took a sip of her tea, welcoming the burn as it slid down her throat.

"Not enough. She needs to know her place in this family, Raine."

Setting the china cup down, Raine took a deep breath so she didn't explode. "Mother, she's three months old. Her place right now is as my child. Nothing more."

"I didn't call to argue. The luncheon has been rescheduled for next Saturday, and I expect you and Abigail to attend."

"Her name is Abby, Mother."

"Abigail is more dignified."

"But that's not her legal name, so if you refer to her again, call her by the name I chose for her."

Her mother sniffed into the phone. "I don't know where I went wrong with you," she cried. "I just want what's best."

"For whom, Mother? Best for me, or best for you and your social status?"

Silence settled in on the other end of the line and Raine knew she'd gone too far…again. This is how nearly all of their calls went, and in the end Raine always felt guilty and mentally drained.

"I'll talk to you later, Mother."

Raine hung up and rested her palms on the edge of the chipped countertop. Why did she let her mother get to her? For twenty-eight years the woman had tried to make her feel like an outcast, and the majority of that time she'd succeeded. The only person who'd ever really understood her had been her grandmother; but when she had passed eight years ago, Raine had been truly alone.

The wind picked up outside, rattling the old windows. She took her cup and headed to her favorite room of the house. The room where she felt at home, where she could be creative, and no one was there to stifle the process.

Her grandmother's old bedroom, where Raine mixed all her lotions and made her specialty soaps. This was the perfect place to work, since it was right next to the nursery, and she felt so much closer to her grandmother here. But as Raine pulled a few ingredients off the shelf, she thought of Max. At one time he'd consumed all of her thoughts, all of her heart and soul. And, damn him, he looked even better now than he had when she'd been totally in love with him.

Hollywood had put him on this pedestal, elevating him to superstar status in no time, and she'd been back home soaking it all in via media outlets talking up the hottest newbie on the scene.

And amid all that talk, flashing cameras and Max throwing that signature dimpled grin to the reporters, Raine had been back in Lenox, nursing a broken heart…and coming to grips with an unexpected pregnancy.

Max had never known he'd been a father. Had never known the grief, the anguish, she'd gone through in losing the baby. He'd been living the dream and loving life while she'd been burying the last bond of love they had.

But now Raine had a second chance, and she wasn't going to blow it just because Max was back in town. No matter how much her heart fluttered when she'd seen him, no matter how sexy and handsome he looked, no matter how heated his gaze was when he looked at her.

Raine had more important priorities now, like making sure this legal guardianship of her cousin's baby went through and keeping her grandmother's home from going into foreclosure. Since she wasn't exactly flush with cash, Raine had used the rest of her meager savings and had taken out a loan against the property in order to pay for the adoption.

However, none of that had felt like a sacrifice to her, because Jill had entrusted Raine with Abby…and Raine wasn't about to disappoint her. So there was no way in hell she'd go down without a fight…not after getting nearly everything she'd ever wanted. Where there was a will, there was a way, and Raine had more will than anything else.

* * *

Max helped his mother to her bedroom, which was now a guest room on the first floor. With her being a little lethargic at times, he'd made sure all of her things were on the first floor so she didn't have to climb steps.

Although she would say she was fine, he could see that she was tired and just being stubborn. He knew she'd be even more so when her radiation treatments started. So he'd let her keep her pride and just keep his mouth shut, but he would make her as comfortable as possible, which was why he'd made sure the nurse who had been here the past two days would stay on and come by for a few hours a day.

As he settled her into bed, he eased down to sit beside her.

"Care to tell me what Raine was doing here?" he asked.

His mother rested against her plush pillows. "She brought me a lovely gift bag."

Narrowing his eyes, Max gave her a skeptical look. "So she just stopped by, because she knew you'd had surgery, and now you two are all chummy?"

Elise laced her fingers together across her lap and smiled. "Actually, no. During the past several summers when I've been staying here, she's taken care of the landscaping, brought me fresh vegetables, fruits and eggs."

"Wait, back up." Max held up a hand, even more confused than he'd been seconds ago. "Raine does the landscaping?"

"During the summer months, she does a great deal of it. Just the flower beds, Max. You don't have to look so angry. We have another man do the grass cutting."

Raine worked for his mother? What the hell had happened to her dreams? To her trust fund? She shouldn't have to work odd landscaping jobs for his mother. The thought of those small, dainty hands marred with calluses bothered him.

Most of the shallow women he knew back in L.A. wouldn't dream of doing their own landscaping, let alone someone else's.

"Who else does she work for in the summer?"

Elise shrugged a delicate shoulder. "Several families around here. Not her own, of course. Her mother is mortified that Raine does so much manual labor."

"And what kind of manual labor does she do?" he asked.

"She's quite the gardener and farmer. She prides herself on growing her own organic plants to keep them as natural and healthy as possible. Her grandmother would be so pleased."

Max knew Raine had never felt a familial bond with anyone other than her cousin, Jill, and her grandmother. He'd seen firsthand how that elderly woman had catered to Raine, showed her all she would need to know about running a farm, raising animals and growing gardens. Raine's maternal grandmother was accepted in Lenox because she was sweet and elderly but when a twenty-something woman tries to follow in those footsteps…well, he assumed that bohemian lifestyle didn't go over so well in the posh, hoity-toity land of tea sippers and pearl wearers.

"I just saw her house," Max stated. "It needs quite a bit of work. I can't believe she'd let it get like that."

His mother shrugged. "None of my business. But if she doesn't take care of it, the Historical Society will come in and make her. That house is a landmark in Lenox, even with the barns. In fact those barns are kept up better than her house. That girl cares more about the animals and the people around her than she does her own comfort."

As much as Max wanted to know more about Raine, his mother looked tired as her eyelids were growing heavy. He would be here for a few months, so there was no doubt he'd find out all he wanted about Raine and her new life.

His life was always splashed all over the internet and

in the tabloids…or the life the media tended to fabricate. There was no doubt Raine knew more about his life over the years than he knew about hers. It wasn't like he'd find anything if he did a Google search on her name…at least nothing of use.

"Is there anything I can get you before I go?" he asked, turning his attention back to his mom.

His mother grabbed his hand and squeezed. "No, I'm just glad you're here."

"I wouldn't be anywhere else, Mom."

"Please, Max, don't make this about your father." Her eyes held his, a sad smile forming on her lips. "He's busy this time of year."

Max nodded, really not wanting to get into this argument again. "He's been busy his whole life, Mom. I'm not here to fight, but I also won't pretend that it's okay to put work before family, because it's not. I work across the country, and I'm here."

Her eyes misted. "All I've ever wanted is for the two of you to make peace. That's all."

Guilt weighed heavily on Max because he knew of his mother's wishes, but he and Thomas Ford would never get along, because they viewed life from opposite ends of the spectrum.

Max leaned forward, kissing his mother on the cheek. "Good night, Mom. See you in the morning."

He turned off the light on his way out of the room and pulled the door shut behind him. It was odd spending the night in his old home. The memories that filled these halls, these rooms, played through his mind like a movie. The glimpses he caught seemed like another lifetime, another person.

As he went back downstairs, he recalled the time he'd snuck Raine in after they'd first started dating. His parents had been out at some charity dinner and wouldn't be home for hours. He knew they wouldn't approve, and to be honest, that just made the clandestine encounter all the more appealing.

He'd never forget how it had felt kissing her in that dark foyer as soon as they'd stepped through the door. As he stood at the base of the steps now, he could still see that young couple, arms intertwined, lips locked. Max had waited weeks to get her alone to kiss her, and she'd been so worth the wait.

Max sighed, raking a hand over his face. Teenage love was so complicated at the time, but looking back, he realized that was the best experience of his life. He and Raine had had something special, something he'd convinced himself could stand the test of distance and time.

But no matter how many letters he had written, emails he had sent or calls he had made, she'd never acknowledged him after he left. And he refused to tell anyone how deeply her rejection had hurt. Then and now. Although years had passed since they'd last seen each other, they'd once been very much in love. So how could Raine be so cold and act like they'd shared nothing?

Max was still recovering from that heartache—and seeing her up close, knowing she had a baby, a life, only twisted that knife a little deeper into his already wounded heart.

Three

The snow wasn't letting up at all and neither was Abby. Raine had no clue how mothers had more than one child. And twins? Mercy, those women deserved a special place in heaven. She was having a hard enough time just focusing on this one kid, not to mention holding down a job, fixing dinners, showering, taking a bathroom break…

But Raine had always wanted to be a mother, and she would not trade a moment of the sleepless nights for anything. Especially since Jill had needed Raine, and there was no way Raine could turn her back on her cousin when she needed someone the most.

Being shut out of your family because of decisions you made was the common connection she and Jill shared. They'd always been close, but this baby truly secured that tight band around their love.

And regardless of genetics or DNA, Abby was 100 percent Raine's. From the moment the precious baby girl had tightened her chubby little hand around Raine's finger, she knew no greater bond could exist. Even those accidental gassy smiles were like another stamp on her heart, solidifying the fact that Raine couldn't love Abby any more even if Raine herself had given birth to Abby.

Hearing the growing cries, Raine shook the bottle on

her way back to the nursery. Early morning sunlight spilled through the window, and she picked up the fussy baby and prayed to God that, after this bottle, Abby would sleep for a couple hours. Because Raine truly didn't know how much longer she could go on little to no sleep.

Sweet dimpled hands came up to grip the sides of the bottle, and Raine sank into the cushy rocker in the corner of the room. Resting her head against the back of the cushion, she closed her eyes as Abby greedily sucked down the milk.

Thankfully they had nowhere to go today, seeing as how the snow kept coming down in big, thick flakes. And when she'd glanced out at the driveway, her car had been there. The tow service must've brought it after she'd gone to bed, and she had no doubt there would be a hefty bill on her credit card statement since she had to give them the account number when she had called.

From what she'd seen, only the headlight and the grille were damaged, but she hadn't waded through the snow to find out any more.

Raine opened her eyes and glanced down at Abby whose own eyes had drifted shut.

"Now you want to sleep," Raine said with a smile. "When I'm holding and feeding you, but when you're alone in your bed, you want to scream."

Raine knew the feeling of being alone, left out and neglected. But there was no way this baby would ever feel anything less than secure. Perhaps that's why Abby kept crying. She instinctively knew that Raine couldn't handle it and would hold her to calm her down. The truth was, Raine just hated the thought of the baby feeling scared or abandoned.

There was no worse feeling in the world.

"We have each other," she whispered to Abby. "And you'll always know what love is."

Finally when the bottle was depleted and Abby was

breathing peacefully, Raine swiped the milk from beneath Abby's soft, full lips and laid the baby back in the crib.

Raine slid the curtain from the hook and blocked out the bright sun. Tiptoeing as quietly as possible, Raine eased the door closed behind her.

Should she go finish making the rest of her lavender soaps, take a brief nap and then start in on filling the on-line orders, or throw a load of laundry in, and fold and put away the two baskets waiting on her?

Did the to-do list never end?

She'd just gone into her workroom when she glanced out the window and saw a full-sized black truck pull up her drive. In a mad dash, she ran down the stairs, because, if someone rang her doorbell, she'd not be greeting them with the most pleasant of smiles. She'd personally murder anyone who woke Abby from her long overdue nap.

Raine jerked open the door just as Marshall Wallace lifted his hand to the bell. She resisted the urge to ignore this unwanted visitor, not that she didn't like Marshall, but she knew why he was here, and she wasn't in the mood.

"Hey, Raine," the young, polished man said with a wide smile. "Your father wanted me to drive out here and check on you."

"Hi, Marshall." She curled her hands around the door. "As you can see, I'm fine. So go back and tell the mayor he did his civic duty."

God forbid her father trek out here in the elements to see how she and Abby were doing. The salt and snow would probably ruin his designer shoes.

And that was just another common thread she and Max had shared. Their fathers always put work ahead of family. Even though Max was one of the most recognized men in Hollywood, he'd dropped everything to be with his mother. Not that she needed a lot of care, but he was here for the love and support.

"Have you thought any more about my offer?" Marshall asked, shoving his hands into the pocket of his thick brown coat.

Raine sighed. Another reason why she always cringed when Marshall came to her house. The man was relentless in his quest to date her. He'd started pursuing her years ago after Max had left. He'd been so persistent and in her face, she'd let it slip that she was pregnant so he'd back off. Then she'd regretted her decision and had sworn him to secrecy.

She'd given into his advances once, though, and they'd gone out. The entire evening Raine felt like she was dating her brother…if she had had a brother, she figured that's what it would be like.

"Marshall, I'm just so busy right now with Abby, focusing on the adoption and working on my online orders. You wouldn't want to go out with me. You should look for someone with more time and freedom."

"I'd be more than happy to come here with dinner. We don't have to go out."

Oh, Lord. If he thought he'd come over, eat dinner and play house, he was sorely mistaken. Even she wasn't that desperate.

Raine dodged his less-than-subtle approach and returned his smile. "Tell my father I'm fine, and so is the baby, not that he ever asks about her. I appreciate you coming out, Marshall."

As she started to close the door, a big black boot stepped over the threshold and blocked her.

"I hope you'll at least consider my offer, Raine," he told her, easing his body just inside the door frame. "That time we went out, I felt a connection with you."

A connection? This was worse than she thought. Surely whatever he felt was just like…indigestion. There was no way that lame date sparked something romantic on his end.

Of course, he could just be horny, and that was a whole other matter she didn't want to get into with him.

"Marshall, I don't have time to date right now. I'm sure a busy man like you understands."

There, she'd appealed to his male ego and even stroked it a little. If he didn't back off, she'd just have to be blunt and tell him to get the hell off her property. But her mother *had* raised a lady, despite her mother's views to the contrary, so Raine would make every effort to be polite.

Marshall nodded. "I won't give up on us, Raine."

Before she could sputter a "There is no us," he'd turned and was heading back to his truck. Was this dude for real? She'd never once led him to believe there was hope. Even after their date when he'd gone to kiss her good-night, she'd done the swift head turn, and he'd caught her cheek.

Closing the door, Raine sagged against it and squeezed her eyes shut. Why did life hate her? Why, within the span of twenty-four hours, did she have to encounter the only man she'd ever loved and now was fighting off the one man who wouldn't take no for an answer? Apparently Cupid had struck Marshall, and now he was determined to make her his Valentine. No thank you.

Damn, Valentine's Day was two days away, and Marshall was probably looking for a date. That was a big hell no.

The only Valentine she wanted was asleep upstairs. Besides, Valentine's Day didn't mean much to her. She'd spent nearly all of them single, except when she had dated Max. He'd given her this little gold locket and had told her that she'd always have his heart.

She should've known an eighteen-year-old boy was only out for sex, but those pretty words had made her fall in love with him even more. And she'd die before she ever admitted she still had that locket. So what? She had kept quite a few things from high school. Just because that particular piece was in her jewelry box didn't mean anything.

God, she couldn't even lie to herself. She'd kept that locket because she'd wanted to hold on to that hope that one person truly loved her for her, for the quirky way she was.

But that love was not only naive, it was a fabrication.

The banging on the door jarred Raine's body, making her jump. Pressing a hand to her chest to try to control her rapid heartbeat, she turned back to the door. Marshall really didn't give up, did he?

She threw open the door, ready to be brutally honest with the man, but it wasn't Marshall standing before her. It was Max.

With the collar of his black coat up around his neck and his dark knit cap pulled low on his forehead, he looked mysterious...sultry even. And that sexy stubble along his jawline only made him look more ruggedly handsome. With those dark eyes staring back at her, Raine felt that gaze all through her body, infiltrating places she wished would stay dormant where this man was concerned.

"What are you doing here?" she asked, blocking him from seeing inside.

"Wanted to make sure you had your car back and to see if you needed anything. The roads are pretty bad, and they're calling for several inches per hour for the next day."

Raine didn't want her heart to melt at his worry. And she didn't know why the notion of Max checking up on her made her belly dance with nerves, when the visit from Marshall had simply annoyed her.

She didn't want the belly-dancing nerves. She wanted to stay angry with Max for the rest of her life, but seriously, she had to get over the teenage attitude. They now led different lives. It was over and way past time to move on.

"I'm good right now," she replied.

"How bad was the car?" he asked.

Raine peered out around him to assess the damage. "I haven't gone out to see up close, but it looks minimal. I'm sure I can still drive it."

"Not in this weather, you can't." He pointed to the four-wheel-drive truck he had. "I used the truck dad keeps in the garage, because there was no way my rental would've gotten me here."

Abby's screeching cry sounded through the house, and Raine resisted the urge to cry herself.

"I'm sorry," she said. "I need to get her."

She turned from the door and ran up the steps. Abby was clearly not happy, but the second her eyes landed on Raine, she calmed down.

"You really just want me here, don't you, sweet pea?" she cooed as she picked Abby up and laid her against her shoulder. "You need to learn to sleep without me coming in here all the time."

But how could Raine be upset? Even though she was in a zombielike state nearly every day, there was just no way she could be angry or even feel put out by this precious bundle.

"You're just tired yourself, aren't you?"

Reaching into the crib, Raine grabbed the yellow blanket and wrapped it around Abby. Maybe she would be entertained in her swing while Raine worked on the soaps. Perhaps Abby would fall asleep there and get some much needed rest.

As she turned from the crib, she froze when she saw Max standing in the doorway.

"I thought you left," she said, trying not to cringe over him being in her home. Her run-down home.

This man was used to Beverly Hills mansions, probably threw lavish patio parties where guests mingled over champagne and caviar. And here he was in her home, with its carpet tearing, linoleum peeling, ceilings chipping...the list went on and on.

"I wasn't done talking."

Raine snickered. "I wasn't under the impression we had anything more to discuss."

"Is she okay?" he asked, nodded toward Abby.

"She's fine. She doesn't like to be alone."

His eyes returned to hers. "Sounds like she takes after her mother."

Raine started to correct him, but technically Raine *was* Abby's mother. Just because she was adopted—or would hopefully be soon—didn't make the relationship any less real. And Max wasn't going to be sticking around anyway, so really anything she did or did not do was none of his business.

Shifting Abby to the other shoulder, Raine patted her bottom and swayed side to side. "What did you need to talk about that you braved this weather to come see me?"

He opened his mouth, but Abby started screaming right in Raine's ear, and Max straightened in the doorway. "What's wrong?"

Raine pulled Abby back and looked at her. Abby was rubbing her eyes, fussing and puckering that little lip. It was the pucker that always got her.

"She's just tired," Raine explained. "She fights sleep."

"Fights sleep?"

"Trust me. It sounds insane, but there's no other term for it."

Raine moved over to the rocker and started singing "You Are My Sunshine." Usually that song calmed Abby down. Raine had gone through the song twice before Abby relaxed against her. Max eased out into the hall, and Raine appreciated the privacy. It wasn't that she was uncomfortable with him here, but… Oh, who was she kidding? She was extremely uncomfortable. Here she was all frumpy in her fleece socks, paint-stained sweatpants and a hooded sweatshirt that read Meat Sucks in big, block letters.

Added to that, the house was a mess. She hadn't been able to really clean since Abby came, and the past week had been hell because there was no sleep happening in this house…for either of them.

And she wasn't even going to get into the repairs that needed to be done. Basically the house and everything and everyone in it needed an overhaul. Too bad none of that would be happening anytime soon.

"I need to rock her again," Raine hollered over the baby's cries, hoping Max would take the hint and let himself out.

He nodded. "I can wait in the living room. We need to talk."

Talk. One word. Four simple letters that sparked myriad emotions…fear being the number one contender.

What did he want to talk about? Okay, that was probably a stupid question, but did he really want to rehash the past, or did he have an ulterior motive?

Before she could question him, Max had turned and walked from the room. Raine attempted to shift her attention as she moved toward the rocker, swiping the pacifier off the changing table first. Maybe this would work. Raine wasn't a fan of the thing because she dreaded weaning Abby from it in the months to come, but something had to help this poor baby sleep, and if the pacifier worked, then, hey, Raine was all for it.

Abby instantly started sucking, her moist lids lowered over her eyes, and she sniffled a little, but for the most part calmed right down.

In no time she was asleep…again. Hopefully for a few hours this go-round. Raine couldn't keep coming into the nursery every time the baby cried, but she couldn't just stand outside the door and listen to it, either. Surely there was a happy medium.

Raine placed Abby back in the crib and eased out of the room. Now, if she could just get Max to leave, she'd be able to dodge this inevitably awkward chat. And not only would their talk be awkward, but her emotions were bound to make her more than uncomfortable. The man kept sparking things within her…she just couldn't let that flame rekindle.

When she passed the hall mirror, she caught a glimpse of herself and resisted the urge to straighten up the lopsided ponytail and all the tendrils that had spilled from it. Max had already seen her, and she wasn't out to impress him, anyway. It wasn't like she could even compare to the supermodels and A-list actresses that had clung to his arm through the years.

Besides that, she wasn't sorry for who she was. She was happy with her meager life, and she wouldn't feel ashamed simply because her high school sweetheart was in her living room.

At the top of the steps she straightened her shoulders and silently applauded herself for the mental pep talk. Now she had to face Max, figure out what he thought they needed to discuss and get him out of her house. Because she couldn't afford for those old feelings to come creeping back up again.

Four

Max glanced at the various photos spread across the mantel. Most were of Raine with her grandmother from years ago, but now newer ones had been placed in frames. Pictures of Raine with Abby, Abby sleeping, a black-and-white picture of Abby's hand holding onto what he presumed to be Raine's finger.

But he never saw a picture of the baby with a man…or Raine with a man for that matter. The fact she was alone with this baby shouldn't make him feel relieved, because in reality, that just made him a jerk, but he'd be lying if he didn't admit that he'd gotten a sick feeling in the pit of his stomach when he had thought of her creating a family with someone else.

When he'd decided to come home, he knew the chances of running into her were pretty good, and he'd dreaded the thought of seeing some lucky man standing at her side.

Max was supposed to be that man. Max had spent day after agonizing day trying to reach Raine once he'd hit L.A. He just couldn't figure out why she'd lied and said she'd be right behind him. Why not just cut ties before he left and spare him that misery?

But she'd strung him along, and her rejection had sent him into a downward spiral which eventually culminated in his near-fatal motorcycle accident. He'd cared for nothing, living recklessly and damning the world around him. But the wreck had really opened his eyes.

Max released a deep, slow breath. He had no idea what possessed him to drive out here today when the weather was so bad, but he'd seen her stranded in the snow, then socializing with his mother, as if there was no history between them, and couldn't get over the fact that so much had been left hanging between him and Raine. He knew they'd both moved on, but that didn't stop him from wanting closure.

He needed answers, and he wasn't leaving until he got them. Raine may have shut that chapter in her life, but he was about to reopen it.

As Raine descended the staircase, she held all the poise and glamour her mother had raised her to have, but he couldn't suppress a grin because of her bedhead, the verbiage on her T-shirt and the way she tried to be so regal when she looked like a hot mess.

But that's one of the things he'd always admired about her. She never cared what people thought of her image; her only worry was caring for others.

"You should go," she stated. "The weather isn't getting any better."

Max glanced over at one of the photos on the mantel. "I snapped this picture."

Her eyes drifted to the photo he was pointing to. A young Raine had her arms thrown around the neck of her grandmother, both women were laughing for the camera. Max could practically hear the laughter, and he was instantly transported back to that day.

"She always loved you," Raine murmured. "She thought for sure you were the one."

Max stared at the elderly woman in the photo and swallowed the lump in his throat. "Life happens. Plans change."

"What do you want from me, Max?" she asked softly.

Max turned his attention back to her and noted her defensive stance with her arms crossed over her chest, but he could also see how visibly tired she was. "I want closure."

"So bringing up the past will…what? Suddenly make things better?"

He shrugged. "Maybe I figured after all this time I deserved some answers."

Raine held his gaze a moment before she burst out laughing. "Did you come here to humiliate me?"

"What?"

She shook her head and moved farther into the room. "Max, we're living in two different worlds. Why on earth would you find it necessary to come all the way here just to discuss a period of our lives that really isn't relevant anymore?"

His cell vibrated in his pocket before he could utter a comeback. Not relevant? The absence of Raine in his life had nearly destroyed him. There wasn't a day that went by that he hadn't thought about her, wondered what she was doing. No way in hell was she not relevant in his life.

The number on his screen belonged to his mother, and a moment of panic set in when he answered. Sasha, the nurse, was there with her, so surely nothing was wrong.

"Honey," his mother began. "Have you left Raine's house yet?"

"No, why?"

From across the room, Raine studied him.

"Sasha just went out to get something from her car when a trooper pulled up, thinking she was leaving. We're under a level three advisory, and unless it's an emergency, no one's allowed on the roads."

Max shot his gaze to the wide window in the front of Raine's living room. "You're kidding?" he said, as he watched big fat flakes cling to the window.

"Afraid not."

"I can't leave you alone," he told her. "I'll head out right now and be there shortly."

"Don't risk getting fined or even hurt, Max. Sasha is here, we're safe and warm. There's nothing she can't provide for me. Besides, I'm fine. I'm tired, but nothing a nap can't fix."

Max knew all of this, but it was the fact he was going to be stuck here with Raine that was giving him fits. Trapped with Raine *and* a baby. What the hell, Fate?

"I know, but I came back home to help you, and I can't do that if I'm not there."

"I'm sure it will be fine later tonight or maybe tomorrow. We need it to stop snowing so the state workers can keep the roads clear."

He continued to watch the snow come down, showing no sign of letting up. The dark gray skies weren't looking too kind even though it was still early in the morning. Shouldn't the sun be out?

"I'll get back to you as soon as I can," he promised. "I'll call and check in, too."

Max hung up with his mother and eased the phone back into his pocket before turning back to Raine.

"Looks like I'm stuck here," he said.

Her eyes widened. "I'm sorry...*what?*"

"Seems the county is on a level three advisory, and no one is allowed out unless it's an emergency."

Raine jerked her attention to the window. Her shoulders slumped, and she released a heavy sigh. "Life sucks," she muttered.

Max shook his head. "I'm no happier about this than you are."

She focused her narrow gaze on him. "Don't even think of taking advantage of this situation."

"Excuse me?"

"The snowstorm, the stranded victim." She pointed a finger at him. "I hope you don't think we're going to bond or have some passionate reunion."

Max laughed. "You're still just as outspoken as you used to be."

Raine dropped her hand. "I'm nothing at all like I used to be," she groused. "That girl grew up when life smacked her in the face."

Max wanted to know more, wanted to know what had happened. God, did he ever want to know. Something made Raine hard now, and he hated that. He wanted to see that free spirit he'd fallen in love with, but at the same time, maybe it was better this way. Maybe having her hate him was for the best, because he certainly wasn't too thrilled with her, either.

"Go on with whatever it is you were doing," he said. "Pretend I'm not here."

"Not so eager to chat now?"

He shook his head. "Not when you're so upset. Besides, looks as if I'll be here for a while."

"No matter how long you're here, I won't want to discuss the past."

She turned on her heel and nearly stomped off. Max smirked. Now what the hell was he going to do? He had work he needed to do, but his laptop was back at his mother's house, and there was no way in hell he'd ask Raine for her computer.

He pulled out his phone and checked his emails. This movie deal he was working on could not be put on hold. He'd waited years to prove he was worthy of directing his own film, and, with the help of Bronson Dane, producer of every film worth any mention in Hollywood, Max knew this was the big break he'd been waiting for.

When Bronson had approached him with this project,

Max had nearly cried. Seriously, he'd never been so close to happy tears in his life.

And this snowstorm and being stranded with Raine for God knew how long would not put a damper on his work. He could communicate with his phone and her computer... if she let him use it. And when the snow cleared, he was getting the hell out of here.

Raine mixed a touch of aloe and a hint of jasmine, but her shaky hands tipped the bottle and made a mess over her scarred countertop. Resting her palms on the edge of the work space, she hung her head between her shoulders as the recent events took control of her emotions.

Why? Why did he have to come back just when she was really starting to turn her life around? The sales from her lotions and soaps were really promising, and next month the Farmer's Market would reopen, and she'd start pulling in even more money with the vegetables she'd been growing this winter. She already had several potted plants thriving in her meager indoor greenhouse, and it wouldn't be long before she was outside gardening again. Things were looking up.

And most important, she had Abby who had come into her life just before Christmas and she couldn't be more blessed.

So why did her ex-turned-Hollywood-hotshot have to show up at her house, looking like he'd just stepped off the ski slopes in Vail, and wreak havoc on her hormones?

Raine laughed. There, she'd admitted it to herself. She was as attracted to Max now as she had been years ago, but, just because he was still the sexiest man alive, it didn't mean she would act on her lustful feelings. She had no time, nor did she have the inclination, to travel down that path of heartache again.

Heavy footsteps sounded outside her door, and she froze.

When those steps moved into the room, she closed her eyes and willed him to go away.

"You okay?" he asked.

No, she wasn't okay, but the standard answer was "Fine," right?

She turned, leaned her butt against the edge of the counter and crossed her arms. "You need something?"

His eyes searched hers as if he was looking for answers only she could give. Yeah, she had nothing. No emotions, no feelings. Right now she felt as if she'd been wrung dry.

"I hate to bother you, but if I'm going to be stuck here, I need to get some work done. Do you have a laptop or computer I could use?"

He wanted to work? Great, that would keep him out of her hair for a while.

"I have a laptop in my bedroom," she said. "I'll go get it."

As she moved forward, he stepped in her path, stopping her with his wide, muscular body. His hands came up to gently grip her forearms.

Her eyes lifted to meet his, and that clench in her heart nearly brought her to her knees.

"Max," she whispered. "Don't make this any harder."

"I'm not doing anything," he said. "No matter what happened between us in the past, I can see you're wearing yourself thin. You look ready to fall over, Raine."

Yes, those were the words she wanted to hear. Nothing like a blow to the self-esteem to really perk up an already crappy day. She hesitated to tell him this was her everyday appearance, and he was just used to women who popped up in the morning with makeup in place and hair perfectly coiffed.

"I'm fine," she assured him. "I have a lot on my plate right now, and I hadn't anticipated being stuck with you. It's thrown me off a little."

"I'm not too thrilled about being stranded here, either.

My mother is recovering from major surgery, and I promised I'd help."

Raine pulled back the throttle on her own anger and self-pity. "I'm sorry about your mom, Max. The doctors got all the cancer out, and Elise told me after her radiation treatments, she'd be fine. But I'm sure you're still scared."

Max nodded, taking a step back and resting his hands on his hips. "When she first called me, I was in a meeting with a producer who was asking me to be part of his next film. He wants me for the director."

Raine listened about this other life Max had, a life she knew nothing about. Other than seeing him in movies, which was hard to watch at first, she'd not heard a word about any behind-the-scenes stuff.

"I've wanted to direct a movie for years, and the moment my big break was happening, my world back home fell apart," he went on. "Cancer. It's amazing how one word can make you rethink your entire life, every minute, every word you've said. I knew I had to get here, but she assured me that the nurse and my father would be with her through the surgery in Boston, and I could come here later, because she planned on undergoing radiation here in Lenox."

"You're here now," Raine told him softly. "I know she's happy to have you back."

Max's sultry blue eyes met hers. "What about you, Raine? Are you glad to have me back?"

Raine swallowed, looked him in the eyes and…couldn't come up with an answer. On one hand she loathed him for not fulfilling his promise to her, for hurting her at such a young age, but, on the other hand, how could she hold so tightly to the past? He hadn't tried to contact her in ten years…that was hard to let go.

But he was here now to care for his sick mother. Technically she didn't need him, but he'd come to show his love and support. How could she find any fault in that?

"It's okay," he said, taking a step closer and closing the narrow gap. "Under the circumstances, I'm not thrilled to be here, either."

She knew he referred to his mother's state, but a part of her wondered if he also meant her. Was he bitter toward her? All she was guilty of was falling in love, being naive and waiting for her Prince Charming to send for her.

And the baby they'd created.

Seeing him after all this time only brought back that rush of emotions associated with knowing she was carrying his baby, knowing he wasn't sending for her…and then the miscarriage. Those several months were the darkest of her life, and Max Ford held the key to the past she never wanted to revisit again.

"If we're going to be stuck together for who knows how long, I think it's best if we don't bring up the past," she said. "We're not the same people, and I just can't focus on something that happened so long ago. Not when I have Abby to care for. She's my future."

Max continued to stare at her, holding her with that piercing blue gaze. The room seemed to shrink, but in reality all she saw was him. Broad shoulders, tanned features beneath dark stubble, faint wrinkles around his eyes and mouth. He'd aged, but in the most handsome, beautiful way…damn him.

"Where's Abby's father?" he asked.

Raine jerked away from the shock of the sudden question. "That's none of your business."

"It is if he lives here."

"He doesn't."

"Is he part of your life?" Max asked.

"No."

His hand came up, cupping the side of her cheek. She barely resisted the urge to close her eyes, inhale his masculine scent, lean into his strong hold, but she could afford none of those things and honestly had no idea why he was touching her.

So Raine glared back at him, refusing to let him get past the wall of defense she'd built so long ago.

"You used to be so soft, so easy to read," he murmured. "What happened when I left?"

"Reality." She backed up until her spine hit the counter. "Reality was harsh, Max, and it woke me up to the life I was living, not the life I wanted."

God, it hurt to look at him. The longer he was here, in her home, in Lenox, the longer those memories from fifteen years ago would assault her. The loss of him, the loss of their baby.

"I'm going to go start lunch," she stated. "You're more than welcome to eat with me but no more dredging up the past again. Are we clear?"

He took a step forward, then two, placing a hand on either side of her body to trap her. Leaning in, his face came within inches of hers.

"We can't get past this tension between us until we discuss it. Maybe that makes me the naive one, Raine." His eyes darted to her lips. "Or maybe I'm a fool for still finding you just as attractive as I did then."

Raine couldn't breathe, all air had whooshed from her lungs the second he'd locked her between his sturdy arms. But just as soon as he leaned in, he pushed away.

"Don't worry. I know we're two different people," he stated as he neared the door. "And no matter what I feel now, whether it's old feelings or new hormones, I have my own set of worries."

He turned toward the door, then glanced over his shoulder. "And be warned. We will discuss our past before I leave Lenox."

Five

"Yes, Mother, Marshall was here."

Max stopped just outside the kitchen when he overheard Raine's exhausted tone. Seems some things hadn't changed. Apparently her mother could still bring out the frustration and weariness in Raine's voice.

After working for a couple hours on Raine's laptop, he set out to see what she was up to. Now that he knew, Max couldn't help but feel sorry for her.

"No, I didn't need him to stay. I'm a big girl, and I'm fine. Abby is fine, too, not that you asked."

Really? What grandmother wasn't doting over a grandchild? Was the relationship between Raine and her parents still so strained that Abby wasn't even a consideration in their lives?

Or maybe Raine didn't want them to be in the baby's life. Who knows? And to be honest, he couldn't focus on Raine's problems. If he did, he'd find himself deeper entrenched in her world, and he could not afford to get caught there again.

"I have to go," Raine said. "Abby's crying."

Max smiled at the silent house, the obviously sleeping baby.

"Please tell Dad not to send Marshall out here again.

The man is getting mixed signals, and they aren't coming from me."

Who the hell was Marshall? From the tone and Raine's plea, he had to guess someone her parents deemed suitable to be a boyfriend or the perfect spouse. Yeah, he had never fit that mold when he had wanted the title. Her parents had delusional thoughts of Raine marrying some suave and sophisticated political figure. Did Raine look like First Lady material?

Obviously her parents didn't know her at all, or they chose not to care what she wanted. He firmly believed the latter.

And that phone call answered the "man in her life" question. Apparently her mom and dad were relentless in trying to find the right "suitor," which made him laugh on the inside. Would her parents ever give up and see that Raine was a grown woman more than capable of making smart decisions?

Max eased into the room. Raine's back was to him, her eyes fixed on the falling snow outside the wide window that stretched above her sink. The paint on the interior of the windowpane had peeled away from the trim, and the faucet was dripping, whether to keep the pipes from freezing or because it was old, Max had no clue. But he couldn't get involved. He was just here to wait out this freak snowstorm.

The old yellow Formica countertops were the exact same as what he'd remembered, but now they were chipped along the edges. The old hardwood floors were scarred and in desperate need of refinishing.

What the hell had Raine done with all that trust fund money she was due to get when she turned twenty-five? She certainly didn't invest it back into her house.

"How long are you going to stand there?" she asked without turning around.

Max moved farther into the room, unable to hide his smile. "Just seeing if it's safe to come in."

She tossed him a glance over her shoulder. "I started making lunch, but my mother's call threw me off."

Max gripped the back of one of the mismatched chairs at the table. "You and your parents still don't have a good relationship? After all these years?"

Raine opened her refrigerator and pulled out asparagus.

"We've never quite seen eye to eye on things," she stated, rinsing the vegetable. "My mother is trying to turn me into some snobby pearl-wearing socialite, and my father is too busy worrying about his political standing in the town to worry about such nuisances as his child or grandchild… unless we're in public."

Max hated hearing this, hated that he wanted to hold a grudge against her, but he also couldn't believe how she was treated by her own family.

"So what are you doing that your parents dislike so much?" he asked, pulling out the chair, turning it around and straddling it. He rested his arms over the back.

Raine laid the stems on a baking sheet and placed them in the oven. "I'm not doting all over the movers and shakers of this town. I'm too different, meaning I grow my own vegetables, make my own soap and lotions, sell eggs, an occasional goat for milk, and in the summer I do some landscaping for a few families. Your parents' second home here is one of my jobs."

Max watched as she busied herself with this healthy organic lunch he'd rather pass on. But now that he was in here, he would probably stay.

"Mom mentioned you worked for her. She's impressed with you."

Still he was dying to know what had happened. In the years that he'd been gone and would visit his parents in Boston, Raine's name had only come up in the beginning.

His mother hadn't mentioned once that Raine had worked at the Lenox house in the summer.

She pulled out what he assumed to be tofu, and started packing it and placing it in the skillet on the old gas stove. "I rarely see your dad, but your mother comes to Lenox quite often. I assume to get away from the city life."

Max nodded. "That's why she wanted to recover from her surgery and take radiation in Lenox—because it's so quiet and peaceful. Since her oncologist expects her to make a full recovery, and has been in touch with the local hospital, he said she'll be fine to continue treatments here." As the skillet sizzled and aromas filled the spacious kitchen, Max kept his eyes on Raine as she turned to face him. Even in her sloppy clothes she looked adorable. But damn, he didn't want her to look adorable. He wanted her to be overweight and have a face covered in warts. An overbite? Thunder thighs? Anything?

Of course even if Raine had gained two hundred pounds and had a blemished face, he'd still see that young girl he'd fallen in love with. And a piece of his heart would always belong to her for that reason alone, no matter who they were today. Her beauty went so far beyond physical, nothing could ruin his image of her.

"I'm sorry you're trapped here with me," she said. "I'm sorry I was grouchy earlier, but I'm just…I'm not sure what to say to you. I mean, our past aside, you're Max Ford, Hollywood's hottest actor, and I'm…"

She glanced down at her boxy outfit and laughed. "You get the picture."

Max tilted his head. "No, I don't. Are you saying you're not worthy enough to be trapped with me? Why the hell not? Just because I'm famous? I'd much rather be trapped with you than any L.A. high-maintenance type."

Raine continued to laugh. "As you can see, I'm anything but high maintenance."

She turned back to her stove and flipped the…meat? No, tofu wasn't meat. Raine hated meat, and her shirt even advertised the fact.

"That's one of the things that drew me to you to begin with."

Her hands froze, her back rigid.

"I liked your simplicity," he went on. "I liked the fact you didn't care what others thought and that you were determined to be your own person. It was so refreshing to find someone else at the theater that day who was just like me."

Raine's mind flashed back to that day he spoke of, and she had no doubt his mind was replaying the same moment.

That day her parents had given her strict orders to go to the local Shakespearean Theater and try out for a role. Any role, just something that would make it look like the family was supporting the local arts and to get her out of the house to socialize.

But she'd seen Max with his mischievous smile and stunning baby-blue eyes, added with that chip on his shoulder, and she had felt like she'd found her new best friend…and for a time she had.

"Seems like a lifetime ago," he said.

Raine nodded, refusing to let this cooped-up ambience cloud her vision. They were kids with immature emotions. But when he'd left… God, it still pierced her heart. She hated admitting that, even to herself, but it hurt like hell being rejected by the one person she'd leaned on and loved so completely. And then discovering the pregnancy…

"Yeah," she agreed. "A lifetime."

Refocusing on lunch, she turned off the burner and slid the tofu burgers onto her grandmother's old floral plates. He had said he wasn't eating, but he had to have something, and she'd made plenty. Once she had all the food on the table, she had to laugh at Max's expression.

"You have something to say?" she asked when he continued to stare at the plate of food.

He burst out laughing, shaking his head. "Looks good."

Raine kept her smile in place. "You're such a liar."

"Yes," he agreed. "I'll have you know I have an Oscar award and several Golden Globe awards to prove that I'm awesome at lying."

"You hate everything on your plate," she said. "Even the best actor in Hollywood can't hide that."

Max picked up his fork, held it above his plate. "You think I'm the best actor?"

Great. Why didn't she just tell him she owned all of his movies and they were in her nightstand? God, that would make her extremely pathetic, and it would seem like she was clinging to a past that had left her vulnerable and shattered.

First the locket she kept, now this. Next she'd have a shrine in her basement like some stalker.

"You know you're good at what you do," she said, picking up her own fork and jabbing a piece of asparagus.

"I love the work I do. I think when you love what you're doing, it comes through, no matter the job."

Raine nodded, remembering that's how their bond had started years ago. They both had had dreams, aspirations that no amount of parental guilt could diminish.

"I suppose you don't have a frozen pizza in your freezer?"

Raine eyed him across the table and raised a brow. "You didn't just ask me that, did you?"

With a shrug, Max grinned. "Worth a shot. I'm not surprised you're still so..."

"Earthy?" she finished.

Max cut into his tofu and slid a bite into his mouth. His slow chew, the wrinkling of his nose and the quick drink of water had Raine sitting back in her seat, laughing.

"God, you're priceless," she said through fits of laughter. "I would've thought you had moved past this. Isn't everything in L.A. about being fit and thin? People wanting to be healthy?"

Max took another drink of water. "Yeah, but most people either use drugs, plastic surgeons or home gyms."

"Well, I prefer to go about staying healthy the old-fashioned way."

Several minutes passed as Max toyed with his food before he spoke again.

"So upstairs, you were making lotion?" he asked.

Popping her last bite of asparagus in her mouth, Raine nodded. "I make organic soaps and lotions. I usually sell gift baskets at the Farmer's Market during the spring and summer, so I'm working on the startup for that right now. I also have an online business that's growing."

"You took a gift bag to my mother."

At his soft words, Raine glanced across the scarred table to find his piercing blue eyes on her.

"Yes."

"Even though my parents never liked us together."

Raine nodded. "Your mother was caught in a rough spot, Max. She just wanted you and your father to make peace."

Max grunted and shoved his chair back. "My father and I never had peace before or after you were in my life."

"Even now?" she asked.

"Especially now," he confirmed.

Max came to his feet, picked up both plates and set them on the counter. He stared out the window which was quickly becoming covered with icy snow. He wasn't getting out of here anytime soon.

"Nothing I ever do will please that man," he said. "Which is why I do whatever the hell I want."

Raine came to her feet, not sure what to say, to do.

"I used to do things just to piss him off," Max went on.

"Dating you for example. I loved being with you, but parading you around him, knowing he disapproved, made me feel like I had the upper hand."

Raine knew all of that, or at least she'd always had that feeling, but she'd never heard him say the words aloud until now.

"I think we used each other," she told him. "I knew my parents frowned upon everything I did, so dating someone who had no aspirations of college or a political career really made me laugh. They were so angry, and I loved it."

He glanced over his shoulder and grinned. "Guess we didn't turn out too bad for rebellious teens."

Raine thought of her depleting bank account, the baby sleeping upstairs who wasn't technically hers until the judge said so and all the repairs her home needed. Spring couldn't get here soon enough, because she desperately needed to sell a couple of goats and get set up at the local market. That was her best source of income.

A loud pop came from the back utility room and Raine jumped.

"What the hell was that?" Max muttered, already moving in the direction of the noise.

Raine was afraid to find out, but she followed him. As soon as they opened the pocket door, she groaned at the sight of the hissing furnace that may date back to Moses's time.

"That's not good," he stated.

Raine leaned against the door. "God, I so don't have time for this."

Not to mention money. What the hell was she supposed to do now that her furnace gave out? Could things possibly get any worse? "I thought the thermostat was going bad," she said. "I had no idea it was the entire unit."

Max squatted down looking at the furnace, jimmying around a few things, but to no avail. When he came to his feet, he turned to her and sighed. "There's no way anyone can come look at this as long as the roads are in this condition." Raine nodded, forcing herself not to cry. What would crying do? Would it keep the three of them warm? No, so she needed to take those frustrations and redirect her energy toward something productive.

"I have some wood in the barn and two fireplaces, one in the living room and one in my bedroom. But the one in the living room hasn't been cleaned out for some time, so I'd be afraid to use it. We'll have to use the one in my room."

Her bedroom. Where they'd all have to sleep tonight if the roads weren't any better. Raine nearly laughed in hysteria at all the crap life was throwing at her.

Oh, well. She'd always heard the saying "Don't pray for a lighter load, pray for a stronger back."

"Let me get my coat, and I'll go get the wood," Max offered.

"No." She held up a hand to stop him, but he ran into her, forcing her to feel those hard pecs beneath his thick wool sweater. "You've only got those fancy city shoes on, and my chickens are like dogs and will bombard you for affection. I'll do it."

"Chickens are like dogs?"

Raine laughed. "Yeah. They would've run up to you when you got here, but they're in the barn staying warm, and you got inside before they could get out of their little flap and onto the porch. You step in that barn, and I guarantee you'll be surrounded." She blew out a breath. "Then you'll trip, fall on your butt into a snow pile and will be of no use to me."

Something sparked in his eyes, and she realized perhaps that hadn't been the best choice of words. "I meant—"

"I know what you meant," Max said, cutting her off. "But I can't let you carry in all the wood that we'll need. You'd have to make numerous trips, and I'd rather do it.

Don't forget, I was a country boy before I lived in Holly-wood. I'm not afraid of some chickens, Raine."

"You will be when they chase after you and knock you down."

He merely raised a brow as if he didn't believe her. She smiled in return, more than ready for the show to begin.

Six

Humiliation had long since settled in.

Max lay on his back, staring up at the sky. He'd barely taken a step inside the barn before he was…attacked by feathers. God, the feathers were everywhere.

Thankfully he'd donned his heavy coat and wool cap, but there was that sliver of flesh on the back of his neck that was exposed to the icy snow. Max shivered and sat up. No way in hell was he turning around to see Raine, because he knew she was plastered at the back door waiting for him to bring the wood back. He had no doubt she was also laughing her ass off when his feet flew in the air, and he landed face up in the mounting snow piles. The bucket had flown to who knows where, because he was just trying to stay upright and not get mauled by feathers and beaks.

Which totally took his mind off the fact that some very delicate areas were going to be bruised and sore. He doubted Raine would offer to rub him down.

Damn, she hadn't been kidding about these chickens. They were everywhere. Clucking, pecking, swarming. Weren't they just supposed to lay their eggs and sit on them?

Max came to his feet, shaking the snow off his back. He found the bucket had flown closer to the barn door, which was one thing in his favor. He moved to the wood pile,

which was located in the corner under a bright blue tarp…
right next to the small flap where the chickens obviously
came in and out of.

"'Scuse me." He waded through the stalking chickens,
feeling even more absurd for talking to them. "Just need
to get some wood."

He stocked the bucket with several pieces and carefully
moved back out of the barn. Thankfully those little hea-
thens wanted to stay warm, so between the house and the
barn he only had to tackle the snow mounds.

As Max stepped up to the back door, Raine swung it
open for him. One hand held the door, the other covered her
mouth. But the way those beautiful eyes were squinting, he
could tell she was dying to laugh and holding it in…barely.

"Go ahead," he muttered. "Get it out of your system."

Quickly she removed her hand and composed herself.
"I have no idea what you're talking about."

He sat the bucket down and picked up the empty one
before turning toward her. His face was mere inches from
hers, causing her to tilt her head back slightly.

"Now who's a terrible liar?" he asked.

Raine's eyes darted to his lips, and he was damn glad
he wasn't the only one having a problem controlling desire. But could he trust what he was feeling? Were these
merely past emotions or brand new ones brought on by her
spunky behavior that he found so refreshingly sexy? And
the way she stubbornly tried to keep that vulnerability of
hers hidden added yet another layer of irresistible appeal.

She'd been private and vulnerable before, but as a
mother, he found her to be even more so now. That protective nature of hers really had a part of him wanting to dig
deeper to unearth more Raine mysteries. But his realistic
side told him to back off.

"I'll unload this bucket," she said, evidently trying

to break the moment. "I think one more trip ought to be enough."

"Trying to get me out of here?" he asked gruffly.

Raine swallowed. "Trying to stay warm."

Max inched closer until her warm breath settled on his face. "There are a number of ways to stay warm, Raine. If I recall, you always loved hot showers."

Her lids fluttered down as she sighed. "Max…I can't…I just can't revisit the past."

"I'm not talking about the past," he murmured, easing his bucket to the ground and placing his hands on her narrow waist. "I'm talking about right here, right now, and the emotions we're both feeling."

"You don't know what I'm feeling," she whispered.

Teasing her by brushing his lips across hers for the briefest of moments, he said, "No, but I know what I'm feeling."

Max claimed her mouth, damning himself for allowing her to get under his skin so quickly. But she tasted so good, so intoxicating…and even after all these years, so familiar. Her delicate fingertips skimmed along his jawline as she cupped the side of his face.

There was no hesitation, Raine was all in, and she gave back as much as he was willing to take. He parted her lips with his tongue, drawing her body closer to his, as she met him thrust for thrust.

A shrill cry broke through the silence, killing any passion.

Raine jumped back, her eyes darting to the baby monitor on the counter. Immediately she brought her gaze back to him, her hand coming up to cover her mouth.

"Don't," he warned her. "Don't say you're sorry. Don't say it was a mistake."

She shook her head, crossing her arms over her chest. "Fine, but it won't and can't happen again."

Stepping around him, Raine left the room and rushed up

the stairs toward the nursery. From the monitor he heard her soft voice as she soothed Abby. Instantly the baby quieted.

And when Raine started to sing, he was taken back to when they'd first met, and she'd tried out for the only solo in the play. Her sweet, angelic voice had instantly blown away the cast and crew. All gazes were magnetically drawn to that shy girl on stage with her prissy little pleated skirt and staid sweater, more than likely chosen by her mother. He'd instinctively known that the prim-and-proper getup really had not suited Raine. She was much more of a jeans and T-shirt kind of gal. Even then.

Maybe she hadn't changed all that much. And if that was the case, he was in bigger trouble than he thought.

Max picked up his bucket and stormed back out into the freezing snow, hellacious chickens and all, because if he stuck around to listen to her much longer, he'd be pulled into a past that he'd barely come out of alive the last time. He couldn't afford to feel those emotions ever again.

Well, so much for the weather cooperating. It was nearly ten o'clock, the streets were dark and desolate, and the snow had shown no sign of slowing down.

Abby had just taken her bedtime bottle and hopefully would sleep a few hours.

Max had put up the Pack 'N' Play pen in the master bedroom, where they had a nice fire going. Thankfully the room was spacious, and Abby could sleep in the corner of the room.

Raine and Max were prisoners as well, considering the rest of the house was quickly becoming colder. Max had brought up plenty of wood to last through the night and into the morning.

So here they were. In the bedroom with a sleeping baby and a whole cluster of hormones and that damn kiss hovering in the air between them.

Oh, and a past that had never gotten proper closure. Great. Just great. Exactly what they didn't need. Why couldn't they both still be angry and bitter? Did passion really override all else here?

"I'm going to go change," she whispered to Max who was sitting on the bed, propped up against pillows and doing something on her laptop.

When Max glanced over, eyeing her from head to toe, all those points in between tingled as if he'd touched her with his bare hands. And she knew from personal experience what those hands felt like roaming up her torso.

Even though a lifetime had passed between then and now, a touch like Max's wasn't one she could easily forget. How could she? When his simple touches, his soft caresses, not only sent shivers racing all over her body, but they also left an imprint so deep, she knew she'd never truly erase it from her mind.

So, yeah, that tingling wasn't going to stop anytime soon if she didn't put a lid on those damn memories and stop letting him affect her now.

Raine turned to her dresser and grabbed the oldest, ugliest set of pajamas she owned. There was no need in putting on anything cute or seductive. That was the dead last thing they needed. Not that she had a great deal of "sexy" lingerie, but she'd better keep anything skimpy out of this room while he was in it…and circumstances all but begged them to get naked and horizontal.

With a soft click, she closed the bathroom door and started to change. She'd just undressed completely and pulled the PJ shirt over her head when the door opened. Raine quickly tried to tug the shirt below her panties, but it just wasn't long enough.

"What the hell are you doing?" she demanded, not speaking as loud as she wanted for fear of waking Abby.

Max's eyes raked over her bare legs, definitely not help-ing the tingling.

"We need to talk, and I didn't want to wake Abby," he said, closing the door with a soft click.

Raine rolled her eyes. "You couldn't have waited until I was dressed?"

Like a predator to its prey, he stepped forward, narrow-ing the distance between them. Apparently he didn't know the term "personal space."

"There's nothing here that I haven't seen," he said, his gaze locked onto hers. "Throw your pants on if that makes you feel better."

"Turn around."

That cocky grin spread across his face. "Are you really going to stand there and act like you're not turned on? That the fact we're stuck here together hasn't had you thinking, wondering?"

It was all the thinking and wondering that was driving her out of her mind. Hormones were evil. They reared their ugly heads when nothing could be done. Well, something could be done, but at what price? Because she sure as hell couldn't risk her heart again.

Not only that, she had to concentrate on the adoption. What would it look like if she were to delve into a torrid affair with Hollywood's hottest bachelor?

"Max, I realize that in L.A. you flash that grin and get what you want, *who* you want." She gripped her shirt tighter. "Yes, I'm attracted, but for all I know that's just old memories rising up."

He took one last step forward until they were toe to toe and brought his hands up to gently cup her face. "What if it's not just old memories?"

Raine sighed, because, if she were honest with herself, she wanted nothing more than to rip off his clothes and see if they were even better in bed than they used to be. And there wasn't a doubt in her mind they would be phenomenal.

"I live in the real world, Max," she said, pushing the erotic image of the two of them out of her head. "If we slept together, what happens next? I have a farm, a baby, here, and, in a few months, you'll be back in L.A., working on your next project, and you will totally forget about Lenox."

About me.

A flash of pain swept through his eyes, and his brows drew together. "My parents may have moved to Boston when I left for Hollywood, but I never forgot Lenox…or the people here."

The ache from his abandonment when she'd needed him the most years ago killed any desire she may have been feeling now. But at least, if she were stupid enough to get entangled with him again, she'd know upfront that he would leave without looking back.

And all she needed was the Family Court judge to get wind of the fact that Max Ford, Hollywood hotshot and rumored playboy, was snowbound in her home.

"Listen," she began, looking him dead in the eye. "We both chose our separate lives. It's ridiculous to act on any feelings we're having now, just because we're victims of the current circumstances."

"I prefer to call this fate."

Still holding the hem of her shirt so it didn't ride up and show off her goods, Raine stepped back, forcing his hands to fall away. No matter the cold she felt once his touch was gone, this was for the best. Distance now would spare her heartache later.

"So you want to…what? Have sex and then when the snow thaws just go back home and pretend nothing happened?"

Max scrubbed a hand over his face and groaned, looking up at the ceiling. "I don't know what the hell I want, Raine."

Before this got too far out of control, she wrestled into her pants while he obviously battled with himself over right and wrong.

He turned, leaning against the edge of the vanity and crossed his arms over his wide chest. "All I know is, since we kissed, I can't shake this feeling."

"What feeling?"

Max shifted, meeting her gaze. "That I want you."

Well, that was a change. She couldn't deny him, couldn't deny herself. Whatever happened in the past could live there. Raine wanted to live for the moment, but she also had to be realistic at the same time. "I want you, too." Unable to help herself, she reached out and rested a hand on his firm shoulder. "But I need more than sex. I want to find a man who will love me and Abby. Getting this sexual tension out of the way by sleeping together won't help either of us in the long run, no matter how tempted I am."

Because if she slept with him again, Raine knew she'd fall into that deep abyss of her past. She'd fall back into that mind-set that Max was the one.

"We may be stuck here for days," he murmured, reaching up to stroke her jawline. "You going to avoid the devil on your shoulder that long?"

Raine swallowed and answered honestly. "I'm going to try."

Seven

Raine had to admit she was quite proud of herself when morning rolled around, and she still had her clothes on. She'd spent the night with Max, in a bed, trapped in a freak snowstorm, and she'd held on to her dignity...not to mention her panties.

Max was not lying beside her in all his fully clothed glory. The only other person in the room was Abby, who had finally fallen back asleep at six after taking her third bottle of the night.

Raine held back a chuckle. She wouldn't be surprised if Max had decided to try to fix the stove downstairs in order to get some peaceful sleep. Abby hadn't had a bad night, actually. She'd only gotten up three times which was good, but in Max's world he wasn't used to being dead asleep one second and woken by a screaming kid the next.

And Raine was still shocked at Max's five a.m. gesture. On the third and final cry of hunger from Abby, Raine had thrown back her covers only to have Max's hand still her movements.

The man had not only gone down to the freezing first floor to retrieve the bottle from the fridge but he had returned and fed Abby. And if that wasn't enough to melt her heart, he'd also sat at the foot of the bed and gently rocked the baby back and forth.

And here she thought Max had been sleeping during the other feedings. Apparently he'd been watching her.

Easing out of bed, Raine tugged her pajama top down and attempted to smooth her hair away from her face. She padded into the bathroom and brushed her teeth, pulled her hair up into a ponytail and did her best not to cringe at the dark circles under her eyes. Yeah, she was quite the catch. If her sexy shoe collection of an old red pair of Crocs slip-ons and her very well-worn work boots didn't reel him in, surely this haggard housewife look would.

Not that she was trying to be a catch, mind you, but still…she should at least try not to look drab all the time. Working from home and raising an infant really did a number on your beauty regime. Not that she'd had much of one to begin with, but she should at least put forth a little effort.

Her mother would be totally mortified if she saw the lack of makeup in Raine's bathroom, the dollar-store shampoo in her shower and the one little bottle of lotion she used after a bath…her own concoction, of course.

Growing up, Raine remembered her mother having pots and bottles of various lotions to firm up this and de-wrinkle that. And the makeup. Good God, the makeup that woman owned could rival any beauty counter at the mall. Raine never wanted to be that high maintenance, that fake, to have to put all of that on just to step out and have lunch with "friends."

Still trying to remain quiet and not wake Abby, Raine left the warmth of her bedroom and went out into the frigid hall, taking the baby monitor with her.

As she hit the bottom of the steps, she shivered slightly but still didn't have a clue where Max went. Then she over-heard him talking on the phone, his voice coming in from the kitchen.

Hand on the newel post, Raine froze, knowing she had no business eavesdropping, but she couldn't stop herself.

"My mother is doing great," he said. "I'm not with her because of this freak snowstorm…yeah, you saw that? I heard another six inches just today, too. It's hell on the East Coast, and I can hardly wait to get back to L.A. Between you and me, I'd trade palm trees for snow-covered evergreens any day."

Why that honest fact bothered her was silly. She knew Max was only here to care for his mother, and he had absolutely no qualms about playing house with her. He'd been here one day, and already she'd gotten comfortable. And after that near fatherly display from him earlier this morning, she was so much more attracted. Damn that man and his power over her hormones.

"I'm not at my mother's," he went on. "I stopped by to visit an old friend and got stuck here. But I'm using her laptop, so…yes, it's a she."

Max's masculine laughter sounded through her house, and she didn't even want to know what the person on the other end had said to garner such a response.

"I'm more than capable of working and playing when necessary," he said, still smiling. "She's an old friend…. Yes, I agree."

Raine decided now would be a good time to make her presence known before he said something she wasn't ready to hear. She moved to the doorway and leaned against the frame, arms crossed over her chest. She simply waited until Max fully turned around, but, instead of looking like he'd been caught, like most people would've, the man merely winked and continued smiling.

Even the way he oozed confidence was a turn on. Granted since he'd come back into town, she hadn't been turned off.

Raine tried her hardest to tune him out as she grabbed a

premade smoothie from the fridge and headed toward the stairs. She had her own work to do, and it didn't consist of watching Hollywood hottie Max Ford parade around her house wearing the same clothes from yesterday, with bed-head and day-old stubble.

Why did he have to be so damn sexy? Stomping up the stairs, because she was mature like that, she sighed. Had *she* been stuck somewhere overnight, she wouldn't have woken up looking sexier…not by a long shot. For some reason her looks deteriorated in the dark hours, because, when she woke, her hair was all lumped to one side in a matted mess, her eyes were bloodshot, and she was always a tad cranky.

Raine checked in on Abby once more before going into her workroom and setting the monitor on the counter. She had a small space heater she kept at her feet so she clicked it on high and closed the door to keep the warmth in.

Whatever Max wanted to do downstairs in the cold was his own business. They were safe and warm, so long as they stayed upstairs, and so far the electricity had held up which was surprising in a snowstorm that came on this fast.

Looking over her spreadsheet of items she wanted to make for the Farmer's Market in six weeks, Raine tried to block out the fact that her furnace had died. She simply couldn't think about that right now—although the blast of icy cold air when she'd gone downstairs had been a very real reality. The unit couldn't be fixed today even if she had the money, so her attention was best suited for work and Abby. Not the pathetic bank account, not the snowstorm and certainly not her handsome new roomie.

Downstairs the backdoor slammed. Raine smiled at the thought of Max going out. Obviously he hadn't learned his lesson the first time he had encountered her loving Or-pington chickens.

But he hadn't met Bess and Lulu yet—the equally loving

goats. They hadn't come out the other day, but it was only a matter of time before they realized a new person was here.

A giggle rose up in her, and, regardless of how cold it was on the first floor, she simply had to know how this all played out. Besides, she would have to feed her animals shortly anyway.

Grabbing the baby monitor, she padded down the hall, ran down the steps and stood just inside the kitchen door to watch Max.

Sure enough Bess and Lulu had gone through the rubber flap which gave them access in or out. The kindly goats encircled him, and, even with his jacket collar pulled up to his chin and his black knit cap pulled down over his ears and forehead, Raine saw the thread of fear and confusion in his blue eyes. Perhaps she should've warned him…

Nah, this was so much more entertaining.

She eased the back door open enough to yell out. "They're like dogs. They love people."

"What the hell does that mean? I've never owned a dog," he called back.

Raine shook her head. "Just pet them and keep walking. They'll go back in the barn when you come in."

She watched as he went into the barn closest to the house to gather more wood. Part of her wanted him to get tangled up in the chickens again, simply because the last episode had been so amusing, but another part of her was a little excited to see this city boy back in Lenox. Once upon a time he'd felt so at home here on her grandmother's farm. They'd ridden horseback, laughing excitedly as teens do, and had had a picnic out in the fields behind the property.

But that was long ago. Her grandmother was gone, the horses had been sold for the new roof, and all that was left were the bittersweet memories.

Tears clogged her throat. Turning back time wasn't an option, not that she would want to endure all of that heartache again, but she certainly missed being so happy, so loved.

By the time Max made it back to the house, she'd blinked away the tears, but the pang in her heart was just as fierce as when she'd first seen him nearly two days ago standing on the side of the icy road ready to assist.

Max brushed by her as she held the screen door open. He stomped his feet on the stoop before stepping inside. Raine took the bucket as Max pulled off his coat, boots and hat.

"It's still coming down," he said, hanging his coat on the peg by the door. "My tracks were covered by the time I came back out of the barn."

"I've given up listening to news reports. It will stop when it stops."

And the longer he was forced to stay here, the longer she had to fall deeper into memories, deeper into those emotions she couldn't afford.

Max turned to grab the bucket, but froze as his gaze held hers. "You okay?"

Raine nodded, pasting on a smile. "Of course."

"I've lived in L.A. a long time, Raine. We're professional liars, and you are holding something back."

Even if he hadn't been surrounded by "professional liars," he'd always known her so well. They hadn't changed that much.

"Seeing you out there brought back a flash of memories. That's all."

"Memories shouldn't make you sad," he said softly.

Raine eased the bucket down beside her, crossed her arms over her chest. "No, the memory was beautiful."

Running a hand through his sleep-mussed hair, Max stepped closer. "We may have gone our separate ways, Raine, but that doesn't mean I stopped caring for you. And even though we're stuck in this hellish snowstorm, I have to say I'm not sorry to be here."

"You're not?"

Shaking his head, he slid his hands up her arms. "Not at all. Maybe this is fate's way of making us talk, forcing us to settle this rocky area that's been between us for years."

Raine glanced down to their socked feet, so close together. Now he wanted to talk? What about when he'd left? What about sending for her and the promise of them starting their lives together? He hadn't been so keen on talking when he'd left her behind, pregnant and alone.

She looked back up, catching a sliver of pain in his eyes as he watched her. "We can't change anything about the past, Max. And you aren't staying in Lenox any longer than you have to. I heard you on the phone. I know you have a big deal waiting for you in L.A., and that's great... so opening up about what happened between us years ago won't solve anything. It won't bind us together, and it won't erase all the hurt."

"No," he agreed. "But it may make this tension between us easier to live with."

Raine laughed. "Tension? We have tension from so many different angles, Max."

Those strong hands curved around her shoulders, pulling her against his solid, hard chest. Raine had to tip her head to look up at him.

"There's a way to get rid of some of this tension," he whispered against her lips a second before claiming them.

She curled her fingers into his sweater, knowing that letting him sink further into her life was a vast mistake, but she couldn't help herself. Leaning against Max, being in his arms again, felt like no time had slid between them. No pain, no hurt.

He teased her lips as his hands slid down to the hem of the long-sleeved shirt she'd slept in. When his chilled fingers hit her bare skin, she sucked in a breath, but he continued to explore farther beneath her shirt.

His hands encompassed her rib cage. Max skimmed his thumbs along the underneath side of her breasts. She'd not bothered with a bra this morning, and she was so glad she hadn't. Not that her barely B cups needed confinement anyway, but, like a fool, she had wanted that extra connection with him. She wanted to feel his skin against hers.

And she'd known the second she'd seen him in her house yesterday that she wouldn't be able to resist him on any level.

Before Raine knew it, her shirt was up and over her head. Wrapping his arms around her waist, he lifted her and strode toward the stairs.

Raine tilted her head back as Max's mouth traveled from her lips, down the column of her throat and to her breast. She gripped the side of his head, trying to hold him there, silently begging for him to never stop.

He held her against the thick post at the base of the steps, pulled back slightly and released her. "Tell me to stop," he said, his voice raspy. "Tell me this is wrong, because I can't even think when I'm with you. All I know is I want you, here...now."

Raine palmed his cheek. "I want to tell you to stop. I know this is wrong, but right now, I want nothing more than to be with you."

In no time Max had shed his clothes and was jerking down her bottoms and panties.

"It's really cold down here," she muttered between kisses and sighs. "Let's go upstairs."

In a swift move, he lifted her and carried her up the steps and into her bedroom where Abby was sleeping soundly in the warmth of her Pack 'N' Play pen.

Max continued on into the bathroom and eased the door shut with his foot before carefully placing Raine back on her feet.

Light spilled through the small window on the far wall

and the sight of Max gloriously naked nearly sent her trembling knees buckling. Over the years he'd filled out in all the right places, but that scar stemming from his chest to his shoulder gave her pause.

She reached out, her fingertip lightly traveling over the faded red line. "Does it still hurt?" she whispered.

He grabbed he hand, kissed her fingertips. "That was long ago."

She knew when it was; she also appreciated the fact he wasn't about to let their past come into this room with them.

He kissed her deeply, wrapping his arms around her waist and arching her back. Raine had to clutch onto his shoulders and hold on for the ride.

As he gripped her tight, his lips left hers and continued their descent, making a path of goose bumps and trembling nerves down her throat and toward her breasts.

"Protection?" she panted.

He froze, rested his forehead against her chest. "I have nothing with me. I wasn't exactly planning on being stranded here."

"I've never been without protection," she said. "I know I'm clean, and I'm on the pill."

Lifting his head, his heavy-lidded eyes met hers. "I've always used protection, too, but it's your call, Raine."

In silent response, she tilted her hips into his and smiled.

Max lifted her, and she wrapped her legs around his waist. He turned and eased her down on the edge of the marble vanity. Raine couldn't wait another second. She maneuvered her body, pushed with her ankles and enveloped him. Then she stiffened. It had been so long since she'd been with someone. But this was Max…well, she wanted it to last. Silly and naive as that may sound, she never wanted their time together to end.

For this moment, Hollywood didn't exist, her problems

didn't exist. Right now all she knew was Max, and that was more than enough to satisfy her.

Max's hands slid up her sides, palmed her breasts, as her hips started moving, slowly at first and then faster as he kissed her, explored her.

Raine held on to his shoulders, using him for leverage as she pumped her hips.

"Raine," he rasped. "I…"

Whatever he was about to say died on his lips. Which was just as well, because right now all she needed was release. She wasn't doing this for sweet words, wasn't with him for the long-term. They both knew that.

Max grabbed the back of her head and slammed his mouth onto hers, his other hand reaching between them to touch her intimately.

Clever man that he was knew exactly what to do to her… he'd never forgotten.

Within seconds Raine's body shivered as wave after wave of ecstasy rolled through her. She tore her mouth from his, needing to somehow break that bond before she was pulled any deeper under his skin.

Max gripped her waist with both hands as he held her as far down as she would go when his own body stilled. For a second their gazes locked, but Raine had to look away. As his climax came to an end, she wondered what she'd seen in those baby blues, but, she knew if she delved too far into what had just happened, she'd be even more hurt when he left this time.

And she wasn't about to make the same mistake twice.

Eight

Well, hell. Awkward, party of two? Your bedroom is now available.

Raine pulled her robe from the back of the bathroom door and shoved her arms into the sleeves. Without a word, she opened the door to the bedroom and left. And Max watched her walk away without a word.

She'd done her best to distance herself during sex, she'd even avoided eye contact as much as possible, but he knew she'd felt something. And try as he might to deny it, he had, too.

Couldn't people just have a good time without feelings getting all jumbled into the mix? Ostensibly they couldn't. All that past between them, the current sexual tension and the fact he kept feeling this pull toward her. Maybe he felt the need to protect her because of her obvious vulnerability with the baby, the old house falling apart, her apparent financial crisis.

And what she'd done with tens of thousands of dollars from her trust fund was beyond him, but she clearly hadn't poured it into this place.

Max sank to the couch and slid his wool socks back on. At some point he would have to wash his clothes and take a shower…that shower probably would've been a good idea before the sex, but he hadn't been thinking. He hadn't been thinking of much other than Raine since he had stepped foot back in Lenox and came face-to-face with his past.

Obviously he had to go down to the freezing first floor to retrieve his clothes because he only had the ones he'd worn over here yesterday.

When he got downstairs, Raine was picking up her own clothes and trying to get into them without removing her robe. Okay, so she was plainly not comfortable with what just happened.

As if they needed another layer of tension.

Raine's cell chimed. He glanced around the room and saw it lighting up on the end table. She rushed toward it, pulling her shirt over her head and over that damn robe. Max shook his head and went to gather up his own clothes from around the room.

Scooping up the phone, she answered it. "Hello."

Max didn't make a move to leave the room once he had his things—if she wanted privacy, she could walk away. Yeah, he was in a mood and had no one to blame but himself. He'd been selfish. He'd wanted Raine, and he hadn't given a damn about the consequences or the fact that he'd have to stay here afterward and actually cohabitate until this damn storm passed.

"No, Marshall, I'm still fine."

Marshall? Who the hell was that? Max made no attempt to hide his curiosity as he pulled on his boxer briefs and jeans while staring across the room at her as she continued to talk. She kept shaking her head, glancing up to the ceiling, sighing…didn't take a genius to figure out she had no interest in talking to this Marshall person.

"My friend Max is here, and he's helping with anything I need."

Friend? After what they'd just done, he sure as hell felt

like more than a friend. But what would she tell the dude on the phone? My ex and current lover is here?

Max felt he was more than friend status, because, well... because he just was. Although his exact title was rather iffy, and he wasn't altogether certain he wanted to delve too deeply into that area.

So, okay, friend it was.

"Yes, he's a good friend," she continued. "No, we're not dating. We dated as teenagers... Yes, Marshall. It's Max Ford, the actor... Yes, I know how famous he is."

As she spoke, her gaze caught his, and then the smile that spread across his face. Raine merely raised a brow as if she dared him to say a word.

Max knew he was famous but hearing her discuss his celebrity status with another man only made him smile wider. Had Raine watched his movies? Had she seen when he'd won an Academy Award?

He found himself wanting to know more and wanting to share that aspect of his life with her.

Share his life? Yeah, sex muddled the brain.

"I don't really think that's any of your business," she said into the phone as she crossed the room and rested her shoulder on the windowsill. "I need to go, Marshall."

She barely got the words out before she hung up and clutched her phone in her hand. With her back to him, she sighed, and he could see her shoulders tense up. Max closed the distance between them.

"Problems with your boyfriend?" he murmured as he came to stand directly behind her.

Raine threw him a nasty look. "Marshall is not my boyfriend, no matter how much my mother and father want him to be because of his political aspirations. We went on one date, and I'm still trying to block it out."

Max slid his fingertip along the side of her neck, shifting her hair aside so he could taste her. He couldn't get enough. Raine was one sexy woman, but, all fired up like this, he was finding her irresistible.

"Sounds like he doesn't know what to do with a beautiful woman," Max muttered against her skin. "His loss."

Raine trembled beneath him, and Max grinned as he allowed his lips to gently roam over her neck. She tilted her head to the side with a slight groan.

"What are you doing?" she asked on a sigh.

"Taking advantage of this situation."

Her head fell back on his shoulder as he slipped his hands around her waist and pulled her against him.

"What just happened in my bathroom wasn't the smartest move we could've made," she said, but made no attempt to free herself from his embrace.

"Maybe not, but it was inevitable."

A low cry came filtering through the house from the strategically placed baby monitors.

"Does this mean playtime is over for the adults?" he asked as Raine stepped around him and headed for the steps.

She gripped the newel post and stared at him from across the room. "I think maybe it shouldn't have started," she whispered.

Max watched her ascend the steps to the second floor and couldn't help but laugh. Her words held no emotion, and he knew, in her mind, Raine was saying what she thought the situation called for.

But he'd felt her come apart in his arms, when he'd held her, kissed her, tasted her. She had allowed that wall of defense to come down, and she'd let herself feel.

Through the monitor he heard her consoling the baby. She was such a wonderful mother. He wondered, if she'd have come to L.A. when he'd tried to contact her, would they have had a family of their own? Would their baby have

Raine's earthy nature and his creative side? Would he or she have Raine's soft green eyes or his bright blue ones?

Max wasn't one to get caught up in domestic bliss, but just being in her home one day and seeing this whole new side to her made him think. They'd shared the same dreams once, and she'd fulfilled the majority of hers—so had he for that matter, but at what cost?

Max glanced into the kitchen where bottles vertically sat in the drying rack, a can of formula beside that, a stroller folded up in the corner of the living room, a bouncy seat over by the window.

All of these obvious signs of a baby had him trying to picture his immaculate home in West Hollywood. Yeah, he didn't think all this brightly colored plastic would go with the black-and-chrome features his interior designer had meticulously chosen.

Raine came back down the steps cradling Abby against her chest. The sight of her fresh after intimacy and holding a sweet baby tugged at his heart, and there wasn't a damn thing he could do about it. He didn't want to play house with her; he didn't want to get swept into this crazy world of organic foods, overly friendly goats and diaper changes.

He wanted to get the hell out of Lenox once his mother's treatments were over, and he wanted to start working with Bronson Dane on this film that would launch his career to another level. But the pull he was feeling toward Raine was growing stronger and stronger by the minute.

"I'll put more wood in the fireplace in your room." Max went into the kitchen to retrieve the forgotten bucket of wood. "Mind if I grab a shower?"

He watched as Raine used one hand to jiggle the baby and one hand to mix a bottle. The woman truly was a natural mother. Another tug on his heart had him pausing.

Max's own biological mother had abandoned him, and the Fords had taken him in. Elise had been the best mother he could've asked for. She'd been patient, loving and so nurturing.

Max saw those same characteristics in Raine.

"Not at all," she told him. "Use my bathroom. If you want to leave your clothes on the bed, I'll wash them real quick for you. There's another robe in there hanging by the shower. It's big and thick, and shouldn't be too bad for you to wear for a couple hours."

"Um…okay. Thanks."

"I'm going to get a large space heater I have in the garage. We can see how well it does down here," she added. "It's not like we can keep staying up in the bedroom."

No, wouldn't want to tempt fate any more than necessary.

"When you're done, I'll grab a shower if you can watch Abby for a few minutes."

Babies didn't necessarily make him uncomfortable, but he wasn't quite ready to play nanny.

Although getting up to feed Abby had been…nice. Holding someone so precious and innocent had flooded him with a mix of emotions…namely love. Falling for Abby was not the smartest move.

Max shook off the impending feelings and concentrated on the here and now. This first floor was turning into an icebox. He needed to call someone about that furnace and have them look at the fireplace, as well. His mother surely knew enough people around this town that they could get a reputable name to come out as soon as the roads were clear.

"Sure," he said. "I'll be right back down."

After he showered, he'd call his mom and check in and get that name. Max knew his mother was in good hands, but he still wanted to keep touching base with her. The plow trucks should be coming through, and hopefully he wouldn't be stuck here much longer.

Because he had a sinking feeling that the longer he was here, the more he'd slide into that life that he and Raine had planned out. A life they were meant to have with kids and a house and him fulfilling his acting dreams.

Yes, they'd had their lives all perfectly drawn out like a blueprint. And they'd each gotten what they'd wanted out of life, but they were technically alone. So much time had passed that Max wouldn't know what to do if he were to be in a committed relationship. He had never made time for one, so he'd never really thought much about it.

For the past couple years his main goal had been career oriented, and getting that directing job with Bronson had been at the top of his priority list. But now, being with Raine really opened his eyes to his personal life…and the lack thereof.

So, yeah, getting the hell out of here would be the best thing for both of them.

"Not one word."

Raine had to literally bite her lips to keep from speaking, laughing, even cracking a smile. She totally failed on the latter.

"There was no thick robe hanging by the shower, and I didn't think to look to make sure it was there until I was out of the shower, at which point you'd already nabbed my clothes."

Across the room, Abby swung in her baby swing, and Raine was looking toward the doorway where Max stood with bare feet, bare legs and a silky, floral robe that barely came together in the middle. He was gripping the material together with both hands in an attempt to keep his goods hidden.

Like she hadn't just seen them. Not only that, this look was certainly not a turn on. It was, however, quite laughable.

"Maybe I put that robe away," she muttered, swallowing the laughter. "At least you have something to wear until your clothes are done."

His eyes narrowed. "You did this on purpose."

Now Raine did laugh. "Oh, I wish I'd thought that far ahead. I swear I thought I had a big white bathrobe on the back of the door. I can go find it for you."

She started to pass by him when he grabbed her arm. "What do I do if she cries?" he asked, his eyes darting to Abby.

Raine looked to the baby who was smiling up at the miniature spinning mobile of bears above the swing.

"She seems pretty happy," she said. "I'll only be a minute. It's probably in the other bathroom or in the laundry room. Besides, you were amazing with her in the middle of the night. I never thanked you."

Max shrugged. "You'd been up enough times and needed to rest. I figured if I did anything wrong, you'd intervene."

Raine smiled. "I was so glad to just lay there, I wouldn't have stopped you."

She moved away before he could stop her again. The image of Max Ford in her living room wearing a silky robe, watching a baby while waiting on a fluffier robe made her chuckle. If only his dad could see him now.

As much as Raine had despised Max's father, she knew, even to this day, Max wanted approval from the man. But no matter how many awards, how many movies or charities Max worked with, his father had never accepted Max was following a dream and loving what he did.

She recalled Max telling her one time that his dad had always wanted him to go into the family business. Since Max was adopted and an only child, there was no one else to inherit Tom Ford's dynasty.

But even before Max became famous, and a power broker in his own right, he'd had zero desire to be a restaurateur.

Within moments, Raine had found the robe and met him back in the living room. He hadn't moved an inch, and his eyes were locked on Abby.

"How long will she stay in that thing and be content?" he asked.

Raine shrugged. "She really is self-entertaining. She's just cranky through the night."

Max took the other robe, peered down at it, eyed the baby and then looked to her.

Laughing again, Raine rolled her eyes. "You can change. I swear Abby won't look."

Dropping the silky robe at his feet, Max displayed all his glorious muscles and potent male virility right in her living room. Keeping his blue-eyed stare locked on Raine the entire time, he grabbed the new robe and slid into it.

The man was gorgeous, and he knew it. Jerk.

"Looks like the snow is finally letting up," he stated, tying the belt as best he could around his waist. "You have plans for Valentine's Day?"

Raine crossed her arms and smirked. "Oh, yes. Abby and I plan on wining and dining on bottles of goat milk and decadent chocolates."

Max laughed. "I'm serious. You don't have any plans?"

"Do you really think I would've just had sex with you if I had plans to be with someone else in two days?"

Max nodded. "No, but I thought I should ask."

"It's after the fact now," she said.

He stepped forward, looking both ridiculous in that robe, yet sexy. "Maybe we could do something, since we both don't have plans."

Raine took a step back, holding up her hands before he could reach out and touch her. "Wait a minute, Max. I'm not looking for a Valentine or a date. What just happened between us was only you and me working off some tension and past memories. That's all."

"Old friends can't go out and enjoy the day?"

Go out? Sleeping together had been one thing—an amazing fantasy come true that she wouldn't soon forget—but to go out where people could see her on a date…

She couldn't afford *any* misstep in this adoption. And Max Ford was so recognizable that there's no way they'd go unnoticed.

"Old flames gallivanting around town where my father is mayor? Uh, no." She hated her father's status, except when she could use it to her advantage. "Besides, Valentine's Day doesn't mean much to me."

"Because you're single?"

Raine laughed. "Because it's just a day. I don't need a sentimental holiday to remind me of what I don't have."

She turned from him, not wanting him to read any more into what she said…or didn't say. She squatted down in front of Abby and flicked at the spinning bears. The baby smiled, eyes transfixed on the toys.

"Don't be embarrassed, Raine."

Her hand froze on the swing as she threw him a glance over her shoulder. "Excuse me?"

"That didn't come out right." He took a seat in the chair closest to the swing and rested his arms on his knees, leaning forward to look her in the eye. "We all had dreams. Some didn't come true, others did. I just don't want you to feel embarrassed that I asked about Valentine's Day. If you don't want to do anything with me, I understand. But the offer is there if you choose to."

Raine resisted the urge to snicker as she turned back to Abby. "I'll be fine."

Because his offer of a pity date was really topping her list for Valentine's Day. She'd much rather spend the day alone than be with someone who was only passing through and felt obligated to throw extra attention her way.

And the sex did not count. She'd been on board with that, and its sole purpose was to clear the tension between them.

Yes, that was the second time she'd thought that, but she wasn't trying to convince herself. Really. It had meant nothing. Just two people, taking advantage of the situation of being forced together.

Raine came to her feet. "I need to get this wood upstairs before I hop in the shower."

Max stood, placing a hand over her arm. "I'll get it."

She watched him walk away in that ridiculous robe and didn't know whether to laugh or cry…or take a picture and sell it to a gossip magazine.

"I'll go check on your clothes," she called after him.

Raine stopped the swing and lifted Abby out. "You're so lucky you have no clue what's going on. Word of advice? Stay a kid."

Because adulthood truly sucked sometimes. Sexual tension, worry over making a wrong decision, anxiety over making family happy…at one time she'd wanted to please her parents, but, as Raine got older, she quickly learned pleasing her mother was an impossible feat.

That was one thing Raine swore on her life that she would never let Abby worry about. Raine would be her baby's number one supporter and Abby would never have to wonder where she stood.

Nine

Max resisted the urge to groan as his mother rambled on about how this prime opportunity would be perfect for him and would help the community as well. It was a win-win… or so she kept telling him.

"The timing is perfect," she informed him.

Day two was coming to a close, and the snow had stopped, but the streets were covered, and cars were still parked in their little snow mounds.

"Mom, you know I love theater, but this is such short notice." He gripped the phone and turned from the bedroom window. When Raine had finished her shower, he'd come up here for privacy when he'd called his mother, and he'd also wanted to check the fire. Plus he felt putting some distance between him and Raine was best for now. After they'd had sex earlier, his libido had decided to join the party late, and he wanted her even more now.

And seeing her with dewy skin and silky wet hair hadn't helped. He'd had to get out of her presence quickly, but now that he was up in her room, the steam from the bathroom billowed out as did her fresh jasmine scent, probably from some exotic lotion or soap she made.

"Honey," his mother went on. "This is what you do. The play won't open until the first of April. You have almost two months to prepare, and since it's only a week long, you'll finish just in time to get back to L.A."

She had a point, several in fact, and they were all valid. And he really did love the Shakespearian Theater in Lenox. That's where he'd gotten his start. And where he'd met Raine.

Her soft voice filtered up from the first floor. She was singing again, as she did most of the time when she thought he wasn't around.

When they'd been teens and she'd sang on stage, he'd fallen so hard, so fast. Returning to the same stage suddenly didn't sound so bad.

"I'll do it," he conceded. "Can you have someone email me the script? I'd like to know a little more about what I'm getting into here."

His mother squealed with delight. "I knew we could count on you, Max! This will really raise a lot of money for the theater. It needs renovations that only a good chunk of funding can repair. You don't know how proud I am of you."

Max chatted a bit longer, making sure Elise was doing okay and feeling good. She assured him that she was fine but worried about him being alone with Raine. He blew that off because there was no way in hell he would discuss his out-of-control emotions where his ex was concerned.

And he would not analyze the fact he felt it his civic duty to help fix up the place where he had first fallen in love with Raine. So he wanted the theater to be back to its perfected state…so what? That didn't mean anything more than it was. When Max hung up, he glanced at the clock and realized it was Abby's bedtime. He turned off the overhead light and clicked on the bedside lamp to get the room ready for her. Not that he was growing cozy with this baby routine; he was just trying to help, that's all.

By the time he started toward the steps, Raine was coming up, clutching Abby to her chest and a bottle in the other hand.

"Sorry," he said as they met on the landing. "I didn't mean to be in the way."

"Oh, it's fine. I was working on some seed packets downstairs, so we're good."

When she started to move on up, Max touched her shoulder. "Can you come back down and talk, once she's asleep?"

Raine's gaze held his, and he didn't know if she was worried or scared of why he was asking her for more time alone.

"Just to talk," he added. "I'd like to talk to a friend right now."

Her eyes softened, shoulders relaxed and a sweet smile spread across her face. "I'll be right back down. I think that heater is doing a good job in the living room. I'll meet you there."

Somewhere along the way, tripping over chickens, getting felt up by goats and having sex on her bathroom vanity, Max felt as if they'd forged this new bond, something deeper than they'd ever had before. That could be the sex talking, but he truly didn't think so.

In any event, that didn't stop him from wanting to know more about the past—about what the hell had actually happened.

Max headed down to the kitchen to check the fridge, but when he glanced in and only saw goat cheese and some other questionable items, he decided it may just be best to avoid a snack. If he stayed here any length of time, he'd lose weight.

He was used to caviar, steak, fine cuisine. God, at this point he'd settle for a hot dog as opposed to asparagus, but Raine would probably kick him out in the snow if he mentioned the mystery meat.

After several minutes, Raine came back down, empty bottle in hand. As she rinsed it out in the sink, she eyed him.

"So, what's up?"

Leaning against the counter next to her, he shrugged. "Just spoke with my mother. She asked me to do some theater work while I'm in town."

Raine held his gaze for a moment before turning back to her task, shaking the bottle and resting it vertically in the strainer. She dried her hands and Max waited. Surely she'd have some input, some reaction.

But she said nothing as she walked over to the back door and checked the locks, flipping the back light off.

"It's cold in here," she stated, then walked into the living room.

"She said it's for some charity to benefit the arts and that the theater needed some major renovations," he went on as he followed her into the comfy room. "I know it's short notice, but I'm warming up to the idea. Might be nice to go back to the place where I got my start."

"I wouldn't know," she muttered as she strode toward the couch.

Max stood in the wide arched doorway watching as she picked up a few toys and a pink blanket from the floor. She stacked everything up into a neat pile in the corner and turned back to him.

"What?" she asked.

Resting his hands on his hips, Max shrugged. "You tell me. You don't think I should help out?"

"Not my business to say one way or another."

"Really? Then what did you mean a minute ago by you wouldn't know?"

Raine raked a hand through her messy hair and sighed. "It's been a long day, Max, and I kind of need to sleep when Abby does, because, in case you didn't notice last night, she's not the best sleeper."

"Why do you do that?" he asked, stepping farther into the spacious room.

"Do what?"

"Run. When things are uncomfortable, you run to avoid them."

Her glare searched his for a second before she laughed. "You're kidding right?"

"Not at all."

He stood directly in front of her, ready to battle it out if need be, but she wasn't going anywhere. Not this time.

"I thought we weren't going to rehash this," she said. "If you want to talk about running, then maybe you should turn that judgmental finger away from me and point it at yourself."

"I never ran, Raine. I wasn't the one who got scared."

In a split second her palm connected with his cheek, shocking the hell out of him.

"Scared?" she repeated. "You have no idea how scared I was when you left. You have absolutely no clue what I went through, so don't you dare tell me about running and being scared."

Max rubbed his stinging skin and took in her tear-filled eyes. "What happened, Raine? What terrified you so much all those years ago that it would resurrect such strong emotions?"

She blinked back tears and looked away, shaking her head. "Dredging up the past won't change a thing, and trying to do so is just making this time between us now uglier. There's no reason we can't be civil."

He grabbed her shoulders. "We were a hell of a lot more than civil earlier. Don't you dare even think of denying the fact we were good together."

"You don't get it, do you?" she asked, jerking free of his grasp. "You are here by chance, Max. I have a life here, a baby who depends on me. As much as I wanted what happened between us to be simple and not get to me, it has." She released a deep, shuddering breath. "It made me remember, made me think of things I have no business reminiscing about. And when you mentioned the theater, that was the last straw, and I was taken right back to that time we met."

Max listened, his heart clutching, as her voice cracked on the last word. Right now he hated himself. Hated how he'd upset her, hated that he'd left—even though he had done everything to get her to follow—and he hated that fate had slammed him back into her life so suddenly that neither of them knew how the hell to handle all these emotions. Shaking his head, he sighed. There was so much between them—anger, resentment, betrayal.

"Listen," he said softly, meeting her watery gaze. "I didn't bring that up to make you remember or to hurt you. I just wanted a friend to talk to, and you understand me. Despite all the time that's passed, Raine, I'm still the same man."

"The same man as what?" she whispered. "Because the man I fell in love with shared the same dream as me. The man I adored and felt safe with would've never hurt me."

"Hurt *you*?" he asked. "You think I wasn't hurt? You ignored me, Raine. I worked damn hard to get a place ready for us. I had a small apartment with a little balcony, and I couldn't wait to show you."

Raine jerked back. "What? But…I waited to hear from you."

Max's heart thudded in his chest as he absorbed her shocking words. "I called." He wanted so bad to reach out and touch her, but not yet. Not when emotions were so raw. "I called every day. Your mother told me that you weren't home or that you were sick. Finally she told me that you couldn't bring yourself to call me because you'd changed your mind, and you were dating someone else."

Tears slid down Raine's pale cheeks. "She lied."

Max watched as confusion and doubt washed over her,

and that pit in the bottom of his stomach deepened. All this time he'd thought she'd purposely given him the brush-off, but, now, seeing her shock, he knew they were both victims here.

"You didn't have a clue, did you?" he whispered, his own shock spearing his heart, causing the ache to settle in all over again.

He didn't know what was more agonizing—Raine ignoring his plea or someone else sabotaging their dreams.

"No." She opened her tear-glistened eyes. "You wanted me?"

Max stepped forward, closing the distance between them. "I couldn't wait to get you out of here, Raine. I hated leaving you behind, knowing you wouldn't be appreciated and loved like you were with me."

"Your career took off so fast," she said. "I kept seeing you with women in the tabloids, and, when I didn't hear from you, I just…"

Max closed his eyes, unable to see the hurt he'd involuntarily caused. He was a coward. Knowing he'd caused even a moment of anguish for Raine put a vise grip on his heart.

Why did he take her mother's word for it? Why didn't he fight harder? Hindsight was layering guilt upon his shattered heart, and he deserved every bit of angst. He'd brought this upon himself for not going after what was most important in his life.

"When I couldn't get in touch with you, I worried I'd made a mistake in leaving. I thought about coming back." His voice was thick with emotion. "Instead, I turned reckless when your mother said you'd moved on. I didn't care what happened to me."

"The motorcycle wreck you were in not long after you left." She spoke aloud as if talking to herself. "That's where that scar on your shoulder is from?"

He nodded. "I was so angry at you for shutting me out,

and all that time you had no clue how much I wanted to be with you. My God, can you forgive me?"

Raine smiled through her tears. "We were victims, Max. There's nothing to forgive. We both know who's at fault here."

Anger bubbled up in Max. Fury and bitterness soon followed.

"Did your parents despise us together that much?"

Raine swiped at her damp cheeks. "My mother offered me my trust fund early if I would stop seeing you and date this boy who planned to go to law school and had aspirations of running for State Senate further down the road. Needless to say, I refused."

This was news to Max, which just proved how strong and loyal Raine was. Too bad her parents never saw what a treasure she truly was.

"What are we going to do?" she asked.

He focused his attention back on her, on the glimmer of light at the end of this long, dark tunnel. "You need to confront your parents."

Raine nodded. "You want to join me?"

"If I come along, things could get ugly. How about I watch Abby while you go pay them a visit?"

Raine stood stock-still. "You'll watch Abby? Alone?"

Max shrugged. "I think I've got the hang of it. Feed her, change her and let her sleep. Does that cover it?"

Raine's sweet laughter filled the room. "That covers it for the amount of time I'll be gone."

She reached for him, wrapping her arms around his waist and resting her head against his chest. "I have no idea what to say. I know they'll defend their actions, but they stole everything from me. You were my life, Max."

How could they get over this massive hurdle that seemed to constantly be placed in front of them? Could they move past this revelation? So much time had elapsed, but his feelings were stronger now than they were when he and Raine had been eighteen.

Emotionally, if they could move on, where would they move *to*? He had a life in L.A., and she had a life here with her work, her baby.

Abby. He couldn't let Abby or Raine out of his life, but how the hell did he make this work? Had they missed their opportunity?

"After I talk to my parents, where does that leave us?" Raine asked, searching his eyes for answers he wasn't sure he had.

"It leaves us with a lot to discuss." He reached out, stroked her rosy cheeks. "And to decide if we think this will work again."

Her lids fluttered down as she brought her hands up to clasp his wrists. "The stakes are too high."

"Does that mean you won't try?"

"It means I'm scared," she murmured, raising her gaze to his.

Max slid his lips across hers. "Me, too."

Coaxing her lips apart, he wrapped his arms around her waist, pulling her body flush with his. He wanted to take away her pain, make her forget all the bad between them. He worried she'd push him away, but, when her hands traveled to his shoulders and around his neck, he knew they were meeting in the middle.

With a patience he'd never known before, Max lifted the edge of her shirt until she helped to rid herself of it. He fused their mouths together once more, taking her bra straps and sliding them down her arms.

Raine arched her back, allowing him perfect access to her neck, her chest. All that smooth, silky skin waiting to be explored. He took his time, making each stroke of his tongue, each simple kiss, count.

They may have screwed up in the past, and he could

very well be making a colossal mistake now, but damned if he could stop himself.

He pivoted her until they hit the wall. Sudden, frantic movements had them shedding the rest of their clothes. Garments lay all around them in random piles.

Max took his fingertips and traveled over her bare hips, into the dip at her waist and up to her breasts. Her body trembled beneath his gentle touch. Goose bumps sprung up all over her skin.

"What are you doing to me?" she whispered, searching his face. "The things I want with you…"

"I want them, too, Raine."

He only prayed to God they were talking about the same things, because, even though he'd be leaving Lenox in a few months, he wanted to spend time with her. He wanted to get to know her all over again. And when the time came for him to leave…well, they'd deal with that bridge when it was time to cross it.

Ten

Whoever was pounding on the door would be very sorry.

Didn't people in this town know she had a finicky baby who didn't sleep too well? No? Well, they should. This was the second time someone had pounded on her door, and she was about to put up a Do Not Disturb sign.

Springing from the bed, Raine grabbed her robe and tip-toed from the bedroom, careful not to disturb Max or Abby.

She nearly twisted an ankle racing down the steps, because, if whoever was at the door decided to reach for the doorbell, that would surely wake Abby. And Raine wasn't *about* to let that happen.

Making sure the robe was tied and everything was tucked in, she yanked open the door.

"Marshall," she said, jerking back. "What are you doing here?"

His eyes raked over her body, and Raine so wished she'd grabbed the thick terry cloth robe because the blast of cold air was doing nothing to hide the fact she was completely naked underneath.

"I wanted to check in on you, and let you know that the roads have been downgraded from a level three to a level two. Which means you can go out, but only if necessary…"

Behind her, Raine heard the steps creak. She didn't have

to turn to know who was there, but she glanced over her shoulder and nearly swallowed her tongue.

If she had thought Max Ford was sexy as hell before… well, now she needed some water. The man had on only his jeans—unbuttoned—and was cuddling Abby against his bare chest. Yeah, he may not want this family life, but he looked damn good wearing it. If Abby had woken up fussy, she surely wasn't now. She was nestled against Max's warm, broad chest.

A sliver of sorrow slid through her. This could've been their life…but their baby had died along with her dreams.

And even though she and Max had uncovered a major secret last night, she hadn't been able to confess that she'd been pregnant. Max had already been dealt a blow and was beating himself up. There was no way she was going to drop another life-altering bombshell.

They had enough issues to sort through as it was.

Marshall lifted a brow. "I see you weren't alone during the snowstorm," he stated.

Max came to stand directly behind Raine and she turned her attention back to Marshall. "Thanks for letting us know about the roads."

Marshall didn't take his eyes off Max. "I'll be sure to let your father know you're okay, Raine."

With that he turned and marched off the snow-covered steps.

Raine closed the door, flicked the lock and spun around to lean against it. "Well, that was awkward."

Max held Abby out toward her. "Awkward is not knowing what to do when she wakes crying and smells like… well, you know what she smells like."

Raine laughed and took the baby. "Don't be afraid of a dirty diaper, Max."

"I'm not afraid of the diaper," he said defensively as he followed her back up the steps. "I'm more afraid of the baby in the diaper. What if I did something wrong and hurt her or got crap all over the place?"

Heading back into the nice toasty-warm master bedroom, Raine laid Abby on the bed and grabbed a fresh diaper from the dresser.

"First, you can't hurt her by changing her diaper." Raine unzipped the footed pajamas. "Second, the wipes are here for a reason, and, believe me, I've gone through my share."

Raine quickly changed the diaper and picked Abby back up, patting her back. When she turned to Max, he had his arms crossed over that wide chest sprinkled with dark hair. He stole her breath.

"You're a wonderful mother."

Needing to lighten the tension, she shrugged. "Being a good mother has nothing to do with changing diapers."

"No, but I've see how loving you are with her, how patient and gentle. I'm a nervous wreck."

Raine smiled. "I was a nervous wreck too when I brought her home for the first time. But I learned quickly, and I'm still learning. I'll screw up at some point, and all I can do is hope she loves me through my faults."

And she prayed Abby would love her when she learned she wasn't her biological mother. No matter the genes, Raine loved this baby more than anything in the world. And she'd do everything in her power to give her a life full of choices and opportunities...not demands and expectations.

"So you think Marshall has run back to your dad, yet?" Max asked.

Raine cringed. "I have no doubt he was on his cell the second he got back into his truck. But who cares? My parents don't control me."

Moving around Max, she took Abby and laid her back down in the Pack 'N' Play pen with her favorite stuffed cat. She turned back to Max and sighed.

Now that the damage was done, Raine could only hope

the news of Hollywood's hottest bachelor playing house with her wouldn't hurt this drawn-out adoption process.

"My parents have never been happy with my decisions," she went on. "Finding both of us half naked is nothing that will disappoint them. I'm almost positive I'm at the bottom of the list for Daughter of the Year, anyway."

Max eased down on the edge of the bed and stared at her. "I know your father barely mentions her, but, surely they love having a grandchild."

Raine shrugged. "I'm sure they do in their own way, but they've already asked if I've put her on the waiting list for the private schools because so many of them are years to get into. They can't believe that I've considered home-schooling."

Max rested his elbows on his knees and continued to study her. "So they want to control her?"

"The way they couldn't control me," she confirmed, rubbing her arms. "I won't let it happen. Abby will make her own path in life, with my guidance, not my demands."

"You really are a single mother," he murmured. "You have no one to help you."

Raine lifted her chin. "I don't need any help. I sure as hell don't want help in the form of control."

"Good for you," he stated. He reached out, took her hands and pulled her toward him. "But that has to be hard on you…being alone, doing it all. Is Abby's dad nowhere in the picture? Surely he could give financial support."

Raine shook her head. There was no need to get into the whole backstory of Abby's life. If she and Max could work through their past problems—and that was a big *if*—then she would come clean about everything. And that meant both babies.

"It's just me," she reiterated. "But we're making it work. And as soon as I get back to a heavier volume of work in the spring and summer, things will really look up."

The way he studied her made her nervous. She didn't want him to dig deeper into her life, into her closet of skeletons. He would only end up more hurt, and she couldn't do that to the man she loved.

And she'd never blamed him for deserting her when she was pregnant…because he had had no clue. But she *had* blamed him for killing their dreams. Now she knew the truth, and the guilt consumed her for hating him all these years.

"I'll pay to have your furnace replaced."

Raine jerked her hands from his. "Like hell you will! I'll pay for it. We're okay right now as long as my firewood holds out. These old stoves heat really fast. I should have enough wood for another month anyway. Plus that space heater downstairs didn't do too badly."

"So what will you do when the wood runs out if the weather is still cold? You know the East Coast is finicky."

Raine shrugged. "I'll figure out something. I always do in a pinch."

"Why not just let me help?" he asked.

Raine glanced over at Abby who was waving her little arms and sucking on a stuffed cat's furry tail. "Because you're here for a short time." She turned back to him and offered a smile. "And I won't always have someone to come riding to my rescue."

"Because you won't let them or because you are alone?"

Why did he have to put things into perspective so simply?

"Both," she replied honestly. "I'd rather do things on my own than pretend to be someone I'm not just to have the help and support of my family."

"What happened to all the money you got when you turned twenty-five?" he asked, then shook his head. "I'm sorry…I shouldn't have asked that. I'm just surprised that you're struggling when I know you had a good chunk of change coming your way."

Raine backed away from him and moved to the dresser, pulling out a pair of black yoga pants and a sweatshirt.

She didn't care that he watched; she wanted to get dressed so she could start her day, and then he could be on his way since the roads were clear. They both needed time to think about the past…and the future.

"My parents had that little rule changed when I rebelled and decided that the money could be mine, provided that I adhered to their 'simple' guidelines."

Max's brows drew together. "They kept the money from you? That's…archaic. Why did they do that?"

She pulled out a pair of heavy socks and yanked them on, as well. "Because I loved you, because I planned on leaving and because I ran into some…trouble when you left."

"What kind of trouble?"

Oh, no. There was no way she could get into that conversation. Not after they'd succumbed to passion so many times over the past two days, and not when her heart was starting to gravitate toward him again. She had to steel herself. There was already way too much hurt hovering between them.

"We'll save that for another time," she promised.

Max looked as if he wanted to say more, but he merely nodded.

"I need to get some wood, feed the chickens and the goats." She grabbed a ponytail holder from the top of the dresser and pulled her hair into a top knot. "You care to watch Abby for a minute?"

He glanced over and nodded. "She seems harmless, but, if I smell something, I'll let you know."

Raine laughed, grateful he didn't push the issue. "Thanks. I'll hurry."

"Watch that one goat," he called after her. "He likes to get all up in your business."

Raine laughed and headed out of the room. Max was starting to enjoy it here. He hadn't said so, but she could tell. After only two days of living in her crazy farm-girl world, Hollywood icon Max Ford was comfortable, content and liking it. He smiled, he opened up, and he even let down his guard.

If the paparazzi got wind he was here, they'd be all over him. Raine giggled as she went to the back door and shoved her feet into her rain boots. The paparazzi at her house would seriously tick off her parents, and, if she was a teen again, she'd so be calling the media, but she was a mother and an adult. Pettiness had no place in her life.

And there was no need in starting any more fights than necessary, though she knew her mother or father would be calling shortly to confirm that Max had indeed been stuck here.

As she stepped off the back step, Bess and Lulu came through the weatherproof rubber flap and ran out to her, the chickens following behind. She nearly tripped but caught herself. She loved her life, loved raising a garden, loved her chickens and goats, loved her home that needed more repairs than she knew what to do with, and she loved being a mother.

The adoption progression was beyond frustrating, but her attorney had assured her everything was fine, and sometimes the process took longer than others.

So, now Raine played the waiting game…and tried to figure out just what to do with her heart and Max Ford.

Eleven

Abby started fussing; and Max tried shaking her stuffed cat, holding up another toy that had tag things all over it and even a silky blanket. Nothing was making her happy. And she wasn't in full-fledged-crying mode with the red face and snot, but he seriously wanted to avoid that type of confrontation.

So he bent down into the Pack 'N' Play pen—he thought that's what Raine had called it—and picked Abby up. Instantly she stopped fussing.

"Are you kidding me?" he asked her.

Drool gathered just below her bottom lip and slid down her chin, and Max wasn't repulsed. She was so damn cute he wanted to squeeze her. He refrained, but held her against his chest, inhaling the sweet scent.

He'd worked with babies on a couple of films, but his actual interaction with them was slim because the mother was always nearby, and once the scenes were shot, the baby would leave.

Max took a seat in the chair closest to the fireplace. He'd be kidding himself if he didn't admit that seeing Raine as a mother clenched his heart. They'd had the perfect life planned for themselves, and kids were a huge part of it.

As he looked at Abby, he realized her features were

nothing like Raine's. Where Raine had soft green eyes, Abby's were dark brown. Raine had pale skin and Abby's was a bit darker.

Apparently she took after her dad. And Max hated the man…a man he didn't even know. But how could Max resent a man for making a child with Raine? Raine was a victim just like Max. They'd both moved on as best they could once their lives together had been ripped apart.

Abby squirmed a bit on his lap, so he sat her on the edge of his knee and bounced her. "I'm not sure if I'm doing this right, but if you start screaming, I guess I'll know you don't like it."

Raine's cell chimed from the dresser, and Max nearly laughed. He had no doubt that was either Raine's mother or father calling to confirm that their daughter had a sleepover.

Who the hell took away money rightfully due to their child? Not only that, who kept it when there was a baby in the mix?

Max had no idea really what to do with Abby, so he came to his feet and starting walking through the house.

And there was no way he could let this furnace situation go. He'd already asked his mother who to contact, and she'd done some calling of her own to cash in on some favors. Raine could hardly argue once the furnace was paid for and installed.

"Your mama is stubborn," he told Abby as they paced through the hall.

He stopped at the room where Raine had been making lotions and smiled. She'd been fiddling with things like that when they'd dated. She was always trying out some new homemade soap or making candles. She didn't care that she wasn't popular or that her mother's high-society friends thumbed their noses at Raine. And that was one of the main things Max had found so attractive about her.

He wondered when she'd be making that visit to have a

come-to-Jesus meeting with her parents. But he wouldn't push. She needed to approach this in her own way, on her own time.

And he would be there to support her.

Figuring she'd be back in soon, he headed downstairs toward the kitchen. Abby started fussing a bit more, and he assumed she was probably hungry. Raine had given her a bottle somewhere around five this morning, but then Abby had gone back to sleep. How often did babies eat?

This parenting thing was beyond scary, but Raine seemed to know exactly what to do and when to do it. Were there books? An instruction manual?

Abby started to squirm and cry. This was going to get ugly real fast if he didn't do something. He prayed to God Raine already had bottles made up, because he'd only seen her make a few, and he had no idea how to do one himself. Sometimes she used goat's milk; sometimes she used a powder and water mix.

He sincerely hoped there was goat's milk in the fridge, because he had no clue the ratio for the powder and water, and there was no way in hell he'd be milking any farm animal. He'd risk the roads and hit the nearest grocery store first.

Max opened the fridge, saw two premade bottles, thanked God above for small mercies and grabbed one. Holding onto Abby, he pried the top off and quickly stuck the bottle in her mouth like plugging up a dam.

Blessed peace. He only hoped he was doing the right thing. He cradled her in his arm and propped the bottle up with the other hand. He paced around the room and from the wide window over the sink, he saw Raine go from the barn with the chickens, into the goat barn. She moved slowly over the mounds of snow, but she looked so comfortable in her daily chores. He couldn't even imagine her trying to do all of this on her own, but she was managing somehow.

As he continued to feed Abby and pace, he walked by a small built-in desk area in the corner. Papers lay strewn across the top, but it was the paper tacked on the wall beside the desk that brought him up short. It was a court date regarding…custody?

Was she in some sort of custody battle? He glanced closer at the paper and noticed another name. Jill Sands.

Max drew back. Jill…as in Raine's younger cousin? What the hell was going on?

He glanced down at the baby who had closed her eyes and continued to suck the milk.

Max knew whatever was going on in Raine's life wasn't his concern, but why hadn't she said anything? Obviously Abby wasn't biologically Raine's, yet she hadn't said a word.

The stomping of her boots on the stoop outside the back door had him moving away from the desk. Even though he felt a bit hurt at not knowing, he couldn't exactly expect her to open up to him after all these years apart.

The back door opened, letting in a cold blast of air. Raine slid out of her snow-covered boots and stepped onto the linoleum before shrugging out of her coat and hanging it on a peg. She shoved her gloves into the pockets and hung up her small red cap.

When she turned around, she froze, then smiled.

"Well, I certainly didn't expect you to be feeding her."

Max smiled back as he glanced down at a very content baby. "She was quite vocal, so I assumed that's what she wanted. Hope I didn't mess up."

Raine's eyes roamed over his chest and up to his face. "You're doing just fine."

"You better stop looking at me like that," he said with a

slight grin. "The roads are clear, and I should probably get back home to check on my mom."

The passionate scrutiny that had been visible seconds ago vanished from her eyes. She nodded and reached for Abby.

"Let me take her." With ease she took the baby, bottle and all, and cradled her. "I wasn't thinking."

She'd erected a wall. Just like that she'd taken the baby, stepped back and wouldn't look him in the eyes. Oh, no. This was not going to end this way…hell, this didn't have to end. Did it?

"Raine." He waited until she looked back at him. "Don't do this. Don't shut me out just because our forced proximity is over. We are working toward something here."

"I'm not shutting you out, Max. I'm just scared."

"There's nothing to be afraid of."

He seemed so confident. But that was Max. He'd always had more confidence than her.

"I expect to see you again soon," he said, easing closer and running a hand up her arm. "Will you be coming to my mother's for anything?"

"She hasn't placed any new orders, but I may stop by to check on her. And I need to discuss a couple of things about her gardening, since I'll be placing more seed orders soon."

Max nodded. "What can I do before I go?"

She glanced to Abby and shook her head. "We're good. Thanks for everything, though."

"I didn't really do anything," he said.

Her eyes held his. "You did. More than you know."

"I want to see you," he stated. "Outside the house. Just because I'm leaving now doesn't mean I don't want to see where this goes."

Raine nodded. "I want that. And as we discussed, I'm going to confront my parents soon."

"Let me know when. I'm here for you and Abby."

Raine stepped closer, easing the baby to the side and rising up on her toes to place a soft kiss on his cheek.

"My door is always open for you, Max."

The door to her heart was also wide open, but she couldn't tell him that, couldn't risk him leaving for good again. He would leave, she had no doubt. But would he fight for them?

"Glad to hear it," he said.

"You don't know how much I appreciate you being here, helping with Abby and gathering wood." Raine glanced down to Abby and back to Max. "It's hard being a single mom. I try not to complain, but sometimes I worry if all these balls I have in the air are just going to come crashing down on me."

Max laid a hand on her shoulder, another on Abby's tiny arm. "As long as I'm in the picture, I won't let anything crash down on you again."

Her heart throbbed. Now she could only hope and pray Max wanted to stay in that picture.

Raine didn't want to jump up and down, but when she saw the tiny little green sprouts popping up from the rich soil, she nearly did. Not everyone could grow vegetables in the winter. Well, they could, but she doubted they'd go to all the pains she did to ensure organic seeds and chemical-free soil.

The warm light was perfect and so was the rotation schedule of moving the pots around in the light. Raine was so excited about the little bean sprouts and kale. And her clients would be happy too that they were getting a jump start on their crops. When the weather broke and the risk of frost was gone, she could transplant these vegetables into the ground for her clients, and they could have their fresh produce before most other people.

And the stash she'd be able to take to the Farmer's Market would be larger than last year. Thankfully each year her business grew. She had no less hopes for this spring.

Her cell vibrated against the worktable, and Raine smiled at the number on the screen.

"Hi, Jill," she answered.

"Hey," her cousin replied. "I haven't called for a while but got a break from classes and wanted to check in. I heard you all got a crazy amount of snow. Everyone okay?"

Raine leaned back against her counter and crossed her arms. "Yeah, we're all good now. The furnace went out, but I have enough wood to last until the warmer weather gets here."

She hoped.

"Oh, Raine, I'm sorry. I swear, you really do always look on the bright side of life. I wish I could be more like you."

Raine smiled. "You're more like me than you know."

"How's Abby? I loved the picture you sent me last week of her in that cute little crocheted hat with a pink bow. She's getting so big."

"She's doing great. Still a bit cranky at night, but much better than she used to be with bedtimes."

Jill sighed. "Sometimes I wonder if I burdened you."

"Never," Raine said, coming to stand fully upright. "That beautiful baby has never been, nor will ever be, a burden to me. I love you, and I love her."

"You're the best thing that's ever happened to me…and to Abby," Jill replied with a sniff. "I know I made the right decision in letting you adopt her. She's getting more love and care than I ever could've provided."

Raine's heart clenched because, for a very brief moment, Jill had considered an abortion.

"I've always wanted a family," Raine told her cousin. "And Abby is such a huge part of my life now. I can't recall what it was like without her."

"I'd like to come visit over summer break," Jill said. "If that's okay with you."

"That's more than okay with me," Raine said. "I'm really proud of you for putting your baby's needs ahead of your own."

"I know I made the right decision. There's no way I could've taken care of a child and continued my schooling…and I couldn't abort her. The thought now makes me sick. So adoption was the only other choice."

Raine teared up. She couldn't wait for that official piece of paper.

"I need to get to my next class," Jill said. "But I wanted to make sure you all were okay. I love and miss you, Raine."

"Love and miss you, too. See you soon."

Raine hung up, clutched her phone to her chest and closed her eyes. Jill was doing what she should be, with no help from her parents. Jill's mother and Raine's mother were sisters. They were certainly cut from the same snotty, holier-than-thou cloth, as well.

When Jill had become pregnant, it was like déjà vu for Raine all over again. Things happen…Raine hated to tell her mother that they were all human, and not everyone was perfect.

Raine may not have been in the best financial position to adopt, but she was much better off than Jill, and Raine's business was continuing to grow.

There was no way Raine would've sat back during Jill's struggle. Jill needed support like Raine never had, and when Abby was old enough to understand, Raine and Jill would sit down and tell her the truth.

But for now, Abby was hers and Raine would love her as her very own.

Twelve

Max made sure his mom was comfortable in her favorite chair in the patio before he went to get her lunch. The nurse had left, and Max was doing what he'd originally come here to do.

While he was beyond thankful for the time he'd spent with Raine, he was needed here. He also wanted a break from Raine and her sultry curves, her snappy comebacks and the maternal love he saw in her eyes each time she looked at Abby.

If he was going to fight for them, Max had some serious thinking to do. While he would not give up this movie opportunity with Bronson Dane, he also could not walk away from Raine again without seeing if they could make things work.

There had to be a way. Fate wouldn't be that cruel to throw them together just to rip them apart once more.

But now that he was home again, he figured his mother would be a good source of information. Plus, knowing her, she'd want to hear about his three days snowbound with his first love.

As Max brought his mother a tray of sandwiches and fruits, she smiled up at him.

"Thank you, sweetheart." She picked up the glass of

water and took a sip before looking back at him. "How are Abby and Raine doing?"

Wow...that didn't take long.

"They're great," he said, taking a seat in the floral wing-back chair. "So just ask what you want to know, and let's skip the chitchat."

Elise laughed, reaching for a grape. "I'm a mother, Max. It's my job to put my nose in your business."

"Well, that guy you called about the furnace phoned me, and I gave him the go-ahead to replace the unit and repair her stove, so she could be warm sooner rather than later."

His mother's eyes widened. "She agreed to let you do that?"

"Oh, no, but I'm doing it anyway."

"Good for you," she murmured. "She needs someone to help her. God knows that snooty mother of hers won't. And don't get me started on her father."

"Yeah, when did he become ruler over Lenox?"

"Not long after we moved." Elise waved a hand in the air and reached for another piece of fruit. "That man can't control his family, so he tries to control the city."

Max could see that. Raine's father had been an arrogant jerk when Max and Raine had dated as teens. Little did he know it was Raine's mother who was so underhanded.

"I think Raine is a lovely girl, and I'm just sorry I didn't see it years ago," his mother finally said, her eyes seeking his.

Max jerked his attention to her and eased forward in his seat. "She's no different now than she was when we were teens. What changed your mind?"

"I never truly had a problem before," she admitted. "But I wanted peace in my house. You and your father already had so much tension between you...I didn't want a girl to drive that wedge deeper."

"I loved her."

"I see that now," she said. "My own shortsightedness had a hand in keeping you two apart."

Max shook his head. He wasn't getting into the real reason he and Raine had parted ways.

"Raine is the hardest worker I've ever seen," Elise continued. "She goes out of her way to make sure her clients are well informed of exactly what they're getting with their plants and seeds. She's very concerned about chemicals and unnatural gardening. The fact that she does all this research in order to have the best is really remarkable."

"How many clients does she have in town?"

His mother shrugged. "I'd say around thirty or so. She's quite busy in the summer. I don't know how she'll juggle the business with Abby when the time comes. Of course, I'll still be here, so it would be no hardship to let the little princess come inside while her mother works."

Max had so many questions. Too many and he almost felt guilty gossiping about Raine with his mother. God, he'd resorted to being one of the busybodies in town. Now all he needed was a teacup and matching saucer.

"Her mother has tried to get the ladies not to hire Raine, and some of them have listened," she said. "I personally need someone here when I'm not around in the summer, and, since Raine started several years ago, she's been nothing but a blessing to me."

Max stared at his mother. Was this the same woman who had tried to convince him as a teen that Raine wasn't right for him and he should move on?

His mother smiled softly and eased back in her seat, ignoring her lunch. "I know what you're thinking. I know what I said in the past, and I believed what I said at the time was what was best for that point in our lives, Max."

"You told me not to see her anymore," he reminded her. "You said she wasn't good for our family."

"And at the time she wasn't," Elise insisted. "Max, your

father didn't think she was good for you. And no matter what I thought, I couldn't stand to see our family torn apart by teenage hormones. You were two rebellious teens, and you fed off each other's defiant ways."

"I loved her, Mom," he repeated. And he still cared deeply for her. "I would've married her had she come to L.A. when I tried to get her there."

"I know you would've," she said softly. "I know how much you cared for her, but at the time I just couldn't have my family ripped apart. You two weren't ready to be together, to be that far away on your own. You had stars in your eyes. Your father used to have that same look."

For the first time when discussing his father, Max really looked at his mother. Her eyes had darted down, her mouth no longer smiling. Max loathed his father. The man was nothing but a careermonger who did anything and everything to get to the top, to be the best. He had sacrificed his family, his personal life and ultimately the relationship with his son. There was no way Max was like his father. He wouldn't sacrifice his family…at least not intentionally.

But he was so far past caring what his father thought. He did, however, care about how his mother was being treated.

"When will Dad be here to visit?" he asked, already figuring the answer.

"He's so busy, Max. You know how he is…"

Max nodded. "I know. I just assumed he would take some time off."

He didn't push. No need in stating the obvious and making his mother feel worse about a marriage that was obviously one-sided. Did his father see what all he was missing in life? Was a chain of five-star restaurants that important when your wife was recovering from breast cancer surgery?

Max stewed in silence as his mother ate, but a few more questions kept gnawing at him. Did his mother know about the adoption or guardianship or whatever the hell was going on with Raine? Surely she did, because Raine hadn't been pregnant, and his mother would've known. Hell, the whole town more than likely knew about this, so why wouldn't she tell him the truth?

Didn't she think he'd understand? He was adopted himself for pity's sake. Perhaps that was another reason he'd fallen so hard, so fast, for little Abby.

But he wasn't done with Raine. They were just getting started. He'd get her to open up, he'd break down that wall of fear, and then he'd figure out just how the hell they could make this work.

As Raine assembled her last basket for the morning, her doorbell rang. She glanced over at Abby, who was pleased as punch in her Pack 'N' Play pen, and left her to head downstairs to see who her unexpected visitor was.

She frowned when she peered out the window alongside the door and saw a man in a blue work uniform standing on her front step. Cautiously easing open the door only a couple inches, she kept her hand on the knob. "Yes?" she asked.

The man held out a clipboard with what appeared to be an order form. "Good morning, ma'am. I'm here to install your new furnace. I was informed the old one has not been removed, so I'll need to do that first."

Raine stared down at the order, then back up at the man. "Excuse me? New furnace?"

Then it hit her. Max. Damn it. Most women got flowers and got all weepy. She got a new furnace and tears pricked her eyes. She was so not normal.

"Um…no. No, the old one hasn't been removed." She allowed the furnace man to enter. "It's right back here."

As much as she wanted to protest, she knew this worker didn't want to get caught in the middle of a feud, and she also knew when to just let someone help. And that was a totally new concept for her, since Raine didn't get reinforcements from anyone. Yet, stubbornness aside, how could she deny that Max had been there for her more in the past several days than her parents had been most of her adult life?

When Raine showed the man where the furnace was, he went back out to his truck and another man came in as well to assist. Raine wasn't too comfortable being alone in her house with two strange men, but that was life. She was a single woman, and this was just how it worked.

Once she realized they didn't need her standing around staring at them, she went back upstairs, grabbed her cell from her work area and then picked up Abby.

She quickly dialed Elise's house and wasn't surprised when Max answered.

"You seriously paid for a furnace?" she asked, not beating around the bush.

"I seriously did," he said with a chuckle. "Did you try to kick out the workers yet?"

Raine smiled and shifted Abby's weight. "I thought about it, but then realized I would only be hurting myself and Abby if I didn't accept your very generous and much appreciated gift."

"Wow. The old Raine would've fought me tooth and nail over this."

Her smile spread across her face as she started to head back downstairs. "Yeah, well, I'm not the same Raine, and I'm not an idiot. I need a furnace and you want to gift it to me. I'll take it."

Max laughed again. "I'm very impressed with the new Raine. Would the new Raine happen to have any plans for Valentine's Day?"

Was he flirting with her? She hadn't flirted since...way too far back to remember.

"Sorry. The new Raine has a baby and no sitter."

"I'd like to have both of you for my date," he stated. "I'm kind of greedy."

"What about your mother? Will a nurse be watching her that night?"

Abby's little arms were waving about and nearly knocked the cell from between Raine's shoulder and ear. Raine eased her head the other direction to ward off slobbery fingers.

"Well, Mom claims my father is coming to town to spend the day with her."

Raine stepped into the living room, settled Abby into her swing and turned it on. "You don't sound convinced."

"I believe he wants to come, but work always gets in the way."

Raine watched Abby as she swung back and forth. The men in the other room were making quite the racket, and Raine couldn't believe she was contemplating a date with Max. Seriously? And if they went on a date, where would that lead? Back to bed?

Marshall had already seen Max at her house, so that secret was no longer well kept. Perhaps if that became an issue with the adoption, this "date" would go a long way in proving Max wasn't just a fling. Even though she couldn't necessarily define what they were at the moment, they'd definitely gone beyond just sex.

But was she ready to take that next step and go on a real date?

"I'm not sure," she said.

"I don't want you to be uncomfortable, but I know we have a good time together. What do you say?"

"Can I think about it?"

Max chuckled. "You can, but you have a day to do it."

"If I did agree, what would we do?" she asked.

"I have plans in place if you say yes. That's all you need to know."

Shivers coursed through Raine. How could she refuse

a man when he'd already given her and their time together so much thought and consideration?

He was right in the sense that they did enjoy each other's company, and she didn't have anything else to do.

Oh, who was she kidding? She wanted this date like she wanted her next breath.

"If you're sure you can handle me and Abby, then I guess we're available."

"Perfect," he said. "I'll be at your house tomorrow at five. Does that work?"

Giddiness swept through Raine, and she spun in a little circle. Max couldn't see her, and, even if he could, she didn't care.

"Where will we go?" she asked.

"All you need to worry about is being yourself. Don't get all fussed up. I just want to see the natural Raine I spent three days with in the snowstorm."

Raine wrinkled her nose. "You're serious? Because natural Raine isn't worthy of public places."

"You'll be fine," he assured her with a laugh. "Promise."

By the time she hung up, Raine was intrigued as to what he had planned. Max being back in town had already turned into something she'd never expected. How could she not fall for him again? Especially when she ached for him with all her heart and soul.

Although she knew she should probably keep her distance, deep down she knew there was no way she could stay detached from him. Her emotions were too profound, their bond too strong. And since they'd been intimate and had begun to confront their past issues, that bond had only grown.

He was extending this olive branch to her. She had no doubt he wanted to see where this newfound relationship led. She did, too.

But as much as she wanted to savor this time together, she knew they both needed to proceed with caution.

Because neither of them could afford another emotional landslide.

Thirteen

When Max took his first step over the threshold of the Shakespearian Theater, he had to stop and take it all in. The large red-velvet curtains draped from the stage at the far end. The slanted rows of seats and the tiered balconies on either side were completely empty, but in a few short weeks would be overflowing with an eager audience…he hoped.

This play was for charity, and they needed to raise an insane amount of money for the theater's renovations. Of course he'd donate a large sum as well, perhaps double the amount brought in from the play.

And since he'd just been faxed the script yesterday morning, he'd barely had time to look it over, but he did know he was playing a Roman soldier. Just what he wanted to do—sport a sheet, a metal chest plate and wield a sword. But for the sake of the arts and as a favor to his mother, he'd do it. God knows he'd played worse characters over the course of his career.

As he made his way down the aisle, that thrill shot through him of doing live theater again. There was nothing like that immediate feedback, the cheers, the standing ovations…and the ego boost that inevitably followed. The vanity of acting was just part of the process, and he'd learned long ago to face it head-on, but not let it consume his life. Too many talented actors had fallen, because their ego had gotten in the way of their dreams.

Max made his way to the back of the stage where he'd told the director he'd meet him.

An elderly man was bent over in the corner mumbling something about cords and wiring. Max smiled and cleared his throat to get the man's attention.

"Oh, oh. I didn't know you were here." He came to his feet, extending his hand. "It's an honor to meet you in person, Mr. Ford."

"Call me Max," he replied, pumping the other man's hand.

"I'm Joe. I'm the director here. I can't tell you how thrilled we were when your mother said you'd take on this part. We had a local man scheduled to play the role, but he had to bow out at the last minute."

"I'm happy I can help."

Joe slid his hands into his pockets and rocked back on his heels. "How is your mother doing? Hated to hear about her illness."

"She's on the mend and doing remarkably well," he told the older gentleman. "We're really lucky they caught the tumor in time. The doctor expects a full recovery and no chemo, so she's happy."

"That's fantastic news," Joe said with a smile. "We all just love her around here. She's always been such an advocate of the arts and it's nice to have someone like her in our corner."

Max nodded toward the wires. "Having some problems over there?"

The director sighed, shaking his head. "I can't get this mess figured out. We need to have the lighting updated, and I'm trying to get through this one last play before having it replaced."

"Is it the time or the money that's the hold up?" Max asked.

"A little of both." Joe laughed, moving over the squat down again. "I really need to get an electrician in here before we do this production at the end of the month…"

"Call someone and I'll cover all costs. See how fast they can get it done."

Joe's head whipped around. "You're serious?"

Max nodded, squatting down beside Joe. "Absolutely. I can do some things, but this may be out of my element."

Joe grinned. "Yeah, I heard rumors there may be collaboration between you and Bronson Dane. Any truth to that?"

Shrugging, Max smiled. "We'll see." Coming to his feet, he rested his hands on his hips. "Now, why did you need to meet me today? Don't tell me you're spending Valentine's Day working."

Joe laughed. "My wife would kill me. I wanted to talk to you in person before any other actors arrived. Now that you've seen the script, are you comfortable with it? Do you want any changes?"

"I thought the script was great. I'm really looking forward to doing live theater again."

"Wonderful. That's such a relief."

Max studied the man and noticed he was much more relaxed now. "Did you think I'd come in, throw my weight around and try to take over your production?"

Joe raised his brows. "We've had that happen before. Not with you, of course. Last summer we had a certain A-list actor who wanted some things changed before he'd commit."

Max knew who Joe referred to. Even though L.A. was on the other side of the country, the acting industry really was small, and word traveled fast…especially when other performers were all too eager to slip into some diva's shoes.

"Well, I assure you," Max went on, "I'm thrilled to be

helping out with the charity and to get back to my roots. Are we starting rehearsals Monday?"

"Yes. Since we're pushing the envelope with the lead role change, you'll be coming in at the start of dress rehearsal, so I'm afraid there's not much time to get acquainted with the cast."

"I'm flexible." Max walked around behind the stage, checking out the lighting, looking at the various exits. "This place hasn't changed since I started here fifteen years ago."

"Not too much has. I've been here for almost ten years, and we've replaced the sound system and done some minor updating, but that's about it."

Max glanced to the small dressing area in the corner for the quick changes that were sometimes needed between sets when there wasn't time to change in a dressing room.

As if he were watching it happen, he saw a younger version of Raine and himself sneaking into that room and closing the door. They'd fooled around for hours on end in there. They'd arrive early for rehearsal and while the director and sound manager were busy talking, he and Raine would make out. Pathetic, but they were in the throes of a teenage love that consumed their every waking moment.

"If that's okay with you…"

Snapping out of his reverie, Max turned back to the elderly man. "I'm sorry, what?"

"I said I was going to have you and Patricia come in earlier on Monday. Since you're the leads, I thought you'd want to go over some key scenes without the rest of the cast here."

Max nodded. "That should be fine. If my mother is feeling up to it, I may bring her to a few of the rehearsals just to get her out of the house."

"We'd love to have her."

Max shook the man's hand again and walked around the

theater, taking in all the familiar surroundings, letting the nostalgia seep through him.

After several minutes of strolling down memory lane, Max knew he needed to get ready for his date with Raine. He was pretty anxious for their time together. Granted being around Abby made him a little uneasy, but he was starting to get more comfortable with her. It was just…she was so tiny he seriously feared he'd hurt her.

The snow was still stark white, except for the black slush that lined the side of the streets, but, for the most part, it remained beautiful and crisp.

As Max maneuvered his way back home, he realized how much he'd missed this weather. He hated to admit it, even to himself, but he'd once loved the winters here. When he'd been a kid, they'd had so many snowstorms. Canceled school, sleigh rides and sneaking off with Raine had been the major highlights from his youth.

He may not know what the hell he was doing with her, but he knew for sure that, when he was with her, he had that same feeling he had always had when they'd been together in the past…*perfection.* There was simply no other way to describe it.

L.A. would be waiting for him when he returned in two months. But for right now, he wanted Raine. He wanted to spend more time with her, with Abby, and, when it came time to leave again, who knows, maybe she'd come this time.

Raine didn't have much in the way of going-out clothes, but she settled for her nice jeans, black knee boots and a pink top that rested just off her shoulders. A bit sexy, but not obvious and trampy.

She nearly snorted. She was so not the poster child for seduction. She'd had to scrounge to find some makeup so she at least looked a little feminine.

And Max had called earlier, upset and frustrated because his father's plans to come visit had fallen through so they would either have to cancel their plans or spend Valentine's Day with his mother.

So did this really constitute a date since his mother and her baby would be there? Um…no. Apparently fate had intervened and taken the romance out of the most romantic night of the year. She nearly laughed. This whole *spending the evening with his mother* bit felt a little like working backward. Shouldn't they have done this *before* falling back in bed together?

Raine left her bathroom and picked up Abby from the Pack 'N' Play pen. Abby looked absolutely adorable with her red leggings, black-and-red shirt with hearts and black furry booties. There was a matching black hat with a red bow on it, but Raine wasn't so sure Abby would keep it on. Raine would at least try.

She had just descended the last step when the doorbell rang. Nerves settled low in her belly. This was nothing major. Just because it was Valentine's Day and just because Max had invited her and Abby to spend it at his house didn't mean anything. They were old friends. Okay, so they were old lovers. No, wait, they were new lovers.

Biting back a groan, Raine headed to the door. She honestly didn't know what they were right now. They'd slept together, argued, rehashed a very rocky point from their past and now they were having dinner. If she didn't know better, she'd think they'd slipped right back into their old pattern…except now she had a baby in the mix.

She jerked open the door, and Max stood there with a potted…basil plant?

Raine laughed. "You never were predictable."

"Why should I be? I always prided myself on standing out in a crowd."

"Basil, Max?"

He shrugged, stepping into the foyer. "You like to grow your own things so I thought you'd like an herb."

Unable to resist, she went up on her tiptoes and kissed Max on the cheek. "You're very sweet." Raine didn't want to think about how handsome he looked in his perfectly pressed dress pants and cobalt blue shirt, matching his eyes. Nor did she want to think about the lengths Max had gone to in order to get this plant at this time of year. The fact he didn't do the traditional roses on Valentine's Day warmed her heart and touched her in places his niceties had no place touching. He was leaving in less than two months, and she refused to let her heart go with him this time. Spending time with Max was going to happen, she refused to deny herself. But she was older and wiser now, and she had to be realistic.

"Are you two ready to go?" he asked, holding his arm out waiting for her to take it.

"I need to get the car seat from my vehicle first."

Max shook his head. "I bought one and put it in already. Well, the store manager had to install it because I was afraid to screw it up, but it's in and ready to go."

Oh, God. That was it. Her heart tumbled and fell into a puddle at his feet. Damn this man. How could she even consider handing him her heart again when it had been shattered in so many pieces last time? For heaven's sake, she was still recovering, if she were completely honest with herself.

"Everything okay?" Max asked, searching her eyes.

Raine offered a smile and shifted Abby in her arms. "We're good. All ready to go."

He slid a hand over her cheek, brushing her hair aside. "You look stunning, Raine. Too bad we can't stay in."

"Perhaps it's for the best."

"You don't believe that."

She stared up into his crisp blue eyes and held his stare.

"I do. As much as I love being together, we both know you'll be leaving soon. So let's just enjoy the time we have and worry about everything else later."

He captured her lips softly, then eased back. "I couldn't agree more."

Raine followed him out, angry at herself for the pity party she waged deep inside. There was that sliver of heartache in her that wanted him to stay. Wanted him to deny that he'd leave.

And didn't that make her naive?

Did she honestly think that they'd make love a few times, set up house with Abby, and he'd be all ready to throw his life in L.A. away and play daddy? She wasn't that gullible as a teen, so why now?

Because she wanted what she'd never had. Because she wanted to have that family, and, dammit, she wanted it with Max.

Once they were settled in his SUV, she forced herself to calm down. Wishing and wanting things that would never come to fruition was an absolute waste of time. She had other worries in her life, other people who loved and depended on her.

Like Abby. Each day that passed without a word from the courts made Raine more irritable and nervous.

Hopefully spending the evening with Max and Elise would provide the perfect distraction.

Fourteen

"She is just precious."

Max watched as his mother's eyes lit up while she held Abby. The baby kept trying to suck on the side of his mother's cheek, and Raine went to the diaper bag.

"She's getting hungry," she explained, mixing formula into the bottle. "Here, I can take her."

His mother looked up at Raine and smiled. "Would you mind if I fed her?"

"Not at all."

Raine shook the bottle and handed it over, along with a burp cloth. Max watched as his mother nestled Abby into the crook of her arm, and instantly Abby took to that bottle, holding onto his mother's hand.

Max couldn't stop the smile from spreading across his face. Just this alone was worth spending Valentine's Day with the women in his life.

"Why don't you two go for a walk or something," his mother suggested, looking across the sitting room to him. "I'm fine with this little angel, and I'm sure the last thing either of you want to do is babysit me."

Max laughed. "I'm not babysitting, and this is no hardship to spend my evening with three of the most beautiful ladies I know."

"Cut the charm, Romeo," Raine chimed in. "We already agreed to be your dates for the night."

His mother laughed. "Go on, you two. I've taken care of a baby in my time. Abby and I will be just fine."

Max really hated his father right now. Absolutely hated the man for always putting his work ahead of his family. Granted Max's mother wasn't sick at the moment, but she was just coming off of major surgery, and it was Valentine's Day, for pity's sake. What the hell could possibly be more important than your own wife?

He wasn't even married to Raine and still wouldn't have thought to spend today with anyone else. He wanted to have a good time with her while he was here. He wanted to make memories…and that revelation scared him. They'd already made memories in the short time he'd been here, but part of him wanted more. A lot more.

Max glanced over at Raine. "I have the greatest idea. Grab your coat."

Raine quirked a brow at him, and he shrugged, waiting for her to argue. But, surprisingly, she grabbed her coat, hat, scarf and gloves and bundled up as he did the same.

Max whispered his plan to his mother before he left the room, and she smiled up at him, indicating he should take his time and not to worry about Abby.

He grabbed Raine's hand and led her from the room, through the kitchen and into the attached garage off the utility room.

"What are we doing?" she asked as he flicked a switch, flooding the spacious three-car garage with lights.

"You'll see."

He went to the far wall where two sleds were hanging. More than likely these old things hadn't been used since before he left for L.A., but he knew his parents never got rid of anything and kept everything in an orderly fashion.

"Are you serious?" Raine asked when he held the sleds up.

"Very serious. This California transplant can't let all this good snow go to waste."

Raine glanced back toward the inside of the house, then back to him. "But your mother…"

"Is fine," he finished. "She knows we'll be a little bit. Let's have fun. Mom is loving this baby time, and I haven't been sledding in years."

He saw the battle she waged with herself, and then a wide grin spread across her face. "Oh, all right."

They headed out the back of the house where there was a good-size slope leading down to a large pond out in the distance. Max had loved this house as a kid. Sleigh riding in the winter, fishing in the summer. Of course his dad had always been too busy for either activity, so Max usually had a buddy over.

He took his boot and cleared a pile of snow out of the way before tossing down his sled. "Let's go slow a couple times to get this packed some, then we can race."

"You're on."

By the time they'd climbed back up the hill the third time, they were both out of breath.

"Apparently I'm not in as good of shape as I thought," he said, panting.

"Well, I'm blaming the heavy meal in my belly and carrying this sled. It's not me."

Max laughed. "We'll go with that. You ready, hotshot?"

She sat the sled atop the snow and settled onto it. "Let's see what you've got."

"On three." He sat down, placing his hands beside him in the snow to push off. "One…two…three!"

They shot down the hill, her sled turned at the last minute, slamming into his and knocking them both from the sleds and into a pile of snow. Even though snow slid into the top of his coat and made his neck cold and wet, he couldn't deny he was having a blast. And Raine's sweet laughter resounded through the night, wringing his heart and making him wonder again "What if?"

With her body half on his and half in the snow, he rolled over to his back and pulled her fully onto him.

Her wide eyes stared back at him, her smile still in place.

"You're the most beautiful woman I know," he whispered. "I love to hear you laugh, to know I'm the one who brought a bit of happiness into your life."

"I'm really glad you came home. Not for the circumstances, but because I needed this." Her eyes dropped to his mouth. "I needed you."

Because anything he said at this point would be too heavy and emotional, he made better use of his mouth and slid his lips against hers. She returned his kiss softly, gently, then eased back.

"Your mom is looking better and better. I'm so glad we came tonight."

"Me, too."

"She really loves Abby."

Just as he was about to bring up Abby and the court documents he'd seen, cold, wet snow went up his shirt… thanks in part to Raine and the snowball she just shoved beneath his coat.

"Raine," he yelled, laughing as she came to her feet and started running away. "Payback's coming, sweetheart. You better run."

He quickly rolled and fisted a huge ball of snow and launched it at her back as she retreated. On cue, she squealed and returned a ball of her own. Max chased her around the flat part of the yard, volleying one ball after another until he'd had his fill, and then he charged after her and caught her around the waist. His arm wrapped around her from behind as he lifted her up. Her laughter filled the night, and Max didn't know when he'd felt this alive, this free, this in—

No. Love didn't come into play. He was just getting caught up in nostalgia. They'd been apart too long. How could he trust that he'd truly fallen back in love?

When she wiggled, Max eased her down to her feet and turned her around to face him. He smoothed the hair back from her face that had escaped her knit hat.

Raine's eyes searched his, and he knew she wanted more. He knew she wanted everything they'd dreamed of years ago. He knew it, and part of him even still ached for that. But going slow was the only option, because, if this was going to work, they had to nurture the relationship and protect it at all costs.

"You're so special, Raine," he said huskily. "You'd really like L.A. If you ever wanted to visit, I'd love to show you around."

"I'm pretty happy here."

"I am, too," he admitted. "More than I thought."

Raine gasped, and, before she could ask questions or he could say more asinine things without thinking, he captured her lips and pulled her tighter against him.

When he pulled back, she fluttered her lashes up at him, and he knew those questions hadn't left her mind, but he still wasn't ready to answer them.

"What do you say we go inside and get some hot chocolate?" he suggested. "We can relieve Mom of baby duty."

Raine nodded. "You know we aren't done here, right?"

He knew exactly what she referred to. "I know, but let's just enjoy this for now. I'm in a territory I had no idea I was heading toward, and I need to think."

"Neither of us planned this, Max. We were both blindsided, but I have to consider Abby first."

"I wouldn't expect any less from you."

She continued to hold his gaze. "And I can't afford to

let my heart get wrapped up in you again if I'm going to get hurt."

A band slid around Max's chest, squeezing tight. The ache of hearing her talk about heartbreak meshed with his own.

"I won't let you get hurt," he professed, hoping he could keep that promise. "I care for you, Raine. I care for you in a different way than I did the first time…and I have no idea what the hell to do about it."

She reached up with her gloved hand and cupped his jaw. Such delicate hands, such a strong woman.

"We'll figure this out together," she told him. "But right now I can barely feel my toes, and I need that hot chocolate you promised."

Max kissed her on her icy-cold nose and led her back into the house. He truly had no idea what he would do about these feelings he had for Raine. He only hoped to hell that, by the time he left Lenox, he had some answers, because right now all he knew was that he had the film of a lifetime waiting on him, he had a mother he was tending to, and he had an ex-girlfriend who was starting to work her way into his heart.

A heart she'd already broken once before. They had both been ripped open again upon discovering the truth. Could they risk so much for another chance?

Fifteen

Raine stopped in her tracks as she adjusted the carrier in one hand and the diaper bag in the other. She'd run out to deliver a few of her new lotions and soaps to some clients, and to leave some samples at area businesses.

After a long morning of running errands, all she wanted to do was relax and lay Abby down for a nap. But there was a note on her door, and as Raine grew closer, her smile grew wider.

Surprise waiting for you inside. Had to use spare key.
You need to find a new hiding spot.
M

In the past three weeks since Max had been in Lenox, he'd spent a good portion of his time caring for his mother, but Raine and Abby were oftentimes over there, as well. Their alone time was limited, which meant this newfound love she had for him was not based on sex.

Max Ford was still the one for her. He was the one now, just like he was the one then.

Raine slid her key into the lock and went inside. Eager to see this infamous surprise, she set her stuff down and uncovered Abby from the blanket shielding the cold air from her in the carrier.

Taking the baby, Raine started to walk through the house. She tried to focus on the anticipation, instead of her mother's phone call earlier in which Raine was scolded for spending more time with Max's mother than her.

Raine had simply stated that Elise accepted her for who she was. Granted that hadn't always been the case, but Raine loved Max's mother. She was sweet, loving and not judgmental.

Her mother had been damn lucky Raine hadn't gone off on her about Max's shocking revelation. But that conversation was not to be held over the phone. Oh, no. That would be a face-to-face meeting. Soon.

Shoving aside the hurt, Raine searched the living room, kitchen and entryway. Nothing.

Climbing the steps, she wondered if it was something big and obvious or something small, and she'd already walked right by it.

She glanced in her work space area, in the nursery, but, when she hit the doorway to her bedroom, Raine froze. There draped across the bed was a beautiful long blue gown. Another note lay atop the gown.

I've lined up a sitter. Don't worry, she's trustworthy. Be ready at five, and I'll pick you up. Tonight is all about you. Not Abby, not my mother and not work… for either of us.
M

She read the note again. Tonight was the opening of the play at the theater. Was he taking her? What about his mother? Wasn't she going to attend? Who had he lined up for a sitter?

While she was beyond thrilled with the idea of going

to the show tonight, and, even more thrilled that Max had gone to so much trouble to get this exquisite dress for her, her mind was whirling with questions.

Her cell vibrated in her pocket. Raine sat Abby in the Pack 'N' Play pen in the corner of the room and pulled her phone out, smiling at the caller ID.

"You are determined to get me to the theater again, aren't you?"

"I'm relentless when I want something," Max stated. "And since I know your mind is going a mile a minute, I'm letting you know that my mother's nurse will be watching Abby. You know Sasha from school, and she's very trustworthy."

Okay, Raine was relieved that the sitter was someone she knew.

"Where did this dress come from?" she asked, eyeing the narrow waist and hoping the thing fit.

"That's not for you to worry about. The bathroom should have a bag with shoes, jewelry and new makeup in it. I had a lot of help from some friends, but I want you to be pampered tonight, and I want you in the front row...just like you used to be."

Tears pricked Raine's eyes, and she swallowed hard. "I can't believe you did this."

"I've been planning it for some time," he confessed. "And I knew you wouldn't accept the gifts and theater ticket if I offered, so I made sure everything was in place."

"You're sneaky." She headed to the en suite bath and nearly keeled over at the designer labels on the makeup he'd bought. "Max, I can't even imagine what you spent on this stuff. You're insane."

"No, I just want you to have nice things, and if I want to pamper you one night, I will. Now, rest up because I plan on giving you an amazing night and showing you that sometimes you need to put yourself ahead of others."

"I put myself ahead of others," she insisted.

Max's rich laughter filtered through the phone. "When? From what I've seen, if it's not Abby, it's your clients. And everyone I've talked to has said what a hard worker you are and how you are always running around town delivering plants, lotions, soaps, giving advice on healthier lifestyles."

Raine shrugged even though he couldn't see. "I do what I can for my clients. It's how I make my living and am able to stay home with Abby."

"All the more reason for you to get out of the house tonight."

Raine smiled. "All right. I'll be ready at five."

"Wonderful. Sasha will be there just before, and you can go over Abby's feeding and bed schedule. I plan on keeping you out very late."

Oh, the promise in that declaration sent shivers racing through her body.

"I'll be ready."

After they said goodbye, Raine gathered up the bags of shoes and jewelry, and nearly floated back into the bedroom to look at the dress one more time. Blue was her favorite color; he hadn't forgotten. She knew this wasn't a coincidence. Max Ford hadn't forgotten one single thing about her in all the time he'd been gone.

Thrumming with anticipation, Raine set the jewelry on top of her vanity and gingerly opened the black velvet boxes. Her eyes traveled appreciatively over the expensive sparkling jewels, but she knew exactly what piece she should wear tonight.

The locket.

"Loraine."

Raine cringed as she stood from her front row seat after the final curtain call. There were only two people on this earth who called her Loraine and she knew at least one of them was standing right behind her.

As she turned, she pasted on a smile and came face to face with her parents. Yes, they all lived in the same town, but she still tried to avoid them at all costs.

"Mother, Father." She eyed her mother in her perfectly coiffed hair and her simple strand of pearls around her neck. "I didn't expect to see you here."

"Anything to help raise money for the arts," her father piped up, his voice rising to make sure all surrounding spectators heard him.

Raine nearly rolled her eyes. What he meant to say was *anything to look good for the upcoming mayoral election later in the year.* She had no doubt whatever monies her parents had donated, they were all too willing to share the amount and take all the accolades for their generosity.

"Are you alone?" her mother asked, glancing around.

"I'm here to see Max."

"Is that so?" her father asked. "I suppose you two are... friends? Marshall mentioned seeing him at your house the other day."

And Raine had no doubt if they hadn't been in public her father would've gone into greater detail, because there was no way Marshall mentioned the Max sighting in such a casual way.

Just looking at these two made her ill...a terrible thing to think about her parents, but they'd robbed her of her dreams, her life and her only love with no remorse what-soever.

Raine slid her small clutch beneath her arm and sighed. "What I have going on in my life is none of your business. You made sure of that when you cut me off financially after deciding I was an embarrassment to you."

Her mother's eyes darted around. "Let's not get into this here, Loraine."

"Don't want to air your dirty laundry, Mother?" She laughed bitterly. "I'm pretty sure everyone already knows something happened between us. Besides, no one cares. That was years ago, and if you're still letting this rift consume you, then maybe that's the guilt talking."

Raine's father stepped forward and held up a hand. "Listen, Loraine. Let's not do this. Why don't you bring Abby over to the house this weekend?"

Raine tilted her head. "You know, I don't think so. I'm happy with my life. I don't need pity, and I don't need your money. What I always wanted from you was acceptance and love, but that will never be. And if we weren't in public promoting Max's play, I'd jump right into just how despicable you two are for your actions. Now, if you'll excuse me, I'm going backstage."

As Raine turned, her mother's words stopped her cold. "He was wrong for you years ago, and he still is, but for different reasons. He's a player, Loraine. Don't make a fool of us by chasing after Max Ford."

Oh, there were so many comebacks, but Raine chose the one that would annoy her mother the most.

Raine glanced over her shoulder, offered her sweetest smile and said, "I'm not chasing after Max. I'm just having sex with him."

Shaking and bubbling with anger, Raine gracefully walked away with a class that her mother would normally appreciate…under other circumstances. Raine had to smile as she made her way backstage. She'd never truly spoken her mind with her parents, never sassed or back talked as an adult, because, no matter how cruel her parents had been in recent years, they were still her parents.

But damn it felt good to see her mother's reaction to that proclamation. The woman deserved so much more anger spewed her way, but they were in public, and this was Max's night. Besides, she couldn't risk causing a scandal when she was still in limbo with this adoption.

Max was in his dressing room, a slew of roses in various colors sat on the vanity. He turned toward the door when she entered.

"A packed house and a standing ovation," she said. "From the whistles and roses being tossed your way, I'd say opening night was a success."

Max crossed the small room and enveloped her in his arms. "And having you in the front row was the greatest moment of the entire night."

When he eased back, his eyes darted down to her necklace. "Raine...you kept it? After all this time?"

He brought his gaze back up to hers, and she couldn't help but smile. "It meant too much. Even after you left, I couldn't get rid of it."

Max lifted the locket, popped it open and studied the picture inside. A picture of the two of them smiling for the camera on a warm, sunny day in the park. The picture was too small to capture anything but their faces, but Raine had that moment in time embedded into her mind.

"We were so young," he murmured.

Reaching up, Raine cupped the sides of his face and kissed him. "Don't go back there. Let's focus on now."

He nodded, closing the locket. "This is so much better than the jewelry I'd chosen."

"I was hoping you wouldn't mind," she said.

"Not at all." He brushed his lips ever-so-softly against hers. "You're stunning tonight."

"And you look nice with eyeliner," she teased.

His eyes gleamed mischievously. "I bet you say that to all the guys," he said.

Raine slid her hands up his bare arms. "I think you look sexy as a gladiator. Maybe you could wear this getup sometime for me."

Max nipped at her neck. "I'm wearing it now."

Swatting away his advances, she laughed. "We're in your dressing room, there are hordes of people running around outside this door, and the press is casing the place for glimpses of you when you leave."

Max snorted. "First of all, the press got enough pictures of me when I came in. Second, the door has a lock. And third, you look so damn hot in this dress, I can't wait until we get home."

"Whose home?" she asked, grinning.

"Well, my mother is at my house, and the sitter is at yours." His hand went to the zipper at the back of her glimmering blue gown and slowly unzipped until the top sagged just at her breasts. "Looks like this is it. Ever made love in a dressing room?"

Made love. The fact those two words slipped through his lips had her hoping for more.

"I have," she informed him, sliding her arms out of the fitted sleeves. "I believe it was about fifteen years ago. With you."

"Then I'd say we're past due for an encore."

Raine took a step back and allowed her dress to shimmy down her torso and puddle at her feet. Max's eyes raked down her body, giving her a visual sampling and sending shivers racing through her.

Closing the small gap between them, Max spanned her waist with his strong hands and tugged her against his chest. And, as if the dam broke, he assaulted her mouth. His hands were all over—roaming up her back, combing through her hair, pulling at her panties.

Raine ran her hands over his thick white costume and had no clue how to get him out of it. Finally, he released her long enough to extricate himself from the thing. He shucked his white boxer briefs and was on her again, this time lifting her up against him until she wrapped her legs around his waist.

Her back pressed against the wall as he pulled aside the cups to her strapless bra. Raine arched into him, allowing him all the access he wanted and more.

When he gripped her panties and literally tore them off, Raine laughed. "You really are in a hurry."

He slid into her in one swift, quick thrust. "You have no idea," he murmured against her mouth. "I've barely held it together with wanting you."

Did he mean just tonight...or for longer?

Raine tilted her hips, not wanting to worry about anything beyond right now and how amazing it felt to be with Max. He gripped her waist and slanted his lips across hers as he continued to make love to her.

In no time Raine's body shook as waves of pleasure coursed through her. Molding herself against his bare chest, she wrapped her arms around his neck and held on as he started pumping faster. His body stilled against hers, his warm breath fanning out across her shoulder and neck, sending even more chills all over her bare skin.

In an ironic sort of way, they'd come full circle. This theater held such a special place in her heart, since this is where she'd met and fallen in love with him.

Max leaned his head back, looked down at her and grinned. "I have another surprise in store for you."

Raine laughed. "I'm not quite ready again."

"Not that," he said with a slight grin. "I've arranged a dinner for us."

"Where?"

"Here."

Raine tilted her head. "Here? At the theater?"

That cocky grin spread across his face. "I wanted tonight to be special. And before you worry about the sitter, she was well paid to stay as late as we need."

Warmth spread through Raine. Max had taken care of everything, and he was all about pleasing her, meeting her needs.

But it was time they opened up about their feelings, now and years ago. Where were they headed here? Because this certainly felt like more than just a pass through. Yes, he was leaving, but would he return? Would he want to see where this long-distance relationship could lead?

And Max still didn't know the truth about the baby she'd lost. His baby. Their baby.

This evening may not be the perfect time to address it, but hadn't the past been buried long enough? There would be no ideal time, and her nerves wouldn't get any calmer. He needed to know about this adoption she was facing—fighting—as well, because, if he was truly ready to get involved with her, this adoption would affect him, too.

Looking into Max's eyes, she knew tonight would change their lives, one way or another, forever.

Sixteen

Something was off with Raine. They'd made love, though it was frantic and hurried, and a deeper bond had formed between them back in his dressing room.

But he couldn't chalk up her tension to all of that, because, when she'd stepped into the room, she'd already been wound up pretty tight. He didn't know what had happened between her arrival at the play and when it finished, but something—or someone—had upset her. If he had to wager a guess, he'd lay money on her parents.

With his hand on the small of her back, Max led her up the back stairs to the stage area.

"All of this is going to spoil me," she murmured, throwing a smile over her shoulder. "A beautiful dress, a play and now dinner on stage?"

He laughed. "Don't forget the dressing room."

"I'll never forget the dressing room."

He led her closer to the table that had been set up amid the coliseum decor. With the crisp white tablecloth, a tapered candle flickering, fine china and a single red rose across her plate, Max hadn't left out one single romantic detail.

"You went to a lot of trouble for me tonight."

"No trouble," he replied as he pulled out her cloth-covered chair. "I called McCormick's in town, asked if they could deliver a few things, and then I paid one of the guys on the crew here to set this up. I really did nothing but make a few calls."

Before sitting in her seat, Raine turned, placed her hands on his shoulders and leaned in to kiss his cheek. "You've done so much more, Max. This time that you've been here… it's been amazing. I can't thank you enough for making me take a break and have fun again."

Before she could turn and take a seat, he gripped her shoulders and slid his lips over hers. "You deserve breaks, Raine. You deserve fun. You just needed someone to show you."

Her gaze held his, and he lost himself in their beautiful emerald-green depths. This was not what he'd planned on. Nothing prepared him for all the emotions, all the feelings, he'd be forced to face. He'd pretty much been resigned to the fact he'd see Raine during his lengthy visit and had even assumed he'd be swept back into the past.

But he hadn't planned on looking at her and seeing a future.

"I ran into my parents before I saw you," she confided. "I need to talk to them about what happened."

"It won't be easy, but they need to be held accountable for ruining our lives."

Raine wound her arms around his waist and rested her head against his chest. "I have no idea what to say. I know they'll defend their actions, but they stole everything from me."

Leaning down, Max kissed her gently on the forehead. "We won't let them win."

She gazed up at him with her heart in her eyes, and Max felt a surge of emotion. So much time had passed, but his feelings were even stronger now than they were when he and Raine had been eighteen. However, their future still seemed so uncertain, and he had no clue where they went from here.

Exhaling slowly, he took her hand and helped her into her seat before taking his own. He'd made sure to have her favorites here tonight. Already they'd created memories, but he didn't want the night to end.

When he glanced across the table, he froze. Raine stared down at her plate, not moving or attempting to eat.

"You don't like the menu?" he asked.

Shaking her head, she lifted her gaze. "The menu is fine. But I think we've hit a point where I need to tell you about Abby."

He waited, not letting on that he already knew. She was opening up, and he wanted to take full advantage of this important step she was taking in their relationship.

"You've asked a couple times about Abby's father." Easing forward, Raine rested her elbows on the table. "He's not in the picture…and I'm not her biological mother. Jill is."

Max reached across the small round table and took her hands in his. "You're adopting Jill's baby?"

Raine nodded. "She's just not at a point in her life where she can care for a baby. At first she mentioned abortion, but, once we talked through everything, she realized that wasn't the best decision. I may not be financially sound, but I had to try to make this work. You know I've always wanted a family."

"I know," he whispered. "And you're Abby's mom in every way that counts, Raine. Just like Elise is mine."

A smile spread across her face. "I knew you'd get it. I hesitated on telling you, because I had to wait and see where we were going with this. At first you were just stuck at my house, but now there's so much more."

"You don't need to explain," he said gruffly. "Adopting Abby is remarkable, Raine."

"Actually, she's not legally mine, yet."

Max stroked his thumbs along the back of her hands. "When will everything be finalized?"

Blowing out a breath, Raine shrugged. "I wish I knew. My attorney can't figure out what the holdup is, either. I've been approved through Social Services with my home visits, background check and everything. All my attorney can figure is that sometimes this process takes longer than others."

That threw Max for a loop. If everything was complete, what was the problem? He would look into that, because there was no way this adoption shouldn't go through.

"I'm glad you told me," Max said. "I'm glad you're getting this dream of motherhood because you're amazing at it, Raine."

A flash of hurt flickered in her eyes, but she offered a quick smile. "There are days I question if I'm doing it right, but I just have to keep moving forward doing the best I can."

He raised his wine glass. "Then let's celebrate us, Abby and the newfound life we've discovered. We may not know what's going to happen, but for now we are happy, and I want you to remember this night forever."

Raine picked up her own glass and clinked it to his. "I'll never forget any of the time you've been back in Lenox, Max. It's been the best few weeks of my life."

Max took a long, hard drink of the wine, wishing for something stronger. Hollywood was waiting for him, but the future he'd originally planned sat directly within reach.

No matter how they decided to approach the future, he had a feeling someone would inevitably get hurt. He only prayed to God they survived this time.

Seventeen

Raine had been up all night playing over and over in her head the scenario that would greet her today when finally confronting her parents. She expected denial, defense and even derision, but she would stand her ground and not leave until she had adequate answers. She was owed that much.

Max had been much more understanding, much more supportive than she would've been if the roles had been reversed. The thought that her parents had sabotaged her life, her every dream, made her so mad she could hardly control the trembling.

Without knocking, she marched straight through the front door of her childhood home…or, more accurately, museum. The cold, sterile environment was no place to raise a child. As her rubber-soled work boots thunked through the marble foyer, Raine winced inwardly. She was just grateful that Abby had never been forced to spend much time in this place. Approaching her father's home office, she overheard another familiar male voice. Great. Just who she was *not* in the mood for.

Raine stepped into the spacious room with the back wall of floor-to-ceiling windows and took in the bright, sunshiny day. This day was about to get very dark, very fast.

"I need to talk to you," she said, interrupting whatever her father was saying.

She hadn't heard the specifics of the conversation. She was too overwrought to focus on anything but her past right now.

Marshall turned in the leather club chair he sat in. "Raine," he said, raising a brow. "You're looking…natural today."

Raine laughed, knowing full well he was referring to her farm-girl attire. "I look like this every day, Marshall. I need to speak to my father. You're excused."

"Loraine," her father exclaimed, coming to his feet. The force of his actions sent his office chair rolling back and slamming into the window. "You surely can wait until our meeting is over."

Raine crossed her arms over her chest. "Oh, it's over. I need Mother in here, as well."

Her father shook his head. "I'm sorry, Marshall. I don't know what's gotten into her. I'll call you this afternoon."

Marshall came to his feet and approached Raine. "I hope everything is okay. Would you like to call me later and talk?"

"Marshall," she told him, placing a hand on his arm. "I've been nice about this, but I'm just not interested in you in that way. We went out once, but that was it for me."

Marshall's cheeks reddened. "Can't blame a guy for trying."

More like can't blame a guy for trying to kiss the ass of her father the mayor, but whatever. She didn't have time to think or worry about Marshall's feelings right now.

Raine waited for her father to get off the house intercom. Marshall left, and moments later Raine's mother swept into the room. The woman always felt the need to make a grand entrance…pearls and all.

"What a lovely surprise…" Her mother's words trailed

off as she raked her eyes over Raine's wardrobe. "Heaven's sake, Loraine. Couldn't you have freshened up before coming out in public?"

"I showered, and my underwear is clean. That's as fresh as I get," she defended with a smile. "But I'm not here for you to look down your nose at me and throw insults my way, because you think you're on another level."

"Loraine, that's enough," her father bellowed from behind his desk. "Whatever foul mood you're in, we don't deserve this."

Raine snickered, moved around the spacious office and flopped down on the oversized leather sofa in the corner. Propping her dirty work boots upon the cushion, she glared back at her father.

"Is that so? Do you really want to get into what the two of you deserve? Because I don't think you'll like what I believe is proper punishment for your actions."

Her mother let out her signature dramatic sigh. "For heaven's sake, Loraine, I don't have time for whatever game you're playing. If you have something to say, just say it. I have a luncheon to get ready for."

"Oh, yes. We wouldn't want family to come before your precious tea and cucumber sandwiches."

Her father rounded his desk, opened his mouth, but Raine held up her hand. "No. For once you two will be quiet, and I'll do the talking. And you may want to sit because this could be a while."

Her parents exchanged worried looks and came to sit in the matching wingback chairs opposite the sofa Raine sat on.

"It's apparent you're upset," her father stated. "I've never seen you like this."

Rage bubbled in her, and she clasped her hands in her lap to control the trembling. "Ironically, I've never felt like this."

In all the scenarios in her mind she'd created over the past few days, nothing truly prepared her for this moment of confronting them about the past. She needed to keep the anger in the forefront because if she allowed that sharp, piercing hurt to come into play, she'd break down and cry.

"I'll give you guys one chance to tell me the truth about what happened when Max left for L.A. And after all this time, I believe one chance is quite generous on my part."

When both of them widened their eyes in response, she felt that sickening feeling in the pit of her stomach. A little thread of generosity within her had hoped that her parents hadn't been that cruel, that they hadn't purposely altered her future, decimating her dreams.

But the silence in the room was deafening...and heart wrenching.

"We did what we thought was best," her mother stated, straightening her shoulders. "You were too young to be that serious."

"Was I now?" Raine eased forward on the couch and glared across the space between them. "How many times did he call, Mother? How soon after he left did he try to send for me?"

Her mother shrugged. "I don't recall, Loraine. It was so long ago, I'd nearly forgotten the matter."

Tears burned her throat, but Raine willed herself to remain strong. "So let me get this straight. You'd forgotten the matter like it was a trip to the grocery store? This was my *life* you destroyed. Do you not care? Did you even care when I was crying myself to sleep night after night—or when I discovered I was pregnant? Did it ever dawn on you to tell me the truth?"

"No."

Her father's quick answer had Raine gasping. Who were these people? She'd known that they'd never been supportive but to be this heartless and cruel? The thought of *ever* treating Abby in such a manner was purely sickening.

Raine came to her feet. "I just want to know why. Not that it matters, but why would you purposely do this to me?"

"Because Max was chasing a dream, and the odds were against him of making anything of himself," his father said. "We wanted more for our little girl. Don't you understand?"

Raine laughed, though she was on the verge of tears. "What I understand is you two thought you could run my life. You thought taking away my money would make me see your way. Well, I hate to tell you, I couldn't care less about your precious money or your idiotic expectations for my life."

"You'll understand better when Abby gets older," her mother insisted. "You'll want what's best for her, too."

"Yes, I will," Raine agreed. "But even though I'll try to shelter her, I will let her make her own mistakes—and I won't stand in the way of her dreams. Maybe if you two had an ounce of what I felt for Max, you would've been pleased to see your child so happy and in love."

"You weren't in love, Raine," her father chimed in. "You two were in lust. You liked each other because you felt a connection and got a kick out of being rebellious together. And you thought fleeing to the other side of the country would secure your little fantasy."

"No, we *understood* each other," she countered. "We confided in each other because we knew how important the other's dreams were, and we didn't stifle each other."

"He left you pregnant, Loraine." Her mother came to her feet, crossing her arms over her chest. "He was off living that dream, while you were here degrading yourself."

"How dare you?" Raine asked, her voice menacingly low. "Max had no clue my condition, or I assure you, he would've been here."

Now her father rose, sighing and shaking his head. "You

think Max Ford would've given up his dream of living in L.A. and becoming an actor to stay here and play house?"

Raine leveled her gaze with him and gritted her teeth. "I know he would've. He loved me. And he more than anyone knows the consequences of coming from a broken and unloving home."

"You're still naive if you believe he's back for you," her mother said. "He's only here for his mother, and then he's gone again. Don't set yourself up for more heartache, Loraine. You have Abby to think about now."

"I know how to raise my daughter."

"She's not yours, honey," her mother said softly, as if that would ease the hurt of the words.

"She *is* mine. I am legally adopting her. She's mine in every sense of the word as soon as the judge signs off."

Anger still high and tension mounting heavily between them, Raine knew this conversation was going nowhere. She wasn't sure what she'd expected when she'd come in here. Denial and defensiveness, of course. Perhaps some antagonism, too. But a part of her had really hoped for an apology. Not that it would've changed matters, but Raine wanted to think that her parents cared.

Now she knew for sure they only cared about their image. God forbid she taint their social standing by being unwed, pregnant, with no boyfriend in sight.

But there was still a little girl inside her that had held on to that slender thread of hope that they would accept her for who she was, and not how her actions or aspirations could drive their social standings.

"Now that I know the truth, I doubt you'll be seeing much of me," she told them.

"You're just angry because it's fresh." Her father started toward her with his hands extended. "Don't say things you don't mean now."

Raine stepped back, silently refusing his gesture. "I'll

still be angry years from now, and I mean every word I've said. I will not be coming around, and, as for the trust fund you've dangled over my head for years, keep it. You've tried your damnedest to get me to see your way, but I'll never be like either of you." She released a ragged breath. "I care about helping people and making my little part of the world a better place. And I couldn't care less what others can do for me, and how far in life I will advance by lying and being deceitful."

Raine brushed past her parents and headed toward the door before she turned over her shoulder. "Oh, and stop sending Marshall to my house. In fact, consider this our last contact unless you decide you can love me for me and not for how I make you look to your friends."

Max wanted to feel sorry for himself, considering he was covered in spit up and smelled like baby powder after that very questionable diaper change. How many wipes were too many to use? And more to the point, would a hazmat suit be overkill? Because the stuff that had been in that diaper surely had to be toxic.

As Max laid Abby in her crib for a nap, he thought about Raine and wondered how her talk with her parents was going. But before he could dwell too much on that, Abby let out a wail, and Max had no clue what it meant.

He peered over the edge of the crib, and she looked up at him, her chin quivering, her face red.

"All right, little one," he said, picking her up again. "You know I'm the newbie here, and you think you can sucker me into holding you the whole time your mommy is gone, right?"

When she instantly stopped fussing, Max laughed and patted her back as she laid her head against his chest and let out a deep sigh.

Being wrapped around her little fingers was just fine with him.

Max couldn't stand the thought of her being upset. Yes, she was a baby; yes, they cried. But that special place in his heart, for that family of his own, was starting to be filled with this little bundle of sweetness.

He moved to the rocking chair in the corner of the room next to the window. Early morning sunlight streamed in, and Max cradled Abby in the crook of his arm as he rocked her. She closed her eyes, sucked on her chubby little fist and quickly fell asleep, trusting in him to keep her safe.

Max loved her. Right this moment, knowing he'd made her stop crying simply by his touch warmed a place in him that he had no idea existed. This is what he wanted…what he'd wanted years ago with Raine.

A family had never entered his mind until he'd met and fallen for Raine. Growing up, he'd known he'd been adopted, and he had also known how much his mother had loved him, but his father…well, if that man cared about Max, he had a very odd way of showing it. Max had always sworn, if he ever became a father, he would tell his child every day how much he was loved. Max studied Abby's sweet face, her long lashes sweeping over the top of her full pink cheeks, her perfectly shaped mouth, her wisps of black curly hair. Everything about her was precious, and Max found himself being pulled deeper into her innocent world. First Raine and now Abby. As if resisting one woman wasn't enough.

"You have more love than you'll ever know," he whispered to Abby as she slept peacefully. "Your mama will make sure of it."

When his cell vibrated in his pocket, he carefully shifted to the side to get it out. Checking the screen, he saw Bronson Dane's number. He couldn't take the call. Not right now. Not when he was so confused about what the hell was going on in his mind…in his heart.

And if anybody had told him months ago that he would ignore a call from Hollywood hotshot Bronson Dane, Max would've called them insane. But Bronson would leave a message, and Max would call him back when he was ready. There was so much that hinged on his decision for the future.

He could no longer deny the fact he was totally in love with Raine. More than likely those feelings had never gone away; they were just buried beneath years of hurt. But he also loved Abby, loved being back in Lenox and loved performing at the theater like he used to. Granted he'd only performed the first night, and there were several performances left, but that one live crowd was enough.

There was no way he should've fallen in love with his hometown. He'd never been one for nostalgia or getting enveloped by old memories and letting them consume him. But here he was, wondering how he could make everything work—have a family and keep his career at the status level it was.

On the flip side, there was the movie waiting for him when he returned in a few weeks. And even though his mother was really doing fine and didn't need his assistance, he wanted to stay and support her for as long as possible.

But there was no way he could be in two places at once, and Raine's heart was here in Lenox. Here in her grandmother's old home with these insane people-loving chickens, goats that goosed your rear end when you walked out and a host of renovations that required doing. Yet Raine had never needed the perfect, polished lifestyle that so many around her did. And he was just as guilty of looking for happiness in a lifestyle instead of being content with the blessings he had.

Looking back, he'd truly had it all when he'd been eighteen. Money didn't mean much because he'd been miserable, if he were honest with himself, for the past fifteen years.

And now that he'd been staying in Lenox, mostly in his childhood home, but some of the time in a house that was so much less than what he was used to, he found himself free and happy.

But he was torn between following his heart and staying true to those dreams. The major question now was, which dream did he follow?

Eighteen

Max was ready to put Abby down again when the doorbell rang.

"Who in the world is that?" he muttered, walking from the nursery toward the staircase.

He held Abby against his chest as he opened the door without looking through the side window to see who the visitor was.

And the second he opened the door, he wished he would've looked first.

"Maxwell," his father greeted.

He glared at his father as Thomas Ford eyed the baby, then brought his gaze back to Max's.

"Dad. I'm surprised to see you here." He shifted a restless Abby in his arms. "Is there a reason you came?"

His father stepped forward, causing Max to step back. "I stopped by the house to see you and your mother. When she said you were here, I decided to come see you."

"Because you think your wife doesn't need your attention?"

Max turned, disgusted with his father. Years of unresolved anger bubbled within him. He strode into the living room, leaving his father to follow or go away. He didn't really care.

"I haven't seen you in over a year," Thomas said, following Max into the living room. "I'd think you'd be more excited to see me."

Max placed Abby in her swing and turned it on low before turning back to his father. "And I'd think you'd have been here for Mom during her recovery, but I see even this health scare did nothing to alter your priorities."

Thomas took a seat on the floral sofa and crossed his ankle over his knee. "I didn't come here to argue. I just wanted to see my son, and your mother didn't know how long you'd be gone."

Max didn't offer to take his dad's coat because he didn't intend on his father staying long, so he remained standing and rested his hands on his hips. "I'll be here until Raine gets back."

"Hmm, I had no idea you two were this…involved." After a tense silence, Thomas cleared his throat. "Well, I came by because—"

Abby started fussing, and Max ignored whatever his father was about to say. He turned off the swing and eased Abby's pudgy little legs from the seat and carried her into the kitchen. Thankfully Raine had premade bottles in the fridge. She claimed Abby was okay to take them cold, and it didn't need to be warmed up in the bottle warmer.

Juggling Abby in one arm, Max pulled out a bottle and popped off the lid, letting it bounce onto the scarred countertops.

He lay Abby down in the crook of his arm and placed the bottle between her little pink lips. She greedily sucked away, and Max turned to see his father standing in the doorway.

"You're looking pretty comfortable here," Thomas claimed. "Your mother wonders if you're planning on staying."

"I'm not," he answered. "I'm here for Mom, and I'm

helping Raine, too. I have a movie to start filming at the end of next month. I can't do that from here."

"I was hoping I could talk to you about the future and your plans."

For the first time Max really studied his father. The deep creases around his eyes, his heavy lids. The man was aging, and all he had to show for it was a chain of prosperous restaurants along the East Coast. More memories were made with his work than with his family. And this fact made Max feel sorry for his father. The man's last moment on earth would be at work.

"What about my plans?" Max asked.

"I know you have no desire in taking over the restaurants," his father stated. "And I'm not asking you to give up your life. But I was hoping I could get you to consider assuming the ownership in name only. I have a very well-staffed set of managers at all locations, and I don't plan on retiring just yet, but I do need to slow down."

Max was shocked. Never in his life would he have guessed his father would cut back on work.

"Why now?" Max asked, patting Abby's bottom as she started to drift off to sleep.

"When your mother was diagnosed with cancer, I started rethinking my life. I haven't been the best husband, certainly not the best father." Thomas shook his head and sighed. "I can't go back and change what I did or didn't do, but I can make better decisions from here on out. And that's why I want to set the wheels in motion so I can concentrate on your mother…and maybe even spend more time with you, if you'd like that."

Max had to lean back against the counter, because his father's heartfelt words really rattled Max. The man had come here, seeking Max out, to have this discussion. As much as Max wanted to ignore his father's request, he couldn't. The man may have had an epiphany late in life about what was important, but he was extending that olive branch and only a total jerk would knock it away.

"This is a surprise," Max admitted to his father. "Is this something I can think about for a few days, or do you need to know now?"

"If you're willing to think about it, take your time." For the first time in longer than Max could remember, his father smiled. "I just want us to be able to be the family we should've been. And I want that no matter what you decide about the business."

Abby's lips fell away from the bottle, and milk ran down her rounded cheek as she slept. Max set the bottle on the counter and used the pad of his thumb to wipe the moisture away.

With his heart in his throat, he knew if his father was opening up about his emotions, then Max needed to, as well. He had questions, and there was only one person who could answer them.

"Why did you adopt me?" he asked, leveling his father's gaze from across the room. "I know Mom couldn't have children, but you were always so distant."

Thomas crossed the room, pulling out a chair from the mismatched set around the kitchen table. He took a seat, raked a hand over his silver hair and faced Max.

"I never really wanted children. I wasn't sure I'd make a good father. I was so intent on making a name for myself, making a nice income for Elise, because she never had a lot growing up. I was determined to provide more for her than her family had."

Something tugged at Max's heart. He'd been wanting to provide more for Raine than her family had…stability and—dare he say—love.

"I knew she wanted a child, and I was gone so much," his father went on. "I guess I thought a baby would fill the void of my absence. Hindsight is so much clearer."

Max eased Abby onto his shoulder and gently patted her back. Raine had told him if she didn't burp she could get reflux. There were so many rules for babies, but, surprisingly, Max felt he was catching on…and enjoying this little slice of parenting.

The front door opened and closed. He straightened and met Raine's eyes as she rounded the doorway into the kitchen. Her gaze went from Max to his father.

"Um…sorry, I didn't know you would be here," she said, slowly crossing the room. "Let me just take Abby and lay her down. I'll stay out of your way."

Thomas came to his feet. "No need to rush out. I need to get back to Elise."

Max met Raine's questioning look and offered a smile. "I'll be home in a little while."

Thomas nodded and glanced to Raine. "Good to see you again, Loraine. You have a beautiful baby there."

Raine smiled. "Thank you. I hope I didn't interrupt anything. I hate for you to rush off…"

Thomas grinned. "I think I'm done here, and I'll see Maxwell at home later. You two enjoy your day."

Max watched his father stroll out of the room and waited until the front door shut, leaving just him and Raine and a sleeping Abby.

"What just happened?" she asked, holding the baby to her chest.

"My dad wants to be my dad."

Raine's brows lifted. "That's…great. Why aren't you smiling?"

"Because I'm torn, and he threw a big decision at me. One I need to seriously consider."

"Want to talk about it?"

Max shook his head. "Not right now. I'd rather hear how things went with your parents."

Raine sighed. "Let me put her down."

Max followed Raine upstairs and waited outside the nursery while she lay the baby down. Once she came out and gently pulled the door closed behind her, she motioned for him to follow her into the bedroom.

"They didn't deny it," she told him, crossing her arms over her chest. "They tried to defend themselves by saying I would do the same thing for Abby to protect her from making wrong decisions."

Max felt his blood pressure soar. "How can they justify something so heartless and cold?"

Raine shook her head. "I have no idea. I just want to move on. I can't keep dwelling on the past, and I can't keep getting disappointed by them over and over again."

Max closed the space between them and enveloped her into his arms. "I'm so sorry, Raine. I want to go back in time and change things, but I know that's impossible. The truth is out now, and you can do what you want with it."

"I want to pretend my parents aren't so deceitful, but when they didn't even apologize, I knew they only were thinking of themselves and their social status."

Her arms came around his waist as her head settled perfectly beneath his chin. He honestly had no clue what he was going to do. He had so much waiting for him in L.A., yet all he could think of was what was in his arms right now.

How could he have both? Years ago they'd been ready to try, but now? Would Raine give up her life here? Would she take Abby and follow him, let go of this farm that means the world to her?

He didn't want to add to her angst, but he couldn't ignore the fact he was leaving in a few weeks.

"You mean so much to me, Raine," he whispered.

She eased back, her eyes locked onto his. "You don't sound happy about that."

"I just didn't expect to fall back into your life so easily," he admitted. "I didn't expect to get so attached to Abby."

"Why are you upset about it?"

"Because I can't stay," he said. "As much as I've loved being here, as much as I've loved every minute with you, I have a life back in L.A. and professional responsibilities."

Raine shifted out of his arms and emptiness settled in just as fast as that wall of defense erected around her when she wrapped her arms around her waist.

"I knew you'd leave," she said, her tone low, her voice sad. "I'd hoped you wouldn't, but Lenox isn't for you."

"Last night, seeing you in the front row brought back a flood of emotions for me, Raine. I wanted to turn back time when you used to sit right there and watch my performances. Back then, and now, you love this farm, and I wouldn't ask you to give it up for me. But we're different people now."

Tears slid down her cheeks.

"I know," she choked out, raising her face to meet his eyes. "How can I be upset when we've had such a wonderful time together?"

"Raine—"

She held up a hand. "No. Don't apologize for being who you are. You're Max Ford. You live in L.A., make amazing movies and live your dream. You're getting ready to take that dream to another level. If I asked you to stay, that would be selfish, and you'd resent me later."

Max ran a hand down his face, the day-old stubble scratching his palm. "I wish more than anything things could be the same."

Raine smiled as another tear escaped her bright green eyes. "I know…. Me, too. But I want you to be happy, and I know you want that for me."

"More than anything." He swiped the moisture away from her cheeks with the pads of his thumbs and kissed her lips. "Let me make love to you, Raine. Let's make the most of the time we still have together."

She melted into Max's embrace, knowing their time was limited, knowing when he left this time, she would be even more crushed than the first.

Nineteen

"That's really great, Noah," Max said as he drove through the dirty, snow-lined streets. "I'm so happy for you and Callie."

"You promise you'll be here for the wedding?"

Noah Foster's voice resounded through the speakers in Max's rental car. His best friend had finally set a date for his wedding. No way would Max miss such a special time, especially considering all that Noah and Callie had been through.

"I swear I'll be there," Max promised. "I talked with Bronson earlier today, and they were hoping to start production earlier."

"Aren't you staying with your mother until the end of April?"

Max turned onto another two-lane road, heading toward Raine's parents' house. "My mother is doing remarkably well, and actually my father has taken some time off to take her to her treatments."

"Whoa, that's shocking."

"Seems Thomas Ford had a change of heart where family is concerned." Max still wasn't sure what to think, but he was pretty excited his father had done an about-face. "He would've been here to help sooner, but he was trying to tie up loose ends at one of the restaurants before he took off."

"Sounds like this ordeal with your mom really scared some sense into him," Noah stated. "It's a shame it took that, but at least he's come around."

"He's even coming to the performance tonight to see me."

Max wasn't going to lie. The fact that his father was stepping up and showing support, after all the years of ignoring the fact that Max was an actor and a damn good one, made his heart swell.

"That's really great, Max." Noah was silent for a moment before he said, "You haven't mentioned Raine yet. Everything okay?"

Max and Noah had been friends for a long time, and Noah knew everything, including all about Raine…the early years.

"That's a botched-up mess," Max muttered, gripping his steering wheel. "I'll have to fill you in when I get home. Long story short, our relationship was sabotaged when I left here. I'm on my way to talk to her parents right now."

"Tell me you're not," Noah said. "I don't know what you found out, but doing anything when you're upset is a bad idea."

"I disagree. I think this is the perfect time for me to talk to them."

"Does Raine know what you're up to?"

Max made his final turn, the house in question sitting straight ahead atop a small hill surrounded by white, pristine snow.

"No, she doesn't," Max told his friend. "I can't leave here and not have my say with them. They hurt her, Noah. She's totally devastated, and I won't tolerate them thinking their actions were acceptable."

"You're in love with her," Noah stated simply. "And don't

even bother trying to deny it, because I can hear it in your voice. This woman has always been the one."

Max clenched his jaw because any words at this point would damn him. Noah was right. Raine had always been the one. But at this point in their lives, when they were both settled into what they loved doing, how could he uproot her? She'd promised to follow him once; he didn't think she'd offer again.

And she hadn't made any overtures to indicate otherwise. In fact, when they'd made love yesterday afternoon, it was almost as if she was starting to say goodbye. It was just best this way. Sometimes people weren't meant to be together, and there was only so much love could do.

Which meant he couldn't tell her that he loved her. If he did, he'd surely beg her to come with him. He'd offer to pay off her farm, sell it, do anything she wanted if she'd follow him to L.A. And in time she would resent him for keeping his dreams alive and well, while she relinquished everything she knew and loved.

"You still with me?" Noah asked.

Max pulled into the wide, circular drive and killed the engine. "I'm still here, but I need to go. I just pulled into the drive."

Noah sighed. "Just don't do anything too rash. If this is the woman you love, these people could be your in-laws one day."

Max snorted. "There's no chance of that."

He disconnected the call and sighed. At one time these people would've been his in-laws, but they'd destroyed any chance of that when they had decided to take fate into their own hands and ruin not only his life but Raine's. And for that alone he was going to have a serious meeting with them.

Yes, Raine would probably not like the fact that he was at her parents' house, but someone had to stand up for her.

Someone had to show her just how much support she had. She'd been fighting her battles alone for far too long, so he had to do this for her sake.

He stepped from the car and ignored the biting wind that swept right through his heavy coat. Damn, L.A. weather was so much friendlier.

After ringing the doorbell, Max stepped back and waited. So many thoughts swirled through his mind on what he wanted to say. He truly had no idea how to even begin, but something told him he'd know once he got in there, all those years of pent-up anger and hurt emotions rushing to the surface. A younger lady answered the door, dressed head to toe in black. A maid? Her eyes widened as recognition of who he was set in. That wasn't his ego talking, he was very aware that people knew who he was. But he wasn't about to throw his celebrity status around. This had nothing to do with him and everything to do with the woman he cared about.

"Hello," he said with what he hoped was a charming smile. "I need to speak with Mr. and Mrs. Monroe, please."

"Of course." She stepped back and opened the door wider. "Please, come in. They are upstairs in the study. I can go—"

"I know where the study is," he said, cutting her off. "Thank you."

Dismissing her, he walked past the young woman and made his way up the wide, curved staircase. Fury bubbled within him at the fact these people lived like this, while Raine's house was falling apart.

Selfish snobs.

As he moved down the hall, he stopped when he recognized Marshall's voice.

"I've done all I can to stop the adoption from going through, but there's nothing else I can do to hold it off,"

Marshall said. "Raine passed all inspections and home visits from social services."

Max waited in the hall, just outside the door, and he had a feeling his temper was going to go from bad to worse very, very soon.

"You have a law degree," Raine's father barked. "How can you not find a loophole to halt this adoption? She's a single mother for crying out loud."

Max fisted his hands at his sides but remained quiet.

"And she has no money," her mother chimed in. "This is ridiculous. Why does she insist on being so stubborn?"

"One reason the courts are moving ahead is because this is the home where Jill wants the baby. Hard to argue with the mother's wishes, especially when the guardian is the mayor's daughter."

"And being the mayor you'd think my assistant could pull some strings," her father complained.

"She's going to be even more difficult since she learned what happened years ago." Her mother's tone softened. "Maybe we should've let her go. Maybe she would've learned her lesson and come back home eventually—"

"No, had she gone when Max left, he would've married her," Marshall argued. "If for no other reason than for the baby."

Max froze. *Baby? What the hell?*

"That was a blessing she lost that child," her mother said. "My God, it was nearly impossible to keep that a secret."

The wide hallway suddenly became narrower, as Max's world slowly closed in on him. Raine had been pregnant when he'd left? Why hadn't she told him?

An image of Raine pregnant with his child nearly brought him to his knees.

Max swallowed, raked a hand over his face and planned his next move. First, he needed to talk with those three hypocrites in the room behind him. Then, he'd go have a very long talk with Raine.

Dear Lord. He'd been a father?

Between that crushing blow and the fact these people—who supposedly cared about Raine—were trying to prevent her adoption, Max needed to clear his head and fast. He had come here for a reason, but his motives had just changed.

Stepping around the door frame, Max met the eyes of Marshall and Raine's father. Then her mother turned, her mouth dropping open as she gasped.

"Not expecting company, I see," Max said easily as he crossed the room to stand with the three people he loathed most in the world. "I was able to hear enough of your little powwow to know that Raine's life is still being manipulated by the people who are supposed to love and care for her the most."

"This is really none of your concern." Her mother lifted her chin, then crossed her arms over her chest. "And it is extremely rude to just barge in here."

Max glared at her. "You really want to lecture me on manners? I don't think you want to go there."

"What do you need, Max?" Raine's father asked.

With a shrug, Max met the man's gaze. "I'm just here to stand up for Raine. To let you all know that I'll be leaving soon, but I know enough now to realize that I need to make a few things clear before I go."

Marshall laughed. "You have no business here, no matter who you are."

In a flash, Max reached out and had Marshall by the collar, eliciting another gasp from Raine's mother. "Don't even think of running your mouth to me. What kind of a man would purposely try to keep a child away from a loving mother? You're a lowlife, spineless jerk, and you belong with these two."

He shoved the man away and looked back to Raine's father.

"Get out, Max."

"I will," he agreed. "But first let me tell you, if this adoption doesn't go through, I will raise all kinds of hell in this town. I never use my status to get what I want, but I will do that, and more, if Raine doesn't keep Abby. You remember that the next time you all try to play God with Raine's life."

"She could have a much better life," her mother pleaded. "If she'd just listen to her father and me. She could have her money and find someone worthy to settle down with."

"First of all, Raine doesn't care about the money. She cares about people, though I have no idea where she learned that fact of life from." Max shoved his hands in his jean pockets, rocked back on his heels. "Second of all, you don't get to decide who is worthy for her. Raine is happy with her life, and, when she wants to settle down, she will."

And it would kill him. Knowing she'd fallen in love and made a life with another man would absolutely crush him.

"You altered our lives years ago," he went on. "Now stay away from her if you're not going to be supportive."

"Supportive?" Marshall piped up. "You left when she was pregnant."

Waves of fury coursed through him. "If you don't shut the hell up, I'm going to punch you in the face. I think we all know why I wasn't around for the baby."

His eyes found Raine's parents as he forced himself to remain calm and not go all Alpha male and start throwing things.

"You won't tell Raine—"

Max laughed at her mother's final plea. "About you trying to sabotage her future again? You bet I will. I don't lie to those I care about."

He turned to walk out the door and glanced back over his shoulder. "Oh, and, Mayor? I wouldn't worry about running for reelection. I have a feeling things wouldn't work out for you."

"Did you just threaten me?"

Max smiled. "Not at all. Just letting you know how it feels to have your dreams and future altered."

He all but ran down the stairs and out the door. He needed air. He needed to think.

He needed to get to Raine.

A baby? They'd been so ready to start their future, and she'd been pregnant. Had she known when he'd left? Why hadn't she said anything…then or now? How could she keep something so vital from him?

Nausea welled up, and he had to remember to take deep breaths as he slid behind the wheel of the car. Gripping the steering wheel, he closed his eyes and prayed for strength… because, God help him, if Raine knew about that baby before he left, he wouldn't be able to look her in the eye again.

Twenty

Raine carefully sprinkled two little seeds into each of the small pots lined up along her workstation on the enclosed patio. The small heater kept the space warm enough for the plants to thrive in the winter months and warm enough for Abby to enjoy her little bouncy seat while Raine worked.

The side door to her home opened and closed. Raine eased her head around the patio door to see in through the kitchen. Max stomped the snow off his boots and shrugged out of his coat, laying it over the back of a kitchen chair. He never failed to make her heart skip, make her stomach get all tied in wonderful knots. He was beautiful, all tall and broad.

"I'm out here," she called before taking bits of rich soil and covering each of the seeds. He hadn't mentioned coming by today, but she was glad he had. With his evenings taken up with the performances, she treasured their time together during the day.

"Hey," she said with a smile as he stepped down onto the patio. "What's up?"

"I just came from your parents."

Raine's hands froze in the dirt. "What?"

"I wanted to have a talk with them before I go back to L.A."

Dread settled into her stomach. "But you're not leaving for another month."

He rested a shoulder against the wall beside her workbench. "Bronson called this morning, and he wants to start filming as soon as possible. With my father taking a break from work, and my mother doing so well with her radiation, I've decided to head back at the end of the week when the play wraps up."

She knew this moment was coming; she just hadn't planned on it being so soon. They were supposed to have more time.

Tears pricked her eyes as she tried to focus back on planting. "What did you need to see my parents about?"

"I wanted them to quit making your life miserable," he told her. "But when I arrived, Marshall was there, and I got some bombshells of my own."

Covering the last seed in soil, Raine slid off her gloves and turned to face him. "What's that?"

"Your parents were trying to stop this adoption, and Marshall was helping them."

"What?" she gasped. "They wouldn't do that to me."

Max quirked a brow. But didn't offer a response.

Raine's eyes darted to Abby who had fallen fast asleep in the bouncy seat. Fear clutched Raine, squeezing the breath right out of her lungs.

"Why?" she whispered.

"Because they still want to control you, and you're not the daughter they wanted you to be. You have a mind of your own, and they don't like it."

Raine rubbed her forehead, feeling a headache coming on. How could her parents be so cruel? At what point would they stop trying to ruin her life?

"I learned something else while I was there," he said, his voice low.

She met his gaze, and a muscle ticked in his jaw. The

way he looked at her with heavy lids, flared nostrils…
something was wrong.

"What is it?" she asked.

"We had a baby."

He knew. Her parents had taken one last stab at killing
anything she and Max may have shared. Raine gripped the
edge of her workbench and willed her knees not to buckle.

"Yes, I was pregnant." Her eyes met his and held. "We
had a little boy."

Max's shoulders sagged, and he exhaled as if he'd been
holding it, waiting to hear the truth from her.

"I'm sorry, Max. I'm so sorry."

Raine couldn't stop the tears. Couldn't stop from thinking of that dark time when she'd wanted that baby and this
man in her life. And she'd ended up losing both.

"When would you have told me?" he asked. "Ever?"

Raine swallowed, trying to get her emotions in check,
because this conversation was happening whether she was
ready or not.

"Someday," she said honestly. "I couldn't yet. We were
still so emotionally damaged from everything in our past.
I just couldn't pile on more hurt. And I was scared."

"Of what?"

Her eyes held his. "That you'd hate me."

Max wiped a hand down his face and pushed off the
wall. Closing the space between them, he gripped her shoulders and forced her to look at him.

"Did you know before I left?" he asked.

She stared up at him and shook her head. "No," she
whispered. "I found out after you left. We'd made love that
night before. That's when I got pregnant."

Tears glistened in his blue eyes, and Raine wrapped her
arms around him, as if she could absorb some of the hurt.

"I wanted to tell you, Max. But I waited to hear from
you and…well, you know how that panned out."

"I hate them," he rasped. "I hate them for destroying something we had. Just tell me, what happened to our son?"

"I went into labor at twenty-eight weeks. He wasn't developed enough, and they couldn't save him." Raine forced herself to keep talking through the pain. "He was so tiny, and to me he was perfect. I planned a funeral out of town for him a few days later, but I had to stay away because my parents would only agree to pay for it if I still kept the secret. Heaven forbid people in the town know.

"Ironically, my parents didn't even come to the graveside service. It was pretty much me, Jill, my grandmother and the pastor."

He studied her face and swiped away her tears. "You must hate me for not being here. I can't even imagine what you went through, because right now my heart is breaking."

"It was the worst moment of my life," she admitted. "That's why keeping Abby is so important to me. I can't lose her."

"You won't. I've made sure of that."

His hardened tone told her that he had indeed done something to make sure this adoption would go through. She didn't need to know what, just knowing this man was in her corner was enough to have her heart swelling.

Silence enveloped them before Max eased back, dropped his hands, forcing her to drop hers. "Why not tell me about the pregnancy when I came back?" he asked.

Raine shrugged. "I really didn't know how to tell you. It was so long ago, yet the emotions are still just as raw. Seeing you, it brought all of that back again, and I wanted to get a better grasp on it before I opened up to you."

"I deserved to know, Raine."

She hitched in a breath. "Yes, you did. But I know how much I still hurt over the loss, and I couldn't stand the thought of hurting you that way. Not when I'd fallen in love with you again."

Max shook his head. "Don't. Please don't tell me you love me, Raine. I can't stay here, and I don't want to leave you hurting again."

Too late.

"I can't keep my feelings inside, Max. I know you're leaving, but you have to know how I feel."

"I can't give you what you want, what you deserve," he said. "It's not fair for you to give your love to me again, when I'm not going to be here."

Raine wanted to know; she had to know.

"Do you love me?" she asked. "Honestly?"

Those magnificent blue eyes held hers. "More than I thought I could."

God, was it worse knowing? She choked back a sob.

"I knew you did," she whispered. "I knew it by your actions, but hearing you say it…"

As much as she hated it, she started to cry. Her hands came up to shield her face as Max's warm, strong arms enveloped her. She sobbed into his chest for the love they shared, for the love that couldn't be bridged through the distance. All the years apart had driven an impossible wedge through them.

Raine stepped back, wiped her face. "I'm sorry. I just… I hate this. It's like we were given a glimpse at a second chance, but I knew it wouldn't work."

Max swiped at his eyes, too macho to have a sniveling crying fit like she'd done. "I can't ask you to leave here, Raine. And I can't stay."

Obviously love did have its boundaries, because, if he'd asked her to come with him, she would. Maybe he wasn't ready for the family life; maybe he was too set in his ways in L.A.; maybe he enjoyed living freely without being tied down to one woman and a baby.

Glancing down at Abby, Raine knew there was no

way she'd give up this baby. But giving up this house, the farm—she'd sacrifice all that for Max.

"I need to get to the theater since tonight's performance starts earlier," he said. "My mom and dad are coming. Maybe you'd like to see if Sasha could watch Abby and come sit in the front row one last time?"

As much as she wanted to, she couldn't. Nothing would compare to the other night when they'd made love in his dressing room, had dinner on the stage. She wanted that memory to be the last one in the theater, because she doubted she'd ever step foot in there again.

"I can't," she told him. "It's better this way."

Max nodded. "So, this is it? Are we saying goodbye here?"

Too choked up with emotion to speak, Raine bit her quivering lip and nodded.

Max placed his hands on either side of her face and forced her to look him in the eye. "I do love you, Raine. Never doubt that. And if you ever need me, just call."

She needed him now. She needed him to stay, to be her rock and her partner. But it wasn't fair to ask him to give up his life in L.A. for Lenox.

"I want…" Max stopped, shook his head and dropped his hands. "Will you call me? Keep me updated on Abby and how you're doing?"

"Sure." *God, this was lame.* "I'll let you know when the adoption goes through."

He stared at her another minute, then he turned, squatted down to a sleeping Abby and kissed her forehead. "Take care of your mommy for me, little one."

Raine nearly threw her arms around him and begged him to stay, but she held herself in place as Max spared her one last glance over his shoulder.

"Goodbye, Raine."

"Bye, Max."

And he was gone.

Raine couldn't hold herself together another second. The dam burst, and she buried her head in her hands, resting her elbows on the wooden bench.

How could a heart be ripped apart so many times in one life and still keep beating?

She would get past this; she knew she was strong…and that she had so much to live for. After all, she still had Abby. She'd wanted a baby for years, and here she was a mother. So she had to look to the blessings she had and find a reason to smile again.

And she would…eventually. But right now, she wanted to throw a self-pity party and feel sorry for all she'd lost.

How would she ever be able to look at pictures of Max in the media or see a movie starring him and not remember how those hands had felt on her body? How he'd gone to her parents and taken up for her—and Abby? How he'd looked with tears in his eyes as he had told her goodbye—

When a large hand brushed across her arm, Raine jumped and turned to see Max. His coat was covered with snow, as was his hair.

"What are you doing?" she sniffed, embarrassed he'd caught her having a breakdown.

"I fell," he said with a smile. "Literally. Bess and Lulu came running out and tripped me. Then the chickens joined in."

Raine smiled at the mental image, then reached up to touch his face. "Are you hurt?" she asked.

Max gripped her hands and held them between his icy ones. "Yes. I'm miserable. I said goodbye two minutes ago, and I can't handle it, Raine. How will I live across the country knowing my heart is here?"

Hope spread through her. *Please, please, please, let him be saying he wants more.*

"I don't care where we live," he said. "If I have to live

on the farm and fly to L.A. when necessary, then I will. Or if you want to sell and move, we'll do that. I just can't leave, Raine. I can't leave you."

She threw her arms around him, not caring about the snow wetting her long-sleeved T-shirt. She squeezed him, never wanting to let him go.

"What made you change your mind?" she asked as she eased back.

"When your crazy goats tripped me, I laughed. I mean, how could I leave here? I love everything about it. I want to make a home with you and Abby, if you'll let me. I know that may take more time in the courts for me to be her adoptive father, but—"

"You're serious?" Raine asked. "You want to be her father?"

Max bent down and captured Raine's lips in a soul-searing kiss. "And your husband."

Raine squealed, waking Abby. "Oops," she said, laughing.

"Let me get her," Max offered.

He lifted her from the bouncy seat and rested her against his dry shoulder. "I have the two most beautiful girls in the world," he said, wrapping his wet arm around Raine. "Nothing is more important than this right here."

"But what about the film you're going to start shooting?" she asked.

"You can come with me for a bit until you need to be back for your Farmer's Market."

"You're not embarrassed that I like to make and sell my own things? I mean, you can purchase whatever you want, and I'm scraping by here."

"You have a career you enjoy, Raine. I would never take that from you."

Raine smiled up at him. "I love you."

Max kissed her forehead. "I love you, too. Now, we

need to add some livestock to this farm and get this house fixed up."

"To sell?" she asked.

"Sell? Hell, no, we're not selling. We can keep a place on each coast. I have a feeling we'll be traveling a lot, because I'm going to spend as much time with you as humanly possible. I'm also going to want more babies."

Raine laughed. "You really want it all. Amazing you got all of that from Bess and Lulu tripping you."

"I fell for you long ago, Raine. I know when I have a good thing, and I don't plan on ever letting go." Max slid his arm around her, pulling her in tight against his chest. "I plan on holding both of my girls forever."

* * * * *

TEMPTING THE BEAUTY QUEEN

CAROLYN HECTOR

I would like to dedicate this to
Dr Henry J. Hector III, aka my dad –
The World's Best Father.

Chapter 1

"I was able to find a *Hamilton* ticket easier than trying to find a date for this month," said Kenzie Swayne, Southwood, Georgia's town historian. To say she had problems was the understatement of the century. Her strictly platonic go-to date, Rafael "Rafe" Gonzalez, bailed on her this morning. Something about the time being right to go after the woman he loved. Deep down inside, Kenzie knew she needed to be happy for her friend, but damn, couldn't love wait a month?

With a heavy sigh, Kenzie flipped her word-of-the-day calendar over. "*Lugubrious*," she announced. "Yep, gloomy, bummed and bleak pretty much summarizes my life right now." Where else could a girl get a hot guy who lived in the next town over to show up for important dates and who wasn't looking for long-term commitments?

At the hint of a chuckle, Kenzie glanced up at her dear friend, Lexi Pendergrass Reyes, who graciously hid her laughter behind her left hand, where her blindingly gorgeous wedding ring caught the fluorescent lights of the room. Kenzie grumbled and leaned back in her black leather office chair and rolled her eyes when the chair hit the wall behind her. Sure, her tiny headquarters in City Hall were small but she had bigger problems. She needed an escort for her cousin's wedding tomorrow and the four major events of June, when three friends were tying the knot, along with a gala and a beauty pageant.

"Come on now," encouraged Lexi. She shifted the four teal garment bags into her left hand and leaned against the door jamb. "What about one of the Crowne twins? Surely they're going to their brother's ceremony?"

The last wedding Kenzie agreed to attend and be in was a surprise for the bride. At least with Waverly Leverve, knowing about the nuptials meant she could at least back out of this one. Kenzie shook her head from side to side. The coppery, red-gold hair fell over her shoulders. She frowned as she twisted it up into a bun. She couldn't control her hair in this humid weather, so what made her think she'd be able to control her life?

Last winter Kenzie became fast friends with the handsome Crowne twins, Dario and Darren. They took Southwood by storm when they moved here to run their brother's garage. The single ladies in town were smitten with the twins and their playboy charm but alas, neither Dario nor Darren would work well as a believable date for her cousin's wedding tomorrow. Most of the Hairston clan, her mother's family, coming back to Southwood wouldn't believe Kenzie was involved in a relationship with either twin. Kenzie did not date playboys. Anymore. Playboys were a waste of time and she saw no need to be strung along by a man with a commitment phobia.

Four weeks. That was how long Kenzie was going to have to endure the scrutinous gaze of her kinfolk, especially Great-Auntie Brenda—Auntie Bren for short. She'd be there for Cousin Corie's wedding tomorrow, Felicia Ward's next week and the Southwood Sesquicentennial

Gala. In her mideighties, Auntie Bren was a force to be reckoned with. You'd never know her age by looking at her or witnessing her spunk. At her assisted living home in Miami, Florida, she kept friends like a queen held court. At the hundred-and-fifty-year celebration, more of Auntie Bren's friends would come and hear the story of her twenty-eight-year-old great-niece who was still not married or dating anyone serious. Both the Hairston and Swayne sides of Kenzie's family were attending and everyone would have a date but her.

"The twins offered to split two of the weddings, one with each, and the Southwood Sesquicentennial Gala and thought the three of us could attend Dominic's all together," said Kenzie, "but I can't. I need some*one, as in the same guy,* who will be here every weekend. Dario can do the first two but then he's swapping places with Darren. I think they're working on a project with Dominic, something about the baby's room."

"Aww," Lexi cooed.

"They look alike but not that much. You know Erin Hairston has an eagle eye. She came here last summer to help Chantal pack up for her big move overseas and had to point out to everyone in the studio how I had more freckles from being in the sun so much." Kenzie scowled and pressed her fingers against her freckle-covered face. As a child it was bad enough she sported this distinct red hair, but to top it off with more than a splash of freckles was downright cruel. Cousin Erin...*perfect* Cousin Erin, turned her nose up at beauty pageants to become an occupational therapist. In Auntie Bren's eyes, Erin was the closest thing to a doctor on the Hairston side of the family.

Lexi, gorgeous since the day she was born, rolled her eyes toward the barbaric florescent lights in the room. "Your freckles are what make you, you."

"Whatever. The least these spots can do is shield me when I'm dying of embarrassment when my eighty-five-year-old aunt is quizzing me about my sexuality."

As hard as she tried not to, Lexi laughed. "What? She wouldn't."

"She did with Maggie," Kenzie said of her older sister, Magnolia "Maggie" Swayne. "Auntie Bren started questioning her about whether or not she liked men and Maggie got graphic with the peach in her hand." Kenzie laughed along with Lexi. "So needless to say Maggie won't be seated at the family table."

"With any luck you won't be seated with Auntie Bren then," said a deep voice from behind Lexi. "I'm sure she put a hex on me."

One could hope, Kenzie thought before she realized who the deep voice belonged to at her door. The half laugh she almost shared with Lexi died and in its place came a scowl. By cruel fate, Kenzie's high school boyfriend, Alexander Ward, had been appointed city manager by his best friend, Mayor Anson Wilson. Kenzie was positive Anson had placed Alexander on the same City Hall floor just to annoy her since he held her responsible for not being able to get close to her friend Waverly. Last year Waverly Leverve came to town as a dethroned beauty queen being taunted by mocking memes of her crying when she'd had to give up the crown. Anson thought he could win her heart but Waverly was destined to be with someone better. "What do you want, Alexander?"

"Aw, babe, is that any way to talk to the higher-ups?"

Kenzie sneered and cut her eyes over at Lexi who made room for Alexander to stand in the doorway with her. "When the higher-up refers to me as *babe*, he reverts back to an ex-boyfriend."

Foolish as it sounded, Kenzie had accepted Alexander's marriage proposal at their high school graduation, caught off guard in front of hundreds of witnesses. She'd figured since they were both attending Florida A&M in the fall there'd be no problem. But the problem came when Alexander made several friends of the female kind over the summer semester. Kenzie didn't find out about his extracurricular activities until the first week she arrived on campus and was greeted by several other women who claimed Alexander as their boyfriend.

She'd returned to Southwood for a semester and endured a pity party from family and friends every turn she took. Not being able to take it, she'd left town for Georgia State and come back with her PhD in history. So far all she had done was archive the town's information to bring it into the digital world but Kenzie had been destined to be the first historian of her hometown. Southwood was in her blood and her family made history. The Swaynes, her daddy's side, and the Hairstons, on her mama's side, helped found the town a hundred and fifty years ago. So to come back to town after everything she'd been through, in Kenzie's mind, she'd had the bounce-back of the decade. In her family's eyes, she was twenty-eight and unmarried with no children.

Alexander doubled over with laughter. "She's still in love with me," he explained, giving Lexi a slight elbow to her ribs. Nobody loved Alexander more than Alexander. Everyone had had their role in school. Alexander had been president of their senior class, captain of the basketball team and shared the accolade of most likely to succeed with his best friend, the current mayor. Regardless of the morning's temperature starting off in the high eighties, Alexander wore a dark suit, including the jacket. The air conditioning these days was spotty, having to work overtime to fight the summer heat.

"Anyway, how are you doing, Mrs. Reyes? Ready to expand your studio?" Alexander went on to ask Lexi. "There's space right by your building."

"The building next door to Grits and Glam Studios, is next door to the old barber shop, and it's historic," Kenzie retorted and heard the contempt in her voice as she spoke. A hardware store had already disappeared when Lexi expanded her Grits and Glam Gowns to accommodate her successful pageant training studio.

"It's old, not historic," Alexander corrected. "The block of land belongs to the city, not the *Swaynes*, Kenzie. We're allowed to sell it to developers if we wish."

Kenzie cursed under her breath and shuffled through the stack of folders on her desk—her contribution to Southwood—and found the file she needed. "Here's the decree, marking the barbershop as a historic site. Martin Luther King Jr. had his hair cut here and spoke in front of the buildings in the sixties." The proof shut the city manager up and an awkward silence fell in the room. Both ladies waited for Alexander to leave. He lingered.

"Well, I'm good for now, Alexander," Lexi replied dismissively. "Thank you for the option."

Alexander ignored the dismissal. "What brings you to City Hall?"

When Lexi raised a questioning brow at Kenzie, Kenzie refrained from rolling her eyes.

"She's here to see me," Kenzie answered. "Is that okay with you?"

"You're allowed to have visitors," said Alexander. "It's kind of cramped in here. Would the two of you like to go into my office and talk? I have a beautiful view of the town square. It's beautiful this time of year."

"Yes, it is," Lexi answered, "but I just needed to drop off Waverly's dresses for all four events this month."

"Ah yes, starting with your cousin's wedding. I thought I saw Corie around town, or more importantly, her fiancé, Hawk Cameron."

Everyone who was anyone knew about Hawk Cameron, the star athlete for the Georgia Wolves basketball team. In the Hairston family, Hawk was more known as the man who'd knocked up the golden child of the HFG, the Hairston Financial Group. When Corie admitted her pregnancy, she'd been the topic of brief gossip. All seemed to be forgiven since Hawk stepped up as a father. *No*, Kenzie thought with a frown, since Hawk *the athlete* stepped up to the plate. Meanwhile, Kenzie was considered a pariah in her family's eyes.

"Was there anything you needed, Alexander?" Kenzie swallowed past the irritation growing in her throat.

Alexander admitted he had nothing and then said goodbye, leaving Kenzie and Lexi alone. Finally.

"Must be tough working with your ex?"

Kenzie frowned. "Not as bad as working with him as a boss."

"No chance he'd…"

Kenzie held her hand up to stop her old friend and mentor. "No, thanks. I'd rather run naked through Four Points Park at the height of mosquito season."

Mosquito season in the South was unlike anything else in the world. "I'll take that as a definite no."

"Exactly. I shouldn't be embarrassed or single-shamed just because I don't have a date, or a boyfriend, or anything to pass off as a boyfriend," said Kenzie.

"Hey, last summer you and…"

With a cut of her eyes Kenzie quieted Lexi once again. Days after the abrupt end to her summer fling with *him*, Kenzie had perfected the art of masking her hurt and frustration with spite and irritation. "Do not mention *his* name."

"Don't be so stubborn," Lexi joked. "I don't understand how you can work with Alexander but you can't with—" Lexi gave pause and consideration for saying the name "—*him*. You two *bonded* last summer."

Kenzie didn't miss the way Lexi's fingers bent into air quotes as she said bonded. "And then he humiliated me by standing me up for the party after the Miss Southwood Pageant. You know I hate to be embarrassed," said Kenzie. "And sure, I was mortified when I found out about Alexander cheating back when we were college freshmen. I could at least deal with Alexander when we started college, and thanks to a lot of therapy, I accept he's the one who should be ashamed, not me. Working with him, well, he annoys me but that's it. We have no…"

"Feelings for each other?" Lexi supplied.

An uncontrollable upper lip curl tugged at Kenzie's face. "Feelings?" She scoffed and waved off the notion. "Not a chance. I want nothing to do with *him*."

"That's why you had *his* truck towed?" Lexi mused and played along with Kenzie by not saying the name.

Feigning innocence, Kenzie batted her lashes. "Anyone who parks one inch too close to a fire hydrant needs to be reported, Lexi," explained Kenzie. "I was looking out for the good citizens of Southwood."

"Yeah, right," said Lexi with a knowing smile. "Well, look, let me get out of here."

The back of the black leather chair scraped against the pale gray wall behind Kenzie. It had a deep groove from the numerous times she'd done the exact same thing. "My goodness, let me get these off your hands." She reached for the garment bags and immediately the wave of guilt hit her. "I'm so wrong. Here you are, five months pregnant in the summertime. A woman in your condition shouldn't have to stand and listen to me complain."

Lexi waved off Kenzie's fret. "Trust me, I'd stand here and talk to you longer. I've been hunched over the sewing machine for the last few days getting ready for Bailey's pageant debut in a few weeks."

The two of them headed off to the elevators just outside Kenzie's door. Pressing the circular down button, Kenzie smiled fondly at the image of her seventeen-year-old niece winning Miss Southwood and keeping the Swayne beauty queen dynasty going. It meant a lot to Kenzie to know Lexi saw the beauty queen potential in Bailey. In the pageant world, Lexi was a goddess. Not only did a one-of-a-kind dress designed by Lexi bring good luck, but her guidance as a pageant coach always brought her girls in at least the top five of every competition.

For Kenzie's family, pageantry ran in their veins. So far six older relatives on Kenzie's father's side of the family were former beauty queens and four on the Hairston side, all before the age of eighteen. More had won Miss Southwood between the ages of nineteen and twenty-five, including Kenzie, but Bailey winning would be quite a feat for someone so young. Plus, there hadn't been a Swayne queen since Kenzie.

"I'm so excited." Kenzie beamed. "I know the former Miss Southwood is supposed to hand over the tiara but I plan on crowning her myself."

"Because we both know she'll win."

Kenzie gave her friend a high five and the elevator doors dinged and opened. As they waited, Lexi pressed on. "I can't wait."

After the elevator doors closed, Kenzie crossed the long hallway of her office floor toward the big bay windows to make sure Lexi made it safely down the front steps. Pride filled her heart at the sight of the well-manicured, lush green lawn of the town center. Cobblestone sidewalks encased the stretch of space in front of City Hall. Scattered diagonal parking spaces filled either side of the roads. Surrounding the area were diverse businesses such as The Cupcakery, Grits and Glam Gowns, The Scoop Ice Cream Parlor, Osborne Books and others in attractive brick buildings with colorful awnings.

Kenzie rolled her eyes at the only thing she considered an eyesore: the upscale Brutti Hotel, built last year. With its modern architecture and glassy windows, and height, it stuck out like a sore thumb amongst the quaint, old town setting. There was nothing historical about the forest area where the hotelier, Gianni Brutti, built the spot and it wasn't even considered Southwood land but everything about the place irritated Kenzie. The upscale hotel did push tourism, which kept revenue in town, so she guessed she couldn't be too mad. In the distance a church bell rang. She was reminded once again of her hectic month ahead. Stress over her single status was going to plague her. The second wedding would be worse only in the sense she would be forced to be around Alexander's and the questions from his well-wishing kin, wondering why the two of them never married. There weren't many things Kenzie disliked about her small town—the folks around here always remembered Kenzie and Alexander as a couple in high school but forgot about her heartbreak when she'd returned. His family, never knowing the full story, always felt the need to remind Kenzie that they were both still single.

In the reflection of the glass Kenzie spotted a sparkling strand of hair mixed with her awkward reddish mess. As if the stress of her life couldn't mount any higher, she'd spied a gray strand. Kenzie pressed her head against the cool glass to inspect. To make matters worse, she spotted the silver Ford F-150 truck driving down Main Street. The same tug on her upper lip returned, just as it had when Lexi almost said his name. *Ramon Torres was in town.*

There were a few things that could cause Ramon Torres to break the strict set of rules he lived by. After battling childhood obesity, Ramon had a no-sweets rule. But for the debut of the summer cupcake, the Wedded Bliss, sold at The Cupcakery in downtown Southwood, he made an exception. The cupcakes were so famously known and loved, Ramon took time away from his boutique hotel, Magnolia Palace, on the outskirts of town just to get one.

The other ban he broke was his No Kenzie rule. Southwood's historian had a knack for getting under Ramon's skin and under his covers. At the moment of spotting the unruly curly red hair secured in a high ponytail on Kenzie Swayne's head, Ramon Torres contemplated leaving The Cupcakery. Considering the debut of the dessert, he decided to stay.

What he hadn't planned on was the way his body responded to the sight of Kenzie's backside in a pair of light-colored jeans. She teetered on a pair of red heels and he recalled how her long legs felt wrapped around his waist. He then ticked off the Yankees' last world series starting lineup in his mind. If he planned on breaking a rule, let it at least be one, not two, in a single day.

The dozen people separating them weren't enough. He needed a battalion. Ramon shifted in his boots and tried to blend in with the group of high school–aged football players with letterman jackets. According to the time on his watch, school hadn't let out yet. Skipping class with identifying clothing to get a cupcake wasn't smart, but Ramon understood. A couple of bankers Ramon worked with on occasion waited patiently in line. Even the kids he'd seen hanging around in the park doing nothing but skateboarding and intimidating some of the locals stopped and stood in line for a cupcake. Ramon understood the things a person was willing to sacrifice for a cupcake. In his quest for one, he'd put himself in the path of the wrath of Kenzie.

Last summer had given Ramon and Kenzie the spark they'd needed to enjoy some heated moments together. Their time had been brief, but most of all pleasurable, until Ramon realized what a distraction Kenzie had been. He'd moved to Southwood to get away from his controlling family. Generation after generation, the Torres men and women were successful. Ramon knew how to throw a party. The family always teased him about making a "good time" a profession. His oldest brother, Julio, became the mayor of their hometown. Another brother became a United States Marshal and Raul, just one year older than Ramon, owned a booming nightclub in Villa San Juan. Ramon's own success gene did not kick in until he reached thirty and just as the gears started to grind, he met Kenzie Swayne. Kenzie put a whole new spin on sexy—and bossy at the same time. She'd been a dangerous distraction when he was supposed to get his life together and grow up. He couldn't live on his parents' property forever, so when the opportunity to buy the old, plantation-style home in Georgia came open, Ramon took it. Since he'd been so great at making sure his friends always had a good time, whether at a party or on vacation, Ramon turned that into a profession and opened the doors to the boutique hotel for families to come and enjoy the Southern town. Magnolia Palace was his baby, his investment and his chance to prove to his family he'd matured.

They worked together on a favorite pastime of Southwood's—the Miss Southwood Beauty Pageant—as a favor to his extended family. Lexi Pendergrass, a former beauty queen, had married Ramon's cousin Stephen. Stephen and his brother Nate were closer to Ramon than his own brothers. With Lexi being kin, as they said in Southwood, Ramon helped her out when the theater downtown, the usual beauty pageant venue, flooded by hosting it at his hotel, Magnolia Palace. With hindsight being 20/20, Ramon now knew he had been in no place to start anything. Had he known hosting the competition would get him involved with Kenzie, Ramon would never have done it. Kenzie wanted a man who was ready to settle down and Ramon was getting on his own two feet.

Ahead of him in line, Kenzie dropped something from her pocket when she retrieved her cell phone from her hip. The ample, heart-shaped view of her behind caused Ramon to forget about the No Kenzie rule. Every red-blooded male in line sighed and cocked their heads to the side to unabashedly appreciate the view. A collective sigh of admiration stretched through the store. Unaware, Kenzie straightened and juggled her oversize purse on her shoulder and committed the ultimate sin…she stepped aside. Whoever was on the other end must have been pretty damn important. Ramon's jaw twitched with a twinge of something. He couldn't put his finger on the feeling. He didn't like the idea of someone so important in her life.

"Torres," someone called out.

Ramon willed Mr. Myers to keep quiet until Kenzie left the bakery. The retired history teacher went so far as to wave his arms in the air. Ramon offered a quiet head nod in the direction where Mr. Myers sat with three older women. He breathed a sigh of relief when the glass doors closed behind Kenzie.

"Hey," Ramon said with a head nod in the direction of the table. The line moved forward to the point where the glass counter came into view. Ramon counted the number of people in line versus the number of cupcakes in the display case. If his calculations were correct and if everyone purchased only one cupcake, there would be two left by the time he reached the register.

"Get your stuff and come over here," Mr. Myers ordered. "I want you to meet my fiancée."

Fiancée? Ramon thought to himself. Which one? At seventy-eight, Mr. Myers had earned his reputation as a ladies' man, splitting his time between the two Southwood senior centers. Ramon pointed toward his watch and shook his head, praying the old man understood the silent apology. He didn't want to be here if Kenzie returned. Bad things happened when she was around. Once, and he couldn't prove it, Ramon had gone to sprinkle salt on his fries at the Food Truck Thursday event at Four Points Park and managed to get a snow mountain of salt. And even though he couldn't prove it, Ramon still felt Kenzie had something to do with his name being taken off the Christmas Advisory Council. Anyone with a business in Southwood wanted to be a part of the CAC. The council also helped bring cheer to town. He was also denied membership to a lot of Southwood events because his hotel was slightly outside of Southwood. Also last year, Ramon wanted to invite the whole town to his hotel for a holiday party but the email was somehow lost in the cyber world. And because the committee had gone for an old-fashioned theme last year, guess who had been in charge of all things last Christmas? None other than Kenzie Swayne.

Hell hath no fury like a woman stood up. Apparently Kenzie was the type of woman who didn't appreciate him bailing on her at the last pageant event last year. That was when Ramon decided to keep his distance and work on a No Kenzie rule…meaning, if he knew she was going to attend the same function as him, Ramon stayed away. So far Ramon had managed not to bump into her face-to-face for six months now. Soon everything would change. Ramon planned on starting up a business not just in Southwood city limits but in the historic downtown area. He was going to get a seat at that damn Christmas Advisory Council this year.

As the cashier argued with a customer, Ramon spied the back of Kenzie's head leaving the park. The fact his body still reacted to the sight of her proved he needed the No Kenzie rule. Pavlov's classical conditioning theory went into effect and induced a mouthwatering reaction, much like at his mother's coquito cupcakes. He still craved her. Just like the desserts, Kenzie was bad for his health and bad for Ramon's concentration.

"All right, guys," announced Tiffani, the cashier behind the counter, "after this batch I'm out of the Wedded Bliss cupcakes. I'm shorthanded today, so I'll need to take a break and make up some more. It will be about an hour until they're ready."

Groans from the customers drowned out Ramon's curses. The line moved forward. Folks behind him left the line, uttering their decision to come back later. As calculated, everyone else in line bought their share of cupcakes, except for the high school students who left, probably due to class. By the time Ramon reached the display counter there were five cupcakes left and no one behind him.

"Looks like you're in luck," Tiffani gushed when she realized he was next. "I'll let you have the rest."

"The rest?" Ramon imagined himself eating every single cupcake and then imagined how far he'd have to run to work them off. "I really just want the one."

"But there's no one else in line and these are going to

go to waste once I break out the fresher ones," Tiffani said as she boxed up the items.

"I'll tell you what, if you'll put four in a to-go box and leave them for the next customer who walks in, I'll take the one and pay you for a dozen."

"Sounds like a deal to me."

Once Ramon got his cupcake to go, he turned around at the same time as Kenzie reentered the bakery. Damn, how much was this going to cost him?

Chapter 2

"You've got a lot of nerve, Ramon Torres," Kenzie hollered at his tailored suit. She hated the way her body heated up at the sight of the man. Ramon turned to face her. His broad shoulders slumped. And she even swore he rolled his neck from side to side, preparing himself for battle. The wind blowing between the buildings whipped a loose piece of hair from his annoyingly cute man-bun on top of his head. The man mixed sex appeal with bohemian chic and wrapped it up in a sharp midnight blue suit paired with black snakeskin cowboy boots.

"What did I do this time?" Ramon stopped his long stride in front of the old post office. He didn't bother trying to sound shocked to see her, which annoyed Kenzie even more.

"Tiffani told me you purchased these. I don't need you buying cupcakes for me," she told his backside as she approached.

"So don't eat them," Ramon responded.

Kenzie walked around his large frame to make sure Ramon saw the irritation across her face. If there was one thing that set her off, it was a man telling her what to do.

Kenzie had worked too hard for the last ten years to grow from a naive girl dependent on her boyfriend. But Ramon wasn't her boyfriend. No, he made it perfectly clear last summer he didn't want to be in a relationship with her. "Don't tell me what to do."

Ramon sighed heavily. "Do whatever you want."

"I ought to throw them away," Kenzie went on to antagonize him. These were cupcakes from *The Cupcakery.* No one ever threw them away, especially not out of spite. Besides, she'd already had a bite of the delectable lemony dessert when Tiffani informed her the previous customer paid it forward.

"You're not throwing anything away." Ramon called her bluff with a sarcastic laugh.

With the box in her hand, Kenzie crossed her arms. "Fine. But I just want you to know from here on out I don't want you buy me anything."

"For future reference, Kenzie, I paid it forward for the next person. How was I supposed to know you were going come back into the shop?"

Back? She took in his choice of words and hated the idea of Ramon having the upper hand. He saw her before she did? "So you saw me and didn't bother speaking? What are you, a stalker or something?"

The square jaw of his tightened. "You were on the phone."

Being reminded of the call infuriated her more. Alexander had tried to sneak a project by her without her knowledge. No wonder he'd been so friendly in her office. Had his secretary, Margaret, not given Kenzie the heads-up, Kenzie would have had no idea the old post office was being considered for purchase. "Whatever."

"Well, if we're done here…" said Ramon, taking a step toward the closed doors of the old post office. In two long strides, Ramon entered, disappearing from Kenzie's fruit-less rant. So what if the man wanted to do something nice for the next person? But why did it have to be her?

The wind picked up on the street, blowing the unsecured hair from Kenzie's ponytail into her face. With a sigh she set the box of cupcakes on the top step and twisted her hair into a bun. The doors closed behind Ramon and left her staring at her reflection from the mirrored doors. Growing up she'd hated her naturally frizzy red hair, but she hated her face full of freckles more. Now with a glimpse of herself, Kenzie smiled in appreciation. It took her a while but she found her unique look appealing and if she did say so herself, as she looked down at her attire…she looked pretty damn good today.

Common sense told her to head on back home. She'd already gotten her coveted debut cupcakes. Now she needed to get home and destress about seeing her family at the rehearsal dinner tonight. She wondered if there was someone on Craigslist she could hire…or was that illegal?

The clicking of the lion's head antique brass door knobs on the post office door reminded Kenzie of her nagging suspicions about the building. Alexander planned on meeting his potential client in a few minutes and Kenzie intended to be here. Funny how he didn't mention it earlier. She understood the position of a city manager needing to bring in business, but at what cost? Buildings in Southwood were historic. Some of them were built before the Civil War. And he'd scheduled a meeting, knowing she was taking the month of June. "Spiteful bastard," Kenzie mumbled to herself. Her ex had sworn he would not let their past interfere with working together when he was hired as city manager.

A car sounded off at the end of the street and a couple of high school kids in two different pickup trucks were mock sword fighting with each other. Idle hands, Kenzie thought with an exacerbated sigh. When the drivers spotted Kenzie they honked again and waved. More than likely they were up to something mischievous in the post office. Kids loved to run around in there, regardless of the danger signs. Speaking of which, Ramon didn't need to be in the building playing around, either. Kenzie reached down and picked up her box of cupcakes and headed inside. Ramon needed to leave.

"Ramon?" Kenzie called out his name. Her voice echoed off the empty walls. An old counter filled with dust split the center of the room. The inside windows were boarded up with old newspapers. Sun damage had destroyed the dates of when the papers were put up.

Footsteps sounded off down the hall just beyond the counter. From old pictures, Kenzie knew there was an elevator. The four-story building was also a playground on Halloween. Kids loved to tell ghost stories about using the elevators and getting stuck between floors, but there was no electricity in the building so Kenzie never believed them.

"Ramon." She said his name once more.

"Are you following me?" Ramon's voice sounded through the dark hallway.

"What are you doing in here?" She followed the sound of his baritone voice and swore his footsteps moved quicker and farther away. "Stop playing around in here."

She finally caught up with him. Sun leaked through the paled paper on the back windows and backlit him. Ramon stood in the elevator car, his back against the wall and his arms folded. He could have easily been a model in an ad for sexiness.

"What?" Ramon asked.

Kenzie placed her hands on her hips and stamped her foot. She hadn't meant to, but she did. "Get out of here."

"Are you going to make me?" Ramon offered a cocky half grin and stretched out his arms toward her.

In an attempt to back away, Kenzie slipped on her heels but caught herself in the elevator doors and kept herself from falling. Ramon didn't have the decency to hide his laugh. "You're a jerk."

"Thanks," he replied. "Why are you following me?"

"I am not," Kenzie said standing her ground. Her eyes caught the debris on the ground by her foot and as she glanced up the air in front of her began to snow. *Snow?* A loud rumble above her head sounded off. The moment she craned her neck upward something pulled on her blouse and her body was jerked forward into the elevator. Thunder was followed by a hail of ceiling tiles behind her. Ramon wrapped his arms around her body and turned his back to the falling debris.

Nestled against his chest, Kenzie stood still until the deafening sound stopped. She should have been frightened but she wasn't. With Ramon's arms secured around her frame she remained safe.

Ramon leaned backward and tipped her chin up. "Are you okay?"

Lost in his almond-shaped, dark brown eyes, Kenzie nodded her head. "I think so. What happened?"

"The avalanche was the floor collapsing just outside the doors."

Kenzie peered around his arms. The doors were closed. A light flickered but she didn't know how. The building had no electricity. Then she realized Ramon held his cell phone over her head. She blinked.

"We're trapped," she said rather than asked. The silence was proof. The doors were closed from the fall. They were safe from the falling debris but they were trapped. Kenzie peered again at the doors, which now, in her mind, seemed closer than before. Her eyes traveled up toward the ceiling of the elevator…the low ceiling, which grew lower by the second.

"Hey now," Ramon cooed, placing his hand on her backside. "Breathe with me."

"I am breathing."

"Your breathing is erratic," he pointed out, pressing his hand with the cell phone against her breast. "Your heart rate is accelerating."

"Don't flatter yourself," Kenzie said with a dry laugh. She pushed his warm hand away from her breast. Her nipples hardened with his touch. Amazing how her body could flip from a mild panic attack to sheer desire. Damn him. "I get claustrophobic sometimes."

"Sometimes?" Ramon chuckled.

"Yeah, well, just when I'm stressed and nearly lose my life," she snapped.

"You're welcome," he said.

"What?"

"I just pulled you from danger."

Kenzie backed away from him. The cool bar on the wall braced her backside. "And I am pretty sure you popped one of my buttons off my blouse."

Ramon held the light toward her chest to see. As if naked and exposed, Kenzie crossed her arms over her chest. "I'll let the second floor collapse on you."

"Technically the third floor."

"What?"

"Why would you walk into a building you know nothing about?" Kenzie shook her head back and forth. "Never mind, I don't want to know. You know, if you weren't such a baby and running from me every time you see me…"

"I don't run from you."

Kenzie scoffed at him for interrupting her. "Face it, Ramon. You're scared of a woman like me."

"I'm not afraid of you," Ramon clipped. "I have something to do in here."

"Like what?"

"I have a meeting with Alexander Ward."

Dread washed over her. Thank God for the darkness. Heat crept across her face. She was sure a red tint would cover her freckles right about now. "You're the one he wants to sell to?"

"If the price is right." Ramon sighed. "And if I can make sure I follow some rules."

So Alexander had listened to Kenzie's advice on restoring the old buildings. The fact didn't ease her irritation. "So you're just going to buy up every important building in my life."

"Here we go," groaned Ramon.

"Here we go nothing, Ramon." Kenzie bared her teeth in the dark. "You bought my family's historic home."

"I bought a business, Kenzie."

When she heard the tone of his voice Kenzie's hands went to her hips. "Are you mocking me?"

"No, I am stating a fact. I am a businessman. It goes with the territory and let's face it, you weren't in the position to buy the place."

Though his words were true, it didn't take the sting out of hearing them. It didn't take the threat of tears rimming her eyes when Maggie once pointed out that Kenzie didn't have…what was it she said? *A pot to piss in to buy the place.* Kenzie credited the plantation home for having sparked her love of history. She delved into the Swayne family tree and its contribution to Southwood. The Swayne family had lived there before the Civil War and harvested a pecan farm. Folklore said the family gave up the home in order to save the farm, which worked in their favor. To this day Swayne Pecans was the highest quality pecan seller in the States; it was passed on from generation to generation and still run today by her father, Mitchell Swayne, and his brothers. Technically she'd never lived in the house. No one from the Swayne side of the family had lived in the house for a hundred years. But that didn't stop Kenzie from believing the home would return to a Swayne one day, preferably her. And Ramon had the nerve to turn it into a boutique hotel. Granted, the property never looked better, but she'd never admit such a thing to Ramon.

"You're breathing heavy again." Ramon moved close to Kenzie's frame. Large hands pressed against her shoulders. "Take a seat, calm down."

"I'm not going to calm down. I don't have time for such luxuries, I've got a million things to do and prepare for and I don't need to be stuck in some dark elevator with the likes of you."

"The likes of me?" He flat-out mocked her with a hard laugh and an overexaggerated Southern drawl. The elevator shook a bit. Did the space between the walls get tighter?

Kenzie felt the floor beneath her against the back of her jeans as she sat down. She tucked her feet under her legs and adjusted her frame away from Ramon's when he got down beside her and wrapped his arm around her shoulder. He smelled wonderful, like lemon icing. Kenzie's stomach grumbled. What happened to her box? Did she drop it?

"What other things do you have to do? You can talk to me. Or have you forgotten we used to be friends?" Ramon asked her while his fingers rubbed the nape of her neck. Kenzie tilted her head against his shoulder. They'd been more than friends at one point. If she remembered correctly, this slick move with his hands toying with the hair at the nape of her neck had landed her in bed with him. Kenzie scooted away. "Tell me what's going on."

"I have three weddings to attend, and my baby cousin is getting married before me. Not only is one half of my family coming, I'm attending the wedding solo which means I'm going to spend several hours with the tilt-of-the-head-pity-look from them. Then I've got two weddings for my pageant girls and all of them are trying to set me up with their fiancés' groomsmen and I'm desperate to take them up on the offer because at this year's gala, I'm going to have my entire family in town, the Hairstons and the Swaynes."

"Not *the* Hairstons and *the* Swaynes." Ramon gasped dramatically before chuckling.

Kenzie elbowed him in the ribs and pressed her lips together to keep from smiling. "Shut up. You have no idea about family pressure."

"I don't?"

"No," said Kenzie. "And did I mention the Miss Southwood Pageant is at the end of the month this year?"

"Hmm. Has it already been a year? Seems like just yesterday you were walking through the doors at Magnolia Palace and barking out orders."

"You're not funny."

"Sorry, I feel like I should get you flowers or something."

"Why?"

"Because it's the anniversary of when we first met," said Ramon, no hint of mockery in his tone.

A shiver ran down Kenzie's spine. "And the celebration of the first time I'd been embarrassed in like a decade."

"By me not escorting you to the *final* party? Do you know how many parties and events we went to? You had something planned every day for a week."

"Well, after everything we went through…" Kenzie began clearing her throat. "If you weren't interested, you should have said so, set the guidelines, not leave me hanging to get myself to the restaurant."

"You're mad because I stood you up?" Ramon asked softly. Kenzie responded by rolling her eyes. "I didn't mean to hurt you, Kenzie."

"I'm not mad about just standing me up. If you weren't interested, you shouldn't have started things up with me and then stopped speaking to me. And don't try giving me a lame answer like, 'It's not you, it's me.'"

"What if that's true?"

"Whatever, Ramon."

"Seriously." Ramon reached to his side and found her hand. "I'd just finished the reconstruction on the hotel. I didn't need to get into a relationship at the time. I'd just opened the hotel and you were a distraction."

"A distraction?" Kenzie's bottom lip poked out. "Gee, thanks."

"You're taking that the wrong way," Ramon said. He gave her fingers a squeeze. "Kenzie, you are like your hair, fiery and spirited. I moved to Southwood to start my business, not get into a relationship. One night with you and I almost forgot everything I came here for."

"Yet you still slept with me."

"I am a man," Ramon answered, "an utterly weak man who succumbed to the most beautiful, irresistible, sexiest woman on earth."

And she was a woman, and the two of them together made such a pair in bed. Ramon was the first man able to coax out a primal desire from her. She wasn't sure she'd ever get it again but was glad and irritated at the same time for at least having experienced the pleasure once—

or half a dozen times. Kenzie licked her lips. The anger at him she felt disappeared. "Thank you for your apology."

"Wait a minute," said Ramon. "I didn't apologize."

"Yes, you did," Kenzie replied. She pushed their hands onto his thigh and let go, patting his muscular leg before letting go. "You meant to."

Ramon began to laugh. "What?" He patted Kenzie's leg and chuckled. "I accept your apology also."

Kenzie brushed his hand away. "For what?"

"For all your antics. I know you were the one behind loosening the salt shaker at that food truck at the park."

The image of Ramon's mountain of salt on top of his curly fries evoked a giggle. "I plead the Fifth." She pushed his hand away.

"See, I knew you were behind all the crappy things done to me. At least I tried to be nice to you with my antics."

"Are you going to admit to sending me magnolias this spring?"

"Why would I send you the first batch of flowers blooming this spring?" Humor flooded his tone. Their hand game stopped. Kenzie turned to face him in the dark. Without needing to see his face, she knew he was leaning close to her. She gulped. He'd remembered her favorite flower. Kenzie's lips throbbed at the idea of kissing him again. Her heart raced with the idea of anything intimate between them again. He was a drug to her and getting addicted to him was not good for her soul.

"Kenzie," Ramon said softly.

"Ramon… I…" Kenzie paused but she knew as she waited with her mouth open he was going to kiss her. Her world shook; her heart raced. And she swore her heart dropped.

"I think the elevator is about to fall." In one quick movement Ramon pulled Kenzie onto his lap.

That familiar feeling of being on a roller coaster just before it went down the hill washed over her. Kenzie's bottom lifted off Ramon's lap. Her heart dropped. Ramon cradled her in his arms and absorbed the fall for her, protecting her once again.

There'd been no thought for his safety during the fall. Ramon just knew if the elevator made it to the floor there'd be nothing to absorb the hit. His first instinct was to protect Kenzie. When the elevator dropped, the hydraulics miraculously kicked in and the bounce jarred the elevator doors open to the lower level. Ramon hadn't noticed the windows from the outside but the light spilled into the hallway where the doors opened.

"Okay, so this time I'm going to thank you," Kenzie said, wiping the gray dust and dirt off her face.

The sound of her voice filled him with pride. She was okay. Ramon helped her, using his thumbs against her cheekbones, wiping until he saw the freckles. Relief hit him. His heart ached at the fear of something happening to her under his watch. Aside from family, it felt odd to care about someone enough to feel responsible for them.

Most of the businesses in Southwood had commercial space on the first level and residential on the next floor or two. This was a common usage in old towns. No one wanted to live away from their businesses for security reasons. Ramon understood the terror small African-American towns felt when angry white neighbors sought to destroy their homes. Since then, there had been subdivisions in Southwood, but people still lived in these split-plan residences. Without the use of cell phones or any other modern technology a postman in the past never knew when he'd have to meet an incoming stagecoach with the US Postal Service or send a telegraph.

Focusing back on the woman in his lap, Ramon blinked. "Are you okay?"

"I'm fine." Kenzie's voice was weak but she tried to smile. "Just shaky."

"That's to be expected," he said, easing her off his lap, where the proof of desire grew. That old, familiar, lascivious feeling crept through his veins. Logic fought the uncontrollable rush of excitement and impulse to touch her again. "Let's get out of here before something else happens."

Kenzie stood first but used his shoulders to steady herself, not realizing her breasts were in his face. Given what just happened, Ramon knew this was not the right time to reach around for her hips and pull her back to him. This was how things worked when he was around Kenzie. She took all common sense out of the equation, just as she had last summer when he needed to concentrate on business.

Ramon cleared his throat. "Let's try to find a way out of here."

Once he reached full height Ramon brushed off the debris from his jacket and did the same to Kenzie's body. His hands smoothed over the soft contours of her hips and breasts. Again Ramon needed to mentally call out the starting lineup of the Yankees.

"Are you okay?" Kenzie asked him.

Ramon glanced down at his pants, afraid of what she was asking, but realized she meant after the elevator's fall. "Yeah, I'm good."

Despite the decrepit state of the building the ground floor wasn't in a state of disarray. Dust piled on either side of the hallways. A half dozen doors stood outside the elevator shaft and Ramon grabbed Kenzie's hand to help walk her through the threshold of the door he figured was the exit. A pile of ceiling tiles blocked them and they had to step over it. The red heels she wore were covered with gray dust and the fabric of her jeans was frayed at the knees.

If Ramon had to hold her hand the whole time, he was going to end up pressing her against the wall and kissing her senseless. They needed to get out of here. Alexander Ward should be here by now and Ramon didn't want the man to think he'd changed his mind about buying the place. It did need a lot of work but he couldn't beat the downtown location. "Wait here," he told Kenzie.

Ramon left Kenzie's side and jogged down the end of hall to the exit door. The silver bar wouldn't budge. Damn it. Guided by the glow of her cell phone, he hurried back to Kenzie. "It's locked."

"Still no service. We can check some of these old offices," Kenzie suggested, making her way to the first door. Ramon followed her inside to the empty space. The faded paper covering the glass offered light but not a view of people walking around outside. Since Ramon was taller, he started toward the window to peel off the paper but Kenzie did some cheerleading jump and tore off a corner, bringing the whole sheet down. Impressed with the move, Ramon clapped for her and she took a bow.

"Six years of middle and high school cheerleading," she breathed, "are finally paying off."

"Are you sure? You're breathing heavier, unless you're having another panic attack."

Kenzie's eyes widened and her face flushed a deep pink. "I'm older."

"Ancient," Ramon teased. He held his hand out for her to take. "Let's check another room—no one is out on the street here. Maybe we'll come across the stairs."

"I think the stairs are filled with furniture."

"Why do you think that?"

Kenzie moved out the door and explained. "When I

was in high school, kids loved coming here and running through the halls, especially during Halloween. This place is haunted."

"What?" Ramon scoffed and closed the door behind them.

"I'm serious. I heard some kids came out Halloween Eve and things would be rearranged from the last time. So they'd booby-trap the place with rearranged furniture and come back and things would be different the next day."

"Sounds like kids were playing tricks on each other if you ask me." Ramon imagined his older cousins doing the same thing to the younger group.

"Maybe, but I believe this place is haunted. I grew up hearing a story about the forties. My great-aunt came here and sent letters to her soldier boyfriend off in the war. She came here every day and mailed a letter. Her beau came back and married another woman from Peachville."

Southwood bordered three other cities—Peachville, Samaritan and Black Wolf Creek—and had become home of their first post office. Like Southwood, the other cities were founded by citizens tired of the Civil War. Union soldiers tore through South Georgia and burned old buildings and land. When Confederate soldiers came home to nothing, some left and some stayed. Those who stayed worked with the lasting people of the land, former slaves and Native Americans, and rebuilt each city. All three worked in unison into the next century. With so many single women writing to shipped off military men during wartime, this soldier had probably met another woman.

"I think your aunt's boyfriend was a player."

Kenzie stopped walking and pondered his statement. Her lips twisted to the side and finally she nodded. "I never thought about it like that. But your belief doesn't answer the question about the noises heard here. The theater next door flooded last summer, which is why we had to hold Miss Southwood at Magnolia Palace."

"So?"

"So the flood started from here. The water has been turned off for decades."

"I'm sure there's a logical explanation." They came to the next office. Kenzie took a step inside but Ramon held her back. "Let me inspect first in case there's a ghost."

"Okay," Kenzie sang skeptically. "But if there's a ghost demanding the blood of a virgin, you're out of luck."

His blood pulsed, as he knew firsthand Kenzie wasn't a virgin, then settled with a splash of jealousy. Sex with her was addicting and it took everything he had to keep his distance. Clearing his throat, he entered the room. The smell of mildew assaulted his senses. Like the previous room the windows were boarded up with paper. Ramon moved to take the paper down before Kenzie.

"We're looking out the back windows," he deduced. "Let's try a room facing the street."

"Makes sense," Kenzie surprisingly agreed. She turned and crossed the hall before he had a chance to exit the room and like before, did her cheerleading jump and tore down the papers. Bright light spilled into the room. Dust particles floated through the rays of sunshine. "Bingo!" She banged on the windowpane. Her red-tipped nails sounded off in a rhythmic beat and the hairs on the back of Ramon's neck rose. He recalled what those nails had done to his back.

Ramon cleared his throat again. Kenzie turned and faced him. "I think we need to hurry up and get you out of here. You sound like your throat is closing or something."

"Or something," Ramon agreed. Sweat began to form under his arms. He took the jacket off and laid it on the desk once he entered the musty room. "Do you see Alexander out there?"

Her hand paused in midair, about to knock on the window, Kenzie turned to face him with a scowl on her face. "I'd rather he not be the one to rescue us."

"History between you two?" Ramon inquired before holding his hand up and swallowing down his first bitter pill of jealousy. "On second thought, this is a small town. Everyone has dated everyone else at one point."

"I don't want Alexander to know I'm here. He purposely didn't tell me about selling the place."

Ramon wiped his finger against the dusty, cluttered desk. "Not too sure I want to buy the place after all. Seems like a lot of work."

"Plus you need to make sure you maintain the history of the place," she reminded him with a sweet grin.

"Oh yes, that it's haunted."

The sweet grin disappeared and Kenzie shook her head from side to side. The button Kenzie swore he'd ripped off had indeed disappeared and he was left with a view of her lacy white bra. Ramon swallowed hard and tried not to stare at the swell of her breasts. Dust flew from her curly hair. Her bun was now loose and her curls dangled.

"Laugh all you want. Try spending the night here."

"I have several bedrooms at my hotel to choose from," Ramon said.

Kenzie rolled her eyes. "Yes, I am well aware." She took a step back and craned her neck for a better view out the window. "Let me get on your shoulders."

The idea of Kenzie's legs wrapped around his shoulders did something to him. "No."

"C'mon, I'm not that heavy."

Ramon rubbed his hands together and licked his lips. "As much as I like your legs wrapped around me, I don't think doing it now that we're friends again is a wise idea."

Getting the hint, Kenzie pulled her blouse together. "Oh."

"I'll check." He moved closer into the room and peered out the dirty glass. "There are more people." Like Kenzie had done a few moments ago, he banged on the glass. Behind him his companion began pushing the desk against the wall. Before he had a chance to question her, she kicked her feet out of her heels and climbed on top of the desk. Ramon glanced down at the legs of the furniture wobbling. "That's not safe—get down from there."

"The two of us banging together will make more noise."

Ramon paused at her statement. How could being trapped in a building be so erotic? "Kenzie."

"Hey! Hey!" she screamed at the window.

The jiggling of her body made the desk move more. Ramon wrapped his arms around her waist and pulled her off the top. She kicked the top drawer by accident and the compartment fell down, causing old papers to fall to the dust covered ground. Like a child on Christmas morning, Kenzie squealed in delight and shimmied out of Ramon's eyes. "Oh my God, what's this?"

"Old papers," Ramon answered. He knelt beside her and as she whipped her hair off her neck he whiffed the sweet, magnolia scented products in her hair.

"But what kind? Look here," she said, lifting up what looked like a legal document stapled to a blue construction-like paper. "Bank papers? Deeds? Oh, look." Kenzie scrambled around the floor and found a brass key. "What do you think this is for?"

Ramon inspected it. "It's too big for a desk drawer." He stood up, went to the office door to close it, where he found a closet. "Throw me the key." She did, but it landed on the floor halfway between them.

"I was a cheerleader, not a quarterback."

Grumbling, Ramon retrieved the key. The lock turned but the door wouldn't open. Humidity often caused wood to swell. Kenzie was already behind him when he shouldered the closet open. Musty air hit their noses.

"Son of a bitch," Kenzie said from between gritted teeth. "Someone has been in here and tried putting in an air-conditioning unit."

Ramon followed Kenzie's glare up to the ceiling of the closet. A silver-coated pipe hung from the top tiles. Rust-colored water stained the walls and the floor. Ramon would rather leave the belongings inside and return with a face mask but Kenzie had already started dragging the plastic bags out. She grunted and tugged at the top bag, an old army-green duffel bag. Ramon took it from her hands and tossed it behind them with ease. The next bags, oddly shaped, weren't as heavy. Kenzie pulled a picture frame from the top bag.

"The date," Kenzie breathed. "This photograph was taken over a hundred years ago." She pressed her finger at the date on the corner of the faded, yellowed newspaper clipping. Ramon wondered if she'd paid attention to the picture first. The image in the article was of a sheriff and his men standing over a body. The sheriff held a most wanted sketch and his deputy held up a picture of a newspaper. The fold of a paper obscured the names tagged in the photo.

"I need to look these names up, of course," said Kenzie. "What else is in here?"

They found more photographs, including some of the post office they stood in when it was first built. The streets were filled with mud. Instead of a sidewalk there were boardwalks. Mud tarnished the hems of the proud women's dresses. A box contained old, loose black-and-white photographs from weddings and men dressed up in military garb standing in front of an old bus, being shipped off to war. Another framed photograph showed the original structure of the schoolhouse.

"Before Southwood High and Southwood Middle," Kenzie began, "everyone was taught in the one school. Now it's used as a shed by the elementary school."

"I remember my folks talking about being taught in one school back in Villa San Juan." Ramon had grown up in a Florida island town so small, they'd only needed one for a long time. He realized Southwood and Villa San Juan weren't so different.

"It wasn't until the late fifties the little school had enough students and funding for a total of three brick and mortar buildings. After the Second World War, while African-Americans from other towns were coming back to the same segregation they'd left, Southwood's citizens banded together as they always had since the Civil War."

"Why don't you teach history?" Ramon inquired. "Didn't Mr. Myers retire?"

Kenzie pulled her hair up into a bun, exposing her long neck. "I wouldn't mind. I've substituted before. I can't possibly think about teaching right now. That's all I need my great-aunts and uncles to hear. I'm going to show up at these weddings and be labeled the spinster teacher. And now it looks like I've just hit the jackpot of artifacts. I can't wait to show all this off at the gala this month, providing the new buyer lets me keep them."

Ramon knew she meant him. He shrugged his shoulders. "I haven't decided yet. There is a lot of damage and I've got to keep up the historic regulations."

"True," she agreed, still rifling through the closet.

Ramon glanced around the room. The closet had now been turned inside out. In Kenzie's search, she tossed some things on top of the original bag. Small pieces of paper spilled out from a hole on the side.

"What's this?" he asked, picking up a square card.

"I have no idea," Kenzie said, inspecting it in his hand. "I can barely make out 'Southwood' at the top. Damn the water damage. I can't tell. What do you think it is?"

"My gut says an election ballot," he half teased her. "Maybe the current mayor didn't win."

"I wish." Kenzie frowned. "I hate Anson with a passion. Unfortunately, when he came along, we were doing electronic ballots. No, these look much older. Hmm, the mystery grows. I told you this place was haunted—you may want to rethink buying it."

"I don't believe for one minute it's haunted."

"You don't sound too sure." Kenzie poked his chest. "Scared?"

"I need to come up with a proposal for how I'm going to keep the historic features intact. Maybe I need a historian, someone who can help me with the Economic Development Council."

"Good luck," Kenzie huffed and folded her arms across her chest.

"Kenzie, c'mon, why don't you help me?"

"Why would I want to help you buy this place and turn it into something stupid like a hotel?"

"I already have a hotel. I can offer you something you don't have."

Chin jutted forward, Kenzie squared her shoulders. "What can you offer me?"

"If you'll help me with the proposal, I'll be your date for all your functions this month."

"No thanks," Kenzie quickly responded with a frown. The corners of Ramon's mouth turned upside down. "Oh come on," she breathed, "you don't think I would allow you the chance to stand me up again."

"We've moved beyond that, Kenzie."

"Oh sure," Kenzie said, rolling her eyes. "In a matter of minutes we've moved on. Whatever. Besides, anyone in town will know we hate each other."

"There's a thin line between…"

Kenzie stopped the following sentence from flowing by pressing her two fingers against his lips—that almost kissed her a few moments ago. The same lips that kissed her naked body on a bed of magnolia petals under the full moon.

"You know we can sell chemistry." Ramon wrapped his left hand around her fingers and kissed the tips.

Kenzie waited a beat or two before pulling away with a step backward. "How so?"

Ramon stepped forward and as if in a dance move, Kenzie backed up against the wall, right where he wanted her. He pressed his hands on the wall on either side of her head. Beneath her blouse her skin rippled with goose bumps. When he dipped his head lower toward hers she pressed her lips together and closed her eyes. Chuckling, Ramon caressed the side of her face.

"Because we can't deny it." His lips were practically on hers. He tasted the sweet lemon frosting on her breath.

"Mr. Torres, is that you?" someone yelled and banged on the outside glass.

Kenzie pressed her head against Ramon's chest and grabbed the lapels of his jacket while Ramon cursed in Spanish. "Think my offer over, sweetheart."

Chapter 3

"And what are you going to do?" Maggie Swayne asked, sitting with her legs crossed on Kenzie's pale pink cushioned couch. She grabbed a pink-and-gold-accented throw pillow and placed it in her lap, clearly desperate for more details of what had happened this afternoon.

Kenzie's traumatic episode this afternoon granted her an excuse to not attend Corie's rehearsal dinner tonight. With fifty Hairstons, Kenzie didn't think she'd be missed. Her mother, Paula, had already excused her. Maggie took the pardon to include herself, too. "Corie's wedding is tomorrow."

The big day had been circled on Kenzie's custom-made calendar on her stainless steel refrigerator in her downtown Southwood apartment. Each month featured a picture of a particular tiara Kenzie had won over the years propped up at one of her favorite historic places around town. This month's image was an old photograph of the Miss Southwood crown on a low branch of a blooming magnolia tree last summer. A year ago, when Kenzie took the job, glad to finally put her degree to use, she never thought it would be so unglamorous. She combed through old newspapers, donated family photo albums and yearbooks. Sometimes she went out in around town and took pictures of trees with sweetheart initials carved in the trunk. On one occasion Kenzie brought her well-earned tiaras along with her and made her own calendar. "I don't need to be reminded," Kenzie said from the kitchen entrance in a clipped tone.

"I mean, we can skip the rehearsal dinner tonight with no questions asked but Auntie Bren is going to have questions tomorrow for you."

"I like the way Mama excused *me* from attending and that includes you for everything but Auntie's wrath."

"Because the last time she got on FaceTime with me and asked where my boyfriend was, I reached over into the nightstand and showed her."

Auntie Bren had a habit of being on the stuffy side. Kenzie could only imagine the old woman's face.

"You're so crass." Kenzie shook her head at her sister, who poked her tongue out in response. "And I have answers for her," Kenzie said with a shrug. She joined her sister in the living room on the couch with two glasses of wine.

The windows were drawn open. The bright lights of the nearby amphitheater shone through, changing colors on the high ceiling. One of the perks of her apartment was the free concerts. She saw all the performances without ever having to leave her place. The downside was the noise level for the concerts she wouldn't have paid for nor taken free tickets to. Tonight's event included a young preteen pop singing group. Kenzie wasn't sure what was louder, the music or the screaming little girls in the audience.

Maggie took a loud slurp of her red wine before setting the glass down on the magazine-covered coffee table. "What are you going to say?"

"I'm going to tell her I worked my behind off at Georgia State until I received a PhD in Southern history two years ago, and becoming *Dr.* Mackenzie Swayne has occupied my time."

"Meanwhile your bed remains unoccupied," Maggie mumbled.

"Maggie," Kenzie gasped.

"What?" Maggie blinked her hazel eyes innocently. "I'm merely saying what she'll say."

"I'm not discussing my sex life with her because she won't bring it up."

Maggie snorted and reached for her glass. "Want to bet?" She cut her eyes over to Kenzie. Kenzie concentrated on swirling the beverage around in the glass. "Yeah, that's what I thought. So why won't you take this Ramon up on his offer? Hell, *moan* is in his damn name."

"Because being around Ramon makes me a different person," Kenzie answered honestly. "I was so mad at him I became bitter."

"But the two of you spoke today and worked things out. No one says you two have to sleep together. He needs help and so do you."

Sometimes Kenzie told her older sister too much. Granted, they were considered Irish twins, born nine months apart, but they bared all the features of twins. Kenzie was outgoing and loved to be around people. They favored each other in looks, with their reddish curly hair, although Maggie's maintained a better hold than Kenzie's. But Kenzie and Maggie were complete opposites. At eighteen Maggie couldn't wait to get out of Southwood. She'd planned on never coming back to live here and had almost lived up to her promise. The Swayne family fortune in pecans made it possible for the kids to never have to work. Kenzie and her brother chose to work for a living. It helped keep their parents out of their lives. Maggie opted not to.

Right now Maggie lived in Atlanta as a socialite living off her trust fund—her true calling in life. Coming back to Southwood was a step back for Maggie, yet when she did, she always scheduled a secluded, two-week break in the family's cabin in the woods over in Black Wolf Creek, away from her social connections in Southwood. Kenzie partly understood her sister's dilemma. Their last name was Swayne but everyone always asked them if they were Hairston girls. As a teen, Kenzie hated the reminder but going away to college, she missed the recognition. The red hair gave them away. Maggie's was lighter than Kenzie's and Maggie wasn't plagued with freckles.

"Maybe I'll tell him something next week for Felicia's wedding."

Maggie rolled her eyes. "I can't believe you're going."

"She was one part of the tiara squad."

"I'm not friends with the girls I competed with," said Maggie. "For Christ's sake, it's called a *competition*, not a friendship pageant. You almost lost your chance to be the last Swayne to ever win Miss Southwood."

"Felicia is always nice to me. When she found out her brother was moving back to town, she sent me a box of magnolias."

"You were banging her brother," Maggie pointed out, then shivered with a gagging noise. "Alexander was a creep then. He just wanted to date a beauty queen."

What Alexander wanted was none of Kenzie's concern. At least Maggie knew to drop the subject. Both girls glanced over at the curio cabinet filled with beauty pageant memorabilia. Maggie had her own set. The Swaynes were big on pageants, a tradition passed down from generation to generation. Their mother, Paula, met their father, Mitch, through a pageant, when Paula *allegedly* stole the tiara from his sister, Jody Swayne. Mitch had fallen in love immediately. The Swaynes didn't speak to their son the first year of their marriage.

Aunt Jody held on to her bitter loss for ten years and stayed away from Southwood. Aunt Jody attended family reunions but she vowed never to step foot at another Southwood pageant ever again. And she kept that promise, even when Maggie and Kenzie competed. Kenzie forgave Aunt Jody for not coming to her crowning and she secretly hoped she'd come back to Southwood, especially with the sesquicentennial gala right around the corner. With the one-hundred-and-fifty-year celebration one week away from the Miss Southwood pageant, Kenzie prayed Aunt Jody would stay.

"Can you believe Bailey is ready for her first pageant?" Kenzie asked. She reached for the photograph on her end table of the seventeen-year-old beauty.

"It's about time," Maggie said, throwing the pillow to the side and reaching for the picture in Kenzie's hands. "I love our brother dearly but Richard nearly tarnished the Swayne dynasty."

"Hairston-Swayne dynasty," Kenzie corrected. After their mother won her pageant, her relatives also tried out and won several if Swaynes weren't in the competition.

"There you go with your history."

Kenzie shrugged her shoulders and took another sip. "I can't help myself, it's in me."

"You could help it if *someone* was *in* you." Maggie laughed at her own joke while someone knocked on the door.

As if on cue, Kenzie's stomach growled. Setting her glass down on the coffee table, Kenzie smoothed her hands down the back of her green cotton shorts. Since she and Maggie weren't attending the rehearsal dinner tonight, there was no need to concern herself with the doz-

ens of buttons on the back of the skintight black dress.
The sexy dress lay across her bed, next to the outfit Kenzie planned on wearing tonight—her bathrobe. Kenzie's
stomach growled again. She hadn't eaten since the cupcake earlier this morning. The box of desserts she'd left
upstairs on the second floor of the post office had been
lost in the rubble. Thankfully the pizza she'd ordered ten
minutes ago came earlier than expected.

"What am I going to do with you?" Kenzie asked as
she opened the door.

"Dressed like that, you can do anything to me you
want," answered a deep baritone voice.

Kenzie realized she hadn't bothered peeping through
the peephole. No one knocked on her door other than delivery men. "Ramon?"

"Ramon?" Maggie repeated, leaning off the couch so
far to peer down the hall she fell over. Kenzie heard glass
break and winced.

Ramon Torres stood before her, dressed in a black suit
and crisp white shirt sans a tie. Gone was the manbun
from earlier and now his hair hung loose around his neck.
A lavender box protruded from his hands with The Cupcakery logo on the top. In his other arm he held a bouquet
of flowers—daisies. *So he decided to pop up at my place
with the wrong flowers?*

Kenzie rested her hip against the door frame to block
him from entering. So many questions ran through her
mind right then. How did he know where she lived? Last
year their fling took place at Magnolia Palace, while she'd
stayed for the week and where Ramon had never formally
picked her up for a date. Why was he decked out on a Friday night? Why hadn't she cleaned her apartment? Kenzie hated having to clean. Considering she lived alone, one
would think Kenzie could keep up with her own mess. Her

project this week had been painstakingly combing through the old photo albums of Southwood High and scanning the pages to archive. But she chose sleeping in a few extra minutes over than tidying up every morning. Irritated with herself, Kenzie blew out a sigh. "Why are you here?"

The thick black brows hooding his eyes rose as if in question. Visibly taken aback by her annoyed voice, Ramon maneuvered his gifts under his arms and pressed his hands together to make the international sign for time-out. "I thought we moved on from the animosity."

Remembering how the afternoon went between them, Kenzie nodded her head and rolled her eyes. "Habit, sorry."

"No worries."

When Ramon flashed his million-watt smile Kenzie's insides felt all warm and fuzzy…something she did not need. "What brings you to my place?" It dawned on her Ramon might have come to the conclusion of her being in need of an escort tonight for the rehearsal dinner. "Oh, God, wait a minute. I hope you didn't get any ideas earlier. It's presumptuous to think I needed a date tonight."

"Whoa, I am about to go on a date but it's not with you," Ramon clarified.

Kenzie felt a draft of cold air sweep against her tongue as her mouth gaped open. "Oh."

To recover from her embarrassment Kenzie narrowed her eyes. "How are you going to propose taking me to all of my events when you're not available?"

"I am going on one date, Kenzie, not getting married."

To add insult to injury, Maggie cleared her throat as she shuffled down the hallway in time to witness Kenzie's embarrassment. "Are you getting some paper towels to clean up your mess?"

"That and I came over here to see who the sexy voice

belonged to," Maggie cooed and extended her hand as she approached. "Swayne. Charmed, I'm sure."

Kenzie cut her eyes at her sister. "The stain?"

"I am getting to it." Maggie said but she kept a firm grip in Ramon's hand.

"Maggie," Ramon said with a friendly smile. "Nice to meet you. How are you doing this evening?"

"I'm better now," Maggie flirted with a goofy smile.

Kenzie's grip on the doorknob tightened. Her other hand went to her hip. "The wine, Maggie."

"I was just heading to the kitchen," Maggie tried to explain but Kenzie pointed to the left, where her kitchen was. "It's over there."

Maggie's eyes widened. "She's bossy, isn't she?"

"No comment," replied Ramon.

"Maggie, go." Kenzie ordered her sister out of the way and stared at Ramon. "So what brings you to this side of town?"

"I realized I've been outside your building but never been in your place," Ramon began with a sly grin. Kenzie read his mind immediately. They'd slept together, several times, yet he'd never been to her apartment. Ramon cleared his throat. "I wanted to replace the cupcakes you bought today."

"Technically you bought them," Kenzie clarified and accepted the cupcakes. "But thank you just the same."

His large foot kicked a box into the doorway. "I also went back inside the post office and grabbed one of the boxes of old Southwood memorabilia you were fascinated with."

Excited, Kenzie knelt and squealed. "I can't wait to go through this stuff."

"I figured," said Ramon. "I'm also having those ballots reviewed."

"Cool," Kenzie breathed. "I love a good mystery. Maybe somewhere in this box is justification for keeping the post office as a historical site."

"Have you thought about my offer?"

Coming to her feet, Kenzie pressed her index finger against her chin to dramatically ponder his question. "Remind me again?"

Ramon shook his head from left to right. Dark strands of his hair spilled over his shoulder. "I know you know. You're struggling whether or not preserving the building is worth spending ten events with me."

"Ten?" Kenzie repeated.

"Three weddings mean three rehearsal dinners or at least receptions, along with the sesquicentennial gala and the pageant, right? Plus the times we need to spend together getting me up to speed."

Kenzie pressed her lips together. "What do you know?"

"I come from a large family myself, Kenzie."

"You never told me."

"Well, we never got around to talking when we were alone," Ramon declared with a wink and a lopsided smirk.

A feverish chill crept down her spine. Intimate moments flashed in her mind, of being tangled in the black cotton sheets of his bed. Kenzie cleared her throat and replaced the wanton thoughts with remembering how she'd sat at her window waiting for Ramon to show up and the humiliating way she'd smiled blankly at everyone at the after party who'd asked of his whereabouts or stated how they'd expected to see the two of them together that night.

"Either way," she said, finding her voice, "I appreciate your offer."

"But your pride and ego won't allow me to help you?" Ramon asked. "I'm not the same guy as last summer."

"Pride and ego?" Kenzie forced herself to scoff. It was easier than believing him.

Ramon nodded his head. His hair was loose around his shoulder and brushed back. The open collar made him sexier. *Damn him.* "Of having to tell me yes."

"Boy, you have her pegged, don't you?" Maggie laughed, coming back through the hallway with a roll of paper towels.

"Judas," Kenzie muttered and clutched the brass doorknob.

"Don't tell me you're going to cut your summer events short? Why aren't you dressed for the rehearsal dinner?" Ramon asked. "Isn't it standard for the close family to attend?"

"We're excused from going," Maggie called out, "on account of what happened today to us."

In question, Ramon turned and looked to Kenzie for an answer. She rolled her eyes. "She is piggybacking on the excuse."

"We're twins," said Maggie. "When you hurt, I hurt." She said it with such conviction Kenzie wanted to offer her sister an Oscar or Golden Globe Award.

"I didn't realize," said Ramon.

"We're not twins."

"We're Irish twins," said Maggie. "Close enough."

Ramon chuckled at the sibling banter. He'd mentioned he came from a big family; Kenzie wondered where he stood in the lineup. She pictured him as the overprotective big brother type—especially after the way he'd looked after her today.

"Well, thanks again for the replacement cupcakes," Kenzie said, wanting to end this bonding moment with Ramon.

"Have you given my offer any consideration?" Ramon asked.

"I'm good."

Ramon licked his lips and glanced down at her frame. "I know. But I asked if you needed an escort in exchange for helping me win the bid for the post office."

"As a historian invested in the community, I'll help," said Kenzie. "But I don't need help with finding a date. I am a well-rounded woman with a PhD and a beauty queen pedigree and tiara to match. I can handle a wedding with my family."

"So who were the cupcakes for?"

Ramon made it back to his cousin Stephen's house in the suburbs of Southwood with his sleepy niece, Philly. Technically Philly would be his second cousin because her father, Ken, was Ramon's first cousin. But given the age difference and how Ramon considered his Reyes cousins as brothers, Philly was his niece in his eyes.

"Uncle Ramon?" Kimber asked, turning down the booming music from her cell phone.

"What?"

"The cupcakes. Tiffani told me you bought a dozen just before closing."

There should be a baker confidentiality clause somewhere. Ramon chuckled and shook his head. "Shouldn't you be off somewhere backpacking through Europe like most college kids?"

"Don't change the subject on me," said Kimber, scrambling from her place on the couch in the family den. School books clunked to the floor. The kid amazed him so freaking much. Kimber lost her father four years ago. Her uncles, Stephen and Nate, had uprooted their real estate business from Atlanta to sleepy Southwood to move into their brother's family home and take care of Kimber and Philly. Of course his first cousins had had a few ups and downs trying to raise the girls but they all came out just fine. Stephen married and he and his wife, Lexi, lived at the home, raising Philly and their almost one-year-old son, Kenny. Kimber was home for the summer to help Lexi out with Kenny and wait for the arrival of the latest addition to the Reyes family.

"I didn't change the subject," Ramon said, "I just don't plan on having a conversation about my love life with my niece."

"A-ha!" Kimber exclaimed and pointed her finger at him. "So you admit to having a love life."

"Love life?" Nate Reyes repeated, coming down the hall from the kitchen. "Sex life maybe, but love? Never."

Nate was not known for his cooking skills and Ramon wondered if he needed to call the fire department or an ambulance for anyone who'd eaten his food. Thank God Philly and her sleepover gang ate breakfast at the hotel.

"There are children present." Ramon nodded his head in Kimber's direction.

Kimber glanced all around her with her hazel eyes. "Who, me? I'm grown. I am almost nineteen."

"We'll talk when you can buy me a drink." Ramon laughed.

"Hey Kimber," said Nate, "I couldn't find the sofrito in the freezer. There are like a dozen tubs of butter, though."

Ramon bent from the waist and hollered as Kimber headed out of the living room, grumbling about Nate burning down the house. "If that ain't Abuela's granddaughter, I don't know who is."

"Tell me about it," said Nate. "Her RA at school offered to switch dorm rooms with Kimber since her kitchenette is bigger so Kimber can cook more food."

"*Switch*, though, right?" Ramon clarified. "Last I checked, Kadeci Hall was coed."

When not living in Southwood and taking care of her family, Kimber spent her time at school as a linguistics major at Florida A&M down in Tallahassee. Ramon had helped her move into the dorm. Tallahassee wasn't too far away, just a few hours, but still far enough her uncles wouldn't be able to pop in on her. Being close but not too close was perfect for Ramon. Most of his siblings and parents lived in Villa San Juan, a small island city off the northwest coast of Florida. Even in Southwood, Ramon resided at Magnolia Palace, which was on the outskirts of town.

"*Switch*," Nate emphasized with a nod. "So how did last night go with Philly and the girls?"

"Great. I used your advice and got a set of earplugs and everything was cool. Full disclosure though, we ate nothing but junk food." That reminded Ramon to give Jessilyn a bonus. Ramon had sent the hotel chef to the supermarket with his black card to get the girls anything they might want for their evening together. Jessilyn, anticipating the needs of preteen girls, made sure to have plenty of toppings for individualized pizzas and a boatload of ice cream sundae toppings, as well. "I didn't make the girls go to bed at any particular time, so I'm pretty sure Philly's tired."

"No problem. Thanks again for taking them."

"Any time. I love spending time with the girls," said Ramon. His newfound maturity and stability got Ramon to thinking about having kids one day. One day. "This was the best time to have them. The hotel officially opens back up for summer vacation today and we're booked solid."

"So you're going to be busy," Nate noted.

"Busy, but don't forget I have tickets to the monster

truck rally next month. We could never get one to come to VSJ."

"I know, right. Hey, speaking of monsters," Nate began. He took a seat on the edge of the blue plaid couch. "I heard you're going to put in a bid for the post office building downtown. The city council has been trying to sell off the block for a while now. Pretty big job to tackle along with the hotel. Why didn't you tell me? You know I'm your construction man."

"News travels fast." Ramon nodded and leaned against the arched door frame of the living room. "The hotel is in order and running itself."

"I notice you didn't say whether the news was good or bad."

Ramon shrugged his shoulders. "Depends on who you ask."

"What if I ask Kenzie Swayne?"

A pulse in his veins quickened. Ramon cleared his throat and raised his brows. "What?"

"Aw, don't 'What?' me, *primo*. News…good or bad… travels fast in Southwood. I heard the two of you were stuck in an elevator all night."

"I just brought back Philly from her sleepover at the Magnolia Palace, so we know the rumor is false."

"But you two got locked in an elevator?"

"We were able to get out after a while," Ramon answered, recalling the moment before the elevator dropped again. They'd almost kissed and he was pretty sure kissing fell under the No Kenzie ban. Of course now that they were friends… Ramon shook his head and cut off his inner monologue, only to find Nate staring at him with bewilderment in his green eyes. "Don't ask."

"I'm not going to ask a thing." Nate laughed. "But you

will have to excuse me for staring. I've never seen you so taken with one chick in my life."

"I'm not taken."

"*Smitten*, as Amelia would say." Last year Nate took himself off the perpetual bachelor list by marrying Amelia Marlow, a local from Southwood who'd tried hard not to return to town. Now she ran her family's ice cream parlor and supplied Magnolia Palace with fresh homemade treats.

Ramon pushed off from the wall. "You're just as bad as Kimber. I'm out of here."

"Wait," Nate said, coming to his feet. "What are you doing later today?"

Even though Kenzie turned him down for the offer to escort her to her cousin's wedding, a niggling feeling bothered him all morning long. "I'm not sure. What's up?"

"Stephen and I were thinking about playing some basketball later before it gets dark and the mosquitos come out."

So they weren't planning on going out at all? South Georgia was known for its flying pests in the summer. "I may have plans."

"Doing who?"

Ramon shook his head. "Don't try to live vicariously through me since you decided to get married."

Nate held his ring finger in the air. The gold band caught the fluorescent light from the foyer. "Don't knock it 'til you try it."

With a shiver, Ramon said, "I'll pass."

"So where might you be going this evening?"

"Funny you should ask." Ramon chuckled. "I think I may attend a wedding."

Kenzie took a deep breath, regretting the fact she had let her Uber driver leave. Folks were still entering the church, which she found a blessing. She could literally disguise herself as a regular guest. Walking shoulder to shoulder with a young female guest, Kenzie walked through the stained glass doors. The party she strolled in with parted but not before a baby in the arms of its mother began to wail. Everyone seated in the pews turned to see the commotion. Kenzie stood stock still. In the first five rows all of the bride's side of the family turned and beamed their gazes down at lonesome Kenzie. The redheads stuck out the most with their empathetic smiles, all of them surely thinking she couldn't get a date or keep a man. Aunt Shelly once asked Kenzie why she couldn't keep a man. This was the same woman who kept a man…or different men…in constant rotation—nonetheless, Kenzie tried to smile at the staring group. She even offered a shy wave. The strapless lavender summer dress failed to keep her from feeling exposed. Heat crept from her ears and along her jawline and she knew it split in two directions…up to her cheeks and down her neck. She cursed at her choice of clothing.

Perfect Erin Hairston, born the same year as Kenzie, hiked up the hem of her dress and made her way toward the front of the church. She was Great-Grandma Bren's favorite out of this generation of Hairstons. Erin was not only beautiful, with her sleek, chic, dark brunette pixie cut, but she was also smart, too, and looked down at beauty pageants. Kenzie tried to remind herself she was a gem, that she deserved respect from not only a man but from her family, as well. She was Dr. Kenzie Swayne, damn it. Despite all her credentials, Kenzie felt inadequate. Erin made fun of her so much when they were kids, Kenzie had this underlying complex when her cousin and family came around. This would be the point where Maggie would smack her up the back of her head and tell her to get over herself.

"Kenzie," Erin cooed halfway down the aisle. She waved at the guests in the pews, loud-whispering to a few of them about having to grab her little cousin who still lived in town. Kenzie rocked forward in her strappy summer sandals. The height fairy had skipped her when she was growing. Everyone Erin passed turned their heads in a ripple effect in Kenzie's direction. "You made it."

Was it too much to ask for the ground to open up and swallow her whole? Was it too late to duck back outside and take Ramon up on his offer? Seriously, all the man wanted was some insight on the historic building he wanted to purchase. Kenzie gritted her back teeth together, finally understanding the meaning of cutting off your nose to spite your face.

"And with a date no less." Erin's voice trailed off and her mouth spread into a bewildered smile.

At the same time as her chastising cousin spoke, a warm hand pressed against the small of Kenzie's back. Kenzie glanced to her right and craned her neck upward. Ramon, dressed in a black suit and a lavender paisley tie, glanced down with a wink.

"I didn't agree," Kenzie said in a low voice while gritting her teeth.

Ramon's warm breath pressed against the back of her ear. Anyone watching would have easily assumed the gesture was a kiss. "This one's a freebie."

Hell, at this point she was willing to do anything he needed.

Chapter 4

Twenty-four hours ago, Kenzie didn't think she'd be able to hold her head high at Corie's wedding. She hated to admit that even a few hours ago she'd almost turned around and left the ceremony. *Thank God for Ramon.* Those were words Kenzie thought she'd never think. But he'd come through in a bind. It pleased Kenzie beyond reason to watch Erin get all miffed. Sure, her cousin tried to sweet-talk her way with Kenzie, but deep down inside she knew she couldn't trust a word coming out of Erin's mouth.

Thankfully Auntie Bren was too occupied at church to pay attention to Kenzie and her faux love life. CJ, the bride and groom's two-year-old son, had everyone eating out of his hands. Kenzie smiled as she headed back to her table with two champagne flutes. After her embarrassing breakup with Alexander in college, Kenzie gave up trying to plan a family. There were enough kids in Southwood who filled Kenzie's life now. She loved helping out the cheerleading squad and then of course she worked with a lot of the toddlers at Grits and Glam Studios, the premier training studio for budding beauty pageant queens.

"You appear to have a whole basketball team willing

to accompany you today," Ramon said, leaning close to Kenzie's ear as he rose from his seat to let out her chair.

Kenzie approached the back table where she and Ramon were seated for the reception. She didn't mind. In her opinion the farther away from the bridal table she was, the closer she was to the exit door. The basketball team Ramon spoke of was actually five grown men huddled together, leering over the single Hairston women. "Who, them?"

"Them—" Ramon chuckled "—as in the University of Tallahassee's former starting lineup."

"Those are Hawk's friends." A little tug of disgust lifted Kenzie's upper lip. One of the players had had the nerve to approach Kenzie at the open bar and ask if the carpet matched the drapes. "I never pegged you for a sports fanatic."

"Fan," corrected Ramon. "And not of them particularly. Their team beat my school so I have a bit of animosity built up toward them."

"Well, aren't you childish?" Kenzie cooed, pressing Ramon's forearm in jest.

Ramon covered her hand with his and grinned. "Do you want to bring up childish things?"

Rolling her eyes, Kenzie pulled her arm away and sat back in her seat. "We're not going there since we're new friends again."

"New friends?" Ramon questioned.

"Yeah." Kenzie offered Ramon a half smile. "You did save my butt earlier."

"Does this mean you're willing to help me with the project if I escort you to the rest of your events?" Ramon ran his index finger along her bare forearm. "No one would question a thing. There are enough guests from Southwood who can attest to seeing us around town last summer."

The touch evoked a set of goose bumps down her arm.

The memory gave a wave of whiplash. He pulled his hand away from her skin but the space still burned with fever. Too much champagne? Kenzie cleared her throat and pushed the stem of her drink away from her slice of double-layered white cake with the raspberry filling. She blinked in Ramon's direction. He did look good in his suit. That didn't even begin to describe Ramon.

"Yeah, that's because…" Kenzie let her train of thought die down. For a moment Kenzie had forgotten about the deal Ramon struck with her.

"Auntie Bren loves me."

Kenzie's mouth widened. "What? When did you meet her?" Kenzie had made painstaking efforts to keep Ramon away from her nosy family members. After the official "I do," sealed with a kiss, Kenzie took Ramon by the hand and led him out the side door of the downtown Presbyterian church. She waited in Ramon's truck with him and fiddled with a new layer of lipstick before they headed into the reception being held in the recreation annex of the church. The photographer had to finish taking pictures of the happy family at the altar. When a typical summer shower fell while the wedding party made its way across the lawn to the reception, Ramon drove Kenzie over to drop her off at the front door. When did he possibly have time to meet anyone? The minute she turned her back on him, he'd make himself a part of the family.

"Maggie introduced me when you went to speak to the bride."

Kenzie glanced over her shoulder and spotted Maggie dancing on the center floor with a few of the members of the starting lineup. As if awaiting the death glare, Maggie turned toward the table where they sat and shimmied her shoulders with her tongue hanging out. "She had no right."

"Why?" Ramon asked. "Your Auntie Bren seems nice. Why are you so worried about what she has to say?"

"Don't call her that."

"She asked me to," said Ramon.

Of course she would, Kenzie thought bitterly. Who could resist Ramon's charm? All the man had to do was smile and women were putty in his hands. Well, she'd be the first to resist him.

Ramon continued boasting about how Auntie Bren adored him. "She expects to see us together at the sesquicentennial gala in a few weeks."

"I did not agree to your deal."

"But you're going to now, right?" Ramon asked.

"You realize you're not the only one eyeing the spot."

Ramon sat back in his seat. His thick brows rose. "What?"

"Yep." Kenzie pressed her lips together. "So whatever you thought your buddy-buddy deal with Alexander was, he offered the same slimy offer to everyone."

"All right, all right."

"Tell me, what it is you want to do with the building?" There, Kenzie thought to herself, best to change to something safe. Yet as Ramon licked his lips while processing her question, she only thought of the moment before he kissed her in the elevator.

"Southwood needs a Caribbean restaurant." Ramon puffed out his chest with pride.

Kenzie felt the corners of her lips turn down. "I don't mind another restaurant but the post office has four floors."

"Five if you count the basement," Ramon said, wiggling his brows up and down. Kenzie inhaled deeply and shook her head.

"There's a Caribbean restaurant over in Samaritan,

owned by the Rodriguez family," she said. "They have a variety of items on their menu."

"Been on lots of dates there?" Ramon asked.

As a matter of fact, she had. She and Rafe ate there on several occasions. Despite this not being a date between her and Ramon, Kenzie did not want to think about another guy, especially not the one who supposedly bailed on her. Kenzie folded her arms across her chest. "Where did you take your date to eat last night?"

"We went back to my place," Ramon answered with a laugh as if remembering what a good time he'd had. "We got pretty dirty in the kitchen."

Kenzie refrained from rolling her eyes by biting her lip. What Ramon did and with whom he did it was none of her business. "Just the kitchen?"

"And the living room, but I wouldn't let anything happen elsewhere, you know, like in the bedrooms."

A bizarre streak of possessiveness washed over Kenzie… she just wasn't sure if it was for his house or the man. Silly for either. But just who did receive the flowers last night? Was it someone she knew? "Just the two rooms?" Kenzie asked, turning the corners of her lips downward. "You must be losing your stamina in your old age."

"Well, if you must know—"

Kenzie held her hand in the air to stop him. "Spare me the details," she said drolly, hoping to mask any shred of jealousy. "Back to the ideas of things to do with the building. The Economic Development Council is going to want to see a business that will bring tourists to our historic district. Southwood used to have a printing shop."

"I'm not a publisher," Ramon answered. "Sports bar? Each floor will have a different sporting event playing on a flat-screen TV."

"The Teagues over in Samaritan have the closest thing to a sports bar," Kenzie countered.

"Are you preserving Samaritan or Southwood?" Ramon asked.

"I'm just helping Southwood maintain its originality. It has retained the same structure and sleepy culture since it was founded. We don't need to compete with the other towns, just enhance what's here and what we need," Kenzie informed him. "What do you think of a tutoring center? The district wants to step up its testing in the fall and having a quiet place to study would be fantastic."

"Now I know where I know you from," said Erin, sliding into the empty seat on the other side of Ramon. Kenzie glared at her cousin for the interruption. Oblivious, Erin continued. "You're the dude who bought the old Swayne plantation, Magnolia Palace."

"Guilty," Ramon responded with a proud smile. "Have you seen the recent renovations online?"

Erin waved off his question with the back of her slim hand. "I only saw pictures of the old place when I spent the night at Kenzie's. It was broken-down then. I would love a personal tour to see what you've done with it."

Of course she would, Kenzie seethed. She didn't know why Erin's flirting with Ramon irked her. Whom Ramon did things with was no longer her concern. They were friends now and she'd be happy for him if he found love... just not with Erin.

"The doors open tomorrow for the summer."

"Oh man, that would be awesome," Erin cooed. "Don't you think, Kenzie? We can have a cousin day. I wanted to discuss some things with you."

"I've seen it already." At first Kenzie feared her words came out sounding possessive; when Ramon's face lit up with amusement and Erin clutched the pearls around her neck, Kenzie gave her head a light shake. "I mean, Ramon was kind enough to allow the Miss Southwood Pageant to be held in the theater on the property."

"That's right, the Swayne family tradition," said Erin. "Ramon, do you know a Swayne always wins when they enter? Well, except for when my dear Auntie Paula, Kenzie's mother, won?"

"Interesting." Ramon wrapped his arm around Kenzie's shoulder. "And you carried on the tradition?"

Kenzie took a deep breath and prepared a slew of words for her cousin. Erin's side of the family had always looked down on the Swaynes until they started winning. She leaned forward against the table but Ramon slipped his arm around her shoulder.

"Coming from a family of four successful brothers, you will understand why Magnolia Palace means so much to me."

Erin cocked her head to the side and smiled. "And where are you from?"

"Villa San Juan."

Snapping her fingers on one hand while slamming her French-manicured hand on the table, Erin laughed. "That's where I know you from—you're of the Torres family."

Ramon lifted his brows in Kenzie's direction. He'd mentioned his family's name before. She knew Stephen and Nate Reyes were his cousins. Ramon reached over and grabbed Kenzie's hand. "Let's dance."

Without protest, Kenzie followed Ramon. The fast music slowed and blended into a ballad. Ramon brought Kenzie up against his hard frame.

"Your family is interesting."

"And what about yours?" Kenzie allowed Ramon to settle his hand against her lower back. His right hand engulfed her left. For a moment she worried about her palms sweating. The heated dance floor was overcrowded with guests. At six-foot-three, Ramon towered over Kenzie by a foot.

"My family isn't here," said Ramon.

Pressed against his solid body, Kenzie gulped. "Why does it sound like your family is off-limits?"

"It's not. We're just here with yours."

"Fine," Kenzie huffed.

"Why don't you tell me about what you think I should do with the building?"

Immediately she answered, "A youth center."

Ramon pulled his head back. His thick eyebrows furred together with question. When he used to question her antics, he'd give her the same look. Kenzie gulped and tried to block out the image of them last summer. Suddenly her mouth went dry. She licked her lips.

"Why a youth center?" Ramon asked, spinning her around in his arms.

Grateful for the brief break of contact between their bodies, Kenzie tightened her grip on Ramon's hand. She needed to focus on the topic. "Did you not notice the trouble the kids around town get into?" Kenzie asked him. "Think about what they did in the abandoned building. They need a place to hang out."

"Hanging out doesn't generate money."

"Does everything have to be about money?" Kenzie asked.

"I bought Magnolia Palace," Ramon stated as if she didn't know. Of course she knew. He'd called upon her services last summer—or rather she'd offered up her services. Ramon had taken her advice then, but something in his eyes told her he wasn't going to be as accommodating this time around. "What part of that makes you think I'm not a businessman?"

Kenzie rolled her eyes. "Well, you asked me what I thought."

A warmth spread over her body. Ramon drew his fingertips along the edge of the fabric where her dress and her skin met. In an attempt to pull away, Kenzie pressed her hand against his chest. His heartbeat thundered against her palms. He nuzzled his mouth toward her earlobe. Heat rose from Kenzie's core. Her bottom lip trembled with anticipation of what might come next.

"What are you…?"

"Shh," his warm voice said against her collarbone. "Auntie Bren is watching us."

Like with every wedding, the time came for the bouquet toss. The timing was out of order from what Ramon had witnessed in the past, but the garter toss had to come first while the bride verified the single status of all her potential catchers. Kenzie became the first person Corie confirmed as single. The way everyone pointed the fact out amused Ramon, who stood back and watched the single ladies line up like a football team ready for battle on the field. Ramon held his tumbler of rum in his hand and rolled his finger along the glass. Coming from a family who built its island city on the backs of a rum refinery, Ramon considered himself a connoisseur of the alcohol. Not Torres rum, but not bad, either. Ramon tried to focus on the drink rather than the commotion.

The dude who caught the light blue garter held the material over his mouth to insinuate a sexual gesture. Somewhere in the mix of single women stood Kenzie. If she was standing there the way she had when she left his side, Ramon pictured her arms were folded against her chest with a scowl across her face. Ramon laughed to himself.

"Enjoying the party?"

Ramon turned to his left and reached out to shake the hand of a man he met earlier, Kenzie's father. "Indeed I am, Mr. Swayne."

"Please, call me Mitchell."

"All right, Mitchell," Ramon said, trying out the name. "How about you? Enjoying the wedding?"

Mitchell Swayne's light brown features pinched together. "The wedding is fine. The bouquet toss is my least favorite part."

"Oh, really?"

"Yeah, if one of my girls catches it," Mitchell said, "I'm going to pay out the nose."

"Fortunately just one woman will catch it," provided Ramon.

"Let's hope it's the one who would rather take her eye out with a hot poker than get married."

Ramon was willing to bet the hotel that the least likely to get married would be Maggie. Last summer Kenzie had started making future plans for the two of them. Back then he'd been in a foggy haze of Kenzie and almost saw himself falling for the commitment lifestyle. Generation after generation, members of the Torres family married the first person they fell in love with without ever testing the waters. Ramon grew up not wanting to sell himself short when it came to beautiful women. Besides, he sincerely doubted the happiness of his family members. He heard his parents argue all the time. Roman never wanted that for himself. If he couldn't get along with his significant other, it was time to bounce.

If she was anything like his sisters and cousins, Kenzie had probably been planning a dream wedding since middle school. Kenzie struck Ramon as a planner. He bet she scheduled everything down to when she woke up, what she ate and when she took a shower. *Mmm.* His thoughts trailed off with the idea of Kenzie naked in his shower. It was one activity they had not gotten around to sharing. Ramon inhaled deeply and remembered who he was standing next to.

Oblivious to Ramon's nefarious thoughts, Mitchell leaned forward on his dress shoes as his shoulders bobbed and weaved, swaying to the rhythm. Ramon glanced up in time to see a bouquet hit the overhead spotlight. The crowd of women—and Mitchell—gasped and waited on bated breath. Petals rained down on the well-dressed women. Ramon wondered what the protocol for him would be if Kenzie caught the bouquet. Photographs were taken of the bouquet catcher and the catcher of the garter belt. He cut his eyes toward the table of basketball players and scowled. Did he truly want a photograph of some dude with his hand up Kenzie's dress to exist in history in someone else's wedding album? Ramon's grip on the glass tightened and the sweet brown liquid sloshed around.

In the center of the onlookers, a half dozen redheads darted down to the dance floor and formed a huddle over white buds of baby's breath mixed with deep green oval leaves and stems. Thanks to his six-foot-three height, Ramon had a slight advantage over the scene.

"Oh God," Mitchell groaned.

Ramon felt like a rock had sunk in the pit of his stomach. Baffled, he darted his eyes between the garter holder, who now leered and sinuously rubbed his hands together, and the mysterious light arm holding the coveted bouquet. Raised Catholic, Ramon understood the power of prayer but couldn't for the life of him remember going to mass, confession or even saying a prayer. But somewhere deep inside he heard his own voice under his breath pray…beg…for the winner of the bouquet toss to be anyone but Kenzie. While he remained unsure about a future or marriage, the idea of

Kenzie being photographed with the guy who caught the garter didn't sit well with him, either, even if she challenged him all the time. Ramon held his breath for a beat before deciding he couldn't watch. He tossed back the drink until he saw the bottom of the tumbler. Through the clear glass came a blurry vision of a woman dressed in yellow and jumping for joy. Beside him Mitchell cursed. Ramon did a double-check—positive Kenzie wore a purple-colored dress.

"I'm next!" Maggie shouted.

Kenzie waltzed back over toward Ramon. Her face softened with a smile and a sigh of relief. "Squeaked by another one," she boasted.

"Thank you, peanut," said Mitchell, opening his arms to embrace his daughter.

"Wait." Ramon chuckled. "So you're *not* the daughter who wants the huge wedding?"

Kenzie and Mitchell looked at each other, then back at Ramon before playfully nudging each other as they cracked up with laughter. Ramon scratched the back of his head at their inside joke.

"There is no way I am getting married."

"Thus increasing her slice of her inheritance." Mitchell laughed.

As the two carried on the hysterics, Ramon wondered what bothered him more, the fact that Kenzie didn't plan on marrying…or the fact she no longer wanted a commitment from him. Hell, last summer Ramon needed to walk away from their budding relationship because he just knew she'd wanted more than what he could deliver, especially when he needed to focus on his business. Now to find out they were on the same page all along? Ramon scratched his chin, still bothered and oddly offended, and wondered if he proposed to her whether she would say no.

"Your glass looks empty," Mitchell said, bringing Ramon out of his funk.

"Don't forget to get us some champagne, Daddy."

Now alone with her, Ramon cleared his throat. "I've never met a woman who did not want to catch the bouquet."

"I didn't see you muscling your way to catch the garter," Kenzie countered.

Ramon nodded. "True, but I don't know anyone here."

"You knew the table of Hawk's friends."

"But no woman I'd want to be photographed with. Wait." He shook his head at the frown on Kenzie's face and the fact he'd started off like a jerk. "It wouldn't be fair to have a complete stranger in their album for the rest of their lives."

"Or at least until they divorce." Kenzie shrugged, casting a skeptical glance over her shoulder at the newlyweds on the dance floor, and folded her arms across her chest.

Ramon tried not to stare at the way her breasts swelled in her strapless gown. He cleared his throat. "You know, there was a moment in the sermon where you didn't have to hold your peace forever."

When Kenzie looked back over at him, she gave an overexaggerated eye roll. "It's not my place and we're not that close."

"*We*, as in you and your cousin aren't close? Or *we* as in you and I aren't close?"

Kenzie studied him for a moment before speaking. She rested her hands on her hips. "Both."

Pressing his lips together, Ramon feigned hurt. More people began to fill the dance floor for the next slow song. Ramon took Kenzie by the hand and led her to the center of the group. Despite their height difference, they were a perfect fit. He assumed the strappy heels she wore helped. Kenzie's small hand fit in his, her purple nails clamped down into his flesh. He looked down into her eyes and continued their conversation. "And here I thought we'd reached a new level."

"Oh, we did." Kenzie laughed and allowed him to lead them to the beat of the song. "Just not the level where I'm going to start sharing my feelings with you."

"This is going to make this month awkward for all our events."

At the key word—*our*—Kenzie's eyes widened. "What are you talking about? I never agreed to your deal."

"Yes, but now that your family's met me, don't you think it will be awkward if I don't escort you to the ses- quicentennial gala?"

"What makes you think I'm going?"

Ramon dipped Kenzie backward. He caught her full weight in one arm. "You're the town historian and you're the emcee for the event."

Kenzie opened her mouth to protest.

"Auntie Bren already told me," Ramon said before set- ting her upright again. A strand of hair escaped her updo. Gently he reached out and tucked it behind her ear. "I know you don't want to disappoint her. She loves me and said she's looking forward to seeing me again. Did you know your entire family is staying in Southwood for the next two weeks? Had I known, I would have offered up a special at Magnolia Palace."

Kenzie's eyes narrowed on his throat. With the inten- sity behind her eyes Ramon wondered if he needed to be worried about his life.

"Again, let me remind you that I never agreed to your deal."

"But I'm already here. Did I mention your family loves me?"

"Half."

"Is that a challenge?" Ramon asked with one raised brow. "I am sure the other half of your family will love me just the same. I believe your father is fond of me." He enjoyed spotting the dimple in her cheeks when she tried not to laugh. They used to laugh together and then when they'd ended things...or he had...the only thing Ramon received from Kenzie was a scowl.

"I'm not challenging you to a thing," said Kenzie. "And don't think you showing up today means I need you for the other things."

"And prove Erin right if you show up stag next weekend at Felicia's wedding?" For once Ramon knew something Kenzie didn't. He smiled smugly and reveled in it.

After a moment of sheer surprise Kenzie closed her gaping mouth. Her throat bobbed as she found words to speak. "What do you know?"

"I know you're in a wedding next week and Erin will still be here," said Ramon. "While you're in the wedding party, she's a guest. She just RSVPed this morning."

"How long was I gone getting my drink?"

"Your cousins speak fast," Ramon replied.

"I am not sure which is worse," Kenzie said, licking her lips, "facing my cousin again or saying yes to you."

"One makes you feel bad and the other makes you feel good."

"Whatever. I am not in the wedding," Kenzie corrected him. Questions formed in his mind but she answered quickly. "I declined."

"Great, that's more time we get to spend together at your place, for a history lesson of Southwood, of course."

Kenzie's eyes widened and her cheeks got a light red tint. Whether she said yes or no, Ramon planned on being there for his new friend. It might make it easier for him to win his bid for the post office and become an acting member on the Christmas Advisory Council, and they would have to work together.

"Thank you again for coming to my rescue," Kenzie said as she and Ramon walked out of the reception hall. A half-moon filled the evening sky, dousing the flames from the day's burning sun. The moment Ramon rested his hand on the small of her back, she shivered.

"You're cold," Ramon stated and slipped off his jacket. "My vehicle's this way."

Stunned by his chivalry, Kenzie ran her hand along the lapels as he rested the garment across her shoulders. The inside of the jacket was still toasty from the heat of his body. Her soul oozed with warmth. "This summer weather is so moody. Hot one hour and a torrential downpour the next."

"I'll take the weather here over the weather in Villa San Juan," said Ramon.

"We get hit with every type of rain possible."

A set of keys jingled in his free hand while he guided her across the paved parking lot. Cars of all shapes and sizes and ages filled the vertical lines. Thanks to Crowne Restoration, a lot of locals were able to drive their classic cars. Kenzie scanned the parking lot for Ramon's truck.

"I'll have to remember to pick you up in my car next week," he said.

"Two cars," Kenzie said. "Aren't we fancy?"

"Or practical," Ramon replied. "I love my truck but it's a gas guzzler on the highway to Villa San Juan."

The mention of his hometown caused Kenzie to think of his family. It felt like he had been avoiding the subject earlier tonight. "How often do you get to see them?"

"I was there a few months ago," answered Ramon. "I took my cousin Philly to visit her grandparents."

Kenzie nodded, understanding the family dynamics. Technically Philly was his first cousin once removed. Her grandparents were Ramon's aunt and uncle. Lexi drew a diagram last summer of the Torres family tree. Ramon led her to the passenger's side and opened the door for her. She climbed inside. After closing it, Ramon jogged around to his side and slid in. Their shoulders brushed and Kenzie tried not to think about the desire pumping through her. This was a simple case of hero worship. Ramon had saved her from an evening of embarrassment.

"Have you ever been?" Ramon asked Kenzie. She blinked at the words. "To Villa San Juan?"

"Oh, um, no."

"It's nice." Ramon pulled his car out of the space and began traveling through town.

How did they end the evening with small talk? Kenzie cleared her throat. "Maybe I'll take a trip when it's not raining so much. Humidity is my enemy." To prove her point Kenzie tugged at a stray curl.

Ramon chuckled. "I'm not sure when it isn't going to be humid. It's right off the water."

"Sounds lovely."

"You'd really like it, considering how much you seem to love history. The town isn't very different from South-wood."

Kenzie settled in her seat, crossing her legs at the ankles. "Well, now I'm intrigued."

"And like you, I come from a long line of founders. The Torres family," he said.

While they drove through town Ramon told Kenzie about growing up. His great-great-great-grandfather had settled the Florida island and named it for his home in Puerto Rico. Torreses had been governing things there ever since, including his life.

"And that's why you came to Southwood?" Kenzie asked, suddenly feeling more than just a sexual connection to Ramon. For a moment she understood him. "To get away from your family?"

"When you say it like that, no, that's not the main reason, but a part of it," he explained. "I had everyone telling me what I needed to do with my life. And even if I started my life in Villa San Juan, I'd never truly know if I earned it or if I got it because of my name."

Under the glow of the passing streetlights, Kenzie nodded. "I get it. I felt the same way about winning Miss Southwood."

"But you won?"

"Narrowly," Kenzie said, nibbling her bottom lip and leaving out *no thanks to Erin*. Erin campaigned with and coached Kenzie's opponent.

"Well, there was more to me coming here than getting away from my folks," said Ramon. "I like helping out my cousins with the girls, Kimber and Philly."

"I never had Kimber in a tutoring session at Southwood High School," said Kenzie. "She always had her act together and never needed help."

"She is something else," Ramon agreed. "I don't know how many teenagers can lose both parents and manage to graduate as valedictorian."

"Don't forget, she's a Southern Style Glitz Queen," Kenzie said with a grin.

"Ah yes, the whole queen thing. It is beauty queen season around here."

Kenzie turned and smiled at him but as they drove by the old post office a light flashed on the first floor.

"What the hell?" Ramon maneuvered the truck to the curb and got out of the car without turning the engine off. A group of kids scattered from the front step and out from a broken window. There were too many of them to catch. Some even took sport in the game and ran parallel to each other, breezing right by Ramon, although he did reach for a few of them. By the time he returned to the car, Kenzie was in tears with laughter.

"I guess it's safe to say it's also teenager mischief season," Ramon grumbled, gripping the steering wheel.

Wiping the corners of her eyes, Kenzie said, "Now you see my reasoning for wanting some sort of youth center? These kids have nothing but idle time on their hands."

Ramon cast Kenzie a glance accompanied by a flat smirk.

"Too soon?" She asked him.

"Just wait until I get my second wind," Ramon growled before shaking his head and joining Kenzie's laughter with his own.

Chapter 5

"Everyone knows women are masterminds of revenge. The better the sex, the eviler their plans might be for you."

An echo of deep laughter from the other guests of Magnolia Palace filled the weight room the following morning. Nate Reyes and his wild comments were the exact reason Ramon made sure his hotel had two gyms. Ramon tried to finish his eighth rep of bench presses but his cousin's off-the-wall statement made it hard. Nate stood unapologetically by his statement with a straight face before he rubbed his hands together and reached for his dumbbells.

The three-hundred-and-seventy-five-pound weights clinked into place as Ramon struggled to catch his breath and he sat upright. The blurry vision of Stephen jumping rope became clearer. The comments didn't faze Stephen. Meanwhile the other men in the gym could no longer pretend to be into their own workouts. Everyone nodded as if agreeing with the statement. Southwood didn't have the *appropriate gym* Ramon needed to keep in shape so he'd made sure Magnolia Palace had one. His cousins made sure the facilities were constantly in use.

"Nate," Stephen scolded.

"Clearly, since Lexi is going to have your second child before your oldest is one—" Nate sighed, dragging his hand over his light brown face "—she hasn't worked out the kinks of you outbidding her on the piece of property she wanted to buy."

Ramon choked on his laughter.

"You're laughing but I don't know why, *primo*," Nate went on. "You volunteered to take a woman to two more weddings," Nate stated and added, "the same woman who had your car towed for being parked a fraction over the line near a fire hydrant by her fireman friend."

Ramon nodded his head and accepted the verbal taunts that were reminders of incidents between Kenzie and himself. At least now the antics would stop. If yesterday was an inkling of what a friendship between them would be like, Ramon couldn't wait to hang out with her again.

"Pay no attention to Nate," Stephen said with a chuckle. "He's still mad about fireman Parker Ward's history with Amelia."

"Hey, their history was in high school," Nate interrupted and puffed out his chest. "Amelia chose me."

By Ramon's calculations, Nate was the one who needed a history lesson. Before becoming Mrs. Reyes, Amelia had spent ten grand at a bachelor's auction just to get even with Nate. Of course, Ramon would love to hear what his cousin-in-law, the reality TV show producer, would do after hearing this non-scientific theory.

"Whatever, Nate," said Ramon. He reached down for his bottled water and took a long swig. The beverage cooled the heat in his chest. When he finished, he stood up to flex his muscles in the mirror. The black tank top he wore exposed the well-defined guns he took care of. Ramon lifted his arms, flexed and kissed his biceps.

"Primp all you want in the mirror," said Nate, "but you will never fetch ten Gs."

"Can we get back to this wedding business?" Stephen asked.

"What about it?" Ramon inquired.

"You don't have to make such a commitment just to secure your bid for the old post office," Stephen stated. *Always the voice of reason.* Ramon nodded his head and agreed with his older cousin. "There's always the archives section in the library."

Shaking his head, Nate cleared his throat. "Not really. I took Kimber last year for her final history project and she said she couldn't find anything good in there."

"I know," Ramon said with a shrug. "I prefer to study with a buddy."

Nate laughed in approval. "I ain't mad at you. I just want to make sure you're aware of the calculating ones."

"She's not a evil-genius-revenge-mastermind, Nate," Ramon verified.

"Does she show up at the same places you are?" asked one of the men at the pull-up bar.

"She's got this eagle eye," Nate answered. "She manages to know when he arrives someplace and finds a way to make his life miserable."

Nate's statement warranted a collective *hmph* from everyone.

"You're leaving out the main part, Nate. Amelia and Lexi have worked with Kenzie on numerous projects, so it's only natural we're at the same place at the same time."

Another round of disapproving *hmphs.*

I'm the one showing up places now, like the wedding last night."

"Wait, though—" Ramon struggled to gain control of the situation "—there is more to these weddings than

I thought. I can't let her face the wrath of her cousins. They're not like us."

Stephen sighed and laughed out loud. "Do you think Lourdes wants to face Rosa and her perfect husband at any wedding? Especially after being stood up at the altar?"

"That was cold." Ramon winced and recalled the time his then eighteen-year-old cousin Lourdes invited everyone down to Miami Beach for a wedding that never happened. At the last minute her fiancé chose business over love. Ramon inhaled deeply. He never wanted to be one to hurt his family but he understood the dude's perspective. Women wanted to be a certain weight before getting married. Why was it hard for women to understand men wanted to be financially ready?

"It's not like Lourdes is hurting in the financial department," said Nate. "I think she mentioned something about planning a wedding for one of the ex's brothers."

Last week Ramon had doubted Kenzie would lift a finger to help his family but after last night he was sure they'd made headway. Though she hadn't let him walk her to her apartment door, Kenzie had allowed him to drive her home. *It made sense to leave the wedding together*, she'd said.

What Kenzie had failed to say was the word *yes* to him. So should he attend the next wedding? According to Aunt Bren, a friend of the Hairstons was getting married and Kenzie was attending. A squeal from outside snapped Ramon out of his daydream.

"What is that noise?"

"Sounds like Jessilyn." Ramon chuckled. "My new chef gets excited when the food she ordered arrives on time."

Stephen rubbed his stomach. "My kind of cook."

"Are y'all staying for lunch? The guests this week are from Canada, so Jessi thought it would be a treat for them to try some down-home cooking." Ramon made sure to use the Southern drawl he'd perfected over the past few months. "I'm sure she'd be happy to fix extra."

"I'm sure she won't mind." Nate patted his stomach.

"I'll take anyone's cooking over his," said Stephen, hiking his thumb toward his brother.

"Hey."

Ramon shook his head and laughed. "Great. I'll let her know to set a few more plates."

Exiting the gym, Ramon thought about his cousin's words. Nate was a hoot and would deny everything if Amelia heard him talk. No… Kenzie disproved Nate's theory. She was sane and damn near gifted in bed. Ramon's body stiffened at the memory of her beneath and on top of him.

Before stopping by the kitchen to give the lunch order, Ramon headed toward his office on the first floor to grab his phone before taking a shower. He took in a deep breath at the banister in his sprawling digs and shook his head. This was his. There were times he still couldn't believe he turned a dilapidated plantation home into a thriving hotel. All sixteen rooms were booked for the entire summer. Guests buzzed through the foyer, prepared to get out on the lake. Children waddled barefoot with brightly colored pool-floaties around their arms and bellies. A lifeguard was already on duty, had been since sunup, for the sake of the guests who wanted an early-morning row out on the calm water.

Ramon slipped into his study to glance at his schedule. He'd learned from Kenzie to write things down on a planner instead of just assuming he'd remember things. Thank God for her. Kenzie had her act together, whereas the ladies he dated in the past were a bit on the vapid side, concerning themselves with climbing the social ladder. He smiled to himself and breezed over to his desk. The blotter listed off all the activities scheduled for the guests. For himself, he had nothing on the schedule. With the help of his chef and housekeeping staff, this place ran itself. Ramon co-ordinated the activities by a signup sheet when the guests registered. Maybe he'd travel into town today and acciden-tally run into Kenzie. It was odd his heart skipped a beat at the thought of her name.

Anxiety over how she might seek revenge against him always lingered in the back of his mind. Could Nate's words be true? Was she a vengeful mastermind tricking him to fall for her, just to reject him down the line? Nah, he laughed off the idea. But today's nerves were more from excitement. He learned last night Kenzie didn't want to tie him down. *Not like tying up is off the bedroom menu*, he thought with a devilish grin.

Satisfied with his free schedule, Ramon headed out of his office down the hall toward the oversize kitchen in the back. He spotted Jessilyn seated at the table with an abnormally large bowl piled high with fresh green beans.

"There's the man of the hour." Jessilyn beamed. "We were just talking about you."

A few weeks ago Jessilyn had approached Ramon about a job opportunity. She was young, fresh out of culinary school and needed a chance. He tested her with a few of his grandmother's recipes, tasted her specialties and agreed to give her a chance this summer.

"We?" Ramon asked.

When he stepped farther into the kitchen he spotted the backside of another person seated adjacent to Jessilyn. Red hair piled on top of her head and twisted into a tight bun, Kenzie turned in her chair to face him. He swore her fresh, freckled face lit up at the sight of him.

"We were," Kenzie answered. She stood up and smoothed

down her turquoise sundress. Freckles were sprinkled across her shoulders. He remembered kissing them last summer.

Ramon gulped. "Hey, I was hoping I'd run into you today."

Kenzie's left brow rose. "Afraid I'd run off with your jacket?"

"Huh?"

Reaching onto the chair next to her Kenzie lifted the jacket he'd wrapped around her last night when they stepped out of the church. "I forgot to give this back to you when you dropped me off."

"Oh?" Jessilyn breathed, giving life to a potential rumor.

"It wasn't like that," Kenzie said, shooting down the gossip. "Ramon helped me out of a sticky situation at Corie's wedding."

"How'd that go?"

"It was lovely."

"So were her groomsmen," Jessilyn said with a giggle. "They were out partying up at the club in Samaritan."

The only nightclub Ramon had gone to was Throb. It didn't surprise him to hear the basketball players were hanging out there. Anything trendy came through Samaritan. Southwood preserved the important history of the area. Ramon had partied a few times at Club Throb. Peachville, well, the name spoke for itself. This season Ramon made sure every room in the hotel had a bowl of fresh peaches.

"Hence why you were out of it when I saw you this morning," Kenzie said to Jessilyn.

Ramon lifted his brows and Jessilyn hit Kenzie playfully in the shoulder and shushed her. While Ramon enjoyed his chef's cooking, he understood she was young and made some irresponsible decisions, such as going out when she had work in the morning. As long as she came to the kitchen ready to work, he wasn't going to judge.

"Do I need to be concerned?" Ramon asked.

"Not at all," said Jessilyn. "Kenzie was just helping me finish up snapping the beans and then I'll start lunch."

"Great, that's why I came to see you," said Ramon. "I have my cousins downstairs working out and they want to stay for lunch."

The idea of cooking for more people didn't faze Jessilyn one bit. As a matter of fact her smile broadened. "I'll make sure they have plenty."

"They have wives," reminded Kenzie as she returned the playful swat against Jessilyn's forearm.

"Sheesh."

Ramon pressed his lips together for a moment. Kenzie, however, did not bother trying to contain herself. Her infectious laugh brought all of them to a full chuckle.

"Seriously, though." Jessilyn sobered. "Bring whomever you wish. Kenzie really saved the day snapping these beans with me."

"Kenzie—" Ramon cleared his throat "—would you like to stay for lunch?"

"Thanks but," she began, rising from her seat, "I have plans."

With whom? Ramon's mind screamed and then he glanced down at the ground and wondered if the hem of her dress covered her purple-polished toes he'd spied last night. "We have mimosas if you're interested."

"Thanks, but I better get going. I really stopped by to return your jacket."

Without thinking, the two of them began walking out of the kitchen. "I could have picked up the jacket next week when we attend Felicia's wedding."

"I'm supposed to meet up with some friends at Felicia's wedding," said Kenzie. "I don't know if I'll be there or stay late to catch up with them."

Ramon clasped his hands behind his back. "But we're still going?"

"I haven't agreed to your proposal."

Shaking his head, Ramon kept walking. Their footsteps were drowned out by the children screaming with excitement. He liked the way Kenzie smiled at them. "Let me guess, you've got canoeing on the agenda."

"I do. How'd you guess?"

"Been there, done that," Kenzie said, looking up and batting her lashes. "Or have you forgotten?"

"How could anyone forget how this home once belonged to the famous Swaynes of Southwood, who so graciously opened the doors for public access for vacations?" Ramon imitated Kenzie's Southern drawl as he spoke. When he bowed at the waist Kenzie pushed her hand against his shoulder.

"Don't get hurt," teased Kenzie.

"Sorry, I couldn't help myself." Ramon grabbed hold of Kenzie's hand before she poked him for a second time. Kenzie wiggled her fingers against his. Everything else in the room ceased for him. The noise of the children, the dishes clanking in the dining room and the screeches from the teenagers outside went away. He was sweaty from his workout but touching Kenzie brought a whole new level of heat.

"Did you really come here to return my jacket?"

"I did," said Kenzie. She stopped struggling against his grip. "And I wanted to thank you for showing up last night like you did."

Ramon jutted his chin outward. "I was pretty heroic."

"Dear Lord," Kenzie groaned.

"What? I came in looking all sharp and won your family over."

Kenzie rolled her eyes and blew a lock of her red hair out of her face. "First of all, Erin is nosey and hung on to your every word to get the tea."

"And Auntie Bren?" Ramon genuinely liked the matriarch of the Hairston side of the family. Like Kenzie, Auntie Bren was tightly wound with a pile of red hair on top of her head, although Ramon suspected a hairdresser might be helping her by now. Either way, both women were firecrackers.

"Don't call her that," Kenzie said from between gritted teeth.

"She asked me to." Ramon gave Kenzie's fingers a squeeze. "Are you jealous?"

"Of?"

"Of the idea of Auntie Bren wanting me."

"I'm leaving now." Kenzie yawned. She yanked her hand free once more and freed herself.

Ramon stopped himself from taking a step forward and capturing her in his arms. "Hot date?" Too bad he couldn't stop his mouth from saying anything stupid.

The corners of Kenzie's mouth turned up into a grin. "Didn't you have your own date Friday night?"

"If by date you mean a slumber party here at Magnolia Palace for my preteen niece after taking her and her friends to a concert in the park down from your apartment. Maybe you heard it?"

Judging from the look on her face, Ramon guessed she had. Also accompanying the annoyed look was a flash of relief. Was she happy to know he hadn't been on a date?

"How sweet of you," Kenzie finally said.

"Sweet was letting those girls do my hair."

Kenzie covered her face to hide her laugh. Her eyes

crinkled at the corners and gave her attempt away. "Please tell me there are pictures."

"None I'm willing to share. Besides, you might try to blackmail me into escorting you to your events."

"Really?" Kenzie cocked her hand on her hip and rolled her eyes.

"Nah, I'm still waiting on you to say yes to my offer," said Ramon. "Remember, I still need you to teach me about the history of the post office so I can decide what to propose for the planning committee." Reaching for the door, Ramon held on to the jamb. Kenzie paused under his arm. Sun backlit her face like a halo. "I need your help, Kenzie."

Wordlessly Kenzie ducked under his arm. Like a puppy he followed her to a white convertible with pink leather seats. They both reached for her door at the same time. Electricity bolted through his skin.

Kenzie had to have felt it, too. She rubbed her hand. A red tint spread over her freckled cheeks. Kenzie cleared her throat. "Well, I am off this month but I've got a few new items to archive, so my desk isn't overflowing when I get back."

"What do you do there?" he asked.

"Well," she started, "I am a historian for the town but that's all glorified. Basically I am a city worker. Until I have my own space, I am an archivist, as in, I'm bringing Southwood's history into the digital age."

She certainly knew a lot about the town, he thought to himself.

"Meet me in my office at City Hall tomorrow," she said. "We can talk there."

Ramon nodded and waited before Kenzie got in her car and headed down the drive before turning toward the wide porch. Nate and Stephen waited for him.

"So she just happened to be here at Magnolia Palace?" Nate asked.

"Shut up, Nate," Ramon said with a laugh as he flipped his cousin the middle finger.

"Well, I hadn't heard from you so I thought I'd check and see if you ended up eloping with Mr. Save-the-Day," Maggie's voice sang out from the cell phone on the corner of Kenzie's desk.

Though they weren't on video chat, Kenzie rolled her eyes toward the florescent lights of her office. "Please don't ruin my Monday with any of your craziness," said Kenzie.

So far Kenzie's month off work wasn't turning out as she'd planned. Monday morning, knowing Alexander intended to sell off—on behalf of the city—all the property downtown, Kenzie came in to work to check and secure all requests. Her morning started out with a tutoring session with one of the football players from Southwood High as a favor to the parents. After the first session ended quickly, the potential quarterback came in for tutoring and thirty minutes stretched into close to lunchtime, as her second appointment took longer than she anticipated.

A stack of requests from local businesses for historic preservation teetered on her desk. Everyone coveted a prestigious plaque posted on their buildings. It helped garner more tourists. This was the part of her job she loved. She followed the paper trail to verify each claim. Even though she grew up in Southwood, she loved hearing the stories people passed on from generation to generation. The only thing she hated about her job was having to tell people no. The last time Kenzie denied a family entry into the registry she felt horrible, but in retrospect, having a peach in the shape of Fat Albert did not make the home or land historic. Ever since Kenzie took on the job as town historian last year she had been busy.

"Don't act like you can't hear me," Maggie persisted. "You're not even supposed to be working. Don't tell me Alexander made you come in."

"Alexander can't make me do anything," Kenzie said with a frown. Thank God Margaret gave her his summer schedule. It was bad enough she was going to have to see him this weekend for Felicia's wedding. How many folks in his family were going to recommend they give each other another shot? Kenzie would rather eat a bowl of rocks. "He never comes in Mondays."

"So why are you there when you're off?"

"I helped out the Stanfield boy about a half an hour ago and then I noticed some work that must have come in when I left early Friday. I wanted to take a peek at some of the homes and businesses requesting to be on the docket for preservation this fall."

"So?"

"So I can take a look at these places this month and maybe even have an announcement for the entries to the state historic registry at the sesquicentennial."

"For which you'll have a date, right? Auntie Bren told me Danielle and Michelle were proposed to last night."

Of course her other Hairston cousins would follow suit and get married. Dani was a physical therapist and Michelle worked with Erin in Orlando, Florida, at their big-time sports agency. "You should have seen their rings. Auntie Bren was going on about the rocks."

"For crying out loud," Kenzie moaned. "I have a freaking PhD."

"So?"

"So?" Kenzie snorted. "Paper beats rock every single time."

Maggie's sigh caused a static sound through the phone. "You say that now, but wait until you have your own set of gems."

"I have my own," she responded, "It's called the Miss Southwood crown. Since I won—"

"Oh-so long ago," Maggie interjected.

"No one on either side of the Hairston and Swayne family has won since."

"Whatever. What's going on with you and Ramon? Is he escorting you to Felicia's wedding?"

A smile tugged at the corners of Kenzie's mouth. Heat spread across her cheeks at the memory of Ramon asking her the same thing. "I haven't really accepted his offer."

"I thought I heard you say you would help."

"I'm helping anyone who wants to place a bid on the historic buildings in Southwood, not just Ramon. There are other places up to be sold. And as the town's historian…"

Maggie grumbled on the other end of the line. "You're the only person with the credentials who can help."

"The only way I can help is to make sure the buyers are aware of the historicity of the structure," Kenzie said, trying to sound authoritative. "Whoever buys one of the buildings downtown has to keep in mind they can't just add a porch to accommodate, let's say, a sports bar. They'll have to stick with the original work as close as possible on the interior and exterior."

"Let me guess, you're going to give an extra lesson to the person who is going to put in a business of your choice, right?"

"Dear older and much wiser sister," Kenzie said, "you know me so well."

"What I do know is you and Ramon were a hit at Corie's wedding. Auntie Bren is looking forward to dancing with him at Felicia's wedding—she said something about making some man jealous."

The last thing Kenzie wanted to do was encourage Auntie Bren to get close to Ramon. What would it look like for two grown men to be fighting over an old lady? Besides, Kenzie didn't want to get comfortable with the idea of Ramon taking her anywhere. What if he decided to stop helping and stood her up for one of the events? It happened before. Kenzie hated being humiliated and the memory of waiting for Ramon to pick her up for the final crowning for last year's Miss Southwood Beauty Pageant was still fresh. The two of them had spent the entire week together; it had been only natural for everyone to assume they'd arrive together. She'd spent that whole evening avoiding questions about his whereabouts and the pitying glances from the people involved with the pageant. Being embarrassed was one thing but she couldn't take being the subject of a year's worth of gossip. Not again.

"Everyone has been talking about you two… Speaking of which, why didn't you come to church yesterday?"

Kenzie choked on the air. Her eyes watered. "What? You went to church?"

"I had to get my church on. I'm not a complete heathen."

"Of course not."

The elevators outside her door dinged and Kenzie's heart raced with the idea of Ramon coming to visit her here. This was her playing field. He couldn't charm her or throw her off her game. Here she was a professional.

"Damn," some of the ladies by the water cooler collectively sang out.

The sweet smell of magnolias filled the air. The pit of her stomach dropped and her nipples became acutely aware of his presence. *He was here.*

A bouquet of blooming magnolias filled the doorway

and covered his face. Kenzie found herself leaning in her black leather chair for a glimpse. He wore a pair of khaki pants with a blue sports coat. His massive hands wrapped around a thin paper blanket cradling the bouquet.

"Ramon," Kenzie breathed. She stood up from her chair and the back of it hit the wall.

"Ramon's there?" Maggie's voice came from the pink cell phone.

As Kenzie maneuvered around her desk, she swiped the screen to disconnect the call and pulled down her black pencil skirt. The peach silk blouse she wore clung to the skin on her back.

"Hi," Kenzie said, trying to play it cool. She clasped her hands behind her back.

Ramon lowered the flowers to reveal his devastatingly handsome smile. "Aren't you going to take these?"

"Well, I wasn't sure. The last time you arrived at my doorstep with flowers you made sure to let me know they were for another woman."

"A preteen niece," said Ramon, pushing the flowers toward her. "And I thought I explained about the concert."

If ever there was a time to crawl into a hole, it was now. How jealous did she sound? "Well, thank you then." She accepted the flowers and glanced around for a vase. "I'm afraid I don't have anything here to put these in."

"We can head back to your place."

Kenzie offered him a tight smile. "No thanks."

"How about lunch?" Ramon asked. "Have you eaten yet?"

"One of my students brought me a muffin earlier."

Ramon leaned against the door. She hated to admit how cramped he appeared in her office. "A muffin, huh? Sounds like a great, healthy choice."

"You know once you lick the frosting off a cupcake it

becomes a muffin, so that counts, right?" she joked and rolled her eyes when he smirked. Kenzie pressed her lips together. "Whatever, we can do lunch. It's not Food Truck Thursday, but there are a few locals, and we can meet up with everyone."

"Everyone?"

There was no mistaking the disappointment in his voice. He didn't bother covering his feelings with a tawdry grin. Kenzie inhaled deeply and steadied her libido. "Yes. I mentioned before you're not the only one interested in property around town. So since Alexander is serious about selling off vacant pieces, to generate revenue for the town, I thought I'd give everyone a history lesson."

Ramon's upper lip curled. "Uh, didn't you already tutor today?"

"What are you here for?" Kenzie turned with her butt against her desk. Ramon cocked his head to the side and licked his lips. A team of goose bumps marched along her arms. All he needed to do was kick the door closed and in two seconds flat she'd be his.

"I thought you were going to give me a private lesson about Southwood," he said, advancing closer.

"You thought we'd do it alone?"

Thankfully someone behind them cleared their throat in a soft manner.

"Kenzie," said Margaret as she cleared her throat at the doorway. "The *package* I thought shipped out is on its way back here."

Alexander. Kenzie sighed to prevent her upper lip from curling. "Thanks, Miss Margaret," she said sweetly. "By the way, this is Ramon Torres. Ramon, this is Miss Margaret Foley."

Charming as ever, Ramon kissed the back of Margaret's hand. "Pleasure to meet you."

Margaret, fifty years of age, beamed. For the last six months Margaret had decided she was going to stop coloring her hair and embrace the gray. Right now a trim of gray circled her head like a headband. She blushed and batted her eyelashes in Kenzie's direction. "Well, hello."

"Foley, you say?" Ramon cut his eyes at Kenzie. Her heart thumped against her rib cage. "One of the footlockers in the basement of the post office belonged to a Priscilla Foley. Any relation?"

After a moment of thinking and twisting her lips, Margaret shook her head. "Not that I can think. I'll let you know if I can remember anyone by that name. Okay?"

"Don't worry about it," Kenzie replied, remembering why Alexander's secretary was here in the first place. "We were heading out for lunch. Can we bring you anything back?"

"Aren't you sweet? But you're supposed to be off work for the rest of this month, dear."

"Yes, ma'am." Kenzie did not miss the way Ramon cocked his eyebrow toward her. The last thing she wanted was him aware of her free time.

"Good. Now, you two go on and grab some lunch." From the door, Margaret shooed the two of them out of Kenzie's cramped office and picked up the flowers. "I'll get these sent over to your apartment, okay, Kenzie? I also got a call from the front desk—the other person interested in the old post office is waiting downstairs for you."

Kenzie reached around and grabbed the stack of requests and her purse off the coat rack beside the door. "All right. I'll get in touch with these people."

"Mr. Torres." Margaret drew her attention to the man taking the folders from Kenzie's hands. "I expect you to make sure Kenzie has a good time."

"Oh yes, ma'am."

One of the ladies from the office already pressed the button for them and Ramon and Kenzie entered wordlessly. Once the door closed, Ramon shifted the paperwork under his arm and leaned against the wall. "Did we just get kicked out of your office?"

If that's what Ramon needed to believe, then sure. Kenzie did not want to bring up her past relationship or scarred friendship with Alexander. And she definitely did not want Alexander to try to sell Ramon another building.

"Margaret is sweet."

"And so you're off for the month?" Ramon asked.

The light in the elevator lit up and dinged with each floor. Kenzie concentrated on the numbers. "Yep."

"Great," Ramon exclaimed. "How about I take off and you can deal with the person who is going to lose the bid to me?"

Kenzie laughed. "Confident, aren't you?"

"Always."

"What if this person listens to my suggestion for what to do with the place?"

Ramon waved off the notion with his free hand. "I've got this. Southwood needs a martial arts or CrossFit gym and I am sure everyone on this council panel is going to agree with me."

"A gym?" Kenzie balked and frowned. She could imagine oversize, bulky men in tank tops and women dressed in see-through yoga pants walking through the center to get to the establishment. "Please don't."

"All right." Ramon laughed out loud. "That was me just being vindictive against one of my cousins. What about a smoothie shop?"

The light lit up on three. Was the elevator slower than before?

"Okay, I get it. Dry cleaner?"

Kenzie rolled her eyes. "Southwood has one in the Brickler Hotel off Main Street."

"You want me to walk my clothes into enemy territory?"

"You're worried about Brickler Hotel when the Brutti Hotel sits smack-dab in the middle of Four Points Park?"

"They're a chain," said Ramon. "It's not the same or as historic as the original structure of the first hotel in Southwood."

The history fact won him brownie points. "You're the one who decided to turn Magnolia Palace into a hotel," Kenzie reminded him with a wink.

Winking in his direction didn't help her at all. Ramon flashed a smile and Kenzie prayed for the elevator to stop midfloor. Caving in to Ramon's decadent lips would be justified if the circumstances deemed it so. Unfortunately the elevator kept going. In anticipation of reaching the ground floor Kenzie reached for her paperwork. Ramon held on to it, managing to tug her close to him.

"Why are you doing this?" Kenzie asked.

"What?" He had the nerve to sound innocent. "I'm trying to be chivalrous. Haven't we moved beyond the hostility between us?"

"There's nothing between us," Kenzie lied.

The smirk on his face proved he didn't believe her, either. "We need to get some things out of the way before we work together on this post office proposal and Felicia's wedding. All this tension between us is going to make Auntie Bren wonder."

"Stop calling her that," Kenzie started to squawk. Before she knew it, Ramon had lowered his hand and captured her lips with his.

Any sense of irritation or anger fell to the wayside. Kenzie pressed her hands against Ramon's broad chest. Her thumbs brushed against the buttons of his oxford shirt, tempting her to rip the material open. The familiar dance of their tongues excited her. Ramon broke the kiss and straightened to his full height. Kenzie wanted to smack and kiss him at the same time.

"Good," he breathed, "I needed to get that out of the way."

Maybe they *had* needed to kiss—to get these confusing feelings out of their system. The problem? She wanted more.

The doors opened. Guiltily, Kenzie took a large step backward.

"Hey, just the person I'm looking for," Erin said cheerfully. She stepped inside and wrapped her arms around Kenzie's shoulders. "I hear you're the one who's going to show me the old post office."

Chapter 6

The heavy knock on the apartment door the following Saturday morning led Kenzie to believe Maggie had not yet arrived. Someone masculine stood on the other side and Kenzie assumed it would be her brother, Richard, who, like the rest of her family members, had come into town. Wrapping her pink terry cloth robe tighter around her waist, Kenzie yanked the door open. Instead of the reddish-haired brother she expected to see, Kenzie came face-to-face with Ramon Torres. Thanks to attending practice with her niece Bailey for moral support for the pageant, Kenzie hadn't run into Ramon for the rest of the week. She thought Ramon might have been scared off listening to the bickering between her and Erin. She shot down Erin's idea for building a rehab clinic for athletes in Southwood. Erin felt downtown Southwood was perfect for rehabilitating patients. Kenzie found her cousin ridiculous. Sports figures would only bring in reporters and disturb the quiet. At one point Kenzie hushed Ramon for defending Erin and because of it, she was sure Ramon was intentionally avoiding her. But just because she didn't see him during the day didn't mean he wasn't haunting her dreams.

How many nights had she woken up from fevered dreams since the kiss back at City Hall? The night after the post office tour Kenzie had dreamed of what would have happened in the elevator. What was it with them and elevators? Finding him now standing in front of her gave Kenzie pause and she wondered if she'd fallen asleep after her shower this afternoon. She blinked her eyes and he didn't disappear.

"I truly need to start asking who it is," Kenzie said with her hand still on the door.

Ramon's dark eyes glanced over her body. "Or you could look through the peeph—" He cut his words off by covering his mouth with his large hands, stifling a laugh. His dark eyes roamed her body, then his head cocked to the side. When their eyes met, he dropped his hand and chuckled. "Sorry, I wasn't going for the short jokes."

"Whatever." Kenzie offered him a dramatic eye roll and straightened to her five-foot-three height. She'd known him for almost a year, slept with him after a week of knowing him, and yet this was the second time Ramon had appeared at her door. The one time she'd expected him to show up for her, he hadn't. Kenzie gripped the handle until her knuckles felt tight, but she remembered they'd called a truce to their feud. Unfortunately she couldn't stop the tone of annoyance in her voice. "Why are you here?"

Ramon didn't bother waiting for Kenzie to invite him; he simply strolled into her living room, wearing an inky black suit with a white-and-cerulean-striped oxford and a matching cerulean blue print tie. Kenzie blinked several times and glanced toward her bedroom where her dress hung on a soft padded hanger on the door. Lexi had designed the dress just for her.

The bedroom. Kenzie's heart skipped a beat. Ramon was here…in her place, with only a robe covering her body.

If he attempted to reach under the fabric, she doubted she'd want to stop him. *Damn his kisses*, she swore to herself and followed Ramon into her living room. He stood in front of the mantel of her fireplace where her framed PhD rested next to her Miss Southwood tiara.

"Felicia's wedding starts in an hour," he said out loud with his back to her.

After an appreciative stare at his backside, Kenzie said a silent prayer for strength to keep from giving into the idea of tempting this man for a romp on her couch. But if she did…thank God she'd cleaned up this morning. It wasn't like she had anything else to do this morning. In order to avoid Ramon or anyone else in her family, Kenzie had hid out in her apartment and ordered takeout for the week. With not having to step outside Kenzie figured she could remain in here for the remainder of her month-long vacation. If she decided to show up at Felicia's wedding, she could do so at the last minute and leave the first chance she got.

"Still doesn't explain why you stopped by." Kenzie sidled up next to her houseguest. "I never agreed to your proposal."

"I know," Ramon said, glancing down. "This isn't part of the proposal. As sweet as she is, I'm scared to death of Auntie Bren."

"Stop calling her that."

He didn't and continued annoying her. "Auntie Bren and I ran into each other at The Cupcakery and we shared a table together. She mentioned how good it was seeing you so happy last weekend and mumbled something about you dating a murderer. Perhaps I heard wrong."

"Great," Kenzie groaned and made eye contact with Ramon. "You heard Auntie Bren correctly," she clarified. "And I'm not dating a murderer."

"That's a relief." Ramon sighed.

"That I'm not dating a murderer or not dating period?"

Ramon's deep laugh echoed against her cream-colored walls. "Both."

"You didn't think I would be dating anyone?" Kenzie's hands moved to her hips.

"Need I remind you of your predicament for the month?" Ramon reached for her hands. The pads of his fingers stroked the length of her thumbs. The intimate touch sent a shiver down her spine. "If you were dating someone, he'd be a fool to not be here for you."

Kenzie's lips formed an O. Why, whenever he was this close, did he make her feel like a stereotypical lovesick fool? Her knees threatened to buckle and her lips threatened to twitch into a pucker and her heartbeat sped up. Ramon dipped his head low and cocked it to the side until their mouths neared. His thick lashes blinked as he looked down at her lips. Kenzie's throat went dry. She inhaled deeply and exhaled and tried to ignore the fact that she was naked as a jaybird beneath the robe. The faint smell of his fresh and woodsy cologne filled the tight space of air between them. The scent was just enough to set her nostrils open. *Wide-open*, as Auntie Bren would say, whenever a person was aroused. Kenzie exhaled a shaky breath and took a step backward.

"Auntie Bren expects to see us together tonight." Ramon smirked, straightened and turned back to the mantel. He adjusted a skewed photograph on the wall of Kenzie and her family at one of Maggie's charity Southwood events she hosted where everyone got together, including Richard. Despite the genuine smile on Richard's face that evening, her brother hated the limelight. Maggie and Kenzie often thought their parents must have found him on the stoop as a baby.

Ramon's hands swiped across the glass protecting her doctorate. A vulnerable shiver ran across her skin. "Why isn't this hanging in your office?"

Kenzie rolled her eyes. "Have you seen the size of my office?"

"Yes?"

"This thing will take over the space," she explained. "Besides, I don't need a document to tell everyone who I am or what my job is."

Ramon nodded and smiled for a moment, as if contemplating what she'd said. "You're right. Everyone does know who you are."

Was he teasing her again? Kenzie crossed her arms against under her breasts and raised a brow. "Meaning?"

"Meaning the Swaynes are an important part of the making of Southwood."

It was hard not to grin at a time like this. Kenzie realized Ramon had been paying attention during the tour she gave downtown earlier this week. Erin, with her ridiculous idea of moving back to Southwood, had failed to remember the Hairstons' contribution to the town history. She kept trying to interject her knowledge. Barry Hairston, Erin's great-great-great-grandfather, had been a founder, but he'd been a farmer and hadn't built anything in town. It was important to Kenzie that anyone buying downtown property respected the painstaking work her ancestors had done when they built this town. She wanted to remind them of what it took for African-American families to prosper post–Civil War. Reconstruction was a hard time for families starting over. In Southwood, the town came together to educate and protect one another.

"Do I get an A for remembering?"

"I am not a teacher," Kenzie replied.

Ramon scratched the back of his head. He wore his hair

in a bun on top of his head, which shook with the motion of his long fingers. Kenzie licked her lips. "Pardon me, but weren't you tutoring some kids Monday?"

"Tutoring and substitute teaching is more like it," said Kenzie.

"Your degree is in history, *Dr.* Swayne," he said.

A twinge jolted her heart. "No one ever calls me that."

"You earned it. Maybe I'll start calling you Dr. Swayne regularly." Ramon wiggled his brows up and down. "Or do you prefer to be called Miss Southwood?" He brushed the back of his hand across the crystals of the three-foot-high crown propped up on a small table by the shelf.

"I'm proud of both titles," said Kenzie. She squared her shoulders.

"Is it because you're the last Swayne queen?"

Kenzie bit the inside of her cheeks to prevent from laughing. "Erin meant to embarrass me with that the other night."

"Why?" Ramon asked as he turned toward her with a raised brow.

"Because she knows I don't like to be embarrassed," Kenzie said with a shrug. "Cousin rivalry, I guess."

"Maybe cousin adoration?" Ramon suggested. "I don't know how many cousins consider moving to a town to be with family they dislike."

No, Kenzie thought to herself. Ramon and his cousins were close. She refused to believe Erin seriously wanted to move back to Southwood to open a clinic for pampered athletes. Kenzie decided she needed to confront Erin this evening. But she didn't want Ramon around for it.

"You don't have to take me to the wedding."

"Of course I do," Ramon said. "I got all decked out in this coordinating suit, just as Lexi suggested."

"You did what?"

"Lexi is my family," he replied. "You don't think I wouldn't call and confirm what she made for you?"

Kenzie pressed her hand to her heart. "Seriously?"

"Yes."

Ramon sighed and clasped his hands behind his back. Kenzie's heart beat faster with his nearness. Without even touching her he made her body shiver. "Now, if you'd rather stay here and continue our kisses…" Kenzie backed up until her legs pressed against the back of the love seat. He closed the gap between them and pressed his hand to the back of her neck. The touch sent a spark through her.

Kenzie's eyes rolled back with her deep sigh, as she hoped to blow out the tension building in her blood. "Last week was because Auntie Bren was watching and I thought the kiss in the elevator was to get this tension out of our systems." Kenzie didn't realize her voice was barely above a whisper until Ramon leaned close. She thought for a moment he couldn't hear but instead, his breath tickled her right earlobe.

"You will never be out of my system."

Kenzie gulped. She clutched closed the opening of her robe. Ramon covered her hand with his and eased her fingers free from the material. The warmth of his hand cupped her breast. Kenzie took a deep intake of breath before biting her bottom lip. She tilted her head backward as Ramon nibbled her neck and then collarbone in that exact spot that sexually charged her body.

Every spot of her body he touched set her skin on fire. While his mouth made its way down her breastbone, Ramon slid his large hand through the opening of the robe. His fingers splayed against the curve of her stomach. While his thumb traced a circle around her navel, four fingers dipped into the curls between her legs. Kenzie sucked in a sharp breath. Pleasure oozed through her pores.

To fix the height difference between them, Ramon lifted Kenzie onto the back of her sofa. Legs dangling, Kenzie clung to Ramon's shoulders and arched her back to meet his mouth for a deep kiss. He felt wonderful. She felt free. No worries in the world. This is what she remembered about Ramon and oh God, how she'd missed this. Ramon's hands moved from around her waist back to the valley between her legs. He kissed her lips and played with her clitoris, rolling it between his thumb and forefinger. His middle finger slid inside of her body. Ramon knew her. He knew when to deepen his kiss and the pressure of his finger. He knew how to bring her right to the brink of an orgasm and when to break the kiss, take both breasts in his hands and suck on her nipples at the same time. Kenzie floated on air. She fell backward on the chair but Ramon caught her before she flipped over. A forefinger stroked the length of her neck as it extended back.

"What's it going to be, Dr. Beauty Queen?" Ramon whispered. He helped her to her feet and readjusted the ties of her robe.

"I think we better leave before my alleged murderer date finds himself free tonight." Kenzie smiled to herself as she headed toward her bedroom and left Ramon in her living room with his eyes open wide.

The Presbyterian church off the corner of Main Street was once again packed later that afternoon. Most of the shops in town closed early on Saturdays, which made getting to the church and parking easy. Ramon and Kenzie arrived just before the ceremony started. They found seats in the back rows. It was easy to spot the Hairstons among the guests in attendance. Auntie Bren had craned her neck to find them. When he waved in her direction, Auntie Bren smiled in approval. Ramon didn't miss Kenzie's elbow in his ribs. The bride was beautiful—well, Ramon had a hard time trying to concentrate on anything else besides his date. He deserved a medal of honor for controlling himself in Kenzie's apartment. How the hell was he going to spend the rest of the evening next to her keeping his hands to himself? The woman was sexy in clothes and out. The low-cut blue dress she wore was not helping Ramon keep his head. A row of pretty flowers lined the bodice of the gown and kept beckoning his eyes. The nuptials for her friend, Felicia, didn't take long and Kenzie shot out of her seat once the service ended.

The Ward-Crawford reception was held at the new hotel overlooking Four Points Park, convenient for the other three surrounding cities. Gianni Brutti, the owner of the hotel, sent over a limousine service for the wedding party, even though the weather was perfect for everyone to walk. Kenzie insisted they drive so she didn't have to run into anyone she knew. Was she embarrassed by him? A cloud of childhood shame briefly washed over him as he remembered the lonely feeling when no one wanted to pick him to be on their sports teams. Ramon might have been a heavy child but he would have been a heavy hitter too, if the kids had given him the chance. It felt like everyone was embarrassed by him.

Because they had left the church earlier than the others to avoid talking to everyone, Ramon and Kenzie arrived at the reception early. They were able to grab a drink at the bar before entering the gold-and-glass elevators to the party.

"I can't believe I am standing here," Kenzie groaned.

Had Gianni not been a close friend of the Torres family, Ramon might have grumbled the same way as Kenzie, but for a different reason. He should feel threatened by Gianni's fifteen-story hotel. Gianni had capitalized on the location of the building and garnered visitors who wanted a closer to town southern visit with all the city life amenities—an upscale restaurant and bar inside, close to the woods without being in nature.

"You don't like one of the nation's best hotels?" Ramon asked.

"Need I remind you this place is your competition?" said Kenzie.

Ramon pressed his hand against Kenzie's lower back to help her sit down on the bar stool. "I didn't realize you cared so much about my business," he said, his mouth close to her earlobe.

Kenzie turned her face toward him. Their mouths were close. A set of goose bumps christened Kenzie's shoulders. "I care," she whispered, tilting her head. Ramon's heart raced, eager for a continuation of their last encounter. "You're living in my ancestral home."

"Cute," said Ramon. He touched the tip of her nose with his index finger and signaled the bartender for two glasses of champagne.

"Are we celebrating something?" Kenzie asked.

"Yes," Ramon replied, taking both glasses from the bartender. "After a day like today, shouldn't we?" A red blush stained Kenzie's cheeks. He liked that about her. For all her toughness, Kenzie had a vulnerable side.

"Ramon," Kenzie began as she cleared her throat, "about this afternoon… Don't you think things got a little out of hand?"

"Not a damn bit," he swore. "We are good together, Kenzie. Don't you agree?"

Kenzie tried to hide her smile by taking a sip of her champagne. He knew she agreed. He didn't need to hear her verbally agree.

"There's more to a relationship than sex."

"So there was more to the relationship between you and this previous guy you dated?" asked Ramon.

"Alleged." Kenzie smiled coyly and wiggled her brows.

A cackle of women's laughter sounded off from the entrance of the hotel's bar. The two of them turned around in their seats. A group Ramon recognized as part of the wedding party and some guests filled the doorway. Each woman wore at least a five-inch tiara on top of her head and screamed at the sight of Kenzie, who slipped off her chair and met the girls in the center of the bar. They all began to jump up and down, screaming with excitement. The group turned in one huge circle and he suddenly noticed a sparkling tiara nestled in Kenzie's curly hair. Ramon blinked twice. When did she get a tiara? She hadn't left the house with it, right? They'd sat through the wedding and Ramon was pretty sure she hadn't been wearing it.

Once the screams died down, Kenzie joined Ramon's side and slipped her hand into the crook of his arm. "Ramon," she said with sweetness in her voice and a squeeze of her hand on his biceps. He wasn't going to question it.

"Yes, dear?"

"These are some of my oldest and dearest friends," Kenzie said. "This is the Tiara Squad." The light touch of her nails sunk through his jacket. If Kenzie was forcing a smile, he couldn't tell. She beamed from ear to ear. Unlike the other women who rushed over to greet her, Kenzie's makeup and long lashes all seemed natural. The foreheads on some of the other ladies didn't even move when they screamed. Damn Botox. The other women also sported another type of bling on their fingers—some wedding rings and others engagement rings.

Ramon tried not to choke on his laughter but failed.

Kenzie elbowed him in the stomach. "Ouch, sorry. It's a pleasure to meet you all. Tiara Squad, eh?"

"With Kenzie as our leader," said the woman named British. It was the only name he remembered because of its distinctness.

Kenzie looped her arm around British's shoulder and bumped her hip. "Oh, be quiet."

"Brit," began one of the two blonde girls, "don't get Kenzie upset. I can't do squats in these Spanx."

"So Ramon," said the other blonde woman, "how do you know our captain?"

"Captain?" Ramon asked, raising a curious brow toward his date. "I knew you were a cheerleader, but captain?"

"You couldn't tell by her bossiness?" This time the bride, Felicia Ward-Crawford, came over to hug the ladies. Kenzie and her friends all fawned over her with another round of screams.

Felicia smiled in approval at Ramon. "And who is this plus-one your Auntie Bren was telling me about back at the church?"

Kenzie made another set of introductions to the bride and her groom, Gary Crawford, who now walked over to the group.

"Kenzie came through for me last summer when she coordinated a pageant that was held at my hotel," Ramon said. He glanced over and winked at Kenzie.

"Magnolia Palace?" British leaned forward.

"You own Magnolia Palace?" a slender brunette asked with eyes wide in disbelief.

"You had Kenzie Swayne working at Magnolia Palace?" asked the blonde.

"And you're still alive?" British rested her arm on Kenzie's shoulder.

"Y'all leave him alone." Kenzie laughed, pushing British's hand off her shoulder.

Ramon took a step backward and watched Kenzie in her element. Last summer she coordinated the whole pageant at Magnolia Palace. After standing her up for the party after the pageant, Ramon hadn't seen a lot of Kenzie—at least not in her element. Last weekend Ramon had felt her tension from being around her family. Right now Kenzie's smile was genuine and happy. Another lady came over to the group and whispered in the bride's and groom's ears.

"Y'all, we all have to get upstairs," announced Felicia. "Kenzie, I insist you walk in with us. It just wouldn't be the same."

As if looking to him for permission, Kenzie cocked her brow at Ramon. He nodded his head and watched the members of the Tiara Squad squeeze themselves into one of the elevators. Through the glass he could see her full lips spread into a genuine smile, which caused Ramon's heart to twinge. *Hmph*, he thought to himself, *that was an odd feeling.* Ramon didn't think he was the type of person with a closed, cold heart. But he also didn't think he'd be the type of person whose heart skipped at the sight of a smile.

"You might as well come upstairs and get a drink with me."

Ramon looked to his left and came eye to eye with Alexander Ward. Ramon thought he'd recognized him as one of the groomsmen at the altar and now extended his hand for a shake. "Mr. City Manager."

The second set of elevators opened up and the two men entered. "You say it as if I have some authority." Alexander chuckled and pressed the button to the top floor. "Right this way."

Alexander nodded and pointed toward the bar in the back of the restaurant in front of the floor to ceiling windows. A pretty bartender entertained the best men with bottle tosses.

Women stopped the city official along the way and, judging from how they reached out for a hug or an air kiss, Ramon pegged him a player. But still Ramon followed. He needed a drink. He needed something to take his mind off how devastatingly gorgeous Kenzie was in her dress and how he almost hadn't let her put it on this evening.

"What are you having?" Alexander asked.

"Any Torres Rum?"

Alexander's face broke out in a grin. "Of course. We have nothing but the best for my twin sister."

"Twins?" Ramon repeated.

Alexander lifted his finger to catch the bartender and gave the man their order. "So how's the research on the building going?"

Ramon looked across the room where he left Kenzie. "It's going fine. I learned from Kenzie's memos that brick lasts one hundred years and that it's overdue for a makeover, which is not something a new buyer wants to deal with."

"We have a great construction company in town," said Alexander, "and we've also partnered up with the surrounding cities at Four Points. Good pricing, too."

"I'm okay with paying," Ramon said, twisting his lips together in thought. "I want to make sure this is understood for anyone else interested. Maybe warn them off."

"You don't think I'd cut Erin Hairston the same deal?" Alexander asked.

Ramon took a swig of his drink and studied the man over the rim of his glass. Did the man think he'd put pressure on Ramon to make a quick sale? Or was Alexander working an angle to get benefits with the contractors? He figured he'd get with Nate, a licensed carpenter, at some point to get an estimate. There was something to be said about buying locally but Ramon trusted family.

"So I thought I saw you come down to City Hall this week."

"You did." The bartender set two glasses in front of them. Both reached for one to take.

"I hope you were able to find what you needed."

The way his drinking partner said it, Ramon wondered if he meant more. Ramon followed the man's stare across the room to the exact spot where Kenzie and her friends were. He wondered which one he was interested in.

"I found what I wanted," said Ramon.

He was up there dropping off some of the ballots he'd scooped up from the basement. In the ruckus of being rescued a week ago, Ramon had left the other items from the closet. At City Hall Ramon found a specialist who'd said it would take a couple of weeks to figure out the slips' dates and coordinate them with what was going on in town at the time. He hated to admit Kenzie's enthusiasm infected him. He hoped the analysis of results on the age of the paper came in before the sesquicentennial. His parents, Ana and Julio Torres, planned on coming and Ramon wanted more than anything to prove to his parents he could make a life outside of Villa San Juan without the help of his family connections. He wanted to show them he contributed and belonged in Southwood, just as his ancestors did in VSJ. Buying Magnolia Palace was just a start.

"It's good to see Kenzie out and about," Alexander said all of a sudden.

Though the statement was out of the blue, Ramon squelched his curiosity by taking another swig. Like Villa San Juan, everyone in Southwood grew up with each other and many were probably related. Ramon recalled some of the names from his history lesson of Southwood. Four major families helped pull the city together, the Swaynes, Hairstons, Pendergrasses and Wards. Ramon drained his drink and nodded, realizing these two must have gone way back.

"Better seeing her with you than with that other dude she drags to all her functions," Alexander went on. "It's just interesting to see her taste in men since we broke up."

Ramon controlled himself to stop from turning and punching this jerk in the face. Was he seriously going to either sell him some property or throw away the deal? Clearly the man was insecure. Given the beauty on the dance floor, Ramon thought, casting a glance at Kenzie, he understood. He wondered how the two of them worked around each other. No wonder Kenzie was in a perpetual bad mood whenever Alexander came around. This was also the second time this murderer Kenzie dated had been mentioned. He wasn't sure what bothered him more, the fact she dated a killer or the fact she dated other people at all. A woman like Kenzie wouldn't wait around for a man like him to come around and make up his mind.

Ramon leaned his back against the edge of the bar. Even though this was Felicia's wedding reception, Kenzie stood in the center of the dance floor in a circle with the bridesmaids, her friends and the bride, laughing and having a good time. Ramon liked the way her head tilted backward. She wore her hair down and kept the long ringlets tamed. Each defined curl sparkled under the strobe lights. Kenzie swayed and shimmied her hips. Her shoulders twisted and bumped against her friend standing next to her as they belted out the lyrics to the song playing. Ramon wanted more than anything to be a part of Kenzie's life right now. The trendy pop song the ladies danced to blended into a Latin trumpet beat.

"Oh, how I love this song."

Ramon glanced down beside him at a feminine form. Auntie Bren, decked out in a royal purple gown and a set of jewels wrapped around her neck to complete the regal look, set her glass of champagne down on the bar top.

"Would you care to dance?" Alexander asked.

The sweet smile Ramon knew Auntie Bren to normally sport faded. "Not with you."

Alexander smiled awkwardly. "She's playing hard to get," he explained to Ramon.

"Not with him," said Auntie Bren. "Ramon, grant an old lady a wish and take her out on the dance floor."

"You have to point me in the direction of an old lady," Ramon teased and took hold of Auntie Bren's hand to lead her to the dance floor.

"Thank you for saving me back there," Auntie Bren said, settling her arms on his shoulders.

Two ladies in one week, Ramon thought to himself. He wasn't surprised his dance partner kept up the tempo so when he felt the time was right to dip her, he did. He just didn't expect Kenzie to almost bump heads with her great-aunt when the elderly man she was dancing with dipped her.

Auntie Bren gripped Ramon's biceps to pull herself up and clung to his shoulders. "Oh dear, there's Oscar Blakemore."

Ramon followed Auntie Bren's glare. "Boyfriend?"

"Hush," she hissed, swatting Ramon's chest. "He wishes."

The Blakemore man stared at them through the crowd toward them. Even though he walked with a cane, Mr. Blakemore didn't let that stop him from barreling onto the dance floor, shouldering people along his way. The song ended. Just as Ramon reached for Auntie Bren's fingertips to apply a thankful kiss, a heavy hand slammed against the side of his shoulder. Ramon knew exactly what to expect—a showdown for Auntie Bren's honor. Shoulders squared, Ramon prepared for battle. The old man's pinched lips sneered, then it was blurred. Kenzie's beautiful face came into focus.

"There you are," Kenzie cooed. "Auntie Bren, you don't mind if I steal my date away now, do you?"

Immediately Auntie Bren nodded her head. Her eyes were focused on the challenger. "Not at all."

"This will allow me the opportunity to keep you company on the dance floor," Mr. Blakemore said, extending his elbow.

Beside him, Kenzie pushed Ramon's arm.

"What?"

"Mr. Blakemore is a decorated veteran and a former boxer."

"Okay?" Ramon asked slowly and then a story clicked in his head. "So that's Auntie Bren's two-timing boyfriend from back in the day?"

"Stop calling her that," Kenzie huffed. "He also could have knocked you out with one punch or with his cane."

Ramon wrapped his arms around Kenzie's waist and drew her against his body. "First you're worried about my hotel competition and now my health. This is the best date ever."

"I never agreed it was a date."

Ramon dipped his head and lowered his mouth to hers for a kiss that tasted of champagne. The Tiara Squad made a bunch of ohhing and ahhing noises. "Too late—you already claimed me to Auntie Bren."

"Stop calling..." Kenzie bit her bottom lip and shook her head. She rose up on her heels and pulled him down to her. "Aw, hell, never mind."

Chapter 7

Kenzie hated to be embarrassed, but kissing Ramon on the dance floor should have been at the top of her charts for embarrassing moments, but it wasn't. Maybe because her friends, including the bride, cheered her on for finally succumbing to his charms. The DJ in the corner played a slow song; Kenzie didn't know which. She barely heard the beat over her own heart thumping in her chest. The crystal ball flickered light across Ramon's face. He smiled down at her.

"I'm digging this PDA," he teased. "What's wrong with it?"

The rhythm of the song set in as Kenzie pressed her forehead against the center of Ramon's ribs. Her stilettos helped balance the height difference between them. "I don't like the spotlight on me."

"Says the beauty queen." Ramon laughed, moving his hand from around her waist to tilt her chin toward him.

"Pageants are different." Kenzie rolled her eyes. "I am proud of my tiara."

Ramon shook his head and blew out a sigh. "What am I? Chopped liver?"

"I mean, I'm proud of holding my title as the last Swayne or Hairston—don't get me wrong," she boasted. "But that's as much of my business as I want to let people in on."

"People in town know about the guy you were dating?"

"Clearly you want to know about my dating history."

"You don't have to tell me," said Ramon, stiffening.

"I'll tell you this one time." Kenzie moved her hands to grip Ramon's biceps. She tried not to pay attention to how solid he felt and how weak her grip was. "Rafe is an old friend of mine. His wife died a few years ago and he was under heavy suspicion."

"Define 'heavy'?"

"While he was away serving our country, she was having several affairs. Rafe came back and found out but according to him he didn't even care."

Ramon snorted. "Didn't care?"

"No," Kenzie said with a shrug. "He'd been in love with another woman for a long time, so I guess his feelings weren't too hurt and he wanted a divorce. So anyway, Fourth of July night, Rafe came home to a bloody scene and no body. He was questioned."

"Did he have an alibi?"

"He told me he did," she answered, recalling the story Rafe had told her. Rafe didn't want to give up his alibi because of the person he was with wasn't fully divorced either. He protected the woman he loved. What had made Kenzie's relationship perfect with Rafe was that his heart belonged to another woman. At least now that lady had come to her senses. And Kenzie was happy for her friend.

Though the music continued, Ramon stopped dancing. "And you're going to tell me you believe him."

Something about the tone in his voice irked Kenzie. It seemed like he didn't believe her or was mocking her.

Kenzie took a step backward. She had shared a personal story about her dearest friend and he was mocking her. A piece of Kenzie's heart ached. "Yes I believe him. Rafe at least comes through for my events."

"And there are so many events," Ramon said, exasperated. "You dragged me to at least a half dozen of them."

The corners of Kenzie's eyes twitched. She blinked in disbelief. Did he seriously just make fun of her? "What?"

"I'm just saying you're standing here gushing about some other guy for taking you to all these things, yet he's not here," said Ramon. "If he were such a standup kind of guy, why isn't he here now holding you? I miss one of your many parties that you planned and I'm exiled to hell and this guy stands you up for your month of stress and you place him on some sort of pedestal."

Kenzie took a step away from Ramon's embrace. "You know what." Kenzie's voice rose with anger. A couple dancing nearby stopped and looked at them. "Never mind," she said, lowering her voice. "I knew there was a reason I never trust you with anything."

"What? Wait, what's happening here?"

"Bye, Ramon."

Kenzie stormed past Ramon, bumping his shoulder in the process. Walking away was the best thing to do right now. She'd been a fool to think he'd changed. Kenzie rushed over to her table and grabbed her blue clutch and stormed out through the doors toward the elevator. She jammed her finger from pressing the button so hard.

"Running away from another man?"

Without having to turn around, Kenzie rolled her eyes at the sound of Alexander's voice. The ice in his beverage clanked against the glass. "Go away, Alexander."

"I can't go anywhere right now," said Alexander. "I'm too infatuated with you. You're gorgeous in that dress."

His speech sounded a bit slurred but it was no concern of Kenzie's. She pressed the already lit button to the elevator again and tucked her purse under her arm. Alexander approached. Rum seeped through his pores. She sighed in annoyance.

"Did you ever stop to think that this could be our wedding?" Alexander went on.

As if choking, Kenzie began to cough. Alexander stepped closer. "What do you say we get ourselves a room and pretend we're on our honeymoon? For old time's sake?"

The heat of his breath sent a twitch of fear down her spine. Alexander wasn't a vicious man but he was lecherous when drunk. Before she had a chance to say another word, Alexander made a yelp-like noise. The elevator arrived with a ding and she didn't bother turning around to give her ex a second thought. She needed to focus on the ride down. Damn Brutti Hotel, Kenzie thought. She rolled her eyes and slowly turned around just in time to watch Ramon give Alexander an odd side hug. Alexander's eyes widened as his cheek began to swell. Kenzie's darted her glare between Ramon and Alexander.

"Thanks for the directions, buddy," Ramon said, all chipper.

Kenzie's eyes scanned the odd way Ramon held his left fist. He kept opening and closing his fingers together.

"Going down?" Ramon asked. The doors sealed closed but didn't keep out Alexander's vulgar goodbye.

"Following me?" Kenzie asked, leveling her eyes with Ramon's. She willed her libido to settle down. Memories of their little afternoon excursion flooded her mind. Her heart raced with the memory of his touch. Damn him.

"Considering you're my date this evening…" he began and pressed the PL button for the plaza level.

Knees locked, Kenzie frowned. "We can cut the charade between us."

"I don't think so." Ramon turned his back to her for a moment and screwed around with one of the buttons. The hydraulics in the small compartment bounced to a stop. Kenzie accidently dropped her purse. "You have the nerve to walk away from me after you stood there gushing over some other man while we're on a date."

"I wasn't…" Kenzie tried to justify herself. "I tried to tell you…"

"About how great some other dude is?"

Judging from his flattened lips, Ramon recalled what she'd said. "I didn't."

"You think it was easy standing there and listening to you go on about Mr. Perfect?"

Bubbling laughter stirred in her sternum. "You're jealous?"

"Nah. I just don't appreciate it." Ramon folded his arms across his broad chest.

The male ego, Kenzie mused. Men didn't want what they had until someone else started playing with it. What made Ramon any different than Alexander? Alexander busied himself with other women back in college. Ten years had gone by and he never gave Kenzie a second thought. Now all of a sudden there was a spark on the dance floor with Ramon and he had something to say? Ramon hadn't given Kenzie so much thought in almost a year and the moment she talked about another guy he became jealous.

"What happened to your hand?" Kenzie asked, noticing his red knuckles.

"Alexander fell."

"On your fist?"

Ramon shrugged. "He was advancing toward you as you were getting on a small, confined elevator."

The reminder of where she was caused Kenzie to gulp. "Alexander is a bad drunk, but he's harmless. Can you start the elevator back up, please?"

"And you know this about Alexander because he's your ex?" Ramon asked without budging.

"Yeah, like when we were in high school. What does it matter?"

"It doesn't," said Ramon.

"Ramon, please start the elevator back up." Impatient, Kenzie stepped closer to him and tried to push the button. She had no idea which one he used to stop the elevator so she pressed them all. The compartment lowered a foot and bounced back up, then not only stopped but the lights also went out. The jolt sent Kenzie into Ramon's arms. "What just happened?"

"You broke the elevator," Ramon teased. "I'm kidding—there must be a short or something. Hang on."

He tried to let her go to turn to the panel but Kenzie clung to him. "Found the phone. Hello? Hello?"

With her hand still on his shoulders, Kenzie felt his lungs sink with a sigh. "What's wrong?"

"I can't get a person to pick up the phone."

"Are you serious?" Kenzie shrieked. "This stupid hotel and its cheap elevator."

"In the hotel's defense, you were pressing a lot of buttons, Kenzie."

Kenzie wanted to dig deep for the anger from earlier. Nothing came. She tried to find something else to be mad at. Better mad than what threatened. "Are you blaming me?" Kenzie inhaled and squared her shoulders.

"Relax," Ramon said, reaching for her. "Someone will come looking for us soon."

"Not likely," Kenzie huffed. "They were getting ready to serve dinner. Free bar and delicious food—no one is going to leave the reception hall any time soon."

"So that's good news for us."

Good for who? she thought. There was nothing Kenzie could do. If she peered against the glass she would succumb to her fear of falling, given how far up they were from the ground. Thanks to the hotel being built in a wooded area, the tops of the trees blocked her view from below. If she stood closer to Ramon, she'd give in to her fear of making love to him right here and now.

"Ever notice every other time we ride the elevator we get stuck?" Ramon teased in the darkness.

The starlit skyline filled the glass compartment. Kenzie wasn't sure which was worse—facing death if the elevator fell or facing Ramon. She took a chance on the latter and was greeted by a smirk across his face. "I am glad you can find the humor in this."

"Humor or opportunity?" he asked, feeling for her hand. The pad of his index finger stroked across the vein in her wrist.

Kenzie's pulse quickened with the touch. She wondered if he felt it, too. "Ramon, I don't think..."

"For once in your life, don't think," Ramon ordered her before reaching for the back of her neck with his large, warm hands. He cupped her neck with his fingers. His thumbs outlined her lips before his mouth came down to claim hers. For the second time this evening Kenzie's heart melted. Knees caving, she leaned into him. With one swoop Ramon lifted her by the bottom and wrapped her legs around his waist. With her back against the glass of the elevator the hem of her skirt rolled up her thighs. Neither of them broke their kiss. Kenzie fumbled with his belt buckle, which prevented her from touching him. She slid the leather from the loops and let it hit the floor with a clank. Nervously her fingers played with the button and zipper of his pants. She peeled away the material until she found what she was looking for.

The hard erection sprang to life in her hands. Kenzie groaned while she caressed the full length of him. A shiver of anticipation crept down her spine. Ramon tugged at the stitches of her panties until they ripped. He broke the kiss for a moment.

"I'll buy you a new pair," he growled, tucking the material into the inside pocket of his jacket. His hands pressed between her legs and fit her body onto him.

They both sucked in a deep breath at their connection. Kenzie wrapped her legs tighter around his waist. Ramon cupped her from under her arms and over her shoulder. He pulled her down onto him as his hips bucked forward.

Kenzie, filled with Ramon inside of her, wrapped her legs tighter. She arched her back and used the glass to help her sink deeper onto him. She gasped when Ramon tugged down her bodice and freed her breasts. Liquid desire coursed through her veins with the heat of his tongue across her nipples. Kenzie cried in ecstasy. Ramon pumped into her, fusing their bodies together. His fingers hung on to her shoulders. Her nails sunk into the fabric of his shirt.

"Ramon," she cried.

"Kenzie," he replied against her ear. His velvety voice against her lobe coaxed every ounce of orgasm out of her. She squeezed her legs around his waist, climbing him, grinding him until waves of pleasure poured from their bodies.

"Oh my God," Kenzie groaned into Ramon's neck. "I can't believe we did this."

Ramon planted a kiss on her forehead. His hands

roamed her thighs as he eased her back to her feet. "Believe it. And this isn't going to be the last time, either."

"We aren't getting back together," Kenzie announced. She found her shoes and slipped them back on, giving her a little bit more height next to Ramon.

A deep laughter filled the space between them. "See, there's your mistake." Ramon cupped Kenzie's face. "You keep looking at us as a couple last summer."

"I forgot, I was just a fling for you," Kenzie blurted out.

"Not a fling," clarified Ramon. "We were just getting to know each other."

"And what have you learned about me?" Kenzie asked.

The pads of his thumbs traced circles around her cheekbones. "I know you love your city. You love your family, and I know you hate being embarrassed."

Kenzie pulled her head away from his touch. "Do you know why I hate being embarrassed?"

"Because you're a perfectionist?"

Scoffing, Kenzie gripped the railing behind her. "I was engaged."

"Okay?" He tucked his shirt into his pants.

"To Alexander." Kenzie waited for another slow *okay* from Ramon as he fumbled with his belt. She expected to hear the jingle of the buckle. When he didn't respond at all she continued. "We were just out of high school and starting college. I thought I knew him but clearly everyone else did, too—both in town and on campus. When I joined him at school I was humiliated when everyone in my dorm had already been with him and when I came home mortified, everyone who tried to comfort me knew all about his ways."

Finally Ramon cleared his throat. He reached for her, draping his heavy arm over her shoulder. His fingers splayed against the nape of her neck. "You don't like being the butt of a joke but you don't mind being the center of attention." The last part came out with a chuckle.

"Shut up." Kenzie laughed.

"Kenzie," he said, reaching for her hands to bring to his lips. "I would never knowingly do something to embarrass you again."

A grinding noise sounded as Kenzie tried to gather her thoughts. The lights flickered a few times before deciding to stay on and the elevator began its descent down to the plaza floor.

"Here we go," Ramon said with a wink.

Kenzie pressed her hands to her face and pinched her cheeks. She must look a mess right about now. The reflection on the doors showed her hair was wild, but that was nothing new. The once-defined curls had their own sense of direction. The flowers of her bodice were crushed and her dress was wrinkled. When the elevator's doors slid open and a gush of air swept through, Kenzie was reminded of the absence of her panties. As if reading her mind Ramon patted the breast pocket of his jacket and cleared his throat.

Three men in maroon jackets met the two of them at the door. Apologies spilled from their mouths.

"Yes, we are extremely sorry for the inconvenience." A man, close to six five, dressed in a dark suit and with a turquoise carnation in his lapel, stepped forward. His black hair was cut short and parted on the side. He belonged on the cover of a magazine, not as a bellboy at a hotel, Kenzie thought. "Ramon?"

"Gianni?"

"Brutti?" Kenzie repeated and then snorted in disgust. Because of the location of the hotel, no one ever consulted with her about building it. Had Kenzie met Gianni Brutti in person, well, she still would have hated the idea of such an eyesore sticking out of the forest in Four Points Park, but she might not have hated looking at the man. Talk about eye candy.

"Ramon, you beautiful bastard," Gianni said in a booming voice. The men hugged and shook hands in that male bonding ritual Kenzie had seen football players do. "Had I known the competition was in my hotel spying, I might have let you stay in there longer."

"Man, what are you talking about? You aren't any competition." Ramon laughed, took a step back and wrapped his arm around Kenzie's waist. "Gianni, I'd like you to meet Kenzie Swayne. Kenzie, this is an old family friend, Gianni Brutti."

Gianni extended his hand and Kenzie, remembering her manners, returned the shake. "Pleased to meet you."

"Kenzie Swayne," Gianni repeated her name. "As in *the* Kenzie Swayne, of the Swaynes of Southwood."

"The one and only." Ramon beamed.

"Your beauty surpasses the photographs, Miss Southwood."

Kenzie rolled her eyes. "What?"

"I have a wedding reception going on upstairs. The bride insisted on having photographs posted upstairs," answered Gianni. "Didn't you two see them?"

"We were kind of busy," said Ramon.

Gianni leaned forward and shook Ramon's hand again. Kenzie watched the way Ramon's cheeks rose in a silent laugh at whatever the man said to him. "Thanks, man," Ramon replied. "Well, we'll see you around."

"Most definitely," said Gianni. "Your mother told me she's made reservations here for the sesquicentennial in Southwood next week."

"Funny. See you later." Ramon escorted Kenzie outside to where he parked his car.

"What was that all about?"

Ramon cast a glance toward the hotel. "What? My folks? I'm sure he was joking. I've had reservations held for my family for weeks now."

"What did he whisper to you?" Kenzie asked.

"Oh, that? Well, let's just say I have already started keeping my promise to you." Ramon opened the passenger door and allowed Kenzie the chance to sit first. She climbed in but kept staring, waiting for his answer. "Let's just say the lights were off but the cameras were still rolling. Gianni is going to erase everything for us."

It hadn't been Ramon's intent, but he woke Kenzie up the next morning by accidently kicking open the door to her bedroom. Last night, instead of walking Kenzie to her apartment door, he'd stayed, continuing what they did in the elevator. And he was glad he had, too, except for the fact he had no clothes other than his dress slacks to change into. In his defense, carrying a breakfast tray filled with a wineglass of orange juice, a bottle of water, two egg-white omelets, toast and two bowls of fresh peaches was a struggle. He made a mental note to give the staff at Magnolia Palace a raise for making it look so easy.

Upon the clumsy entrance, Kenzie sat up in the bed. One side of her hair fell across the left side of her shoulder, covering her bare breast. She brought the pink comforter to her neck in an attempt to be modest.

"Nah," Ramon said shaking his head. He set the make-shift tray on the edge of her bed and reached for the covers to expose her luscious body. "Too late to be bashful now."

Kenzie gave him a lazy smile. "Yet you're so formal in your pants."

"Good thing you didn't have any bacon. I would have been forced to make it."

"No one would force you," Kenzie said with a laugh. She scooted over to make room at the head of the bed. She tucked her long, slender legs to sit crisscross applesauce style, as Philly used to say.

"Oh yes, if bacon is in a refrigerator, it belongs in a frying pan—it's a law," said Ramon, trying to recall the last time he ever brought food or cooked breakfast for a woman in her home. He wondered what made her so special but when she cocked a brow at him, not believing his theory, he realized why. She didn't fall for his BS. "I'm a man—we are drawn to bacon."

"Maybe that's what my brother was doing in my fridge last week." Kenzie pondered, her finger on her chin. "Since he and Bailey moved back to town, he seems to do a lot of shopping from my kitchen."

"Your brother Richard?" Ramon asked, trying to recall meeting him at Corie's wedding last week.

"He has yet to learn that a woman is impressed by a man who cooks," Kenzie mused over the tray. "I'm impressed. Did you once tell me you have brothers?"

"Three of them," Ramon boasted.

Kenzie's pink lips parted for a whistle. "No sisters?"

"No, but we have cousins."

"Your poor mom."

"You mean poor me." Ramon laughed. "Being the youngest of four boys, six if you include how close me, Stephen and Nate are, I got beat up a lot."

"Aw, poor thing." Sincerity was lacking in her voice but because she was naked and eating his food, Ramon was not going to complain.

"That's all right." Ramon snagged the slice of peach off her fork. "My mama took care of me and fed me."

"Fed you what?"

"What *didn't* she feed me." Ramon chuckled. "I didn't always have this physique."

Kenzie took a peach off his plate. The ripe skin matched her nipples. Ramon stirred on his side of the bed.

"So you were a mama's boy?"

Holding his left hand in the air with his right over his heart, Ramon gave his oath. "I cannot tell a lie. It was pretty bad."

For the first time ever, Ramon confessed what it was like for him growing up. He spoke while keeping his focus on the sheets until Kenzie touched his kneecap. When he glanced up, their eyes met. He'd seen her with the kids at the wedding last night. She'd make a wonderful mother. If they ever had a child together, Ramon imagined Kenzie nurturing him and if their boy got teased, he wouldn't march his son back outside like his father did. "And yet you decided to leave the comfort of your mama's side to start anew here in Southwood."

Ramon reached out and ran his hand along her smooth thigh. "What a great decision that was, huh?"

"The jury is still out," Kenzie said with a roll of her eyes.

In a smooth swoop, Ramon pushed the tray farther to the edge of the bed with his legs and with his hands, lifted Kenzie onto his lap. Kenzie pressed her palms against his chest. He wondered if she felt the way his heart beat faster at the mere touch of her skin. "You can't possibly be thinking about going another round," she stated rather than asked.

Ramon's fingers were splayed on her naked hips. "Weren't you the one questioning my stamina last week?" He lifted his hips forward and cursed the restraining fabric of his pants. Ramon cocked his head to the side and kissed her lips. She tasted like peaches. Truth be told, he could go several rounds with Kenzie. He pushed her hair back and kissed her freckled shoulder.

"The food is getting cold," Kenzie moaned. The vibrations of her vocal chords tickled his lips.

"Fine," he said with a sigh, "I don't want you passing out on me when I ravish you later."

"Later?" Kenzie wedged her bottom between his opening thighs, resting her legs on top of his. He was drowning in unchartered infatuation. He had never felt this way with a woman before. He couldn't get enough of her. And the fact she looked at him like she felt the same way he felt drove him over the edge. Desire overcame him when she leaned backward, baring her breasts to him as she reached backward to drag the tray closer to the two of them. He willed himself to behave.

Oblivious, Kenzie continued what she was saying. "I have to meet up with Bailey down at Grits and Glam Gowns."

"Ah, you're going to see my family, Lexi?"

"Speaking of family," Kenzie began, pulling the crust off the buttered toast. Ramon watched with amusement, still waiting for her to finish her statement, while she meticulously pinched off any sign of crust. A red tint splashed across her face when she looked up and found him looking at her. "Crust makes your hair curly."

"I'm pretty sure that isn't true."

Kenzie tugged a few strands of her hair. "Want to make a bet?"

"No." Ramon chuckled.

"Back to your family," she said, poking her tongue out. "I am putting the seating charts together. Are you aware you have a table of twelve at the gala?"

"Yeah," he began with a tsk. "We're keeping it small.

Stephen and Nate's mom is coming to town for the afternoon festivities but she is going to babysit Philly."

The mention of his niece brought a smile to Kenzie's face. Since he assumed she wanted to be married, Ramon wondered where Kenzie stood on having children. He wondered why any of that mattered. Pushing the thought out of his mind, Ramon grabbed the discarded crusts and shoved them into his mouth. Crust spilled out when he tried to give her a toothy smile.

"Ew." She frowned. She lifted her hands to shake his hair out of the knot he put on the top of his head. "Now you're going to have curly hair."

"I don't care." Thanks to the bread in his mouth, his answer came out muffled.

"Now, what would your mother say?"

Chewing, Ramon grabbed the water bottle to wash it down. "I don't know. Let's call her." Ramon leaned back against the headboard and grabbed his phone from his pocket.

"Stop." Kenzie busted out laughing.

"I don't mind," Ramon said.

"I mind," she gasped. "What would your mother think of me if you called her at this hour?"

Ramon set his phone on the night stand. "Well, let's see…how am I going to introduce you?"

"Kenzie Swayne, Southwood historian."

"Okay, Kenzie Swayne, Southwood historian." Ramon mocked her and grinned when she poked her tongue out at him. One more time and he was going to capture it with his mouth. "We can tell my mother the same story we're telling Auntie Bren."

"Stop calling her…"

Ramon shoved a piece of fruit into Kenzie's mouth before she could finish. "Auntie Bren and I have bonded.

Before you took advantage of me last night I was playing the perfect wingman for her."

"I'm sure," Kenzie said after chewing for a moment, "she truly appreciates you helping her."

"I would do anything for her—that's my buddy." He meant it with all sincerity. Even though Ramon had left his large family, it was comforting being around a surrogate one like Kenzie's.

"So anyway," she huffed, "how do you plan on introducing me to your mother?"

"I like that you're eager to meet the family, Kenzie."

"Considering my family is convinced we're in some sort of relationship, I think it's only fair."

"'Some sort of'?" he repeated, feeling let down that this was not a permanent situation between them.

"Well, you know, this thing between us," Kenzie began, wagging her fingers between the two of them.

Ramon sat up and away from the headboard. "You mean my proposal, the one you refuse to give me an answer to?"

"Yet we've already been to two different events and lunch a few times last week."

Ramon shook his head. "Lunch was a work thing. And one of those meals we shared with your cousin Erin." Judging from her frown, Ramon confirmed Kenzie did not care for her family member. "What is the deal between you two?"

Her light shoulder shrug made the juice in the glass slosh. "It's silly, now that I think about it."

"Tell me."

"Erin and I are the same age and it seemed like we were always competing for everything growing up, including Auntie Bren's affection. Auntie Bren never cared for beauty pageants, which of course are in my blood."

"Miss Southwood." Ramon bowed his head.

"Please." Kenzie rolled her eyes. "Erin always said pageants were degrading for women."

"You don't agree?"

"Of course not. Pageants are not just a way of life in the South—they're such a confidence builder."

Ramon felt his eyes widen. "How so? There's only one winner and it's based on beauty."

The bottom portion of her succulent lip poked out. "You're judged on several things—beauty, talent and speech."

"No, someone has to walk away a loser." Ramon reached for her calf, smoothed his hand down to her foot and lifted it to kiss her big toe. As expected, she tried to pull away, but he kept a firm hold. "Don't," he warned. "Don't pull away because I don't agree."

Crossing her arms, Kenzie shook her head. "Not if you're going to sit here and make fun of me."

"I'm not making fun of you, just trying to understand how pageants build egos."

"You attended one last year."

"No, I came after the crowning," Ramon reminded her and then stopped himself. After the crowning, there had been that party that he didn't escort her to, which had landed him in months of torture from Kenzie. He never wanted to go down that road again. "Sorry," he said.

Knowing where the conversation was going, Kenzie offered a soft smile. "You're entitled to your own opinion."

"That means without retaliation?"

"I know nothing of which you speak." Kenzie played coy with him, hiding her laugh behind the glass of juice she picked up.

"I guess my truck getting towed and the salt being replaced with sugar at the food truck thing, and other little antics were just a coincidence?"

"You could look at it that way, or at least look at it like—" she paused and licked her lips "—if I didn't care, I probably wouldn't have felt the need to retaliate."

"Twisted." Ramon wiggled his eyebrows.

"Twisted is my flesh and blood rooting for my opponent."

"Your opponent being the woman whose wedding we attended yesterday evening?"

Kenzie nodded. "Felicia and I are friends. We will always be friends, but knowing Erin campaigned against me…" She shook her head. A curl fell over her shoulder. "That was betrayal."

"How could she campaign against you? Aren't there judges?"

"There used to be," Kenzie explained, "but in order to get people to come out to the pageant, you have to get supporters. Erin backed Felicia, even put money in toward her getting a gown and everything. But I still won," she boasted with a proud smile.

"Okay, I get it," he lied.

Eyes narrowing on him, Kenzie shook her head. "Do you really now?"

"No," he admitted. "I just like the way you smile when you talk about winning."

Once again Kenzie poked her tongue out at him. This time he pushed everything aside and kept the promise he made to himself, taking her once more.

Chapter 8

Instead of meeting up with Bailey and Lexi for a fitting the previous afternoon, Kenzie stayed in her apartment making love to Ramon all day long. All her life she'd prided herself on keeping her word and always being there for people. She woke up this morning kissing him good-bye so he could tend to the hotel as well as talk to some construction teams. If he planned on buying the old post office, it was going to need some work done to it.

When she strolled through the studio side of Grits and Glam Gowns, Kenzie expected to find Bailey highly disappointed in her. Kenzie was faced with four sets of inquiring eyes: Lexi's, Maggie's, Bailey's and Andrew Mason's. Andrew helped run and manage the dozens of toddlers who came to the studio for pageant lessons. At one point Lexi was the coach but with two small children and another on the way things were getting hectic.

Kenzie wrapped her arm around her niece's neck and hugged her. She smelled like Love's Baby Soft perfume and bubble gum. In a way, Kenzie wished Bailey would never grow up. Maybe this pageant wasn't a good idea. But pageants at seventeen and eighteen were a rite of passage.

Once Bailey won, Kenzie knew her baby niece would be all grown up. Next month she would be eighteen.

"I'm sorry for missing yesterday," Kenzie said as she tugged on the frayed hole in the knee of Bailey's jeans. Kenzie had realized that women over twenty-five didn't need to wear holey jeans anymore. She smoothed her hands down the backside of her loose-fitting black skirt and pulled down the hem of her black Grits and Glam Gowns T-shirt with the words Tiara Squad bedazzled in pink and white gems on the front.

Bailey sat on the edge of the black stage where numerous tap dancing lessons had been held over the years. After the hug she sat so her elbows were propped on her knees and her chin propped in her hands. Her big brown eyes blinked and her hair was in two long pigtails; guilt couldn't help but wash over Kenzie.

"I can't believe you forgot about me," Bailey said with a sniffle.

"I—I didn't forget," Kenzie exclaimed and glared at Maggie. "I told Aunt…" She stopped her accusation when everyone started laughing.

"Funny." Kenzie half laughed, half sneered at her sister, who wore a pair of denim short-shorts, a flowy cream-colored blouse and four-inch heels. The wide-brimmed hat on top of her head was obnoxious, Kenzie thought and then corrected herself. She loved the hat and planned on taking it from her sister one of these days.

"Sorry." Bailey held her hands up in surrender. "Auntie Maggie made me do it. I'm glad you're getting busy."

The comment threw Kenzie off for a moment. She scrunched up her eyes but Maggie garnered Kenzie's attention. Unashamed for using their niece to goad Kenzie into guilt, Maggie doubled over on the stage. "Your face."

"My finger," Kenzie sneered, flipping her sister off.

"Aren't you supposed to be some sort of socialite with at least an ounce of poise?"

"But first I am your older sister," Maggie said, sliding off the stage, "and tormenting you comes with the job."

Kenzie thought about her conversation with Ramon the other morning in bed and wondered if his brothers had ever teased him the way her sisters had her.

"Right," Kenzie said with a nod. "My much *older* sister."

"Hey, we're not talking about me here—we're talking about you," said Maggie. "What exactly were you doing yesterday?"

Kenzie cast a glance at Bailey. No way in the world she was going to discuss where or what or especially who she was doing in front of her niece. Almost eighteen or not.

"We should be discussing Bailey," Lexi suggested, fanning out her hot-pink shift dress. The material did not hide Lexi's full belly.

"Great idea," Kenzie and Bailey chorused.

Since the studio session was paid for, the group made the best of the situation. The morning ticked by. Kenzie tried to focus on her niece's dancing, but since the girl had every routine thrown at her down pat, rehearsals ended sooner. Chantal, Kenzie's cousin, was supposed to be the dance instructor at Grits and Glam Studios, but had left to live overseas with her husband; Andrew knew most of the routines and taught Bailey what he knew. Kenzie grinned to herself, remembering how she taught Ramon the pageant wave this morning.

"Bailey," Lexi began, "because you're so talented, I really think you can do your own ensemble, just take over the whole show. I was thinking something like 'Singing in the Rain.'"

"Except it hasn't rained in Southwood in weeks," Andrew reminded them. "How delightful are the judges going to find her number when they are sweating to death?"

"Are we doing it in the theater downtown?" Maggie asked. "That A/C has been spotty again."

Kenzie turned to her sister. "And you know this how?"

"I scoped it out in case I wanted to throw a party there."

"Seriously?" Kenzie scoffed.

"What? My friends have been in search of the small-town feel. No one can believe I'm from here."

"Lexi," Kenzie whined, "don't bring your partying friends to Southwood."

"My partying friends like to spend money, Kenzie."

"Can the two of you stop fighting?" Andrew asked, fanning himself with his hand. "We need to concentrate on Bailey."

"Yeah," Bailey chimed in. "Although I'm not sure about the singing and dancing. What if I get winded?"

"You ran track last semester," said Kenzie. "You will be fine."

They went over the number a few times. Kenzie liked it but she wasn't sold. Given the way Lexi sat, looking pained and uncomfortable, she didn't think she wanted to let her mentor know how worried. An hour into rehearsal, Kenzie sat back in the couch, which was shaped like a pair of lips and set against the window. Break couldn't have come at a better time. Bailey went to check her phone. When the clock in the tower downtown struck twelve, Andrew went off to get some food for them before rehearsal started back up again.

Their afternoon would be given to Bailey's vocal coach, Waverly Crowne. Waverly, last year's Miss Southwood, was a shoo-in for the Miss Georgia Pageant but had found out Christmas Eve she'd had a better title to achieve: that of Mrs. Dominic Crowne. They were already married and expecting their first child but they'd been married in a hurry, and the wedding was largely for Waverly's mother's sake. So far, Waverly hasn't discovered her husband's plans for a second, secret wedding. Waverly was still acting as a vocal coach for all the pageants for toddlers and little kids; fortunately this included Bailey. Thank God the Miss Southwood pageant was the Saturday after next.

A surge of electricity coursed through Kenzie at the idea of the month almost being over. She shifted on the cushions of the red couch. Already two events in and she was sleeping with Ramon. *Again*. How weak did that make her? She was a repeat offender or something. Last summer it hadn't taken long for her to sleep with him, either. This time around things felt different. Ramon shared things with her. When he told her about his childhood, she felt his pain.

Lexi waddled toward the couch and Kenzie got up from her corner to help. Maggie leaped from her perch on the couch, as well, also to aid Lexi down to the cushion.

Lexi swatted her hands in the air. "I've got this."

Stepping back, Kenzie bit the corner of her thumbnail. She wondered where Stephen was and didn't recall seeing his car. Stephen owned Southwood's finest real estate agency, located right next door to Grits and Glam Gowns. If Lexi went into labor now, she wasn't sure what to do.

A loud "Oh my God" penetrated the glass wall looking out onto the street. Bailey stood, talking with someone on the other end of her phone via FaceTime.

"For a girl who didn't want to move to Southwood because she didn't have any friends here," Kenzie noted, watching Bailey, "she certainly is a busybody."

Maggie bowed at her hip. "She's just like her Auntie Maggie."

"God help her," Kenzie groaned.

"Don't worry too much," said Lexi, waddling over to them. "She's adjusting fine and making tons of friends."

"Speaking of making friends," Maggie began, knocking her knees against Kenzie's, "we haven't seen you since Felicia's wedding reception."

Heat bubbled under the collar of Kenzie's shirt.

"She doesn't have to answer," Lexi teased. "Just look at the glow on her face."

"My glow," Kenzie repeated. "Lexi, I'm really worried about you. Are you sure you don't want to go home for the day?"

"No, because if Stephen gets wind that I'm sweaty the man is going to put me on bed rest for the rest of this pregnancy. I have another six weeks."

Kenzie doubted her friend was going to make it that long, but she wasn't going to say anything.

"Let's get back to you and Ramon," Maggie persisted.

"Let's not."

"Stephen said you drove out to the hotel last week," said Lexi, entertaining Maggie's choice of topics.

"And I thought I saw the two of you having lunch in the park," added Maggie.

Although it was none of their business, Kenzie explained how she ended up with Ramon's jacket the night of Corie's wedding. "And if you saw me having lunch in the park with Ramon, you must have just missed Erin. She wants to purchase the post office also."

"What?" Lexi and Maggie chorused.

Kenzie shook her head. "I know, shocking, isn't it? She wants to turn it into a clinic."

"They have that sports center in Orlando," commented Maggie. "Why?"

"Erin hates the tranquility of Southwood." Kenzie

snorted. "She couldn't wait to get out of here because she hated how small and quiet things were."

"Ugh," Maggie groaned. "How will her proposal go over with the council?"

The city council planned on meeting this week. Kenzie already knew she wouldn't recommend Erin's proposal—not out of spite but because if she had her clients here, most of whom were professional athletes, it would disrupt the tranquility of Southwood.

As she told the ladies her decision, Maggie cocked her head to the side and moaned. "Now there's a disturbance for you."

Kenzie followed Maggie's line of sight. Her heart thumped when she found Ramon standing behind her with two coffee cups in his hands. He wore a black tank top, ballers and earbuds in his ears. His hair hung loose around his neck. Behind him Bailey held her phone up...no doubt Kenzie expected to find the photo on social media later.

"Are you ogling him?" Kenzie asked. She waved Ramon in and pushed away from the couch to greet him.

"Jealous?" Maggie called out to her.

"Ladies," Ramon boomed, walking through the studio's side doors.

Stephen, dressed similarly to Ramon, came in through the kitchenette area between the studio and the dress shop side. "It's time for a break."

"We're already taking a break, Stephen," Lexi said. "See?" She fanned her hand down the length of her seated body.

Once reaching his wife, Stephen sat on the armrest and dipped his head for a kiss. The kiss lingered longer than anyone wanted to witness. Ramon cleared his throat.

"Uh, isn't that what got your wife in the situation she's in now?" Ramon asked.

"I can't wait for you to fall in love," Stephen retorted.

Another pang clenched Kenzie's heart. The idea of Ramon falling in love with anyone else didn't go over well with her. She cleared her throat to keep her feelings in check. Ramon remembered the coffee cups in his hand.

"Hey, I almost forgot, this is for you." He handed her the beverage. Warmth touched her hands. "Cream and two sugars."

Kenzie smiled but Maggie gaped. "And how exactly do you know how my sister likes her coffee?"

"Café con leche?" Ramon replied. "Who doesn't like their coffee like that?"

The answer didn't set well with Maggie. She narrowed her eyes on them. "I don't believe you, but since you said it with an accent, I'm going to let it go." She waltzed over to the record table and thumbed through the collection. Bailey came in and went over to Maggie.

"Did we interrupt anything?" Ramon asked Kenzie.

"Just taking a break for lunch," said Kenzie. "Bailey's been working hard all morning on her routine."

"And you've been sitting down?" Stephen asked Lexi. "Of course."

Stephen gave his wife's arm a loving stroke. "Good. Cinderella over here is trying to kill me. Her feet get puffy if she stands on her feet too long."

Kenzie glanced up at Ramon, who hid his laugh behind his cup and gave her a wink. "You guys were just playing basketball, right?"

"Yes," Stephen said with a nod, "I'm not sure if he had a chance to tell you but my little cousin here used to be well over on the husky side."

All Ramon had alluded to was that his mother plied him with sweets as a kid. Looking at him now she found it hard to believe he'd had any weight issues. The man was pure muscle.

"We're not talking about me," Ramon reminded his cousin.

"Hey, Kenzie," Maggie called out, "Lexi has the song from your routine when you ran for Miss Southwood."

Kenzie cut her eyes at Lexi, who shrugged innocently. "It's a classic song."

"What song is it?" Stephen and Ramon asked together.

Kenzie continued to stare at Lexi, willing her not to say a word.

"Mambo," Maggie replied. "Or at least it was the mambo scene from *West Side Story.*"

Beside her, Kenzie felt Ramon's blaze of heat. "Seriously? Do you have any video? Please say there's video."

"No." Kenzie shook her head.

"Do you remember your steps, Auntie?" Bailey asked, using her pleading, sad, puppy-dog eyes. "I need all the inspiration I can get."

Maggie headed toward the record player. "You know it's one of those songs with a beat Kenzie can't resist."

"I can resist," said Kenzie, willing her body to stay still. "Besides, my dance partner isn't here."

Bailey's eyes lit up. "Who was your dance partner?"

"Hank DuVernay," Kenzie replied over the beginning of the song, "and there's no way…"

Andrew, carrying two boxes of pizza, set their lunch on the stage. "Anything my ex can do, I can do better." He swiveled his satin scarf from around his neck to the rhythm of the bongo-driven beat of the song. Ramon took the cup of coffee from Kenzie's hand. Lexi, Bailey and Maggie egged Kenzie on with catcalls and whistles.

Something took over Kenzie, just as the spirit of Rita Moreno had taken her over when she competed for Miss

Southwood. By the time the song finished, people waiting for the afternoon music lesson were gathered around the doors of the studios and folks pressed their faces to the window for the show. Breathless, Kenzie beamed and bowed to Andrew for dancing with her. He was better than Hank. As the people gathered on the studio floor, Kenzie glanced around to find Ramon. Just as Maria and Tony had found each other on the dance floor, he made his way to her. Chest heaving, Kenzie looked away, not sure if her interpretation of the Puerto Rican dance queen was accurate or not. Ramon approached with confidence; he took Kenzie by the arms and spun her around, dipping her backward.

"You're wearing this and doing that exact same dance tonight."

With her hair pulled back into a French twist and armed with her seersucker jacket, Kenzie, well-rehearsed in the speech she planned on giving in a few minutes, confidently pushed away from her desk. She wore a pair of seersucker Capri pants and black high-heeled sandals and felt like a million bucks. Then the back of her chair hit the wall, putting her ego in check. The fancy degree she earned didn't give her a corner office and six-figure salary and so far the only historical fact Kenzie discovered going through the old yearbooks was that Southwood High had a winning football team. The nerves kicked in.

Kenzie paused for a moment and sighed to push her fears away. She hated speaking in front of people. Even at beauty pageants, Kenzie always worried about ranking in the top three when the deep questions were asked. To stutter under the bright headlights, answer incorrectly, or misunderstand the question entirely could be detrimental for a beauty queen's career. Swallowing her fears, she took a deep breath.

In ten minutes Kenzie was scheduled to give her point of view and concerns for the three buildings up for sale—one of them being the one Ramon was interested in. Kenzie would be fair if given the chance to speak about which business proposal best suited Southwood history. Erin, still interested in the post office building as well, wanted to build a clinic. While Kenzie thought a clinic would be perfect, the fact that there was a veterinarian's office right around the corner from the building seemed weird to her. Besides, Kenzie doubted Erin wanted to settle down in Southwood. She was just doing this to get under Kenzie's skin.

"I hope I'm not interrupting," said a familiar feminine voice at the door.

Kenzie glanced up and felt her cheeks move as she smiled at the sight of her mother. "Mom!"

Paula Hairston-Swayne always managed to look as if she'd stepped off the pages of a fashion magazine. Her kelly green top matched her eyes. Her red hair defied the humidity and hung straight down her back and over her shoulder, ending in a perfect single curl. "Good. I thought you weren't speaking to me for a while there."

Kenzie moved around her desk, inwardly cursing at the future bruise that would form where her hip hit its sharp corner. Her hip then brushed against the boxes Ramon had sent over, the ones they'd found in the basement a few weeks ago. She wondered if he'd made any leeway with the washed-out ballots they'd found. A rigged election? A teacher's popular test passed down from year to year? Kenzie made a mental note to come back upstairs after the meeting to bring them back to the apartment for the rest of her time off. She'd promised Margaret she'd stay away.

"Why wouldn't I speak to you?"

"You've been so busy with this new man," Paula said. "I've seen the two of you around town looking all cozy. You and your beau have been so into each other, whether it was at Lexi's studio or the park for lunch. I even called your cell and your house line, and both went to voice mail."

Mother and daughter united in a hug. A twinge of guilt struck Kenzie. How could she begin to explain that what had started off as a front was turning into something more? Ending the hug, Paula placed her hand at Kenzie's temple, by her tucked-back hair. "No product, dear?"

"It's June, Mom," Kenzie said drily and prayed her mom dropped this smothering conversation.

Paula pointed to her perfectly coiffed hair. Besides when she was poolside, Kenzie never saw her mother's red hair out of place.

"Tell me you're going to recommend your cousin's clinic."

"Way to get right to the point, Mommy," Kenzie said, folding her arms under her breasts. Why did she feel like a middle-schooler about to be lectured by the principal?

"Sorry, but I know you're going to speak to the council in a few minutes and I just wanted to plead with you."

Kenzie sighed. "Why is it so important for you to have Erin here?"

Jealousy reared its ugly head. Erin was already Auntie Bren's favorite. Kenzie got that Erin was her mother's niece but did Paula always have to put her needs above her daughter's?

"I think it would do Erin some good if she moved back here for a while."

"Starting a clinic is going to take more than a while," Kenzie reminded her mother. "It's a big commitment and I've already told her starting it downtown is not historically sound. Dr. Fredd's office opened in 1870 just outside of downtown because people paid him in livestock."

"Fast-forward a hundred and fifty years later, Kenzie," her mother said while pinching the bridge of her nose, "and people now use money for currency." Paula paused, clamping her red-stained lips together. "What do you have against your cousin?"

"Where do I begin?"

"Kenzie, Erin's sisters are both married now."

While Paula ticked off the reasons why Kenzie needed to lighten up on her cousin, Kenzie half listened. Kenzie didn't bother bringing up the fact she and Erin were the same age. Why did Erin get empathy?

"And with the business taking off," Paula continued, "she's really just going through the motions at work."

"When do the two of you even talk?"

"We talk," said Paula, "Just as you and your Aunt Jody do."

Avoiding her mother's glare, Kenzie sighed and walked toward the window, her mother hot on her heels. She had spoken with Aunt Jody just this morning to confirm she was attending the sesquicentennial.

"I know you two still talk, even though after thirty years, she still won't speak to me because she believes I stole the crown out from under her."

"C'mon. Mom, you know the title meant a lot more to Aunt Jody than it did to you."

Paula folded her arms across her chest. The bow of the green silk blouse she wore crumpled. "I cannot have this conversation with you, Mackenzie."

"Because I'm a Swayne?" Kenzie cocked her head to the side. "I'm still half Hairston."

Paula snorted. "Your biggest claim to fame is being the last Swayne to win the title."

Actually her biggest claim to fame was earning her
PhD, but Kenzie didn't bother clarifying. "Well, Mother,"
Kenzie said in clipped tones, "I need to hurry and go meet
with the committee so I can get home and polish my tiara."

"Be serious."

"I am." The five-o'clock bell went off in the tower.
"Look, I don't have time to sit here and discuss my issues with Erin, but you should know me well enough to
know that I wouldn't hold my history with her against her
in business." When her mother still didn't smile or look
relieved, Kenzie huffed. "Besides, I am not the sole person deciding which business will open. I am just giving
my professional opinion about the makeup and history of
Southwood."

Her lips slightly moving in a frown, Paula glanced over
her daughter. "I suppose."

"Thank you, Mother."

"Can we talk about your hair?"

"It's the middle of June," Kenzie said, stepping toward
the stairwell. She needed to leave. "There is absolutely
no reason for me to put anything in my hair right now."

"There's always a reason, dear," Paula called out to
her daughter as the heavy doors closed and echoed down
the stairs.

The Economic Development Council was made up of
members of the city council and other local representa-
tives, such as the mayor and his friends. Kenzie made an
inner eye roll at having to face a few of these gentlemen.
As town historian, Kenzie's opinion mattered if Southwood wanted to maintain its historic integrity. The mayor
and his pals wanted to generate revenue, which she understood but in order to remain true to Southwood being
a small town and priding itself on that, they did not need

to bring in franchises. Her purpose today was to prove the town could still survive on local business. People drove from all over for the experience.

"The committee will now recognize Mackenzie Swayne, Southwood historian. Dr. Swayne, do you have anything to add concerning the list of buildings up for restoration?"

Pushing away from the mahogany rolling chair, Kenzie approached the wooden podium. The seersucker suit clung to her elbows, restricting movement as she shuffled her papers.

"Thank you, Miss Leena," said Kenzie, trying not to smile at her friend. When not working on the volunteer committee, Miss Leena manned the administrative desk at Southwood High School and often she was the one making the call for substitute teachers. Kenzie always accepted.

"I'd like the records to reflect the buildings up for sale."

Alexander leaned forward and cleared his throat into the silver microphone in front of him. "Let the records show that this will be Miss Swayne's recommendation."

"Dr. Swayne," Miss Leena corrected.

"I stand corrected," Alexander said with a head nod. "We're just trying to make the committee aware that what *Dr.* Swayne recommends is simply that, a recommendation. I have been hired to ensure Southwood's growth by bringing in new businesses, whether or not the buildings housing them are old."

"Historic." Kenzie savored being able to correct Alexander. "The buildings are historic. And our charming history is what brings visitors to our town. If we want to keep our revenue flowing, we need to preserve not just our physical buildings but also monitor what we put in these buildings." Kenzie took a sip of water from the clear glass on the podium. Out of the corner of her eye she spied Ramon in a light blue oxford, one leg crossed over his other and his hair secured back. She cleared her throat and tried to stay focused.

"Of course, with technology today," she continued, "we can't honestly expect to bring old jobs back like the film store, but we can pay homage to the business with a museum shop. We were already given a lot of historic donations last Christmas when we had our parade. We have clothes and paintings and old pictures to put in a museum if one were built."

"There are several buildings," said another councilman. "Which of those do you suggest the museum be placed?"

"I think the old post office would be perfect. There are several floors to fill. Plus it is smack downtown. I understand Mr. Reyes is interested in the building and we've discussed at length the need for such a facility for the community." Kenzie's heart raced with excitement. The council, Alexander not included, all nodded their heads with approval. Out the corner of her eye Kenzie saw Erin shake her head. Even though her mother wasn't in the room, Kenzie knew her mother was here in spirit…just with Erin. The kelly green dress Erin wore screamed of Paula's influence. She pushed their disapproving frowns out of her mind.

"With all due respect to the people wanting to bring in a commercial business, we don't need a private clinic. Southwood, Black Wolf Creek, Peachville and Samaritan have been thriving with the Four Points General. We don't need private practices. Four Points General has united the four cities since the First World War, and as for a sports bar, we have Shenanigans."

"Shenanigans is a place children can visit," interrupted Mayor Anson.

Kenzie took a deep breath and willed herself not to roll

her eyes. She hated the mayor. Not because he'd hired his best friend, Alexander, but because the man was an obsessive creep. Last year he became obsessed with her fellow beauty queen, Waverly Crowne. His obsession had almost cost Waverly into losing her chance to run for Miss Georgia and he thought he'd gotten away with it. Well, not if Kenzie had anything to do with it. This fall she planned on backing his opponent, whomever that might be.

"There are other sports bars around town, Mayor," Kenzie said, reminding the committee. "They're just not downtown in the founding square. Mr. Mayor, I assure you I am not here to exact some form of moral judgment. I simply was asked my opinion as a historian what was needed and if any of these proposals for the structures work with what's in the history books."

"And you're not a fan of a sports bar, which will bring in revenue?" Anson asked.

I'm not a fan of you, she thought. "As I've stated, this is my opinion."

"And there's a bid for a clinic downtown," said another councilman. The man was elderly and placed his thick black-rimmed glasses on his face. "Or is it a rehab?"

Erin tiptoed to the microphone on her side of the room. "A rehab center, Mr. Silas."

"And you are?"

"Erin," Erin replied with her hands clasped behind her back. "Erin Hairston."

"And you, Miss Historian, do you think a clinic fits the historic entity of Southwood?"

Those on the panel, aware of Erin and Kenzie's relations, leaned forward. Erin stood by her podium and faced Kenzie with her hand on her hip. Kenzie shrugged and leaned close to the microphone.

"No, I don't."

The shocked gasps almost deafened Kenzie. She gave her last recommendation and sat back down in her seat. Blood pounded between her ears. For the rest of the meeting she couldn't do anything but stare straight ahead, well aware of the daggers Erin shot her. When the dismissal gavel fell, Kenzie leaped from her seat in order to catch up with Erin, who stormed out as soon as possible.

Kenzie caught up with her cousin just outside the doors of the meeting room. Late evening sun spilled into the foyer. "Erin, I wanted to talk to you for a moment." Kenzie stepped in her cousin's way before she left the building. Like Kenzie's, Erin's complexion didn't help her hide her emotions.

Stone-faced, Erin turned to glare at her cousin. "What?"

"I don't want you to walk away mad and think I was being mean."

Erin dramatically leaned backward. "You?" she gestured toward Kenzie. "You be mean? Never."

The committee members leaving watched the interaction. Kenzie leaned in close. "Can we go somewhere and talk?"

"Oh, so you don't get embarrassed in front of your co-workers like you just did to me in front of the whole town?"

"Erin, I tried to tell you before I didn't think a clinic downtown was a good idea," Kenzie explained. "I also spoke with Stephen Reyes, who has several places he thought would be perfect, especially a little bit on the outskirts of town, just like Dr. Fredd's."

Erin rolled her eyes. "You just love leaving me out of things."

Ramon stepped out of the double doors, shaking hands with the mayor. His eyes narrowed on Kenzie, then his brows rose with curiosity.

"I'm not leaving you out of anything, Erin. I was asked my opinion about the history of Southwood and I gave it."

Erin smirked and glanced over her shoulder. "And you think a non-profit was a part of the history of Southwood? Let's be honest. We both know why you're doing it. You're so hard up for a man you'll sell your own family out."

Kenzie gasped. "Talk about selling family out—do you not recall a time when you openly campaigned against me?"

"For Miss Southwood?" Erin leaned backward, swaying her hips in dramatic fashion, clearly a habit she learned from Paula. "I was trying to save you."

"Save me?" Kenzie realized her voice had gone up an octave when the people in the hall stopped walking. Ramon came to her side, tugging her elbow.

"Let's get out of here, Kenzie."

"In a minute." Kenzie pulled her arm away. "Save me how, Erin?"

Erin placed her hands on her hips. "You were always more than a beauty queen, Kenzie. I always worried you winning would change you, but I guess deep down inside you are a vapid airhead who is so afraid to attend a public event without a date you had to go and hire someone."

"I—"

Erin silenced her with a wave of her hand. "Save it. He didn't want you a year ago. Clearly your embarrassed, desperate ass still hasn't learned your lesson. He's only using you to get your approval for the building. The building you could have saved for your flesh and blood."

Chapter 9

Once away from the courthouse and just outside of the city limits, Kenzie and Ramon arrived at Magnolia Palace. Cars, vans and SUVs filled the paved parking lot off to the side of the building. A puff of smoke billowed in the sky from the backyard. With it being Thursday evening, Kenzie figured Jessilyn was prepping for the barbecue on Saturday that she'd wanted to bring into town. The young chef's dish smelled like it would be worth eating and getting homemade barbecue sauce all over her suit.

Given what Erin said, doubt crept into Kenzie's mind. Being here on the grounds of Magnolia Palace, alone with Ramon, brought back the memories of their parting. *He's only using you.* Erin's words repeated in her mind. When Ramon led Kenzie on the path on the outskirts of the hotel, Kenzie questioned him. "I have on heels and you're taking me into the woods?"

"I can throw you over my shoulder if you like," Ramon teased.

Tempting offer, but Kenzie digressed and followed him over the pier to a private path she'd never remembered seeing before when she'd been here. Pine needles blanketed the forest floor. Crickets and katydids played a symphony for them as the sun slowly began to sink over the treetops. Any ounce of irritation over Erin's harsh words dissipated at the sight in the clearing of the magnolia trees. White magnolia petals circled a blue-and-white gingham blanket. On top of the blanket sat a brown wicker basket with a loaf of French bread hanging out of one side and a bottle of champagne from the other. Fresh fruit and cheese sat on a white plate with blue trim.

"When did you have time to set this up?" Kenzie asked, turning toward Ramon. He stood behind her, leaning against a tree.

The sleeves of his light blue shirt were rolled to his elbows. Her heart stopped. "Can't I do something nice for my lady?"

Ramon motioned for Kenzie to sit. She kicked off her heels before stepping onto the blanket. He followed suit and helped ease her down onto the blanket. Ramon grabbed the bottle of champagne and opened it. The cork flew off into the leaves. "Now, that's how you end a day like today."

"Should I be afraid to drink this?" Kenzie asked, lifting a flute of champagne in toast.

Ramon raised his glass for a toast. "Why would I want to poison you?"

"Because of my belief in a not-for-profit business in town, something for the kids. If you were still planning on starting up a business franchise, I may have influenced the committee to turn you down." Kenzie chewed her bottom lip and recalled Erin's words. Ramon didn't want her last year. Why would he want her now?

With a half shrug, Ramon shook his head. "We aren't together because of what you can do for me, Kenzie. Let's get that understood." He clinked his glass against hers. A dove in the tree flew away into the blue sky.

"Together?" Kenzie repeated with a smile. "I think it's time we have a talk about that."

"Uh-oh." Ramon set his glass down on the blanket they sat on. "This doesn't sound good. We've got two more events to go to."

"No," Kenzie said with a raised brow. "I never said yes to the previous weddings. You showed up uninvited to the first one and the second one you came to because Auntie Bren invited you."

"In retrospect, don't you find it weird your aunt would invite me to someone else's wedding?"

"You've met her—does anything she says surprise you?"

"No, I guess not."

"Exactly," Kenzie replied smugly.

Ramon leaned back on his elbow. His long legs, encased in a pair of medium-washed denim jeans, stretched over the blanket. "Well, what is it you want to say about your events? Are we not attending the gala together?"

Kenzie raised her index finger. "Let's keep in mind that I never said yes and now that we're done with the committee, I think we should wait."

Ramon sat up. "Wait for what?"

Kenzie set her glass down. "Hear me out first."

"Are you ending things?"

"Have we started things?" Kenzie asked. "If you weren't interested in the building, would we still be here?"

Ramon reached out and took her hand. She loved the security she felt at the touch.

"Kenzie, I broke my No Kenzie rule for you."

"What?"

"I vowed after your recent antics to stay away from you so you wouldn't torment me around town."

Playfully Kenzie squeezed Ramon's hand, for whatever

good that did—his hands were too big for hers to cause him any pain. "Stop playing."

Ramon wedged his hand between her thighs. "But I like playing with you."

A deep inhale didn't stop the chills of desire creeping down her back. "I just want to say I don't need you to escort me to the gala. You don't have to show up for whatever odd reason you've been using."

"'Odd reason'?" Ramon squeezed the thickness of her inner thigh. "I can think of several reasons. Are you saying you don't like when I come over?"

"I didn't say that." Kenzie shivered. "I'm just... I don't..." Her words were lost as Ramon's hand crawled up her legs. His mouth found her neck. "Ramon, I need you to understand that this is confusing and we're getting everyone involved."

"All right," said Ramon, sitting next to her. "Everyone involved how?"

"Everyone believes we're a couple."

"Aren't we? I called you my lady."

Kenzie shrugged her shoulders.

"If you never said yes to my proposal, then what's transpired between us is something real, don't you think?" Ramon bumped his shoulder against hers. "Which is it?"

"But the committee today..."

"We're celebrating right now, Kenzie," said Ramon. "While you and Erin were talking, I got the bid. I start construction on the building next week. The committee wanted your opinion but they valued my dollar amount."

"Please don't tell me you agreed to put in a bar." She scanned Ramon's face for an answer but got none.

"I haven't agreed to anything but the purchase. But if it worries you so much, what if I promise you I won't put a sports bar in the building?"

In truth, Ramon could do whatever he wanted. If the committee had wanted to accept the bid from Erin, they could have. Kenzie pressed her lips together. "I'm trusting you."

"I'm not going to let you down," Ramon whispered. "I don't see how being separated from you is a solution. Because of what your cousin said? Baby, she was mad."

If Erin was mad, she knew the exact low blow to hit Kenzie with. Even her mother had taken Erin's side. Toppled with the realization the committee had truly only wanted her opinion, Kenzie couldn't help but feel utterly useless. "Well, she called me out on my BS, Ramon. I did need someone to take me to the weddings. I was embarrassed to have everyone see me arrive dateless without any prospects."

"Erin attended solo, as well," Ramon pointed out.

Another shrug; Kenzie still didn't feel better. "I guess," she mumbled. "I still would rather make sure we're not together-together at the gala. Will that hurt your feelings?"

"Hell yeah," said Ramon, flopping onto this backside.

The move was so childish, Kenzie giggled. She leaned over his frame. "Can you do that again for me, but this time will you flail your legs in the air?"

"Are you mocking my pain?"

"Pain?"

"You're telling me I can't see you."

"That's not what I said. You're free to attend the gala, just on your own. You're free to attend the pageant, just on your own."

"That leaves one last wedding."

The wind blew, showering them with a sweet magnolia scent. Kenzie closed her eyes and enjoyed the moment. She splayed her hand against his chest, over his beating heart. When she opened her eyes she found Ramon staring at her.

"Jesus, you're so beautiful," Ramon whispered. His hand snaked out and cupped her behind her neck, bringing her head close to his.

Kenzie tucked a stray hair behind her ear. She pressed a sweet kiss against his lips. "Does this mean you're not mad anymore?"

"Oh, I'm pretty mad." Ramon tucked his hand behind his head and turned his gaze. "I have to start obeying my No Kenzie rule again."

"Stop saying that." Kenzie dug her nails into his chest. Ramon playfully continued to ignore her, staring aimlessly into the sky.

"I don't hear anything."

Shifting from kneeling beside him, Kenzie straddled his waist. "You can't hear me, huh? Can you feel me?"

In order to continue his charade, Ramon sighed deeply and closed his eyes.

"Oh well, if you can't feel me, I guess you can't feel this." She lowered her head and kissed his neck. His Adam's apple rose and his gulp echoed. As Kenzie lowered her mouth from his neck, her hands unbuttoned his shirt and slid beneath his cotton undershirt. She loved the feel of his hard muscles underneath his silky skin.

The button of his slacks slipped out of its hole with ease and his zipper coasted downward. A hard erection pressed against the blue boxer shorts underneath and Kenzie was obliged to help free it from its constraints.

Ramon moved to his elbows. "What are you…?"

"Shh." She blew against the tip of his shaft. "You don't hear me, you don't feel me, remember?" Kenzie teased him with a lick before taking him in her mouth. The ground shook when Ramon flopped onto his back. Kenzie smiled to herself, knowing good and well she had his undivided attention. But she was suddenly distracted by the sound of voices.

Stopping, Kenzie came to her knees. "Did you hear that?"

"What?" Ramon asked breathlessly. "No, nothing, don't stop now."

"I'm serious, Ramon."

They were in a secluded area on Ramon's property. They'd taken the path to a private spot. Only Jessilyn was supposed to know where to set up the picnic, and she wasn't coming back here.

"Ramon?" a voice called out to them, a woman's voice.

Kenzie narrowed her eyes on Ramon. Clearly he heard it too and sat up. "That can't be."

"Who is it?" Kenzie asked.

"I think it's my mother."

"You, are you back here?" a deep man's voice asked.

"And my brother Julio," Ramon added. He jumped to his feet, pulling Kenzie with him and adjusted himself. "Cool, you get to meet the family tonight."

"What?" Kenzie exclaimed. "I'm not about to meet your mother when two seconds ago…" She stopped what she was saying and touched her bottom lip.

"You're cute." Ramon laughed, bringing his lips down to hers. "C'mon."

"No, I'm serious. Go cut them off before they discover us and I die of embarrassment."

Ramon sighed heavily. "Only because I don't want you to die before finishing what we're starting."

Kenzie popped him on the arm and turned him around. "Go."

"Okay, fine, twisted woman."

"I'll wait here and meet your parents tomorrow."

* * *

The sesquicentennial celebration turned out to be everything Kenzie said it would be. Residents of Southwood came out in droves for the afternoon picnic and tour through the town. People traveled from as far as North Carolina and south Florida to participate in the activities. Children's activities ranged from sack races to doll- and dressmaking outside Grits and Glam Gowns. Tables were set up for pick-up sticks, a game introduced to Southwood.

The high school's baseball team was scheduled to play an afternoon game against two dozen men. Kenzie suggested anyone who wanted to play against the district champions were allowed to form one team. The list grew to over thirty. Ramon hit one homer, but it didn't make a difference and the newcomers were annihilated by teenaged boys. Kenzie summed up the mercy game with a history lesson. Baseball was introduced to Southwood when a Union soldier from the New York area decided to stay in the cozy town.

The activities for the day kept Kenzie busy and Ramon occupied with his family. She enjoyed hearing the origins of the town and how the family had created their dynasty. It reminded her of her own, without the backstabbing cousins. They knew everything about Villa San Juan, stories were passed on from generation to generation. Kenzie had arranged for horse-drawn carriage rides for the elders over sixty. People were also able to ride in vintage cars courtesy of Crowne Restoration, an automobile shop specializing in classic cars. Vendors set up shop outside of the businesses on the sidewalks and some set up carts and tables in the grassy square in front of City Hall. Business owners dropped their prices for one day and former high school bands from graduating classes of each decade gave an ensemble at the amphitheater.

* * *

As the sun set, free concerts ran downtown but for those who wanted to spend the money to join the black tie gala at the Southwood Country Club. Ramon started the evening off seated at a round table fit for twelve people. His mother and father, Ana and Julio Senior, were across from him. Next to his mother was Kimber, then Lexi and Stephen. Raul, the second-youngest brother, sat next to Ramon, and on the other side of Ramon was his oldest brother, Julio Junior, then Nate and his lovely wife, Amelia, who had a film crew documenting tonight's celebration. Beside Amelia sat Carlos and his wife, celebrity chef Grace Colon.

"Julio," Ramon said, turning to his right. "What did you think of today's events?"

"Spectacular," said Julio. The eldest of the Torres brothers looked tall even when seated. Julio was what Ramon considered a pretty boy and a snob. Women flocked to him. *His personality could be better*, Ramon thought inwardly, but overall, he had to hand it to his brother for trying to be the best he could be.

"I think we need something like this," said Raul, a year older than Ramon and a successful nightclub owner in Villa San Juan. Of course his club was attached to what was probably the most successful restaurant in town in the state of Florida, so Ramon might be biased there.

"There's that lovely Kenzie Swayne," Ana said and gawked, clasping her hands over her heart. "Do you realize she put this whole thing together? We could use her organizational skills at this year's Crystal Coqui. She truly understands the importance of honoring family tradition. I had the good fortune to speak with her this afternoon. She was so kind as to give me a history lesson about Southwood and so generous to tell me more about the surrounding cities."

As Ana held court about her encounter with Kenzie this afternoon, Ramon thought about his night with the belle of the ball. He glanced across the table where his beaming mother looked and spotted Kenzie immediately. It was hard not to miss her. To help get into the authenticity of the time when Southwood was established, she wore an old-fashioned patchwork hoop skirt, bonnet and shawl. Only Kenzie could make the dress sexy.

"Oh yeah," Nate chimed in, snapping his fingers. "It was her family Ramon stole his hotel from."

That's the last time you'll come over and work out, Ramon thought, narrowing his eyes on his cousin.

"*¿Qué*, Ramon?" Ana gasped, clutching the diamond-and-sapphire necklace designed by Kane Diamonds as a fortieth wedding anniversary present. For generations the Torres men showered their women with diamonds. Ramon wondered if it was too soon to buy Kenzie a congratulatory tennis bracelet for doing such a wonderful job today.

As Nate smirked across the table, Ramon's hand wrapped around his glass tumbler of rum. Better the beverage than his cousin's throat. Ana blinked her large eyes in his direction. If there ever was a person Ramon did not want to disappoint, it was his mother. He'd been her baby boy. Growing up and watching his brothers make their mistakes, Ramon learned how to stay on her good side. Some sweet treat—either coconut *tembleque*, a slice of custardy flan, or flakey, cream cheese and guava pastries— *quesitos de guayaba*—was always his reward for good behavior. There were the special times his mother slipped him a couple of *polvorones* cookies for letting her know what his brothers were up to. Ramon blamed his childhood obesity on his tattling. But the melt-in-your-mouth shortbread cookies were divine. "I didn't steal anything. No one lived in the place for over fifty years. I made an investment. I've already spoken to the family and everyone wishes me success."

"Except Kenzie," muttered Nate. Because his cousins had grown up with him like brothers, Ramon's cousins had been collateral damage when it came to Ramon tattling and getting his sweet treats from his mother. So Ramon guessed this playful underhandedness was payback. Just as Nate reached for a piece of red pepper off the crudité plate, his wife, Amelia, must have kicked him under the table. "Ouch."

Thanks, Ramon mouthed to Amelia.

"His investment paid off, Tía Ana," said Stephen. "The Magnolia Palace is the most successful hotel in town."

"And that's with the Brutti Hotel," added Lexi.

"You know, I spoke to Gianni a few weeks ago," said Raul. "He wants to add a nightclub to one of his chains in Miami."

"You'd be perfect to consult," Ramon's mother boasted. "We'll have to stop by and see him while we're in town."

Ramon had put his parents up at Magnolia Palace for the weekend. They'd arrived in typical fashion, loud and carrying food. Jessilyn was a bit overwhelmed when his mother took over the kitchen but like a true chef, she sat back and took notes. It didn't hurt that one of the best chefs in Florida was in his kitchen, as well. Grace was a welcome addition to the Torres family. She was the first to get one of Ana and Julio's boys to the altar.

For some odd reason the idea of marriage made Ramon turn and locate Kenzie. He sat back in his chair and watched Kenzie make her way toward him with a wide smile across her face. His heart swelled and now that he was used to the feeling, he liked it.

"Look at you smiling," Nate said, gaining Ramon's attention again. "Ouch," he added quickly and turned his head toward Amelia. "Why do you keep hitting me?"

"Because you are trying to embarrass your cousin and now is not the time. Behave."

Kimber, seated next to Amelia, snickered. "Don't be too hard on him, Aunt Amelia."

"What?" Stephen and Nate chorused and turned their ears toward the college student.

The matriarch at the table dropped her fork and glared at Nate and Stephen for Kimber's use of the word "aunt." When Kimber's father had passed away, it was discovered she'd never been forced to learn Spanish growing up. It had become a longstanding joke about Kimber and Philly not being able to speak Spanish. Smiling, Grace lifted her goblet of water and coughed. Everyone else caught on. A few years ago, Grace too couldn't speak a word of Spanish. She understood.

When she realized her faux pas, Kimber rolled her hazel eyes toward the chandelier. "*Tía*," she corrected. Everyone at the table laughed. "You all realize I am almost twenty-one and a double major in college, right?" Kimber asked. No one responded. "Ugh. Anyway, *Tía* Amelia, I think it's great to see Ramon all flustered. It serves him right."

"Serves me right?" Ramon blurted.

"Yes." Kimber cut her eyes to him and then back to Amelia. "He's broken many hearts around town."

"What broken hearts?" Ramon asked. "And why am I bothering to ask a kid?"

"*Mijo*, are you meeting girls here?" asked his mother. "Because it is about time you settle down."

"Leave the boy alone," mumbled his father as he pressed his fork through a lemon cupcake, courtesy of The Cupcakery. Most of Ramon's life, Julio Senior had never said much. He went to work at Torres Towers, helped maintain the family name and business and came home. He expected dinner on the table by six and only disciplined when his wife told him it needed to be done. He was a man of few words. Ana clamped her mouth closed.

"Julio and Raul haven't settled down," Ramon pointed out. "Why aren't we having this discussion with them?"

Ana fingered a diamond on her necklace. "All of you need to settle down. I'm not getting any younger and my baby sister already has a grandchild in college."

"*Gracias*, Tía Ana." Kimber beamed. "I didn't mean to say Ramon has been like Tío Nate." Kimber nodded in Amelia's direction. "No offense, Amelia."

"None taken," Amelia said with a light laugh.

"Ramon's been so caught up with work that he never takes time for himself."

The men all frowned. Ramon chuckled to himself. This must be what Kenzie endured with her family. Speaking of which, he noticed she was caught up talking to Mr. Myers, the retired history teacher. Ramon liked the old man but knew talking to him took at least an hour. Ramon was ready to reclaim Kenzie.

"Excuse me, Ma," Ramon said, pushing away from the table.

"Where's he going?" asked Julio.

"To get his beauty queen," Ramon heard Lexi say as he walked away.

At five hundred a plate, the crowd tonight was exclusive, yet the room was still packed. Ramon made his way through the crowd, bumping shoulders with some of the town's prominent members. Kenzie had sat on the decorating committee and brought in the photographs they'd found in the basement of the old post office. People studied the old paperwork and tried to guess whether the bizarre signatures belonged to their family members.

"There you are."

Ramon blew out an annoyed sigh when Alexander stepped in front of him, a dangerous space to put himself in, especially when it stopped him from getting to Kenzie.

"What do you want?"

"Whoa," Alexander said, holding his hands up in the air. "I come in peace."

"I'm not sure what *peace* means to you."

"The word may be lost on you." Alexander smoothed down the front of his white tuxedo shirt. "The last time we came across each other, you sucker punched me."

"You were drunk and advancing on Kenzie with her back turned," Ramon reminded him.

"Kenzie and I go way back," said Alexander.

"Yes, she told me how the two of you were engaged at one point in time," Ramon went on, eager to wipe the smirk off Alexander's face. "And she told me about how you cheated on her." The smirk dropped and Alexander scratched the back of his head. "Yeah, so before you get inebriated tonight, let me warn you—quit while you're ahead."

"Now see," Alexander said, collecting his thoughts, "I came here to discuss the matter of the ballots you brought to my office a few weeks ago to have analyzed."

"I didn't give you anything."

"I understand, but the cute little receptionist downstairs handed me the results."

Ramon studied the man. Clearly the ballots were important to him. "I'm sure somewhere in there is an illegal offense. I'll have my lawyer look into it. But for now, if you'll excuse me…"

"Don't you want to look at them?"

"You would like that, wouldn't you?" Ramon asked.

Alexander shook his head left and right. "I already

know what the contents are, considering I'm the right hand of the mayor."

"So save the two of us the drama and tell me what it is you found out." Ramon tucked the envelope into his jacket.

"The results aren't from an election ballot. Something a little closer to home. Want to guess?"

Ramon stepped forward to leave. He needed to find Kenzie. "I don't have time for games."

Alexander stepped in Ramon's way. "Before you head off to Kenzie, let me warn you, the contents of the envelope concern her."

Gritting his back teeth, Ramon willed himself not to slug him.

Alexander took his moment to continue. "The ballots you found belonged to the Miss Southwood Pageant from ten years ago. Turns out all these ballots belong to my sister, Felicia Ward," said Alexander. "Well, Crawford now. But I digress. I wonder what will happen when this comes to light."

If this came to light, Kenzie would be humiliated. He knew how important it was for Kenzie to be the last Miss Southwood. If she had not won fair and square, this would devastate her and it would kill him to see her so upset. Ramon vowed to never let that happen to her.

"I mean, everyone knows Kenzie as the last Swayne to win a crown, allegedly."

"You'll be wise to keep this to yourself, Alexander."

"Relax," said Alexander. "Kenzie's been through a lot in her life and I don't want to cause her any more pain and embarrassment. I only wanted to tell you ahead of time because I know how nuts Kenzie is about history stuff and I didn't want her to find out this way. There were only twenty-five votes for my sister stashed away. I understand the voting was done by ballots, so there's no telling just how many people voted."

Not like he'd been to many but the last time Ramon had attended a beauty pageant, there'd been a panel of judges. Ramon didn't believe a word Alexander said but right now, it was all the information he had.

"I see you're going to mull it over," Alexander observed. "Like I said, I didn't want Kenzie to be caught off guard looking these over. I'll let you do whatever you want with them." Alexander nodded his head and passed by Ramon.

Ramon turned, still in disbelief about the results and uncertain who knew about them. If anyone got wind of a rigged pageant, Kenzie would surely lose her title. She had her degree and she was proud of it. But knowing she was a fraudulent beauty queen would sting. There'd be no coming back from the humiliation. He wasn't going to let this mar their evening. Ramon turned and watched Alexander grab Mayor Anson by the elbow and head over to the Torres family. Julio rose and shook hands. Ramon felt a tug at his upper lip at the sight of the three of them. He imagined all the smarmy deals Alexander and Anson were trying to throw at his brother. Ramon didn't know how often the Economic Development Council met but he had a distinct feeling Julio might be attending the next meeting.

"There you are."

Ramon's heart lurched at the sound of Kenzie's Southern drawl. He turned toward her and stretched out his arms for her to step into his embrace. He plastered a smile on his face.

"Were you looking for me?" Ramon asked. "Because I was heading over to rescue you from Mr. Myer."

Kenzie cast a glance over her shoulder and then looked back at Ramon.

His heart swelled again. "Hello, beautiful."

Nodding her head, Kenzie blushed. "Thanks. I'm feeling pretty ridiculous in this getup."

"I think this might be the sexiest thing I've seen you in. Lexi did a great job."

"This is an authentic calico dress circa 1870, hand sewn by Elvira Pendergrass, a distant relative of Lexi's."

So dressmaking ran in the family, Ramon thought. He'd seen some of the racy designs Lexi came up with and gave a silent prayer of thanks for Elvira's common sense—she'd left the bodice modest. Considering Alexander was lurking around, Ramon didn't want too much of Kenzie showing. As a matter of fact, he was tempted to take off his jacket to cover her up. At least her legs were fully covered. They were his.

"I had the pleasure of meeting your mother earlier this afternoon." Kenzie looked over his shoulder and waved.

"She was just telling us." Ramon reached out snaked his arm around Kenzie's waist. "It's hard to impress her. How'd you do it?"

Kenzie's dark eyes widened. "Just your typical five-minute afternoon thunderstorm brought us together. I saw her walking by herself and pulled her into Osborne Books. We sat and had tea with Miss Gwen."

The only reason Ramon knew Miss Gwen was because Kenzie insisted they visit her and the bookstore to get more information about the photos of the old city. Kenzie amazed him. With everything going on today, she'd taken time out to have tea with a stranger. He inhaled deeply, his heart thumping against his chest. Ramon dipped his head toward hers, liking the way she bit her bottom lip and hesitated.

"Public affection?" Kenzie asked, looking around.

"You're damn straight." He brought his mouth down to hers.

Chapter 10

"It is about time you and Ramon figured things out."

A short while later Kenzie found herself cornered in the ladies' room by Maggie. Kenzie ran the curve of her summer-strawberry-red lipstick over her bottom lip, which was becoming her favorite product from Ravens Cosmetics. Every time she wore it she ended out in some form of make-out session with Ramon. Her pulse raced with excitement. She needed to hurry and get back out there to him.

"What are you talking about?" Kenzie asked her sister.

"Don't act like you're reapplying your lipstick because you left it all on your wineglass," Maggie teased. "We both know you and Ramon have been sneaking off kissing."

"Well, he has been trying to help keep Auntie Bren off my back." Even as she said the words, she didn't believe them.

Judging from the scowl on Maggie's face, neither did her sister. "Sure, say whatever you want to fool yourself. I'm not going to argue with you."

"Thank you."

"On another note, good job on getting Aunt Jody into town."

Kenzie cleaned up any stray lipstick in the margins of her lips.

"I know, right? I am amazing," Kenzie boasted playfully.

Maggie rolled her eyes. "Whatever."

"Seriously, though." Kenzie sobered. "I was shocked she came. I pulled the great-niece card."

"Bailey," Maggie said with a thoughtful sigh.

"Who can resist?"

Kenzie turned and rested her hip against the white-and-gray marble countertop of the bathroom. "She certainly can't resist seeing another Swayne win another crown."

"Are you ready to give up your reign as the last Swayne to win?"

Kenzie shook her head from side to side. "It is going to be an honor to crown Bailey myself."

Maggie turned too, folding her arms across her gingham period dress. With her hair tied in two pigtails, Maggie reminded Kenzie of a stand-in for Dorothy in *The Wizard of Oz*.

"And soon Bailey will be crowning a new little baby Torres." In an attempt to be funny, Maggie reached over to rub her sister's stomach.

Kenzie slapped her hand away. "Cut that out."

"Don't want me to hurt the baby?" Maggie continued to tease.

Kenzie rolled her eyes.

"See, this is the point where you'd stop me and tell me nothing has happened between you and Ramon and that there's no way you could even remotely be pregnant."

"There is no way I can be pregnant, Maggie," Kenzie said with a straight face. She didn't want to discuss her intimate moments with Ramon with anyone else. Last summer Maggie knew too much. Plus, this way, if things didn't work out between her and Ramon, she wouldn't be embarrassed in front of anyone. Sure, last summer, Kenzie should have picked up on his noncommittal attitude. Things were different now. She felt in her heart things had changed.

"You keep kissing him."

"There's no harm in kissing." Kenzie twisted the gold tube of lipstick in her hands.

Someone flushed one of the stalls and the door opened up. Kenzie and Maggie shared a look, their eyes wide at the sight of Auntie Bren waltzing out toward the sink between them. Auntie Bren was dressed in a period piece like those all the founding members of Southwood had worn. She wore a high-necked, off-white gown with black buttons, very First World War.

"If you two think a woman gets pregnant by kissing," she began slowly in her haughty voice, "it's no wonder you're both still single."

Maggie cackled. "Auntie Bren, aren't you still single?"

Kenzie reached around her aunt and pinched Maggie's elbow. "Hush."

"I'm single by choice," Auntie Bren answered coolly. "Meanwhile, if you put down all of your electronic devices, both internet-ready and battery-included, you might find a man."

Maggie gaped. Kenzie tried not to laugh. No way had her eighty-five-year-old aunt just alluded to a vibrator.

"C'mon, Auntie," Kenzie said, trying to lighten the mood. "We saw you with Oscar Blakemore last week."

"That old guy?" Maggie reached in the breast lining of her bodice, took out her phone and flipped through it. "This guy?" She angled the phone for both of them to see a beautiful photo of Auntie Bren, in all her royal purple, and Oscar in an embrace.

The corners of Auntie Bren's lips turned up in a smile

but quickly turned down again. "That's the man I chose not to be with."

"I don't understand," said Maggie. "Is this the guy you wanted to make jealous with Ramon?"

"Mission accomplished," Kenzie said with a low whistle. "I thought he was going to knock Ramon out."

At the mention of the incident, Auntie Bren smiled softly. "I'm sorry to have placed him in jeopardy like that. He was such a good sport."

Maggie rested her hip on the porcelain counter. "Are you going to tell us who that man was to you?"

"That was a boyfriend of mine when I was fifteen."

"Fifteen?" Maggie and Kenzie chorused.

"What?" Auntie Bren asked innocently. "I wasn't always the matriarch of this family. I used to have a wild side."

"So what happened with you and Mr. Oscar?" Maggie asked.

Other women began trickling into the ladies' room in twos. Auntie Bren took Kenzie's lipstick and used it on herself. "Oscar went off to serve in World War II. When he returned three years later he was engaged to another woman."

"And you were heartbroken?" asked Maggie.

"Of course I was. I thought we were going to get married. I doubted myself because of him. I never learned to trust anyone."

Heartbroken, Kenzie shook her head and reached to hug her aunt. She hated the idea of her aunt being so devastated over one man that she closed her heart to future possibilities. It seemed so lonely. She had a brief taste of that loneliness last summer and compared to the closeness she felt with Ramon now, she never wanted to revisit that dark period in her life. "I'm so sorry. I didn't realize that."

"It's okay. I've chosen to be alone so I can concentrate on my girls," Auntie Bren said with a smile. "And can I say, dear," she said to Kenzie, "it's been a pleasure watching you and Ramon together these last few weeks. I can return to Miami knowing you're in good hands."

Ah, there was that, Kenzie thought. A shiver drove down her spine at the idea of Ramon's hands all over her. She wondered how long it was going to be before she got to spend the night with him again. With his parents and family in town she didn't expect him to leave them at the hotel, nor did she think he expected her to spend the night with him.

"Wait a minute." Maggie interrupted Kenzie's thoughts. "What is going to happen with you and Oscar? Is he going to move down to Miami, or will you move here?"

Kenzie shot her sister a glare. A month of Auntie Bren was enough.

"I mean, or will you guys move some place other than Southwood?" Maggie tried to recover but she sounded so awkward.

Auntie Bren handed Kenzie her lipstick back. "I am done with him."

"What?" The girls gaped.

"At eighty-seven years old he's still lying."

"About what?" they asked again in unison.

Auntie Bren rolled her eyes. "Grown folks' business," she said as if they weren't all adults here.

"What is it you kids say? Ain't nobody got time for that?"

Maggie choked on air.

Kenzie stepped backward. "Lord, let me get out of here."

"Well, wait," Auntie Bren said, taking hold of Kenzie's arm. "Have either of you seen Erin?"

Maggie shook her head from side to side. "Cousin Danielle told me Erin took off yesterday to meet a client, but wouldn't say who."

"You know she wants to open a clinic in town?" Auntie Bren asked Kenzie.

Kenzie shook her head and looked away, knowing what was coming next.

"What's wrong with Erin moving here and starting her business? Are you still mad at her for your beauty queen thing?"

"Nothing, I guess," Kenzie huffed and squared her shoulders. "Look, I tried to tell her I had another place in mind for her but she went off on me after the meeting the other night."

Auntie Bren tipped Kenzie's chin down. "She's family. Now, if you'll excuse me, I am going to mingle with my friends."

"By friends, do you mean Oscar?"

"By friends, do you mean your battery-operated ones?" Auntie Bren crassly responded as Maggie stood there with her mouth wide-open.

Kenzie linked her arm with her sister's. "Serves you right."

"Serves her right if I have a male stripper sent over to her nursing home in Miami."

"It's an assisted living facility," Kenzie corrected.

"Whatever. So you wouldn't care if she moved back here?"

"Not really."

"Because you're so preoccupied and in love with Ramon?" Maggie sung Ramon's name in a low, husky voice.

"Girl, let's go." Kenzie headed out the interior door of the women's bathroom. Maggie, still taunting her, mumbled and questioned if she needed to hurry up and leave so she could get back to Ramon. In truth, yes, Kenzie thought with a smile. Her heart fluttered against her rib cage. Of course she couldn't wait to stand next to Ramon's side.

These last few days with Ramon had been wonderful. After winning the bid for the post office, Ramon started working with his construction team. Top that off with his successful business at the Magnolia Palace, and Ramon was a busy man.

Eager, Kenzie pushed hard on the outer door and immediately hit someone.

"Jesus, girl," Aunt Jody snapped, shaking her hand. "Are you trying to kill me?"

Kenzie hugged her aunt. Even though it wasn't kosher to say, her father's sister was Kenzie's favorite relative. To Kenzie, Aunt Jody was always glamorous. She kept her chestnut-brown hair straight and in a trendy style like a bob, a flip, or even shaggy. Tonight Aunt Jody was participating in dressing up with the other founding family members. She didn't dress in the 1870s clothing. She chose the Roaring Twenties and was able to tuck her hair under and secure a white band around her head. She wore six strands of white pearls varying in size around her neck that hung down the front of her black flapper dress in a knot.

"Oh, dear child," Aunt Jody cooed, patting Kenzie's back. They were the same height. "I have missed you so much."

"What about me, Auntie Jody?" Maggie asked.

Aunt Jody scoffed in Kenzie's ear at the sound of *Auntie.* "Don't call me that. That's my aunt's deal. And Maggie, darling, how am I supposed to miss you when you're forever on the social media?"

"I get no love from this family," Maggie said with a

pout. "And to think, I have been off the grid since I've been here."

Aunt Jody moved to hug her other niece. "Your poor followers must be worried sick wondering where you are."

Kenzie hid her laugh by looking the other way. Aunt Jody grabbed her by the wrist and gave her a tug and held her back. "Where are you going?"

Kenzie shot Maggie a warning glare to keep quiet. It was one thing to have Auntie Bren or other people in her family think she was in a relationship until the month ended but she didn't want to lie to Aunt Jody. But would it really be a lie? Kenzie knew she was falling hard for Ramon. She just prayed he felt the same way. "I wanted to check on the guests."

"This isn't just *your* event," reminded Aunt Jody. "Let some of the other family members around town do some work. Where are the bastards? The Hairstons need to help."

Maggie giggled.

Kenzie made an apologetic smile toward the ladies walking up to the bathrooms. "Aunt Jody," she whispered close. After the overpowering scent of hairspray Kenzie got a whiff of gin. "Have you been drinking?"

Aunt Jody's dark eyes were red around the rims. "No wonder you have a doctorate."

Not everyone in the family spoke of Kenzie's education. She beamed but tried to remember now was not the time to brag. "Let's get you over to the table."

"I'll get some water," said Maggie, taking off.

Kenzie slipped Aunt Jody's arm over her shoulder and escorted her toward a private table away from the center of everything. They were close to the balcony door and Kenzie prayed the fresh air would do her aunt some good.

"You're such a dear," said Aunt Jody. "I was so afraid I messed things up for you."

"Messed what up, Aunt Jody?" asked Kenzie. She picked up a Martin Luther King fan with a Sinkford Funeral Home advertisement on the other side and began cooling off her aunt's face. Sweat beaded under the white band around her forehead but started to disappear with Kenzie's use of the fan.

Aunt Jody grabbed Kenzie by the wrist. "I fear you were involved with the beauty pageants because of the pressure I placed on you."

"Beauty pageants are in my blood, Aunt Jody," Kenzie assured her. "What's going on with you? Have you stayed away from Southwood all this time because of that?"

"Maybe."

"I entered Miss Southwood when I was eighteen hoping that I could get you to come back to town."

Aunt Jody scowled. "I told myself I'd never show my face around here after your father rigged my pageant so your mother could win."

Ah, the family skeletons.

"I'm sorry you think my mom stole the crown from you," said Kenzie, "but it's been over twenty years. Can we let it go? I mean, look at the first big step you've taken in such a time. You finally came back to Southwood after vowing to never step foot here again."

"Well, I've stepped foot." Aunt Jody giggled.

Kenzie narrowed her eyes. "What?"

"Never mind, sweetie. Where is that hunk you were kissing earlier?"

"You saw that?" The breeze coming in from the open doors didn't cool off the heat singeing Kenzie's cheeks.

"If I didn't want to avoid making my date think I was a crazy lady, I would have whistled at the two of you."

Glad to see her aunt was returning to a normal, sober state, Kenzie sat back in her seat. "Maybe you're the one who needs to start talking. Who is the man I saw you churning ice cream with at The Scoop?"

Aunt Jody waved her hand and shook her head. "I see the way you're trying to change the subject. Let's just call it even. I won't ask you anything, and you don't ask me."

"Sounds like a deal to me."

The cryptic conversation stayed with Kenzie as she walked around the ballroom looking for Ramon. Something Auntie Bren had said stuck with her, too. A month ago she'd made plans with Rafael to attend the gala. She chose Rafael because he was safe. She didn't want anything other than to have someone to attend important functions with. Like Ramon reminded her the other night, although she never agreed to his proposal, he still came through for her.

Kenzie spotted Ramon by the bar talking to the mayor and Alexander, along with what could only be Ramon's brother. Judging from the wrinkles in Ramon's forehead and the scowl across his face, he was not pleased. She wouldn't be, either, if she had to talk to those two. He needed rescuing. She gathered her heavy skirts in her hands and set off.

"Kenzie, dear?"

The accented voice belonged to Ana Torres. When Kenzie looked in the direction of where her name was called, she saw Mrs. Torres, who wore a shimmering floor-length silver gown. Her dark hair was pulled up in a fancy bun with baby's breath sprinkled throughout her locks. Like Ramon and everyone in his family she was tall and lean in stature. When they'd talked in the bookstore Kenzie had figured who she was but didn't want to let on. Now, since Ramon had given her a giant kiss in front of everyone, she feared his mother might have some words for her. Would she approve?

"Mrs. Torres." Kenzie gulped, her eyes averted toward Ramon. The bewildered smile on his face made her smile.

"Ana, please," Ramon's mother corrected. "I was just going over there to bring the boys back to the table when I saw you over here. Julio is the mayor back home and he can talk shop all night long to people."

"I can imagine," Kenzie said with a nod. Though they'd both been heading in the same direction the two ladies stood there for a moment. "Are you enjoying Southwood?"

"I am." Ana beamed. "I plan on going back to the bookstore to get some more of that lovely tea we had today."

Kenzie patted Ana's arm. "I already arranged a box to be sent to your room."

"So sweet!" Ana leaned over and hugged Kenzie. "No wonder my son is in love with you."

The word *love* weakened Kenzie's knees.

Ana tugged her silver shawl around her arms. "Don't look so surprised."

"Ramon and I are just figuring things out," Kenzie responded nervously.

"I don't think Ramon needs any figuring," said Ana, "or he wouldn't have kissed you like that in front of his whole family."

Of course she'd seen it. Who hadn't? Kenzie searched for the words to say. Luckily a set of arms wrapped around her waist. Ramon pressed his lips against Kenzie's neck. "Sorry to interrupt, Ma, but I need to steal my lady for a moment."

"Of course," said Ana. "But Kenzie, you have to promise to come over to the hotel tomorrow for brunch. My daughter-in-law, Grace, is going to teach Ramon's chef how to cook."

"Jessilyn is a fine chef," said Ramon, squeezing Kenzie's body against his.

"You're thin," Ana countered and turned to Kenzie. "He must have lost at least twenty pounds since you brought Philly home. Kenzie, will you come tomorrow?"

"I would be honored, Ana."

"And please bring your family, too. Oh look." She sighed. "Julio will talk that poor mayor's ear off. Let me go get him."

Finally alone together, at least as much as two people could be at a gala event, Kenzie turned in Ramon's arms. First and foremost he kissed her lips, giving a little suck to her bottom lip where she'd placed her lipstick a few moments ago.

"How long before we can leave?" Ramon asked.

"We," Kenzie said, wagging her finger between his chest and her breast, "can't leave together. Not tonight."

"What? Why?"

"Because your folks are in town and you need to spend time with them, and I think my aunt Jody might stay at my place this evening."

Ramon bent down and pressed his forehead against hers. "This isn't how I envisioned the evening going for us."

"Let me guess, it had something to do with stripping out of our clothes?" Kenzie asked. They swayed to the melody played by the DJ.

"Lady, with that dress you have on, nothing needs to come off." He jokingly pushed his hips forward. "Since we can't spend the night with each other, how about we go find ourselves an elevator?"

Confused, Kenzie narrowed her eyes. "But every time we get on one…" When she glanced up he wiggled his brows. What a shame they were on the ground floor. "You're crazy, you know that? No wonder I am falling in love with you." The words just fell out. Kenzie held her breath, shocked.

"That's definitely going to get me through the night." Ramon kissed her, deeply. "I love you too, Kenzie."

"Ramon," Ana cooed the following morning. "I am in love with Kenzie Swayne."

You and me both, Ramon thought to himself. He offered a simple smile to his mother and a gentle squeeze of her hand.

They stood on one side of the brunch table as Kenzie and her family came down the walkway of Magnolia Palace. Silver cloches covered the dishes but not the delicious rich and sweet smells. Ramon's stomach ached for food while his heart ached for Kenzie. Two whole nights without her were too many.

"You aren't the slightest bit uncomfortable with the Swaynes coming over here for breakfast?" His brother Julio asked, watching the family come closer. "Wasn't this their family home? And now you're bringing them here because you're sleeping with their daughter?"

"Awkward." Raul laughed under his breath but loud enough for the family to hear.

"Both of you, shut up," ordered their father.

Ramon gave a silent thanks for one of the few times his father stood up for him. It never occurred to Ramon this morning might be awkward for Kenzie's whole family until Julio had opened his mouth.

If the Swaynes were upset, they didn't show it. Maggie held her phone out, recording herself and occasionally spinning around in panoramic fashion. Everyone wore something in the white or beige family. The men wore light-colored beachcomber linen pants and button-down linen shirts. The ladies all wore one form of sundress or another. Kenzie covered the top of her head with a wide-brimmed hat. He would kill to hide behind the hat and kiss her right now.

Ramon had met Kenzie's niece, Bailey, earlier this week. Bailey's father looked very much like Kenzie's dad. The apple didn't fall far from the tree. The main difference between father and son was that in the summer light, Richard's hair had a red tint. Another woman, not Kenzie's mother, linked her arm with Kenzie's. Ramon wondered if Paula Hairston-Swayne had decided to skip brunch. Was it because she thought Kenzie had sided with him instead of Erin on the building? Surely not.

"Mr. Swayne." Ramon came around his side of the table with his hand stretched out for a shake.

"Ramon, we discussed this—call me Mitch."

Ramon cast a glance over his shoulder at his parents. "I needed them to know that it was okay with you."

"Though his hair may look it, he wasn't raised in a barn," said Ramon's father.

Mitch chuckled and shook hands with everyone from the Torres and Reyes families. "Mitch Swayne," he said to Julio Senior.

"Julio Senior, and this is my wife, Ana. It is a pleasure to meet you."

"Thanks. Thanks for having us today, Ramon."

The dark-haired woman beside Mitch cleared her throat. "Oh, where are my manners? These are my daughters. Kenzie, you all know, and my oldest daughter, Magnolia. We call her Maggie."

Maggie paused to stop live-streaming herself. "Really, Dad? That's how you want to introduce me?"

"I could introduce you as my narcissistic daughter?" Mitch suggested.

"Uh, I am working." Maggie rolled her eyes and went back to her camera.

Mitch shook his head and continued his introductions *Family Feud* style. "My daughter considers being popular a job. But anyway, this is my lovely granddaughter Bailey and her father, my son, Richard."

Richard shook hands with everyone.

"And beside me is my sister, Jody Lynn."

"Jody's just fine," Jody said, stepping forward.

Ramon always thought Kenzie favored her mother but even with the dark hair on Jody, Ramon saw the family resemblance through and through with the heart-shaped face and high cheekbones.

"I love what you've done with the place." Jody gaped.

"Thank you," said Ramon. Kenzie came and stood by his side. He straightened to his full height with pride. "I'll have to give you the tour."

"Don't you think they already know what the place looks like?" Julio asked with a scowl.

"We never lived here," said Richard, putting everyone at ease. "This place once belonged to a distant relative."

"This sounds fascinating," Ana said, waving her hands over the magnolia table-scape. "Please sit. We have a variety of things, some fresh baked Mallorca bread, *pastelón*, and of course grits and eggs. We'll eat while you tell us more about your Magnolia Palace."

Ramon and Kenzie sat together. As Richard told the story of Magnolia Palace, Kenzie held Ramon's hand under the table. The simple touch of her thumb sliding over the top of his hand was such a turn-on. He was pretty sure no one would appreciate it if he pushed everything off the table and made love to her until the sun set.

"The house was really just a frame when it was constructed. My sister loves to paint Southwood as some Norman Rockwell city but even after the Civil War, most Black people lived in the city limits. There were still former Confederates who terrorized the town. To live outside the city limits was rare. Many homes were set on fire, including this one. Each time, the frame stood." Richard went on. "Ramon's done a fantastic job remodeling."

"Speaking of remodeling," his brother Julio said, "congratulations on your new spot downtown. Are you going to turn that into a bed-and-breakfast?"

"Not now, Julio," Jose said over his mimosa. His wife, Grace, pulled his hand under the table.

Julio looked between his brothers. "What? I can't ask my little brother a question?"

"If he wanted to talk about it," said Jose, "he would have brought it up to you. There was a reason that mayor's assistant came to you to tell you about the place."

As a US Marshal, Jose was suspicious of everyone. Usually he wasn't wrong and considering Ramon figured the mayor's assistant in question was probably Alexander, Jose was certainly right about this.

"I haven't decided," Ramon answered honestly.

"We were talking about making it a tutoring place or hangout for kids." Kenzie looked over at him with adoration. Ramon winced, recalling the ideas Anson breezed by him last night.

"Yeah, instead of having them trespassing on the property for thrills." Ramon chuckled nervously.

"That sounds like a great idea." Jody beamed.

"It sounds like you won't be making a profit," Julio sneered. A bang from under the table shook the pitchers of tea and magnolia vases. "Ouch."

"Sorry," Lexi said, sitting back from her seat and rubbing her protruding belly. "I never know when this one is going to up and decide to kick me."

"Well, maybe it's a sign we put an end to the subject of Ramon's potential business," said Raul. "Because I am going to work on him for a nightclub."

"Fat chance," Julio said, then scooted out of the way before Lexi had a chance to kick him again. "All right, I'm dropping the subject."

"Bailey, thank you so much for being able to make it to brunch with us." Ana leaned over. "I understand you'll be sequestered at Brutti Hotel for the week because of a beauty pageant thing?"

"Yes, ma'am," Bailey answered shyly. "I check in this afternoon."

Kimber started to speak at the same time as Lexi. Lexi nodded for Kimber to explain. "They do that so the girls can work on a group dance and practice walking on the stage. Tía Amelia." She paused for approval from the family. Once everyone nodded and smiled, she continued. "She has contacts from her old job at MET who are going to get some footage."

Multi-Ethnic Television was a staple channel in every household, especially in Villa San Juan. Ramon and his family religiously watched *Azúcar*, a popular reality show featuring the Ruiz family from Puerto Rico. The Torres-Reyes family had a former producer in their family now. Seated by her husband, Amelia nodded to confirm. "That's right. The world loves beauty pageants. Are you nervous, Bailey?"

"Oh yes, ma'am," Bailey answered with a soft giggle as she tucked her light red hair behind her ear.

The teenager reminded Ramon of Kenzie. He wondered— if they had a child, would she look like Bailey or at least have the Hairston red hair? Ramon glanced over at Kenzie and smiled.

"Cool," said Kimber. "I would love to come hang out

with you backstage. I know it can become crazy over there. It's nice having a friendly face with you, and since we're practically family... Ouch."

"Sorry," Lexi blurted out. She flipped her blond ponytail over her shoulder. "The baby just keeps kicking me today."

Judging from the red blush on Kenzie's face, she got the gist of the reason for Lexi's outburst. Marriage. Kenzie had made it perfectly clear she wasn't interested in that. She also said she didn't want him to escort her to any events, yet they were together all the time. Being with Kenzie felt natural. The problems from last year were gone. He always looked forward to seeing her and couldn't wait to be with her, even if they were apart for an hour. Damn, was he really ready for this step? Hell yes. Was she? Ramon wondered if a true proposal would get her to say yes.

The conversation switched to beauty pageants. Ramon squeezed Kenzie's hand. Alexander's discovery haunted him. Jody had bragged about Kenzie's win, and how the family tradition would be carried on in the beauty queen world. If it ever got out Kenzie wasn't the true queen, he didn't know what she'd do. The pride in her eyes killed him. The last thing he wanted to do was take this away from her.

Chapter 11

"Ladies and gentlemen." Kenzie tapped her silver sparkled nails against the microphone. The color, Winning by Ravens Cosmetics, was a special edition polish in honor of the Miss Southwood Beauty Pageant. Tradition brought an employee of the cosmetics company to Southwood to sit on the panel as a judge for this year's bunch of contestants. Last year they sent CEO Will Ravens, who at the time had been a newcomer to the cosmetics world. Kenzie was honored to witness the budding relationship between Will and beauty aficionado Zoe Baldwin, now Zoe Ravens. This year they sent Will's brother, Donovan Ravens, the CFO. Like Will, Donovan looked just as uncomfortable sitting on the designated judges' area as the ladies seated next to him. Donovan scowled, looking like a grumpy bear with his arms folded across his chest, clearly not in the mood for the festivities. Kenzie worried that his awkwardness was already rubbing off on the judges, and it might reflect in their scoring.

Kenzie smiled and waved at the crowd in the theater in downtown Southwood. She stood on the same stage where she'd won years ago. "Are we having a great time tonight?"

The crowd responded with a cheer.

"Well, I don't want to keep everyone here longer than need be because we have one killer party tonight, don't we?"

Another roar came from the audience.

"All right, without further ado, let's bring on this year's ladies and they'll all tell you who's sponsoring them."

Each year local businesses sponsored a contestant. Everyone wore a sash promoting their respective business. Waverly insisted Bailey wear last year's sash, sponsored by Crowne Restorations.

Kenzie stood off to the side of the stage just behind the curtains. Aunt Jody wrapped her arms around her shoulders.

"Can I tell you how proud I am of you?"

"Thanks, Aunt Jody," Kenzie said, beaming. "I wouldn't be here without your support."

"Yes, I know."

There was something strange about the way Aunt Jody answered. Kenzie inhaled just to make sure she didn't smell alcohol on her aunt's breath. Last week during brunch, Aunt Jody really put back the mimosas. Granted, they were delicious with the twist of mango juice from Ana's mango tree back home.

"I can't thank you enough for being here for Bailey," said Kenzie, patting Aunt Jody's arm.

"I was here for yours."

The confession caught Kenzie off guard. "What?"

Aunt Jody let Kenzie go and stepped backward. She wore a black knee-length gown and a magnolia tucked behind her ear. "I was. I just didn't want your stank mother to see me."

Kenzie rolled her eyes. "It was bad enough she didn't come to the brunch because you were coming."

"It was a family brunch," Aunt Jody said in a clipped tone. "A Swayne brunch. She's not a Swayne."

"Aunt Jody," Kenzie huffed. "This feud is going on long enough. Mom is right over there," she said, pointing to the front row, where her mother sat with her eyes glued to Bailey at the microphone.

"I wonder if I can throw something at her."

"Even if you could, I wouldn't let you. She's still my mom."

Aunt Jody patted Kenzie on the shoulder. "And I'm sorry for that, dear. Oh look, here comes Bailey now."

It wasn't difficult to quickly plaster on a smile. Bailey made Kenzie smile with pride. Her hair was teased high and combed back like a traditional beauty queen's. "You were so great out there."

Tears welled in Bailey's eyes. "Are you sure? I feel so silly like this."

"If you didn't feel silly, you wouldn't be doing it right, sweetie," Aunt Jody offered.

"Ignore her, okay?"

Other girls exited the stage. Kenzie tried not to show too much favoritism. Being an aunt of one of the contestants prohibited Kenzie from being an emcee but she was given a few responsibilities at the beginning, middle and end. The end was where she fully expected to pass the torch. Kenzie even brought the crown she'd worn ten years ago to place on top of Bailey's head.

"Do I really have to do 'Singing in the Rain'?" Bailey asked.

"What other number do you know?" Kenzie asked her. "We've only been practicing for weeks now."

"I know, but still." Bailey chewed on her bottom lip.

"It's just nerves," Aunt Jody offered, placing her hands on Bailey's shoulder as a coach would for a nervous player.

Suddenly Kenzie felt guilty. She thought about what Erin had said to her, about how beauty pageants were her whole. Was Erin right?

"Probably," Bailey mumbled.

"Bailey," Kenzie said. The emcee announced the bathing suit portion. Some of the other girls who had walked off stage before Bailey were now lining up behind the curtain. Kenzie remembered the excitement. She lived for it. What did Erin know? "Bailey, if you're unsure, you don't have to do this."

"What?" Aunt Jody gasped. "Of course she does."

"No, she doesn't, Aunt Jody," Kenzie said, stepping in front of her aunt so Bailey could only focus on her. "If you want to walk away right now, there's nothing wrong with it. I'll go get the car."

"No," said Bailey, shaking her head. "I want to do it."

"See?" Aunt Jody said smugly. "Let her go change."

"I'll walk with you," Kenzie said, linking her arm in the crook of Bailey's elbow. Aunt Jody hip checked Kenzie and took her place beside Bailey. "Aunt Jody!"

"Sorry, dear," said Aunt Jody over her shoulder as they walked away, "I don't trust you to keep her mind on the tiara."

"Crazy lady." Kenzie laughed to herself and shook her head. Turning back to the swimsuit portion of the event, she folded her arms across her chest and sighed in relief, still glad Bailey decided to stay in the competition.

A set of brown hands wrapped around her arms. "Reminds you of some old times, doesn't it?"

Kenzie jerked forward, hitting the curtains. "What is wrong with you, Alexander?" Immediately she wiped the spot of her skin he'd touched.

"What?" Alexander had the nerve to blink innocently.

"You can't tell me all this doesn't bring up memories of when we were together."

"Yes, I exactly can," Kenzie snapped.

"Remember how we stood backstage waiting to do your number?"

"You mean how you flaked on me and Hank had to step in and help me?" Kenzie countered.

Alexander at least had the decency to look ashamed. "Sorry. I was trying to bring up the good times in our past."

"That's exactly what they are, Alexander. The past."

Alexander tugged at the knot of his green paisley tie. "Is this because of the long-haired freak you've been seeing?"

"Ramon?"

"Don't say his name like you don't know who I'm talking about, Kenzie."

Kenzie shook her head from side to side. "I don't know where this strange nostalgia and this burst of inappropriate jealousy are coming from but they stop now. You had your chance ten years ago, and you had the last six months to approach me correctly, but you weren't man enough then. Don't start now."

"You think your new man is so perfect?"

Hands down, Kenzie thought, Ramon was the best thing in her life. She'd realized this week how she'd kept her heart guarded ever since her breakup with Alexander. Kenzie didn't plan on wallowing in her what-ifs with other men she dated in the past. She focused on the exhilarating feeling she experienced every time she and Ramon were together. "He's better than you."

Kenzie cast a glance from behind the curtain at where Ramon sat between Maggie and Richard. Her heart swelled with pride. Their families blended beautifully together.

The contestants entered and exited the stage in a crisscross fashion. The girls under eighteen wore peach-colored, one-piece bathing suits and flip-flops. The older ladies wore whatever, bikinis, tankinis or one-pieces, with or without heels.

As the girls stepped off stage, Kenzie moved closer to the curtains to keep from being trampled. The next event was the talent portion and Kenzie had the honor of introducing this part.

"He's no better than me," Alexander sneered.

"He is."

"Cute. Well, just hang tight." Alexander grabbed Kenzie by the wrist and tugged her on the stage. The audience, unaware of the tension, clapped as expected. Kenzie focused on the red light of the camera from the television studio. When she'd competed a decade ago, no one had filmed it.

"Ladies and gentlemen," Alexander said into the microphone, "it's a pleasure being here tonight. I don't know about you but I'm enjoying myself. How about you?" Alexander took the microphone off the stand and faced Kenzie, giving her such a smug smile she felt nauseous.

"I know we're doing things different this year, inviting everyone from all four points to enter, but how many of you were here ten years ago when my beautiful companion standing here with me won her crown?"

The crowd answered with applause. Kenzie glanced around, not sure where Alexander was going with this.

"Well, who can believe this beautiful beauty queen grew up to become Dr. Mackenzie Swayne? She's our town historian and she's helping Southwood stay honest to its true form. Why, in fact, she recently spoke to our economics committee about restoring some of our buildings, keeping their integrity and all that smart stuff." Alexander pressed his hand to his chest. "I'm not as bright as Dr. Swayne, but I get her part about keeping up the integrity. So can you imagine my surprise when her current boyfriend, Ramon Torres, the same man who went behind her family's back and bought their historic home, made an offer to the committee we couldn't pass up?"

The crowd hesitated in their applause, also unsure of where Alexander was going with this rant. Kenzie glanced out into the crowd to find Ramon. His seat between her siblings was now empty. "Well, I'm glad to make this announcement with the residents of Black Wolf Creek, Peachville and Samaritan here in the same audience. After meeting with Ramon's people and some of the builders I've used in the past, Ramon's new venture, a sports bar and club, will open downtown next month, and I guarantee all of you are invited to the grand opening."

Kenzie cocked her head to the side, sure she was not hearing correctly.

Proud of himself, Alexander winked. "How's that for integrity?" he asked her with a devious chuckle and glare, but spoke into the microphone. A scuffle sounded off behind her. The curtains shifted and when they steadied, Anson and a few men in blue jackets with the word Security written in yellow, stood in front of Ramon, blocking him from coming onto the stage.

"Oh, and speaking of integrity," Alexander went on, "Ramon and I discovered a box of ballots from ten years ago from this very competition. It seems someone threw out a ridiculous amount of votes, votes that would have assured my sister, Felicia Ward—" he chuckled and shook his head "—Felicia Crawford, received the winning crown."

Over her internal screams, the crowd gasped. Everyone stared at Kenzie. Vertigo set in. Her body swayed. She blinked in disbelief as the news began to sink in. Her legs moved on autopilot, turning in Ramon's direction. Anson released him and he ran toward her.

"Kenzie."

"You knew the ballots were from my pageant?" Her voice choked out in a hoarse whisper. "How long have you known?"

"Kenzie, let's go…"

"How long?" Kenzie screamed. The theater was as quiet as a church mouse.

Ramon scratched the back of his head. "Since the gala."

"The gala was a week ago." Hot tears threatened her eyes. "You could have said something."

"I—"

She pushed his chest. "No, you don't get to say anything now. You knew and you could have said something. Instead you allowed Alexander—" She hiccuped a sob. "You let Alexander of all people be the one to let me know." She felt like such a fool. Her biggest claim to Southwood fame was winning her pageant and now it was lost. Humiliation didn't begin to describe her feelings. She had failed her family and their legacy.

Aunt Jody came out of nowhere, wrapping her arm around Kenzie and guiding her off the stage. For the first time in her life, Kenzie held her head low and slunk away. Once she reached the curtains, Richard stood there waiting for her. Then she fainted.

"Ramon, dear."

Ramon glanced up from his third chocolate cupcake to the hand on his fitted white shirt. He wiped his hands on the back of his jeans and stood up to greet Auntie Bren. The sight of the red hair on the matriarch's head caused Ramon's heart to pulse. Two days had passed since he'd been double-crossed by Alexander Ward. He put a lot of blame on Julio as well for indulging Alexander's ideas of what kind of business to put in the old building. Julio gave the misguided impression to Alexander that he could talk him into anything. Ramon never agreed to anything and now he spent his time turning down venders Julio sent over. Right now Ramon didn't want to have anything to do with the building, not if it was going to cost him Kenzie.

Since the shop had opened, he'd been sitting in The Cupcakery, hoping to get a glance of Kenzie leaving her apartment or walking through downtown Southwood. It was Tuesday, dreaded Tuesday, and Kenzie still hadn't returned his calls. He hadn't heard from her nor seen her in forty-eight hours.

A billow of steam from his fifth coffee floated up and met a disapproving gaze.

"Auntie Bren." Ramon tried to say her name with a smile. It didn't feel right.

"What are you doing sitting here all by yourself?"

Ramon lifted a brow. Had she been under a rock for the last few days? "Just enjoying a cupcake."

"What do you have?" Auntie Bren peered over Ramon's table. "Mmm, Devastating Decadent Chocolate? And three wrappers?"

Guiltily, Ramon nodded his head. "Yep." He owned it. Who said only women drowned themselves in food? Men did, too. And Ramon was miserable.

"May I?" Auntie Bren motioned toward the empty seat in front of the stack of paperwork he'd been signing all morning long for the renovations of the post office.

Ramon expected Auntie Bren to ask about the building. People stopped Ramon in the streets to ask about his plans. Just this morning someone had offered to share his winnings from the bet going on from the local bowling team. Ramon had plans, all right—ones that were going to blow Kenzie away and prove to her he'd been listening. Right now the front of the building remained covered by plywood. Construction went around the clock. Keeping the structure of the building intact was going to cost Ramon a fortune. When Ramon delivered his check to the bank he learned the main reason the council had backed him was because Erin Hairston would have had to build an outside ramp to accommodate her patients and that would have changed the exterior structure. Ramon had a side entrance he could make wheelchair accessible that Erin wouldn't have been able to.

Auntie Bren raised a manicured finger at the counter. Ramon turned to see who her dining partner was and caught a glimpse of the man from the Ward wedding, Oscar something.

"I have you to thank for my temporary boyfriend."

Great, he thought. At least someone got a relationship out of this month. "Congratulations," Ramon said.

"Well, he isn't really *new*," Auntie Bren went on to say. "Nor is he really a boyfriend. I just like saying the word. I'm breaking things off when I leave for Miami next week."

"You two look so happy together." Prior to Auntie Bren coming over to visit him, he'd seen the two walking down the street, heading toward The Cupcakery. Ramon had observed the chivalrous way Oscar caught a kid whizzing by on a bicycle with his cane after the boy cut between them as they held hands. Ramon could only assume Oscar had made the boy apologize because the kid had gotten off his bike and held out his hand for Auntie Bren to shake. Ramon had kept his head low when he realized they were heading into the cupcake shop. It was bad enough he'd run into what had to have been every other Swayne and Hairston family member in town, who had all felt the need to tell him off.

Snickering, Auntie Bren shook her head. "Oscar and I

are familiar with each other. We were sweethearts before he went off to the war."

Which one? he thought.

"When he left, I walked down to the old post office every day and mailed him a letter. I handed them to my best gal pal, Priscilla." Auntie Bren cut her eyes over at the counter and half smiled at Oscar. "He claimed he wrote me one as well, but I never received it."

"I'm sorry to hear that. I assume because you never heard from each other, you fell apart and never saw each other again."

"No, not exactly. I went to visit my family up north in Chicago when he returned from the Korean War—yes, baby, he was a career military man. I came back and I saw him. Saw him with my best gal pal."

The math caught up with Ramon. He pressed his lips together when he realized Oscar's dirty deed. There was no ghost in the old post office. Oscar did exactly what Ramon had tried to tell Kenzie. He was a player.

"I couldn't stand seeing him with someone else, especially when I thought he and I had been so in love, so I moved away. I rarely ever come back to Southwood because I don't want to run into him."

The story sounded vaguely familiar. Kenzie was avoiding him. Unlike Oscar, Ramon had an excuse. Alexander was a liar. A liar with a broken nose now, but still a liar. Ramon clenched his fist. Ramon didn't want another day to go by without talking to Kenzie, let alone a half a century. Right now she refused to see him.

"And here you are with him."

"Sure, for now." Auntie Bren shrugged her shoulders. The knot of her purple sweater shifted and she tugged it back down toward the center of her purple-and-white plaid shirt.

"Auntie Bren, we've known each other for a while," he began with a teasing smile, "so I am sure you're here to give me comforting words of support."

"No, dear, if I wanted to do that, I'd tell you to get off your ass and go make things right with my niece." She reached out and smacked Ramon on the back of his head. "She snuck out of her apartment this morning and is at her office. But you better do something grand to win her back."

"Yes, ma'am."

"These came for you."

Kenzie looked up from her office to find another dozen roses in a glass vase so big they covered Margaret's face from her view. Without looking at the card, Kenzie shook her head.

"No thank you."

"Kenzie," Margaret began, holding the crystal vase at her hip, "you've only been in the office for two hours and already this is the second dozen he's sent today, and while I'm no mathematician, I can only guess there will be six dozen more to come if you stay the rest of the day."

"Then it's a good thing I am working a half day today."

Roses had been delivered every hour on the hour to her apartment. Everyone in her complex received a batch. Did Ramon think flowers were going to smooth things over? He lied to her, not so much about the business but knowing about the missing votes. Losing the Miss Southwood title like that, in such an embarrassing way, devastated her. Sure, her world had not ended and her friends were supportive but the idea still hurt her. And Ramon knew. Anger bubbled inside of her for thinking about it. She stared at Margaret, who waited for an answer. Kenzie guessed today's batches could be split and sent over to the two senior centers.

The only reason Kenzie came into the office today was to collect the box she'd left there. Waverly's surprise wedding was later on today and after that Kenzie planned on going to the family cabin in Black Wolf Creek. Kenzie had informed Dario and Darren Crowne that she had no plans to attend the wedding but she would stop by at the reception to show her face.

After Kenzie gave the instructions for the roses, Margaret shook her head and mumbled something under her breath about appreciating gifts. Clearly Margaret hadn't been at the Miss Southwood Beauty Pageant two days ago. *So what?* Kenzie thought to herself. Eventually the whole town would know.

The tiny office smelled like fresh flowers. How did he even know she'd come into work today? Kenzie hadn't bothered mentioning it to anyone she'd be coming in, except for Alexander's secretary.

Left alone with her thoughts, Kenzie almost wished she hadn't come in at all. The elevator ride up to her office involved a lot of pats on her back and words of encouragement such as *tough break*, *hang in there* and *God always has a reason why.*

And even with those well-wishers, Kenzie still faced the scrutiny of those who thought she personally cheated or at least conspired to cheat. Felicia called from her honeymoon in Barbados to say no hard feelings and it meant nothing to her now. But it meant everything to Kenzie. She wasn't a cheater. And then there was her family. Everyone wanted to know who rigged the vote. Kenzie didn't know if that mattered now.

Aunt Jody showed her true devotion to the bottle. She didn't even bother mixing her vodka with orange juice or tomato juice, or even a glass. From the time Kenzie received the news she was no longer a winner, Aunt Jody stayed by Kenzie's side, even when her mother, Paula, came over.

The two ladies put their differences aside to take care of Kenzie. Not that she wanted help. Her father, Mitch, tried to reassure her that no matter what, she would always be his princess. As much as it killed her to stay away, Kenzie didn't want Bailey to see her like this. And no one wanted to talk about Sunday's results. Kenzie preferred to be left alone and no one seemed to take the hint, not even Maggie.

"There you are!"

Kenzie blinked to get her eyes to focus and found her sister standing in the doorway, hair piled on top of her head like a mop with a gardenia tucked behind her ear. She wore a peach-colored dress. Meanwhile, Kenzie, dressed in the same pair of sweats since Sunday night, stepped forward.

"Why are you here?" Kenzie snapped.

"Why are *you* here?" Maggie clapped back. "You're off work this month. Or did you forget? You took this month off for all the weddings and events."

Kenzie shuffled some paperwork around to seem busy. "Yeah, well, everything is over with, so I might as well get to it."

Maggie waltzed farther into the office and perched herself on the edge of Kenzie's desk. "You have one more wedding to attend."

"Since it is a *surprise* wedding for Waverly, she won't even know I was supposed to be in it. Besides, of all people, Waverly will understand," said Kenzie. Waverly had suffered from internet bullying and was publicly mocked when she lost one beauty queen title before becoming Miss Southwood. Kenzie didn't bother checking social media. She woke up every night in sweats remembering the red light on the *live* camera from Multi-Ethnic Television. "Dominic said it wasn't formal."

Maggie rolled her eyes. "I've met her mother. It's going to be formal."

"Jillian Leverve just wants to see her daughter married before the baby is born," Kenzie explained and went back to shuffling her papers. "They don't need me there for that."

One minute Kenzie was tapping the papers in her hands to a beat and the next her hands were empty. Maggie snatched the documents and held the work over the edge of the desk and sprinkled the papers into the wastebasket.

"Go away, Maggie."

"Not without you."

"I don't want to be around people."

Maggie sighed. "I noticed your luggage is missing from your closet."

Kenzie let asking her sister why she was in her closet slide. "I'm going to the cabin."

"Smart. I'll be there."

"I don't need company," Kenzie said.

"I'm not just company." Maggie pouted. "I'm your sister. How long do you want to stay?"

Snarling, Kenzie shrugged. Did she stay for as long as it took Ramon to build his sports bar? She didn't want to pass by the building every day and see it being ruined, littered with sports paraphernalia, loud games and drunk fans? How had she ever thought Ramon matured? He'd looked her in the eyes and lied. Red-hot anger boiled in her veins. She wasn't sure she'd ever want to see him again. But forever wasn't an option. "A while."

"Long enough to wait out the sports bar?"

If she said she didn't care, Kenzie knew her sister would know she was lying. Instead she answered, "We'll see."

"Well, have you read any of the cards Ramon sent?"

Heart aching, Kenzie wondered if it was time to ban

his name from being said. "I don't want to have anything to do with him."

"A week ago you were in love with him," Maggie reminded Kenzie. "Don't be like Auntie Bren. I took the liberty of reading his cards."

Of course you did. Kenzie stewed.

"He never agreed to build a sports bar. That was Anson and Ramon's brother Julio, who were talking mayor talk. They came up with the idea. You know all it takes is a little inkling for Alexander to find out something bothers you and then he runs with it."

"I don't care about the building," Kenzie interrupted her sister. The words choked her. Ramon had failed her. Again. Now, instead of being humiliated in front of a small group of people, the whole world got to see the moment she was proclaimed a fraudulent beauty queen. He'd promised never to humiliate her and had failed. Again.

"It looks like a florist exploded in here, too," said Maggie, changing the subject.

Kenzie half smiled. "At least the flowers will brighten up the senior centers."

"Aw, there's my baby sis," Maggie cooed. "Do you want to go visit there? That always makes you happy, talking to the lifelong residents of Southwood."

"No," Kenzie said, shaking her head. "I just wanted to grab a few things before going to the cabin. I can't take being at my apartment with Aunt Jody there. And Mom."

"Yeah, they're killing me with kindness toward each other. This morning I saw each of them insisting on the other taking the last lemon cupcake."

"Sir." Margaret's voice carried into Kenzie's office. "Sir!"

The only thing Kenzie could do was stand up. Her chair hit the back of her wall and jutted forward, hitting her behind the knees. She fell back into her seat when Ramon appeared in her doorway. His hair hung loose and surrounded his face and fell down the front of his white shirt. Kenzie hated herself for her body's reaction to the sight of him in his form-fitting jeans. Hopefully, the way she sighed covered her desire. Maggie slid off Kenzie's desk in an attempt to put herself between Ramon and her sister.

"Maggie, I've come to adore you like a sister but right now you need to move."

"No," said Maggie, folding her arms across the peach bodice of her dress. "I'm not going to let you hurt her."

Ramon tossed Kenzie a look. Her heart seized in her chest. "Kenzie, seriously?"

Kenzie lifted her chin. Margaret stood behind him, talking to someone on the other end of her cell phone, giving them the full description of what the "intruder," as she put it, wore.

"Kenzie, you know I'd never knowingly hurt you."

She hated the way his voice pleaded as if he were in pain. Well, she was in pain, too. "Just leave me alone, Ramon." Kenzie turned around in her chair, scraping her knees against the wall.

A static noise from the radio of an approaching security officer sliced through the tension of the room. "Kenzie," Ramon said. "At least look at me."

For some reason she obeyed, spinning back around. Three security officers tried to grab his arms. Ramon pulled away. "I meant it when I said I'd never do anything to jeopardize us."

"I recall you saying you weren't going to hurt me," Kenzie replied coolly. She smoothed her hands against the top of her desk. Her bare fingertips brushed against the leftover box from the basement of the post office. "You knew about the votes."

"Yes, I knew," said Ramon. He pulled away from the security guards and advanced closer. Kenzie pressed her back into her seat. "I made the choice not to say anything to you. I thought Alexander wanted to keep it quiet, as well."

"You thought?" Kenzie squinted her eyes. "By going along with whatever Alexander came up with, you humiliated me. Was it for the seat at the big kids' table? You wanted to be on the local committees so bad you were willing to compromise me?"

"It's not like you think."

"What I think is you knew how he humiliated me before."

"It was the lesser of two evils, Kenzie." Ramon exhaled.

"Well, you chose poorly." Kenzie sniffled. She'd thought she was done crying. "You promised me. You promised you would never humiliate me."

"I didn't."

"You did," she said with a simple smile. "Again."

"Kenzie, if you're not going to talk to me…" he said, coming closer.

"Sir," a security guard said.

Ignoring them, Ramon clamped his hands down on the arms of her chair. He leaned his head close; his sweet breath smelled like chocolate cupcakes. His dark eyes were black, scary black, as they searched her face. Kenzie shut her eyes but he jerked her chair to get her attention.

"I knew you were going to hurt me," Kenzie clipped.

Ramon bowed his head for a moment then looked back at her. The whites of his eyes turned red. "Then you came into this relationship with the cards already stacked against me."

"I want him out of here!" someone screamed.

"What the hell happened to you?" Kenzie heard Maggie question someone outside the door. She and Ramon locked eyes, neither of them blinking. Finally he nodded and stood up, grabbing the box from the post office off her desk. "I'm out of here. I just came to get what's mine."

Once the doors to the stairwell stopped rattling after Ramon stormed out the side exit, Kenzie breathed. She blinked to get her eyes to focus and her brows drew together. Alexander was just outside her door, dressed for work in a suit, but also with one of those nose guards basketball players wear. That, however, hadn't protected him from a flying ball or elbow. It had been too late for that. Deep puffy purple circles were under his eyes.

"Don't worry, he won't be bothering you anymore," Alexander said nasally. "I'm in the process of filing a restraining order against him after he punched me at the pageant."

Finally able to push away from her desk, Kenzie stood up. "I quit."

Chapter 12

Even though Kenzie had quit a month ago, her connections to Southwood High School kept her in good standing to serve on the Christmas Advisory Council. She thought staying in Black Wolf Creek, hiding out, would heal her wounds. But now that she found herself standing outside of the old post office, doubts washed over her. Kenzie bit her bottom lip and glanced up at the building. Whatever name Ramon planned to give the sports bar was covered with a thick white sheet. His clout or whatever he'd bartered got the first meeting for the Christmas Advisory Council held on the same day as his soft opening; the meetings were traditionally held in City Hall, and had been for decades, since Southwood had decided to welcome out-of-towners to experience the holidays in a small town. Shops donated money and items to help make each year grander than the one before.

"You okay?"

Beside her, Maggie linked her arm through Kenzie's and forced a smile onto her face instead of lying. Her heart raced. Her legs shook in her three-inch sandals. Thank God the bright yellow scoop-necked dress she wore covered her legs. Kenzie linked her sister's arm with her own and looked both ways. "Is that our parents' car?"

Maggie followed Kenzie's glance. "I think so. Mama said something to me in a text about coming to more meetings."

"You don't have to be here to babysit me, you know."

"I know, but Southwood is my home."

Kenzie raised a brow at her sister. "You may have been with me for the last month but I know you're ready to be with your followers."

"Does this mean I don't have to wait on you hand and foot?"

"Whatever," Kenzie said, rolling her eyes. "Come on, let's get this meeting over with."

"Fine." Maggie sighed. "But I want to be Mrs. Claus if any of Erin's rehabilitating sports patients are going to play Santa."

During the time Kenzie hid out, Erin decided to look at the buildings Kenzie had recommended and it turned out she liked them. The business was set to open by September. The property offered the privacy that her clients needed.

The pounding of her heart deafened Kenzie. With each step she took the blood in her veins pumped harder. She almost got dizzy and thought she might fall backward. She almost did. Maggie gripped her arm.

"I've got you."

The glass doors opened before either of them touched the brass handles. He kept the handles, she thought. Just from the walk up Kenzie was able to tell Ramon had put in a lot of work to restore the brick.

"Welcome," said a familiar face, with short, tight, curly hair and golden-bronze skin, wrapped in a black tuxedo. "Hi, Kenzie."

"Julio?" Kenzie said slowly. "You're here?"

Julio bowed at the waist and held the door open with his butt. "Temporary situation or penance, however you want to look at it." He extended his hand toward her. "Before you take a step farther, I must apologize to you. I let my greed overtake me when I found out about the building and therefore I placed Ramon's relationship with you at risk."

The apology sounded rehearsed but not forced. "Thank you."

"Right this way," Julio said, stepping aside.

The first thing Kenzie noticed was the floors, still black and white but shiny this time. The postal workers' area was now set up as a baseball-themed bar with bat-and-glove-shaped bar stools. What threw her off for a moment was that there were high school kids in their lettermen jackets sitting at the juice bar where the counter used to be. Kenzie looked around the area further. Pinball machines were surrounded by more teenagers. Beanbag chairs, a popcorn machine and a pool table were farther into the room.

"Is this a rec center?" Maggie asked.

"Right this way," Julio said, not answering Maggie. He led them to the elevator. Kenzie gulped with the memory of the last time she'd been in here. The brass doors to the old-fashioned elevator opened to reveal Raul, also dressed in a tuxedo.

"Good afternoon, Kenzie," Raul said. "Welcome back to Southwood. What brings you here?"

"The Christmas Advisory Council?" Kenzie answered uncertainly. Had no one told him why they were here?

"Ah, yes, I believe it is being held on the second floor."

Okay, now they were getting somewhere. The compartment went up smoothly, no shakes or hiccups. Unlike the noise from the first floor this room remained quiet, even with the dozen students sitting on the couches studying.

Kenzie waved in apology at the students, who looked up from their books.

Raul closed the door. "My bad. I thought the meeting was on the second floor."

Once they reached the third floor the doors opened and once again the area was quiet but still filled with people—older people admiring photographs hanging from the crisp white walls.

"Auntie Bren?" Kenzie asked, stepping off the elevator.

Auntie Bren turned around in her deep purple heels and long purple maxi dress. In one hand she held a glass of red, in the other Oscar's hand. Kenzie's eyes darted to their hands' tender embrace. "I thought you… How long have you been in town?"

"She hasn't left," answered Oscar. He brought Auntie Bren's left hand to his mouth and kissed the back of her hand. "I finally got your aunt to come to her senses."

"Say what?" Maggie hollered. "How long were we gone? Auntie Bren, you told us…"

"I know what I said, girl," Auntie Bren snapped, then quickly recovered. "I know I was set to leave and never return but someone helped me come to realize how much I love him."

Oscar snorted. "You mean Ramon Torres gave you the box from Priscilla's footlocker and you realized she had been keeping my letters to you and not sending yours to me."

"What?" Kenzie and Maggie chorused.

"Oh, sweetheart," Auntie Bren said, "you better get on upstairs to your meeting. You don't want to be late."

"This way," said Raul.

Kenzie's heart began to beat faster. So the first floor was a rec center. The second floor had been turned into a study center; now the third floor was a museum of Southwood artifacts and memorabilia? Tears began to form in her eyes. Blinded, she wiped them away when the doors to the fourth floor opened. Aunt Jody greeted her with a big hug. She smelled more like lilacs than her usual scent of fruity alcohol. Kenzie dabbed the corners of her eyes with her fingertips. Now with the room clearer she spotted her former Tiara Squad members from her generation and more. Felicia, wearing the two-inch runner-up tiara, stepped forward. Was this some form of official dethroning ceremony?

"Kenzie," Felicia said. Lexi waddled to Felicia's side. Waverly flanked Felicia's other side and Bailey brought up the rear with her Miss Southwood tiara. Everyone wore their tiaras. "This is yours," said Felicia. She held out a lavender pillow with gold trimming and Kenzie's old crown perched on top.

"Ramon combed through old photographs of your pageant. He got with the Miss Southwood Organization and discovered the votes were cast by the audience. Everyone received a ballot, just like how prom votes for the prom queen. There were over a hundred people there" said Lexi. "The missing votes weren't enough for you to lose. You're still a Miss Southwood beauty queen."

Felicia threw her arms around Kenzie's neck. "Let's face it, you were always and will always be Miss Southwood."

Someone placed the crown on top of Kenzie's head. The same elation she felt when she received her PhD and shook the chancellor's hand whipped through her. "But I can't take this knowing someone tried to cheat for me. People will always assume I am a cheater."

"No, they won't." Aunt Jody stepped in front of Kenzie. She realized something was missing from the top of her dark head. Kenzie narrowed her eyes but Aunt Jody gave her an assuring smile. "I was in a really competitive stage," she said. "I swapped out some of the votes. I've confessed and I resigned as a Miss Southwood runner-up."

A thousand questions went through Kenzie's mind. But she didn't have a chance to ask any of them. Raul tugged on her elbow.

"Sorry, Kenzie," he said. "I had the wrong floor again. The meeting is in the basement."

Sniffling, Kenzie stepped back on the elevator. Ramon had not only fixed the building like she'd dreamed, but he'd gotten Aunt Bren and Oscar back together, and now he'd restored her tiara.

"Are you okay?" Maggie asked when the elevator doors closed.

"No," Kenzie cried. Her hand shook. "I need to see Ramon."

"I believe he's serving on the committee," Raul answered. "Damn, if only this elevator would stop jamming."

The elevator stalled. Kenzie cursed her luck for always jinxing the things. Finally, after five minutes of tinkering with the buttons and the call service, they began to descend to the basement. Kenzie tried to plan out in her mind what she was going to say to Ramon. She'd spent a month away from him thinking she was over and out of love with him. In a matter of ten minutes and without even seeing him, Kenzie realized she never wanted to be away from him for another minute.

"Here we go."

The doors opened and Kenzie stepped out with quickness, eager to find Ramon. She didn't care who was here for the meeting. She needed him now. She needed to feel him in her arms before she burst.

Jose Torres greeted Kenzie, also in a tuxedo. "Ah, you're here. I bet you're looking for Ramon."

"I am," Kenzie replied, craning her neck.

For the first Christmas Advisory Council meeting, there were a lot of people, enough to stand shoulder to shoulder. Kenzie teetered on her tiptoes to find the top of Ramon's head. No luck. She made her way to the center of the room, spotting her parents first. The Christmas Advisory Council was never a formal event, yet her parents stood out arm in arm, dressed in a cocktail event dress and a tuxedo. No one sat at the tables. There weren't any agendas set out for people to go over. This was not a traditional meeting. As a matter of fact, there was only one chair, in the center of the room, on top of a bunch of magnolia petals.

Jose led Kenzie by the elbow to the center of the room to the chair. "Ramon will be right with you."

For some reason, Kenzie sat. She realized everyone in the room was staring at her. She gulped in anticipation. The group in front of her parted. Ramon appeared, like his brothers, dressed in a black-on-black tuxedo. His hair was cut short. Way short. Tears formed again.

"You're back," Ramon said, approaching.

The last time he'd come toward her, they had not been on the best terms. Kenzie stood to meet him. "You got a haircut."

"Locks for Love." Ramon nodded. "How have you been?"

Kenzie blinked and looked to her left and her right. "Small talk? Can we go someplace private?"

"No," he said, shaking his head. "Are you embarrassed?"

She shrugged. "Maybe."

"Not as embarrassed as I am."

"What do you have to be embarrassed about?" Kenzie asked. She stepped closer and pressed her hand over her heart. "I'm the one who behaved horribly."

"I let you get away from me," said Ramon.

"Looks like you've been busy," Kenzie tried to joke.

"I have. I'm doing everything I can, Kenzie, to ensure you never leave my side again. We're going to have hard times and bumpy times, but I don't want to be like Auntie Bren…" He paused, waiting for her to stop him. She couldn't stop him. After what he'd done for her, he was family. "I don't want any time to pass between us when we fight. And we will argue—it is human nature."

The married couples in the room all agreed with him. Kenzie turned around to see who all found it funny. When she came back to face Ramon, he was kneeling in front of her. "Kenzie, I love you. I don't want to spend one more day without you."

"I love you, too." Kenzie began to weep. Tears rolled down her eyes as Ramon reached into his pocket and extracted a beautiful diamond ring."

"Mackenzie Hairston Swayne, my Dr. Beauty Queen," he said. "Will you do me the honor and please be my wife?"

And for once, without argument or debate, Kenzie said yes.

* * * * *

UNLOCKING THE MILLIONAIRE'S HEART

BELLA BUCANNON

Thank you to family, friends and fellow writers,
whose encouragement and support were
invaluable during the highs and lows
of this particular writing journey.

To my husband, always willing to brainstorm
when I'm stuck for a word or idea,
always reassuring.

To Kim for special insight.

To Victoria and Laurie for their advice
and guidance.

CHAPTER ONE

NATE THORNTON SHOOK the rain from his hair with vigour before entering the towering central office block in Sydney's city centre. He'd had to reschedule planned video meetings to make the train trip from Katoomba at Brian Hamilton's insistence, and he'd been further frustrated by his evasive remarks.

'It has to be Thursday the ninth. I think I've found a resolution for your hero and heroine interaction problem. And there's a publisher who's interested in seeing a revised copy of your book.'

Late-night research had shown Brian Hamilton to be one of the best literary agents in Australia. After initial contact he had asked for, and read, Nate's synopsis and first three chapters, then requested the full manuscript. His brutal honesty on its marketability had convinced Nate he was the contract negotiator he wanted.

Attempts to rewrite the scenes he'd specified, however, had proved that particular aspect wasn't his forte. And when he'd been tempted to suggest cutting them out, the feeling in his gut had told him it wasn't that simple, and to ask if the agent could find a better solution.

It wasn't the possibility of income that drove Nate to his computer. Astute investment of an inheritance and a significant part of his earnings while working abroad meant he was financially secure for years. Or, as his brother claimed, 'filthy rich'—a phrase he detested. Although he envied Sam the satisfaction he'd achieved as a pilot in the air force, currently stationed at Edinburgh, north of Adelaide.

His compulsion to write had been driven by the need to put the hardships and traumas he'd witnessed as an international reporter where they belonged—in his past. Those harrowing images of man's inhumanity to man were still in his head, though for the most part he managed to keep them buried.

There was nothing he could do regarding the way he now viewed life and interacted with new acquaintances. The walls he'd built for his own emotional protection were solid and permanent.

Frowning at the number of floors all six lifts had to descend before reaching him, he punched the 'up' button and tapped his fingers on his thigh. Okay, so he wasn't so hot on the touchy-feely sentimental stuff. Hell, the rest of his hundred thousand words were damn good, and his target readers weren't romantic females.

No disrespect intended.

The street doors sliding open drew his attention. The woman who came in brushing raindrops from her hair held it. He had a quick impression of black tights, then a flash of blue patterned fabric under a beige raincoat as she unbuttoned and shook it.

His mind registered long brown hair, a straight nose and red lips above a cute chin—*great descriptive characterisation for an author, Thornton*—then, as their eyes met, he felt a distinct jolt in his stomach.

Dark blue eyes framed by thick lashes stared, then blinked. Her smooth brow furrowed, and she swung away abruptly to study the board on the wall. He huffed in wry amusement at having been dismissed as un-noteworthy—not his usual first reaction from women.

The lift pinged and he moved aside to allow an exiting couple room. Another quick appraisal of the stationary figure of the woman, and he stepped inside.

* * *

Brian's personal assistant had notified Brian of Nate's arrival, and in less than the time it took her to hang his damp jacket on a stand in the corner the agent was greeting him with enthusiasm.

'Punctual as always.' He peered over Nate's shoulder, as if expecting someone else. 'Come on in. Coffee?'

'Yes—if it's going to be rough and take that long.'

Brian laughed. 'It all depends on how determined you are to have a successful publication.'

He followed Nate into the well-appointed corner office, waved at the four comfy leather armchairs round a long low table and went to the coffee machine on a built-in cabinet.

'Strong and black, right?'

'Please.'

Nate sat and studied the view of nearby commercial buildings: hundreds of glass pane eyes, letting in sunlight while hiding the secrets of the people behind them. He'd need to be a heap of floors higher to get even a smidgeon of a harbour view.

'How was the journey down? Ah, excuse me, Nate.' Brian walked over to answer the ring from his desk phone, said 'Thank you, Ella,' then hung up and went to the door.

'I won't be a moment, then we can get started. Your coffee should be ready.'

Spooning sugar into the mug, Nate added extra, figuring he was going to need it. He heard Brian's muted voice, and a quiet female answer. Distracted by the sounds, he drank too soon, letting out a low curse when the hot brew burnt his tongue. This day wasn't getting any better.

'Come in—there's someone I'd like you to meet.'

A second later he was experiencing the same reaction as he had a few moments ago on the ground floor. The woman who'd caused it stood in the doorway, her stunning eyes wide with surprise. And some other, darker emotion.

The absence of her raincoat—presumably hanging up with his jacket—revealed a slender form in a hip-length, blue-patterned, long-sleeved garment with no fastening at the front. The black tights drew his gaze to shapely legs and flat black laced shoes.

This close, he appreciated the smoothness of her lightly tanned skin, the blue of her irises and the perfect shape of her full lips. Not so acceptable was her hesitation and the glance behind her. An action that allowed him to make out the nuances of colour in her hair—shades of his teak table at home.

One look at his agent's satisfied expression and his brain slammed into full alert. This young woman seemed more likely to be a problem for his libido than a resolution for his fictional characters' relationship. What the hell did Brian have in mind?

With Brian urging her in, Jemma Harrison had no choice but to enter the room, pressing the tips of her left-hand fingers into her palm. The man from the lobby seemed no more pleased to see her than she felt about him. Down there, with the length of the foyer between them, his self-assured stance and the arrogant lift of his head had proclaimed his type. One she recognised, classified and avoided.

She'd dismissed the blip in her pulse as their eyes met, swinging away before her mind could process any of his features. Now, against her will, it memorised deep-set storm-grey eyes with dark lashes, thick, sun streaked brown hair and a stubborn jaw. Attractive in an outdoor, man-of-action way. The tan summer sweater he wore emphasised impressive pecs and broad shoulders. He'd teamed it with black chinos and sneakers, and she knew her socialite sister, Vanessa, would rate him as 'cool.'

'Jemma, meet Nate Thornton. Nate, Jemma Harrison.' Brian grinned, as if he'd pulled off an impossible coup.

Jemma stepped forward as Nate placed his mug on the bench and did the same. His cool eyes gave no indication of his thoughts, and his barely there smile vanished more quickly than it had formed.

For no fathomable reason her body tensed as he shook her hand, his grip gentle yet showing underlying strength. A man you'd want on your side in any battle. A man whose touch initiated tremors across her skin and heat in the pit of her stomach. A man she hoped lived a long way from her home town.

'Hello, Jemma. From your expression, I assume Brian didn't tell you I'd be here, so we're both in the dark.'

Against her will, she responded to the sound of his voice—firm and confident, deep and strong, with a hint of abrasion. The kind of voice that would stir sensations when whispering romantic phrases in a woman's ear.

Oh, heck, now she was thinking like one of her starry-eyed heroines, and feeling bereft as he let go and moved away.

'Brian invited me to come in any time I was in Sydney. He didn't mention anyone else being here today.'

'I'll explain once you have a drink,' Brian said. 'Coffee, tea or cold?'

'Flat white coffee with sugar, please.'

She settled into one of the chairs. Nate retrieved his mug and dropped into the one alongside. She was aware of his scrutiny as she scanned the office she'd been too nervous to admire during her first appointment here. It was furnished to give the impression of success with moderation—very apt for the occupant himself.

Average in appearance, and normally mild-mannered, Brian let his passion surface when speaking of books, of guiding authors on their journey to publication and the joy of sharing their triumphs. In assessment he was never condescending, highlighting the positives before giving

honest evaluation of the low points, and offering sugges-
tions for improvement.

Why had he invited Nate Thornton to join them? She'd
bet he had no idea of the romance genre, and wouldn't appreciate any relevant cover if she held it up in front of his
face.

Brian placed a mug in front of her, sat down with his
and smiled—first at her, then towards Nate.

'We have here an agent's dilemma: two writers with
great potential for literary success, both with flaws that
prohibit that achievement.'

Jemma turned her head to meet Nate's appraising gaze
and raised eyebrows and frowned. Why wasn't he as surprised as she was at this announcement?

Brian regained her attention and continued.

'Discussions and revision attempts haven't been successful for either of you. But, as they say in the game, I
had a lightbulb moment after Jemma told me she was coming to Sydney.'

He took a drink before going on, and Jemma's stomach
curled in anticipation—or was it trepidation? She wasn't
sure she wanted to hear any solution which meant involvement with this stranger by her side.

'Nate has a talent for action storytelling—very marketable in any media. Regrettably, the interaction between his
hero and heroine is bland and unimaginative.'

That was hard to believe. Any man as handsome as he
would have no trouble finding willing women to date and
seduce. She'd seen the macho flare in his eyes when they'd
been introduced, and her body's response had been in-
stinctive.

'Jemma's characters and *their* interaction make for riveting reading. But the storyline between the extremely satisfying emotional scenes has little impact and won't keep

pages turning. So, as a trial, I'm proposing we combine
your strengths in Nate's manuscript.'

Nate's protest drowned out the startled objections coming
from the woman on his right. It took supreme effort not to
surge to his feet and pace the room—a lifelong habit when
agitated or problem solving.

'Oh, come on, Brian. You know the hours and the effort—
physical and mental—that I've put into that book. I can understand bringing someone else in…could even accept an
experienced author…'

He struggled for words. Huh, so much for being a great
writer.

'You expect me to permit an unproven amateur to mess
with my manuscript? Her hearts and flowers characters
will *never* fit.'

'Isn't your "amateur status" the reason you're here too,
Mr Thornton? I doubt you've ever held a romance novel,
let alone read the blurb on the back.'

The quiet, pleasant voice from minutes ago now had
bite. He swung round to refute her comment, so riled up
its intriguing quality barely registered.

'Wrong, Jemma. Every single word of one—from the
title on the front cover to the ending of that enlightening
two-paragraph description—to win a bet. Can't say I was
impressed.'

Her chin lifted, her dark blue eyes widened in mock indignation and her lips, which his errant brain was assessing as decidedly kissable, curled at the corners. Her short
chuckle had his breath catching in his throat, and his pulse
booting up faster than his top-of-the-range computer.

'Let me guess. It was selected by a woman—the one
who claimed you wouldn't make it through the first chapter, let alone to the happy ending.'

Shoot! His stomach clenched as if he'd been sucker-punched. Baited and played by his sister, Alice, he'd read every page of that badly written, highly sexed paperback to prove a point.

Brian cut in, so his plans for sibling payback had to be shelved for the future.

'Relax, Nate. Your hero and heroine's action stories are absorbing and believable. It's their relationship that won't be credible to the reader. I'm convinced Jemma can rectify that.'

'You're asking me to give her access? Let her delete and make changes to suit her reading preferences?'

No way. Not now. Not ever.

'No.'

'No!'

Their denials meshed.

Brian was the one who negated his outburst.

'No one's suggesting such a drastic measure. To start with I'd like the two of you to have lunch. Get to know each other a little. If you can reach a truce, we could start with a trial collaboration on two or three chapters.'

Lunch? Food and table talk with a woman who'd shown an adverse reaction to him on sight?

He sucked in air, blew it out and shrugged his shoulders. What did he have to lose? A book contract, for starters.

He matched the challenge in Jemma's eyes, nodded and forced a smile.

'Would you care to have lunch with me, Jemma?'

'It will be my pleasure, Nate.'

Her polite acceptance and return smile alleviated his mood a tad, though the option he'd been given still rankled. He disliked coercion—especially if it meant having a meal with an attractive woman who was somehow breaching the barriers he'd built for mental survival. Another reason for not entering into a working relationship with her.

He avoided entanglements. One heart-ripping experience had been enough, and was not to be chanced again. It was only his fact-finding skill that had prevented his being conned out of a fortune as well. Any woman he met now had to prove herself worthy of his trust before it was given.

Brian had been straight and honest with him from the start. And Jemma had shown spirit, so she might be good company. He'd enjoy a good meal, and then…

Well, for starters he'd be spending a lot of time reading writing manuals until he'd mastered the art of accurately describing a relationship.

It was warming up as Jemma exited the building with Nate. The rain had cleared, leaving the pavements wet and steamy and the air clammy. With a soft touch to her elbow he steered her to the right and they walked in silence, each lost in their own thoughts.

She was mulling over the recent conversation between the two of them and Brian, and assumed he was doing the same. Agreeing to Brian's proposition would mean being in frequent contact—albeit via electronic media—with a man whose innate self-assurance reminded her of her treacherous ex-boyfriend and her over-polite and social-climbing brother-in-law.

But unlike those two Nate also had an aura of macho strength and detachment. The latter was a plus for her—especially with her unexpected response when facing him eye to eye and having her hand clasped in his. Throughout the meeting she'd become increasingly aware of his musky aroma with its hint of vanilla and citrus. Alluring and different from anything she'd ever smelt, it had had her imagining a cosy setting in front of a wood fire.

Other pedestrians flowed around them, eager to reach their destinations. Nate came to a sudden stop, caught her arm and drew her across to a shop window. Dropping his hand, he regarded her for a moment with sombre eyes, his body language telling her he'd rather be anywhere else, *with* anyone else.

'Any particular restaurant you fancy?' Reluctance resonated in his voice.

'I haven't a clue.' She arched her head to stare beyond him. An impish impulse to razz him for his hostile attitude overrode her normal discretion and she grinned. 'How about that one?'

He followed her gaze to the isolated round glass floor on the communications tower soaring above the nearby buildings. His eyebrows arched, the corner of his mouth quirked, and something akin to amusement flashed like lightning in his storm-grey eyes.

'The Sydney Tower? Probably booked out weeks ahead, but we can try.'

'I was joking—it's obviously a tourist draw. If we'd been a few steps to the right I wouldn't even have seen it. You decide.'

'You're not familiar with Sydney, are you?'

His voice was gentler, as if her living a distance away was acceptable.

'Basic facts from television and limited visits over many years—more since some of my friends moved here.'

'Darling Harbour's not too far, and there's a variety of restaurants there. We'll take a cab.'

'Sounds good.' She'd have been content to walk—she loved the hustle and bustle of the crowds, the rich accents of different languages and the variety of personal and food aromas wafting through the air. Tantalising mixtures only found in busy cities.

She followed him to the kerb, trying to memorise every detail while he watched for a ride. Once they were on their way her fingers itched to write it all down in the notepad tucked in the side pocket of her shoulder bag—an essential any time she left home.

As a writer, he might understand. As a man who'd been coerced into having lunch with her, who knew *how* he'd react?

Erring on the side of caution, she clasped her hands together and fixed the images in her mind.

CHAPTER TWO

THE FORMAL ESTABLISHMENT Nate steered her towards was a pleasant surprise. She'd been expecting something similar to the casual restaurants she'd passed on her way to Brian's office from the station. White and red linen, crystal glassware and elegant decor gave it a classy atmosphere, and made it look similar to her parents' current venture in Adelaide. The difference was in the plush red cushioning on the seats and the backs of the mahogany chairs.

They received a warm welcome, and at Nate's request were led to a corner table by the window. The view of moored yachts and the cityscape behind them was postcard-picturesque, and would be more so at night with the boats and buildings lit up. She made a mental note to return to the area after dark with Cloe, the friend she was staying with in North Ryde.

Occasionally taking a sip of the chilled water in her glass, she perused the menu options carefully. Having grown up experiencing different flavours and cuisines, she loved comparing the many ways different chefs varied tastes.

'What would you like to drink, Jemma?'

Looking up, she encountered a seemingly genuine smile from Nate. Pity it didn't reach his eyes. But at least he was giving her a choice—something her ex had rarely granted. She placed her menu down, food decision made, and flicked back the hair from her right cheek.

'White wine, please. I'm having fish for both entrée and main courses.'

'Any special kind?'

That impulsive urge to rattle his staid demeanour rose again: *so* not her usual behaviour.

'I guess I should pick a local label—though our South Australian ones are superior.' She raised her chin and curled her lips, daring him to dispute her statement.

She achieved her aim and then some.

His eyes narrowed, drawing his thick dark brows obliquely down, and his mouth quirked as he spoke in a mild tone. 'We'll save that war until later. For that quip, *I'll* select.'

His flippant remark left her breathless, lips parted and with tingles scooting up and down her spine. She drained her water glass, incapable of forming a retort. He was smart—a fast thinker. A man not to be toyed with.

Her mind inexplicably recalled the adage *Make love not war*, and a hot flush spread up from her neck. Lucky for her, a young waiter arrived for their orders, and she ducked her head to read from the menu.

I'll start with the smoked salmon with capers,' she told him, 'and have the barramundi with a fresh garden salad for my main.'

Nate chose oysters with chilli, coconut and lime as an entrée, followed by grilled salmon and steamed vegetables.

The wine he ordered was unknown to Jemma, and the hours she'd spent stacking refrigerators and racks had given her an extensive knowledge of labels. She'd also filled and emptied many a dishwasher, so figured she'd earned any offer to dine out for years to come.

'You obviously enjoy seafood.'

Nate's upper body leant forward over his crossed arms on the table, his intent to follow their agent's suggestion of becoming acquainted evident in his posture. Pity there was little affability in his tone, and a suspicion there was more to his manner than giving her access to his writing began to form.

'Barramundi is my mother's specialty. I like to compare other offerings with hers.'

'She's a good cook, huh?'

Jemma laughed. 'Don't ever call her that if she has a knife in her hand—which, by the way, will always be sharp. Both she and Dad are qualified chefs, and live for their profession.'

A speculative gleam appeared in his smoky eyes, holding her spellbound, feeling as if he were seeking her innermost thoughts. His features remained impassive, his voice with its intriguing hint of roughness calm. The only sign of emotion was the steady tapping of two left-hand fingers on his right elbow, an action he seemed unaware of.

'I'm guessing that didn't leave much time for child-rearing.'

'I didn't mean—'

The waiter appeared with their wine, sending the next words back into her throat. She'd have to set him straight—hadn't meant to give that impression. Yet as Nate sampled the small amount of wine poured into his glass she couldn't deny the facts. There *had* been little time for any of the usual parent/child activities, though they'd encouraged and financed Vanessa's modelling courses. They'd gained publicity, of course, when she'd won an international contract.

On Nate's approval, her glass was filled. As she savoured the crisp, dry flavour he raised his glass to her without speaking, drank, then set it down.

'This *is* good. I approve of your choice, Nate.' She took another sip and let it linger on her tongue, waiting for him to continue the conversation about family. He didn't.

I presume you don't write full-time? Do you have another career?'

'I paint pictures of Australian flora and fauna, mostly on small tiles, and work part-time in the gift shop where they're displayed. I also sell them at local markets.'

'Let me guess—koalas and wombats top the list?'

Hearing the hint of condescension in his voice, she clenched her teeth and felt her spine stiffen. She tightened her grip on the stem of her glass and held back the retort his words deserved.

'They're up there. Mother animals with babies are my bestsellers, along with bright native flowers.'

'And where's home?'

Firing questions seemed to be his idea of becoming acquainted. She obliged, giving him only the information she wished to reveal.

'The Adelaide Hills.'

'South Australian bushfire territory? I was there in 2015. The risks don't worry you?'

Nate saw the flicker of pain in her eyes and the slight convulsion in her throat—heard the hitch in her voice when, after gazing out of the window for a moment, she answered.

'That year was my first summer as a resident there. A close friend lost property, some sheep and their pets—a cat and two dogs. Meg and her family were devastated, yet they stayed, rebuilt and adopted from the animal shelter. They taught me how to minimise risks, and although the worry is there every year, it's balanced by living with fresh air in a friendly, small-town atmosphere. Big cities are for holidays and shopping sprees. How about you?'

Sprung. He'd kept his questions basic, complying with the intent of Brian's words if not the spirit. He hadn't expected to hear a familiar story—one he'd heard a few times since he'd moved to the mountains. Given her parents' profession, he'd pictured her living in Adelaide or one of its suburbs.

Bracing himself for her reaction, he answered.

'The Blue Mountains.'

He was treated to a sharp intake of breath between

parted lips, a delightful indignant expression and flashing eyes. Against his will, his gut tightened in response.

'That's the New South Wales equivalent. *You* have flare-ups every year.'

Stalled by the arrival of their entrées, Nate waited until they were alone before replying, surprising himself with an admission he didn't normally disclose to strangers.

'I know. I help fight them.'

She tilted her head as she scrutinised him, as if memorising every feature and nuance. He'd already achieved that in the office. He might not have her reputed eloquent descriptive powers, but her face was indelibly imprinted on his mind. Again, not intentionally.

'You're a volunteer firefighter?'

Her apparent admiration was gratifying, if not truly merited. He shrugged it off. Living in the country meant embracing its culture and values.

'You live in the area—you should do your bit. The training keeps me fit, along with exercising at home.'

He scooped up an oyster and let it slide down his throat, savouring the spice and tang as he watched Jemma arrange salmon and capers on a cracker, and take a delicate bite. Her glossed lips fascinated him, conjuring up thoughts better left unsaid, and his sudden surge of desire was totally unexpected.

He knew the myth that oysters were an aphrodisiac, so maybe they'd been the wrong choice.

Risky selection or not, he ate another before asking, 'How much writing have you done?'

It came out more curt than he'd intended—caused by his inability to curb her effect on his mind and body. If he was attracted to a woman his rules were not negotiable. *Keep it simple, keep it unemotional and don't get too involved.* Strictly adhering to those rules since his short disastrous affair—never discussed with anyone, not even family—

ensured mutually satisfying relationships with women of similar views.

Jemma wrote romance. She'd be a sentimental believer in happy-ever-after who deserved flowers—hell, she even *painted* them—and love tokens. She'd want commitment, and would no doubt one day be a devoted wife and mother.

He might fantasise about her, might desire her, but the pitfalls of sexual entanglement had taught him to maintain control. Whatever feelings she aroused now, they would pass once they'd parted company.

She sipped her wine and made a lingering survey of the room, before facing him with enigmatic features. Not one to open up willingly to someone she didn't know. He waited patiently. As things stood now, his literary career wouldn't be taking off any time soon.

'Poems and short stories since childhood—most of the earlier ones consigned to the recycling bin. A computer file of thirty thousand-word partial manuscripts with varying degrees of potential, plus this finished one.'

'Which Brian deems in need of drastic revision?'

'Ditto, Mr Thornton. Is this your first effort, or are there others waiting for your help too?'

She gave a sudden stunning smile that tripped his pulse, shaking his composure.

She rattled it even more when she added, with unerring accuracy, 'No, you'd see any project through to the bitter end before starting another.' Leaving him speechless.

He scooped out the last oyster, trying to fathom why a woman so dissimilar from those who usually attracted him was pressing his buttons with such ease. Down to earth rather than sophisticated, she had that indefinable something he couldn't identify.

Shelving it to the back of his mind, he pushed the tray of empty shells aside. 'Point conceded. And the name's Nate. Unless you're trying to maintain a barrier between us?'

The soft flush of colour over her cheeks proved he was right. His own rush of guilt proved that his conscience knew his curtness was partly to blame.

He drained his wine glass, set it down, and thanked the waitress who cleared away the dishes. A new topic seemed appropriate.

'How well do you know Brian?'

Jemma blinked as he switched topic again. This was almost like speed-dating—which she'd never tried, but she knew women who'd described it. Except she and Nate weren't changing partners, and she definitely wasn't in the market for one.

'Mostly by email, but I trust him. He read my novel, then when I came to Sydney in December we met in his office. Not my happiest encounter ever, as he gave me an honest, concise appraisal of my writing proficiency. Unlike you, my inept storyline passages way outnumber the good scenes. You?'

'Similar scenario. You're not bothered that agreeing to his proposal means putting your novel on hold while you work on someone else's?'

'No, I'm dumbfounded by the offer, terrified of the implications if I fail, and thrilled that he believes I'm worthy of being part of something he seems keen to see published. If you're as good as he's implied, adapting those scenes yet keeping them true to your characters and story will be beneficial for my career too.'

'Hmm.'

He appeared to be considering her declaration as their mains were served, pepper offered and accepted by Nate, and their wine glasses refilled. She waited for him to continue, but instead he began to eat.

The fish was delicious, and her *mmm* of pleasure slipped

out. Glancing up, she found Nate watching her with a sombre expression.

'How does this chef's barramundi compare to your mother's?'

'As good as—though I'd never tell her. It's different, and I can't pick why. I prefer the natural taste of food, so I don't use many herbs and spices and I can't always identify their flavour. How's your salmon?'

She hoped her answer would satisfy him, and save her from having to admit that her limited cooking knowledge came from her aunt and recipe books, because her parents claimed they didn't have time to teach her.

'Up to the usual excellent standard. I've never had a meal here that wasn't.'

They ate in silence for a few minutes, with Jemma wishing she had her sister's gift to attract and charm people of any age. Apart from when she was with close friends Jemma hid behind a façade of friendly courtesy. Though she had her moments when she couldn't hold back—like when someone irked her as *he* had a few times. Or when her curiosity was aroused. Like now.

'How do you make a living while you're waiting for the book sale royalties to come flooding in?'

Nate's head jerked up, his face a picture of astonishment. Instead of the comeback she'd assumed he'd give, he chuckled, and the deep sound wrapped around her, making her yearn for a time when trust had come easy.

'I'll let you know when they do and we'll celebrate.'

The memory of a similar pledge slammed through her, taking her breath away and freezing her blood.

I'm expecting good news. When it comes we'll have a special celebration.

Two days later she'd found out that the man she'd believed loved her and intended to propose was sleeping with a female colleague to gain promotion. He'd even gone to meet her after taking Jemma home that night.

'Jemma, are you all right?'

She shook her head, dragged in air and looked into concerned grey eyes.

'You're white as a ghost.'

'The ghost of a bad memory. Best forgotten.' She managed a smile and he relaxed into his seat, keeping watch on her pale face. 'Truly, I'm fine.'

'I'm not so sure, but…'

He let out a very masculine grunt and she was totally back in the now, reaching for her wine, sipping it as he gave her a serious answer.

'I was a reporter. Now I'm an investment advisor.'

'A good one?'

'Good enough to pay the bills.'

Jemma pondered on his succinct job description. She could visualise him investigating a story, chasing information to find the truth, but the switch to an office job didn't gel.

'Why the career move?'

She watched his chest expand under the tan sweater, hold then contract. He seemed to be deliberately assessing how much to disclose. Preparing to keep secrets and lie like her ex?

'Things happen and you make choices. My gap year— travelling in Europe with a friend after we graduated from uni—became a rite of passage lasting seven years that made me who I am now.'

She empathised, and was convinced his matter-of-fact tone belied his true feelings. Her parents selling their house—her home—to invest in a restaurant, and her ex's betrayal were the two events that had forced her to re-evaluate her future, and they had a continuing effect on her viewpoint and life choices.

'Four years ago, my father had a health scare, prompting him to semi-retire and move with my mother to the south coast. It was my motivation for coming home for good—a decision I've never regretted in the slightest.'

She heard honest affection in his voice and envied that relationship. She couldn't imagine her parents or sister giving up their careers for anyone—hoped she'd be more compassionate.

Sensing he'd divulged more than he'd intended when he'd agreed to lunch with her, she didn't reply and finished eating her meal.

Nate had no idea why he'd revealed private aspects of his life he usually kept to himself. Or why he found it almost impossible to take his eyes off her enchanting, expressive face. His attraction to a woman had never been so immediate, so compelling. So in conflict with his normal emotionless liaisons.

A growing need for open space was compelling. He had to get away from her—away from her subtle floral perfume that had been tantalising him since he'd stepped near enough to greet her. Native rather than commercially grown city flowers, it was delicate and haunting.

He didn't fight his urgent compulsion to pace and consider all the implications, including any legal ramifications, of collaboration. He needed to think and plan away from the distractions of other people, away from Jemma and his reactions to her, physical and mental.

Noting her plate was empty, he placed his cutlery neatly on his.

'Do you want dessert or coffee here? Or we could take some time apart to consider our options and meet up later.'

This time her scrutiny was short. yet no less intense.

With an understanding smile he'd rather not have seen, she nodded. 'That's a good idea.'

Muscles he hadn't realised were tight suddenly loosened.

'I'll need your phone number.'

Unease flickered in her eyes before she reached for her shoulder bag on the floor. Had it anything to do with her adverse opinion of him at first sight?

He held his mobile towards her, allowing her to input first.

Their empty plates removed, and anything else politely declined, she leant her elbows on the table and cupped her chin on her linked fingers as they waited for the bill.

'Do you commute from the mountains every day?' she asked.

'Electronic media means I can do a fair amount from home. I come in when necessary, or for socialising.'

He hadn't yet bowed to the pressure to commit to full-time employment with the family firm, wary of the daily sameness stretching into his future.

'Like today?'

'Like today.'

And he'd be staying until his flight overseas on Sunday morning.

He settled the account on the way out, irrationally torn between needing to be alone and reluctance to let her go. After saying goodbye, she headed for the railway station without glancing back. He watched for a moment, then strode towards the Harbour Bridge.

CHAPTER THREE

JEMMA TOOK NO notice of the world around her as the train sped to Central Station, and as she deliberated on which way to go when she alighted. Her brain buzzed at the compliments Brian had given her, coupled with the sensations from Nate's few touches and her own responses to his looks and his voice.

Could she handle being in frequent contact with him? Even by email? How would she deal with someone who was averse to allowing her to read anything he'd written?

Consider our options.

Like heck. He oozed the authority of a man who knew exactly what he wanted and rarely settled for less. He'd given no indication of his point of view on their two-way deal, focussing only on his novel.

Brian's appraisal of her work had been honest and unemotional, letting her know the downsides while still giving her hope of a satisfactory solution. Already aware of her weakness when she'd submitted to him, she was open to any suggestion for improvement.

Could Nate remain impartial to the romance genre when he read her work? How did he feel about helping to transform her inept storytelling? He'd been very forthright about his aversion to allowing her access to his manuscript. Her emotions wavered from exhilaration that she might achieve publication to apprehension that Nate's expectations might be hard to satisfy.

She walked out of the station and turned towards Circular Quay. Window shopping in Pitt Street would pass the time and occupy her mind. If he didn't call… She banished that thought. He'd phone—even if it was only to dash any foolish hopes she might have allowed to take seed.

A new dress and two fun presents for her friends later, she was watching the ferries dock and depart as she devoured a fruit and nut bar. She wandered over to where groups of excited people were dragging suitcases towards a huge cruise ship. A holiday to inspire a romance novel? Maybe one day she'd take one.

A brochure she'd picked up on the way showed it wasn't far from here to the historic Rocks area. If she hadn't heard from Nate by the time she'd explored the old buildings she'd catch the next train to North Ryde.

Did he like Jemma? Way too much. Nate had kept his emotions under tight restraint since he'd narrowly escaped being duped into a sham marriage, but he'd had trouble curbing them around her. She'd had doubts concerning *him* on sight, which had him wondering who he reminded her of.

Did he trust her? Not yet. Experience in dealing with the darker side of life had taught him that trust had to be earned rather than given freely.

Did he want her? His body's response to any thought of her gave him an instant reply. But that didn't mean he'd follow through.

Mental arguments for and against dual authorship had got him nowhere, and he was still uncommitted as he reached the waterside. Swinging left, he took the steps leading up to the bridge walkway. After skirting a group of photo-snapping tourists, he took a deep breath of salty air and began to run.

He maintained a steady pace until he reached the apartment block at North Sydney. His grandfather had bequeathed a twenty-third-storey unit jointly to him, Sam and Alice, and all three of them had lived there, alone or together, at various times. It was always available for family and friends when they came to the city.

A long, refreshing shower cooled his body, but didn't clear his mind. Dressed in fresh clothes, and with a stubby of cold beer in his hand, he stood on the balcony, staring at the buildings around him. Not far away by foot was the office block housing the family brokerage firm, which had offered him a lucrative job for life.

Far away up in the mountains was the home he'd designed, with an architect's help, to suit the lifestyle he planned to live. Mostly solitary, with occasional guests, pleasing only himself. Closing his eyes, he pictured the view as he woke in the morning, ate his meals and chilled out in the evenings. And in that instant his decision was made.

Somewhere in the thriving metropolis across the bay was the woman Brian believed could help him realise literary success. All he had to do was have faith and stay in command of his libido.

But before he committed to a trial partnership he needed to reinforce the life oath he'd made years ago, during the lowest point of his life. He took the dog-eared leather notebook he always travelled with, flipped it open to a coded page, and read the vow he'd made never to get involved out loud.

Then he phoned Jemma Harrison.

It took three rings for her to answer, and he heard traffic and the rattle of a train in the background.

'Hi, Jemma, where are you?'

'Taking photos from the Harbour Bridge.'

He surprised himself with a spontaneous burst of laughter.

'What's so funny?' There was a spike in her voice, though she didn't sound offended.

'I ran over it on the way here. Which end are you nearest?'

'Um… I guess I'm about a third of the way along from the quay.'

'Keep coming north. Don't rush. I'll meet you at the steps going down to the road. We can sit in the park nearby. Would you like me to bring you a hot or cold drink?'

'No, thanks. I have a bottle of water.'

'Okay, see you soon.'

He grimaced at the screen after disconnecting, and then went to put on socks and sneakers. Having his pulse hiking and his mouth drying, even his palms itching, was something he might have to become accustomed to if they were going to be in regular communication.

Anticipation of seeing her had him moving faster than normal. It was not the way he wanted to feel.

Nate saw Jemma approaching as he reached the top of the steps so he waited, admiring the natural sway of her hips as she came towards him. The extra bag in her hand and the bulge in the one over her shoulder, proved she'd been shopping. Her smile as they met had him steeling his arms at his sides to prevent greeting her with a hug, and the sunglasses hiding the expression in her beautiful blue eyes was a disappointment.

'Hi—would you like me to carry the bag?'

'Thanks, I'm fine.' She waved her arm in a wide sweep. 'I'd love to sit and view all this on a stormy day—or preferably night.'

'You like thunder and lightning?'

She laughed, causing an unfamiliar and yet not unpleasant effect over his skin. Causing him to take a quick breath. Causing him to fortify the reason he was meeting her. To get his book published.

'From a safe vantage point—oh, yes.'

'They can give you a spectacular display in the

mountains—especially when watched from a heated room with a beer or glass of wine at your side.'

Berating himself for conjuring up an image of them sharing wine and nature's dramatic show, he guided her down to the ground and across to the lawn area at the edge of the water. Partial images of the Opera House and the southern side of the bay were visible through the semi-circle of palm trees. A small oasis of green surrounded by acres of concrete and buildings was behind them, and the expanse of deep water in front.

Jemma placed her bags on the ground, sat and curled her legs to the side. He joined her, leaning on his elbows, legs stretched out in front of him. For a moment or two there seemed no need for conversation. The serenity of the small area compensated for the traffic noise from the bridge.

Having resolved his mental conflict, and acutely aware of her beside him, he accepted that she'd now be a presence in his life. How prominent depended on how often they had to meet in person.

Few women he knew would wait so quietly, so patiently, for a man who'd told her he needed to consider his options, expected her to hike across the bridge, and then didn't initiate conversation. Another difference from the women he dated.

Her profile was as appealing as her full face. Delicate smooth skin invited a caress, thick brown lashes enhanced the dark blue of her eyes, and her slender neck with its curtain of…

Where the heck had all that come from? And where the hell had it been when he'd tried to write such descriptions on the computer?

'Jemma?'

His raspy tone came from the absence of moisture in his throat, exacerbated by the expectancy in her eyes as she faced him. He coughed, swallowed and retried.

'Do you have full virus protection on your computer?'

Her chin lifted and her eyes narrowed in umbrage. 'The best—and regularly updated.'

'Would you be willing to send me some examples of those scenes Brian claims will improve my novel to a marketable level? I'm aware it means one-sided trust, but—'

Her laughter—natural, musical and matched by the sparkle in her eyes—cut him short.

'My text is less than fifty thousand words, a fair proportion of which need cutting or rewriting. Most of your...' She tilted her head and her eyebrows rose in query.

'One hundred and ten thousand.'

'Not only pass muster but have earned Brian's praise. You have the right to be protective. How about I email three chapters?'

He puffed out what little air was left in his lungs. This could either be the start of a new career or the most turbulent phase of his life. Even seeing her face-to-face online would test his tenacity.

Jemma tried to hide the elation coursing through her. If he approved of her style of writing there was a chance he'd send her a partial to test her competence in blending with his. A *limited* partial, if she was any judge of men—a talent she could hardly claim, having had no inkling of her ex's infidelity.

Nate Thornton, with his solemn expression and deep-set thoughtful eyes, was hard to read. He rarely smiled, but when he did he stirred feelings she'd sworn she'd never allow to rule her again. And his touch had her hankering for pleasures she'd renounced, tainted by betrayal. An electronic, detached co-author partnership would be the ideal answer.

'You'll need my email address.' He pushed himself into a sitting position, and took out his mobile. She gave him her ever-present notebook and a pen, and had no trouble reading the neat script, wishing hers was as legible when she jotted something down so fast. He recorded hers in his phone—a much newer model than she owned. Something she might have to research and rectify in the coming weeks.

'I've got a USB back-up with me, so I'll send them tomorrow.' She grinned at him; no use being precious about her failings. 'Try to skim over the boring bits. Brian left me with no illusions on the quality of the storyline, but I hope to amend that failing by taking relevant courses.'

He returned the smile. 'Maybe I *should* read them. They're the reason he recommended you work with me instead of offering your novel to a publisher. I'll do a print-out for my flight to Europe on Sunday morning—preferable to reading off a screen for me. I'll get in touch on my return in a week or so.'

'However long it takes.'

She couldn't seem to break eye contact since he'd smiled at her, and wondered whether she ought to take the initiative and leave. Go home and start preparing dinner for her friends or watch some bad afternoon television. Even better, lose herself in the character charts and life histories of the hero and heroine of her next novel. One for which she intended to have Brian begging her to sign a solo contract.

Nate's sudden rise to his feet broke her reverie and dulled her mood. Now the main issue had been settled he'd be anxious to go, and she understood—she truly did. Accepting his helping hand, she rose, taking her shoulder bag with her. He bent to pick up the other one, and maintained his hold.

'How are you getting back?'

'Walking over the bridge, of course. Who knows when I'll have another chance?'

As he'd met her from this direction, she assumed he'd be staying in this area.

'Suits me, Jemma. I'll shout you coffee on the southern side.'

She had no right to feel elated, or for her heart to beat faster, but both happened as he spoke. And the air in her lungs seemed to have dissipated, making her sound breathy.

'Your offer is accepted with gratitude, Nate.'

Since when had she spoken with such formality?

I don't even allow my characters that uptown privilege. Maybe I will in a future book of mine, and their love interest will have a rougher background for conflict.

Her fingers itched to jot down notes on upbringing, and childhood environment. Instead she set the idea into her head as they returned to the walkway.

On her journey across it she'd become used to the noise of the traffic speeding past, separated from her by a steel and mesh safety fence. On the water side there were shoulder-and-head-high gaps in the corresponding mesh to allow for clear photography.

She stopped a short way along to take photos from this end, turning from Nate as she aimed her mobile upward, marvelling at the size and power of the metal beams and the majestic arches above their heads.

'It's so incredible—so powerful and strong.'

'Walking up there is an entirely different experience. Keep it in mind for another visit.'

Swinging round, she bumped into his body as he stepped forward, pointing his finger to the top of the bridge. Her pulse surged as he caught her by the waist for support, and it didn't ease off when he let go.

'Not for me,' she stated with emphasis.

His eyebrows rose and he grinned—a genuine magnetic smile, stirring butterflies in her stomach. Heat flooded her veins and her heart pounded. Such potency…she was glad he normally withheld it from her.

'You're toned and fit. What's the problem? Fear of heights?'

He'd checked out her body? Fair was fair...she'd checked out his.

'No, I just have no inclination to try anything I consider extreme.'

Or to become involved with the self-assured, super-confident men those activities attract.

'Ah.' He straightened his back and crossed his arms in mock umbrage. The quirk at the corner of his mouth and the gleam in his eyes belied his stance. A new personality was emerging—one that was engaging and amiable, much harder to keep at a distance. With luck it was only transient.

'And that encompasses skydiving, mountain climbing and abseiling, huh?'

His words sounded deeper too, making the abrasion more appealing.

'I'm not *anti* them. I can almost understand the compulsion to try them. But not the repeated temptation for disaster. Everyday life is challenging enough.'

'Don't you ever feel the need for an adrenaline rush?'

'Mine come from seeing a koala with her new baby, or a rainbow appearing over the hills in a rainstorm.'

His soft chuckle evoked an alien feeling in her stomach, warm and exciting.

'Oh, darling, you are *so* missing out on life.'

Her mood altered in an instant and she moved away towards the city. He walked by her side, seemingly oblivious to the word that had rendered her speechless and torn at her heart. It marked him as a man who used endearments as a matter of course, making them meaningless; it had been a habit of her ex.

Glancing at him, she caught his lips curling as if she'd amused him and the penny dropped. He'd listed the extreme sports he'd participated in, was prepared to risk his life for the so-called 'rush' she'd heard people rave about. Nothing they'd said had ever convinced her to try any, and she doubted reading about them—they had to be part of the action in his novel—would change her mind.

Was he even now classifying her as boring, doomed to fail in her attempt to revise some of the passages in his high-adventure book?

She stopped and swivelled to face him, square-on. 'You've done all those activities?'

Nate couldn't deny the accusation. He shrugged his shoulders and nodded. 'Multiple times—plus a few others over the years, here and abroad.'

If they stayed in touch for a lifetime Nate figured he'd never get used to the way she breathed slow and even, her lips slightly parted and her eyes wide and focussed as they studied his face. It made him feel virile, yet vulnerable at the same time—a totally alien sensation.

Better she didn't know that some of those activities had been to gain access to high-risk areas, following leads for stories. Others *had* been for the adrenaline rush—to prove he was capable of feeling after the sights he'd been exposed to had completely numbed all his emotions.

Racking his brain for something to divert her attention, he saw it over her shoulder. 'Where does sailing qualify?' he asked, gesturing towards the water.

She twisted to follow his gaze. A few yachts had emerged from under the bridge and were tacking from side to side, skilfully avoiding impact.

Moving to the mesh protection, she craned her neck to watch. 'Mixed. My sister and brother-in-law in Melbourne own a yacht, and I've sailed with them. I love the wind in my hair, the smell of salt water and the sense of the ocean below us as we skim across the waves. *Wearing life jackets.* Ocean-racing in rough weather—like the Sydney to Hobart some years—is *out.*'

He'd bet any advance he might get on his book that she

had no idea how captivating she looked: features animated, eyes sparkling and hands gesturing. Or how the inflections in her voice proved that she wasn't immune to the thrill— no matter how much she said so.

CHAPTER FOUR

NATE DIDN'T DO YEARNING, or hankering for unattainable dreams. So why did the image of him standing on a boat, his arms on either side of her, guiding her hands on the wheel as they sailed along the coast, imprint itself into his mind?

There had been no conscious thought to move nearer. Had he shifted? Or had it been she who'd taken a step? He'd swear there'd been an arm's length between them a moment ago.

The uneven breaths he took filled his nostrils with her subtle aroma. Time froze. Sounds blurred. And Jemma's face filled his vision. The strong-minded man he believed he was might have fought the urge to kiss her. Here, in this moment, there was no option and he bent his head.

With a shudder she jerked away, remorse replacing the desire in her eyes. Guilt and wanting warred for prominence inside him. Neither won nor lost, and his mind was blank of any words to appease her.

Her gulp of air was followed by a short huff—an unsuccessful attempt at a laugh. 'I don't go there very often. They have full social lives, and I have my work and commitments.'

It was an addition to her last statement, spoken as if those few special moments hadn't happened.

She glanced towards the city, took a step that way, and his regret was heightened at seeing her effort to regain composure.

He fell into step beside her, leaving extra space between them and taking up the conversation where she'd finished.

'In the Adelaide Hills? Apart from the firefighting trip, the only time I've been to South Australia was in my teens, when my family holidayed on the South Coast. Great beaches and surfing. My brother Sam, who's with the air force at Edinburgh, reckons it's a cool place to be stationed.'

'I like it. *Oh!*'

She gasped and he turned his head in time to see a speedboat and a yacht come close to colliding.

'Does that qualify as extreme?' he asked as the vessels swung away from each other.

'Only the attitude of whoever's steering the motorboat.'

'If the yacht's skipper reports him he's in trouble. If not, I hope he's had a sobering scare.'

She didn't reply, and he let the conversation lapse, thinking about their near-kiss and cursing himself for his moment of weakness. It might have screwed up any possible co-writing deal, and that was what this was about.

He presumed Jemma was a stay-at-home girl—painting and writing syrupy love stories, never taking any chances outside her comfort zone. But, no, not quite. It took guts and willpower to send a manuscript to a stranger for assessment and possible negative feedback.

Submitting had been *his* intention from the moment the characters and plot had first formed in his head. How long had Jemma dithered before pressing 'send'? And why this strong attraction when there were gulfs of difference between them?

Jemma opted for a café with outdoor seating near the quay. She ordered a banana and caramel ice cream sundae and a glass of water—well-earned by all the walking she'd done today. Nate opted for sultana cake and coffee.

Having him hold the seat she chose, and adjust the umbrella to shade her, was flattering and she thanked him.

'My pleasure.'

He sat on her left, shuffled along until their knees bumped, then pulled back. The contact sent a tremor up her leg, spreading to her spine. It didn't seem to affect him at all.

He'd told her he'd run over the bridge after lunch, which explained his damp hair when they'd met, and his change of clothes. It also signified that he was staying somewhere on the North Shore. With friends? A girlfriend? She didn't want or need to know, but would be amazed if there wasn't one. He didn't wear a wedding ring, although... *Not going there*—it implied personal interest.

'You run regularly? Apart from the bushfire training?' An acceptable question as *he'd* initiated the topic.

'I like to run or swim every day—sometimes both. There are some great hiking tracks near my home.'

His phone rang. He turned his head and held it to his left ear. She averted her gaze to allow him privacy, concentrating on the passing pedestrians.

'Hi, Dave.' He listened for a while. 'No, we're good. Tess will be there Saturday night, so we'll arrange it then.' A shorter pause, then he said goodbye and tapped her arm.

One side of his lips quirked as he peered over her shoulder 'This looks positively *evil*, Jemma.

Leaning away to allow her dessert to be placed on the table, Jemma felt her eyes widen at its size. And Nate apparently found her dilemma amusing.

She flashed him a fake warning glare and then, with a honeyed tone, thanked the waitress and asked, 'Could we please have an extra spoon for sharing?'

'Of course. I'll bring one out.' She set Nate's plate in front of him and walked away.

'Don't worry about your figure, Nate, you can always run over the bridge again.'

Her laughter slipped back into her throat as their eyes locked and the amusement in his slowly morphed into something deeper. Something perplexed and conflicted. Or was she transferring her own feelings?

He blinked, and she found herself facing the sombre features he'd shown at their initial introduction, as if he'd reverted to his distrust of her. How could he switch so fast? And *why*?

Nate's jaw tightened and his stomach clenched as Jemma's mirth abated and her eyes softened and glowed, mesmerising him. He'd allowed his guard to slip, had forgotten how easily a woman could deceive with her inviting glances and enticing lips.

He'd paid a life-changing price once, and wouldn't ever risk the pain and humiliation again. This relationship must be kept casual and friendly—nothing more. Proximity had to be the reason for the desire Jemma aroused, and that would end when she returned home.

'Water, a long black and another dessert spoon. Enjoy.'

The waitress broke the spell and was gone in the time it took him to refocus. Jemma bent over as she picked up a spoon, her long hair falling forward to hide her face. She didn't brush it away.

They needed to set ground rules and fix boundaries for their own protection. Nate reached across the table and covered the hand dipping to scoop up ice-cream. Ignoring its trembling, he held on until she raised her head, her expression wary.

'Trust me, Jemma, I don't want you to have any regrets for the decisions either of us make.'

Her lips parted and her eyelids fell, concealing her emotions, and her chest rose as she breathed in, drawing his attention, threatening his resolve. Her fingers fisted under his, and he became aware of his thumb caressing her knuckle.

Then, with a sudden loosening of her fingers, a deep intake of air and a challenging message in her dark blue eyes, she replied in a clear, steady tone, 'I won't commit unless I understand exactly what's required of me, and I'm sure I can deliver to your satisfaction.'

Sensation akin to a lightning bolt shot through him at her ambiguous statement. Innocent or deliberate, it created mental images that would keep him awake tonight. Or give him memorable dreams.

He released her hand, tore open two sugar sachets and stirred sugar into his coffee, his mind searching for a topic to discuss that would avoid personal revelation.

'How do you rate a visit to Sydney against Melbourne?'

Her hand froze centimetres from her parted lips and her eyes grew bigger, highlighting their colour. Hell, she was alluring—even when caught unawares. And she was smart, cottoning on to his diversionary tactic in an instant.

'That depends on the season and the reason for going there.'

A discussion followed, with inputs about Adelaide from Jemma, centred on the city's central attractions and the entertainment value of international musical celebrities.

Nate ate the remainder of her sundae without mentioning that he wasn't fond of such sweet offerings. Nor did he protest when she checked her watch and said she needed to leave. He insisted on escorting her to the station, told her he'd be in touch, and shook her hand for slightly longer and with slightly more pressure than convention dictated.

As he climbed the steps up to the bridge he remembered her gentle goad. Setting a steady-paced jog, he recalled their meetings, her reactions to the things he'd said and done and his own to her.

A seagull flew past, soaring upward, and he followed its flight to the top curved girders. If the chance arose in the future, maybe he'd persuade her to take that climb.

Jemma had the electric jug boiling and an open packet of biscuits waiting on the kitchen table for Cloe's homecoming after work. She'd missed the closeness she shared with her best friend since her wedding and move to Sydney. Somewhere in her future there *had* to be a man who'd love her as faithfully as Mike loved Cloe.

The one secret she'd kept from her was the love stories that she'd expanded into full novels. Brian's review had proved her judgement to be right. But if she was ever offered a contract Cloe would be the first to know.

'So how did you spend your day?' Cloe arched her back to relieve the kinks of the day and sipped her tea.

'Window shopping, exploring The Rocks area and walking over the bridge. Plus two meetings that are confidential at the moment. Oh, and I *did* have lunch with someone who'll be involved if the project goes ahead.'

She tried for nonchalance, not mentioning Nate, but heard the new inflection in her tone and felt her cheeks flush.

Cloe jerked upright, scanned her face with narrowed eyes, then clapped her hands. 'You *like* him.' A delighted grin split her face. 'You're blushing, Jemma! You like him *a lot*. Come on—give.'

'Nothing to tell. He was at the morning meeting and we had lunch together. He lives here, and as far as I know may have a wife or girlfriend. I live in South Australia, and am *not* interested in a relationship.'

She told herself it was the truth, attributing her reaction to him as natural in the presence of a ruggedly attractive man. So why hadn't it happened when her friends had set her up for dates in the three years since her break-up?

The back door opened, distracting Cloe. Jemma had often witnessed Mike's loving kisses for his wife, so why the blip of her heartbeat and the sharp wrench in her abdomen this time?

That night, after an evening of reminiscing and lively conversation, she snuggled into her pillow, mulling over the past. Her initial reaction to finding out that the man she'd contemplated marriage with was cheating on her had been gut-wrenching anguish. She'd hidden away and cried, cursing them both to the walls of her bedroom, and had deleted every image of him—even shredding printed copies.

A few weeks later a koala with a baby clinging to her back had trundled across in front of her on a photo-taking walk in the hills. She'd stopped, her hand over her mouth in awe, silently watching their progress into the scrubland. Being that close to an active mother and her joey had been awesome. Inspiring.

She'd laughed out loud, realising that life went on and that it was only her pride and self-esteem that had suffered damage. Her heart might have cracked a little, but it wasn't broken and it would heal with time.

That was the moment she'd decided to move from the city.

Later she'd become aware that her ability to trust had been the thing most affected.

Deep inside she still harboured a dream that there was someone out there who would love her as Mike loved Cloe, and would show it proudly and openly. She'd know him the moment he gazed into her eyes, held her in his arms and kissed her.

Nate Thornton intrigued her, and she'd felt a physical reaction to his smile and touch that was normal for any mature female. It could be a sign that she was ready to move on—though not to trust on sight.

She woke in the morning with a smile on her lips, ready for a day of shopping with Cloe and their friends, plus a lunchtime meet-up which would last all afternoon.

Sunday afternoon at the airport, Cloe hugged her and whispered in her ear. 'Let me know if your meetings lead to anything. Of any kind. Your happiness is my greatest wish.'

* * *

Some time in the early hours of Friday morning Nate jerked upright in bed, throwing the sheet away from his sweat-soaked body. Heart pounding, he swung his feet to the floor and bent over, dragging great gulps of air into his lungs.

The details of the nightmare—his first for over a year—were already fading apart from occasional vague shadowy images, but the aftermath stayed. He strode to the wardrobe, dragged on a pair of shorts and went out onto the balcony, to look at the welcoming view of the city lights.

Why now? Long ago he'd accepted that images of the horrific sights he'd seen in war zones and wherever terrorists preyed on the innocent would have a lasting effect on him. Others reported the sickening acts—he'd chosen to write about the indomitable spirit of the victims and their families, keeping a tight control on his own feelings.

He'd got past the initial bad memories and traumatic dreams when he'd written the novel, repeating the mantra, *These are only words on a page*. Nothing had changed, except...

He gripped the railing as a shiver ran down his spine—always a danger sign.

Jemma. Caught unawares when he'd first seen her, he'd let her slip past his guard, triggering emotions he'd tamped down, refused to acknowledge unless for family.

Fetching a cold bottle of beer from the fridge, and a chair from the dining room, he straddled the latter, leant on the back and drank slowly. He'd joined a tight-knit trauma support group overseas, kidding himself that it was to *give* help rather than receive. Only when Phil and Dave had cornered him in a bar late one night, had he admitted he needed counselling. It was the hardest decision he'd ever made. And the smartest.

As the sun rose he retrieved his mobile from his bedroom

and paced the balcony as he accessed a number, not wanting to wait until the group meeting Saturday night.

'Hi, Phil. No, Tess is fine. It's me. Are you free to talk? Yeah, another nightmare…out of the blue.'

The following evening he walked into the back room of a city hotel, thankful for a restful night and willing to admit to the episode in front of the group.

He hadn't mentioned Jemma to Phil and nor would he tonight, having persuaded himself that the attraction wouldn't go any further. He was flying out tomorrow, with an undetermined return date, and he was certain he'd be able to greet her with impartiality the next time they were in contact.

At six in the morning Nate stashed his carry-on case in the overhead locker, settled into his seat and tucked the document wallet containing twenty-nine printed pages, a clipboard and assorted pens and highlighters by his side.

Before retiring late on Friday he'd followed his nightly habit and checked his emails. True to her word, Jemma had emailed her initial three chapters earlier in the evening. He'd resisted the impulse to ring her, and had sent a standard 'received and thank you' reply.

He'd noted the title, printed the pages and slipped them into a clear plastic sleeve. His intention was to read it all in one session on the plane, have a break, then take it scene by scene. Trial and error had proved that worked best for him when editing his own work.

His usual patience through the pre-take-off safety talk eluded him, and he put it down to the anticipation of finding out if she was as good as he hoped. Once airborne, he ordered a beer, clipped the pages to the board and began to read.

Within a few paragraphs he was reaching for his drink. The confrontation between her male and female characters blew him away. Their believable actions and dialogue were portrayed with a minimum of words. He could pinpoint people he'd met like them, yet wouldn't have nailed it as she had. His characters' interactions paled in comparison.

Jemma was good. Until her hero and heroine parted. Then it was as if someone else had taken over the keyboard.

He suspected that Jemma had been hurt in the past, and had deep-buried misgivings regarding men. But she was also intelligent, and ready to stand up for her beliefs if they were challenged. A stimulating paradox from whom he was having trouble distancing himself.

He flipped the pages, his emotions and his temperament riding a rollercoaster with the changing expertise of the author. In spite of the articulate wording, the basic story was, as Brian had implied, mundane and boring.

His respect for his agent grew for the tactful way he'd handled both him *and* Jemma, along with a surge of sympathy for him at being placed in this position of needing to spell out a truth Nate had struggled to accept.

He replaced the printout in the wallet, finished his beer and lay back with his headphones on. At times like these his choice of music was classical jazz.

By the time he landed in Athens he'd read the printout twice and made notes in the margins with a red pen.

And he was still puzzling over the enigma of Jemma Harrison.

CHAPTER FIVE

ON THE TUESDAY evening after she'd come home to Hahndorf, Jemma had been surprised to receive her limited script back from Nate, with comments in the margin. And she'd been thrilled by his second email, asking her to have a go at his attached first two chapters.

Have a go! As if it were a sideshow stall at a fair.

As she'd requested when she sent hers, he'd included back stories for his main characters.

From the opening paragraph she'd been drawn in and captivated; by page seven she'd begun to understand Brian's proposition. By the end of chapter two she'd known it was too good not to be published—even if Nate did it himself. It was a genre she'd never have chosen, yet if she'd had the whole book she'd have continued reading, glossing over the stilted, uninspiring interaction between the hero and heroine.

She'd acknowledged receipt and spent all her free time from then until Saturday morning revising the four relevant scenes, two of them quite short. She double-and-triple-checked, determined not to leave a single mistake. Unsure of the normal procedure, she'd highlighted anywhere she'd made changes in one version, then deleted and amended in red text in another, allowing him to compare.

Dead on noon, with fingers crossed, eyes shut and her lips mouthing a silent prayer, she pressed 'send.'

Late on Wednesday morning of the following week, as she walked into town, she counted her blessings: the beautiful natural setting of her home, fresh air to breathe and the one she loved most tucked into a cotton shoulder bag clutched to her chest.

There was a cruise ship in Port Adelaide, which she knew meant buses full of tourists who'd keep her too busy to fret over the absence of any response from Nate. And she was right. By mid-afternoon she'd hardly had time to take sips from her water bottle, let alone make tea or coffee, since she'd taken over at noon from Meg, who owned the business.

'My mother's going to adore these miniatures,' an American woman gushed as Jemma wrapped three of them in bubble wrap with care. 'It's so hard to find anything small, light and tasteful to take home.'

'Your grandchildren will love the cuddly Australian animals too,' Jemma replied, placing them into a carry-bag.

'Lucky I saw the kangaroos in the window, else I'd have gone straight past. My husband likes to be back at the coach early—keeps me on my toes when we're travelling. Thank you, dear, have a nice day.'

'And you enjoy the rest of your cruise.'

Grateful for an empty shop at last, she hunkered down to drink from the bottle under the counter, relishing the cool water as the doorbell rang with the customer's exit. The murmur of a voice didn't register as she looked at her watch, which showed it was more than an hour until Meg returned. But by now the last of the cruise buses would be heading back to the port, so there'd be fewer shoppers around.

The hairs on the back of her neck lifted as if caught by a light breeze or someone's warm breath. A quiver ran down her back. Not daring to hope, she came upright with slow ease and glanced across the shop.

Her throat dried, her fingers curled into her palms and everything around her faded into mist as her blue eyes met perturbed storm-grey in enigmatic features. It was as if he was unsure of why he was there. Then light flared in his eyes and he gave her the smile she'd spent all the time since she'd been home telling herself she didn't miss at all.

His unique aroma filled the space between them, stirring her senses. Up close, he looked tired, and she noticed that the fine lines at the corner of his eyes were deeper, more pronounced.

'Hello, Jemma.'

Two everyday words in an unforgettable voice with a rusty edge. Absolutely no reason for her suddenly to feel hot all over. No reason for her stomach to clench and her pulse to race.

Feigning control, she met his gaze with what she hoped was a calm, unruffled demeanour. 'Hello, Nate. You're a long way from home.'

The bell rang and they both turned their heads to watch the door open, hear a male voice say, 'Let's have a drink first,' and then see it close.

Jemma saw Nate frown as he scanned the shop and peered at the open doorway behind her.

'Are you on your own? What time do you finish?' He frowned again, as if aware of how terse he sounded. 'Sorry, I'd like to talk to you. Should have let you know I was coming, but...'

He shrugged, as if that were explanation enough. She ought to be annoyed at his arrogance—wasn't that a major factor against all those she deemed were that type of man?—but instead energising anticipation bubbled through her. The reason for his presence *had* to be to discuss Brian's solution. Why come all this way if he wasn't seriously considering it?

'Would you like coffee? I'm dying for a hot drink.'

She sounded like a flustered teenager. Exactly how she felt.

At his nod and 'Mmm,' of acceptance, she went through the doorway and into the small kitchen, not expecting him to follow. The compact space seemed to diminish when he came in, watching as she filled the electric jug, set out two mugs and measured coffee into both.

'Two sugars, right?'

The sound of the bell impeded his reply and she handed him the spoon.

'I take one and milk, and mine's the mug with a possum on it. There's biscuits in the square tin.'

Leaving the room meant squeezing past him and another intake of musk, citrus and *him*. Another aspect of the man she'd missed—which was crazy, considering the limited time they'd spent together. Fixing a smile on her lips, she smoothed her hair and stepped past the counter to greet the new customers.

In the time it took for the water to boil and for Nate to make the coffee the bell rang twice, and he figured he'd made a mistake coming during shopping hours. He hadn't warned her, hoping to gauge her true reaction to him, but had seen a delightful range of astonishment, pleasure and annoyance, leaving him unenlightened.

He hadn't factored in the lack of privacy. He'd be lucky to find a quick moment to arrange a quieter place for their essential conversation on co-operation. Success was now a feasible goal, and his plan for co-writing depended on her availability and commitment. One read-through of her suggested amendments and he was fully on board. With reservations.

She'd done a brilliant job, bringing fiery passion to the bland interaction between his leading characters. And she'd nailed the way the male he'd visualised would respond to a female whose presence had upset his life's equilibrium. His heroine was now feisty and flawed—a worthy match for his hard-bitten, battle-worn hero.

Mug in hand, he went to take a surreptitious peek at

her. She was showing a couple with a young girl a display of colourful teddy bears. Staying out of sight, sipping the hot drink, he admired her genuine pleasure at serving all three. Two women were browsing the shelves… Another was peering in the window.

Why was she having to cope alone? Was it always this busy? If so, it might affect his proposal. And why the hell did she have to be as alluring in jeans and a loose green top as she'd been in the outfit she'd worn in Sydney?

His fingers gripping his mug were white-knuckle taut. Forcing them to relax, he returned to the kitchen. Hanging around was distracting for him, probably the same for her, and would achieve nothing.

Between customers he brought her a fresh coffee, the first one having gone cold.

'Thank you. This is much more satisfying than quick sips from a bottle of water under the counter. It's been full on this afternoon.' She cradled the mug in her fingers and savoured the invigorating flavour.

'Are you always on your own? When do you get a break?'

Her eyes flashed and she stepped away. He shouldn't have asked so abruptly.

'I can manage. Meg had to go home for personal reasons just after I came in at twelve. She'll be back around four.'

'I'm concerned—okay?'

He pressed one finger to her mouth, preventing the words she'd taken a breath to say from being voiced. Had to fight not to caress a path to her cheek.

'Will you have dinner with me so that we can discuss how good your rewrites are?'

His breath caught in his throat and his pulse tripped, then surged as her face lit up and her eyes shone, as dazzling as the stars he gazed at from his balcony in the mountains.

Idiot! That was the greeting she'd deserved—not the uncivil questions he'd fired at her. His hand fell to his sides.

'You're happy with them?' Her voice was husky and animated, making him feel like Father Christmas.

'Yes—so we need to have a serious discussion on how we proceed.'

She blinked, and appeared to consider the implications of his words.

'There's quite a few good places to eat and I'll be free at five-fifteen.'

'We'll need privacy.'

Again there was that assessing scrutiny he was beginning to anticipate. Then she smiled, as if pleased at his words.

The shop bell rang again.

'I could get to hate that sound.' There was a low growl in his voice, fuelled by frustration.

She heard it, and a light blush flowed over her cheeks, easing his tension. He wasn't alone.

In an effort to hide her expression, she dipped her head to finish her coffee. 'I have a customer. Would you rinse the mugs and leave them to drain, please, Nate?'

For another smile he believed he'd clean the whole kitchen—floors, walls and all. On his way out, he called, 'See you later, Jemma,' and held the door for the teenagers entering.

His replies were a quick wave from her and giggles from the girls.

Jemma relaxed as he strode past the window and gave her full attention to her current customer and those who'd followed until the shop had emptied. She'd been on edge since he'd waltzed in—well, strolled in as if he was expected, barking out questions. In hindsight, remembering his demeanour, he'd obviously been disconcerted at finding her serving alone.

The conflict between anger at his assumption that he could act as if they'd arranged this meeting and her emotional and physical response to his presence was unsettling. He muddled her brain—*not* conducive to giving good service.

She brewed herself a chamomile tea, and drank it while automatically tidying the shelves—a no-brainer task allowing her to imagine future scenarios for his battle-scarred ex-soldier and the girl who'd lost everything because of the military.

Meg arrived and was pleased with the sales, giving Jemma due praise.

'The extra tourists helped. Always eager to buy Australian souvenirs.'

'I'll finish closing up if you want to go home and put your feet up.'

'I'm fine—a friend's coming to meet me at a quarter past five.'

'Going to dinner? That'll be a treat.'

Her words gave Jemma reason to think. She preferred to keep her personal life private, except for the facts she chose to reveal to a few close friends. Yet enough local people knew her to make her being seen dining out with Nate open to gossip. A takeaway at home would be better.

As she unpacked and displayed new stock she found herself glancing through the window every few minutes. By five she was ready to leave, and the instant he appeared she collected her two bags and said goodbye to Meg. Resolving to be calm and businesslike, she joined him outside.

She wished he wasn't so ruggedly attractive—like those guys on television who starred in exotic nature series, travelling the wildernesses of the world in their four-wheel drives.

Quivers skittled up and down her spine as he perused her from head to feet and back...as far as the cotton bag clutched to her chest. A bubble of laughter rose in her throat at his puzzled frown.

Nate jerked as if he'd been sideswiped. A moment ago, he'd been admiring how fresh Jemma looked after a busy day in the shop—now he couldn't take his eyes from the wriggling bulge in the colourful fabric she was hugging.

'It's moving.'

He glanced up as her lips parted in a burst of delightful laughter and then she opened the unfastened top. A small tortoiseshell head popped out, tawny eyes blinking at the bright world.

'Hey, it's cute.' He liked animals, and rued the fact that his travelling prevented him keeping any at the moment.

'Isn't *she*?'

'She comes to work with you?'

He stroked the kitten with his forefinger and she leant into it, then licked him. Lifting her out, he cradled her to his chest, and Jemma's eyes showed approval of his gentleness.

'It depends on my hours and how she seems. I've had her less than a week—it's a learning curve for the two of us.'

'I grew up with an assortment of cats and dogs, along with various other pets my brother and I found or brought home. Until I built my own home I couldn't imagine one without any animals. I assume she's not coming to dinner with us?'

She dropped her gaze to his hands, still wrapped around her pet, seemingly unsure of how to answer.

'Jemma?' His fingers itched to cup her chin and see why she'd hidden her expression from him. Instead he tickled the kitten's ear, and waited.

'I thought...' It was mumbled and faint.

She let out a slow breath, breathed in, and then her eyes, cool and determined, met his.

'I thought we'd go to my home to talk…then order take-away.' Firm and assured now.

It was new and strange, this feeling of being honoured by her offer of trust—a gift he was convinced few men were granted. Having guessed she was vulnerable, he resolved not to break it and kept his tone casual.

'Okay by me. Whatever you choose.'

'It's a fifteen-minute walk along the track—unless you'd rather take the road. I assume you have a car?'

'I'd prefer to go through the local bushland. My hire car's parked behind the hotel I've booked into for the night. May I carry…? What's the little fur ball's name?'

'Milly.'

She took off the bag and slipped it over his neck, leaning towards him. Allowing him to breathe in her floral aroma. Forcing him to fight the urge to find out with his lips if her skin was as soft as it appeared.

As they set off he could feel movement through the bag's material as Milly purred in her sleep, snuggled against his chest. It was a comforting feeling he remembered from nights of having pets sleep on his bed in the innocent times of youth.

Some time in the future he'd persuade her to tell him why she'd chosen the name.

He kept the bag open, allowing him to see Milly, and occasionally stroked her head, causing a deepening of her contented sounds. This was one of the comforts missing from his life that he intended to rectify soon. His dilemma was cat, dog or both.

At the end of the shopping area Jemma led him down a side street and onto a track that wound through native scrub and trees—some recognisable from his mountain home surroundings.

'This is where I find my painting inspiration. All the seasons of nature are right here on my doorstep. I keep extensive files of photographs in my computer because nothing stays the same in bushland.'

Her face lit up as she indicated plants she'd painted, adding the fact that she ensured every tile ended up unique. Her passion for her art moved him, and when he queried the canvas paintings he'd seen on the shop wall she admitted they were hers too, and gaining interest.

As they approached a bend she caught his arm to slow him down and touched her finger to her lips. When she stopped and pointed upwards he followed her finger's direction and felt his throat clog. A koala sat in the crook of a gum tree within climbing reach, a joey clinging to her chest. He couldn't remember when he'd last seen one in the wild.

She didn't stir and appeared to be dozing, completely oblivious to their presence.

After a moment or two they continued on, and Nate waited until they were some distance away before speaking, though he was certain his voice wouldn't have disturbed the sleeping pair.

'That was a rare sighting for me. We don't have koalas in the Blue Mountains—wrong type of gum trees.'

'They're plentiful here, but often hard to spot. She's been in that tree for a week, and I haven't seen her awake once.'

They hadn't gone much further when Jemma pushed between two shrubs, and he followed her onto a narrower, rougher, more overgrown dirt path.

'My hidden entrance. I keep it that way to prevent hikers assuming it's another trail and coming to my back door asking for directions.'

That he understood—though it was rare that anyone ventured near his fenced-off property, which was on a clifftop away from the main road.

The track brought them into a cleared area behind a

stone cottage with a corrugated iron roof, its long garden surrounded by a vine-covered, weather-worn wooden fence. It was classic Australiana, by his estimation over a hundred years old, and the house nearest to town in a row of three.

CHAPTER SIX

JEMMA OPENED THE gate and led the way along a crazy paving path between a vegetable garden and patch of lawn on one side, and fruit trees and a flowerbed on the other. Wide steps ended on a veranda that stretched across the back, furnished with an old-fashioned three-seater swinging seat, a small outdoor table and two chairs, and a number of potted plants.

They entered a compact kitchen fitted with modern appliances, with a dining area through an archway on the right. Jemma placed her bag on the mottled stone benchtop and stepped in front of him to take the kitten.

Nate willed himself not to move a muscle. He was in her home on trial. A wrong action or word could have him banished with no chance of appeal. He leant against the bench, admiring the harmonious blend of old and new decor. Admiring Jemma's supple movements as she crouched down, gently placing Milly onto a blue-cushioned bed in the corner behind the back door.

'Is the house yours or rented?'

He could imagine her scouring magazines for furniture and colours to suit, fired with enthusiasm. Picturing her in an ultra-modern house—like his?—wasn't difficult either.

'I bought it, along with some of the seller's furniture, three years ago this coming June. The only difference is the colour. I painted the walls in the bedrooms, study and lounge.'

'You?'

'Not a big job with such small rooms. Do you want coffee, tea or water?'

He grinned. 'You need to ask?'

This was polite small-talk—a prelude to the serious conversation ahead. Her earlier fractured invitation, and the way her lips didn't quite make a return smile now, had him guessing she was nervous. Because he was a relative stranger or because he was a man?

He watched in silence as she clicked on the electric jug and took two mugs from the hooks on an antique hatched dresser. This was her domain, and the less he intruded the quicker she'd accept his presence.

When the drinks were ready he offered to carry them. She thanked him and walked into the hall that stretched to the front door. The compactness of her sitting room was eased by the light sandy-coloured paint, and the space around the furniture. Two suitably-sized paintings—a stormy sea and one landscape—had been hung on the walls.

He appreciated the furnishings: a traditional patterned sofa and armchair, a wooden coffee table and a classic sideboard with mirror, all smaller than regular size. A television sat on a mobile trolley in one of the nooks either side of the stone fireplace. The other held a packed floor-to-ceiling bookcase. And, although modern, the imitation log heater suited the setting.

Polite as always, Jemma thought, as he waited until she'd taken her coffee and settled into the armchair, sliding back, keeping her body erect, and crossing her ankles to one side.

From this position he appeared to dominate the room the way he had the kitchen in the gift shop. Her heartbeat skidded to a stutter as his eyes held hers captive. She refused to be the one to initiate the discussion. He'd requested it—he should air his views first.

Breaking eye contact, he flicked a glance at the window behind her, huffed out a solid breath and sat on the two-seater. He took a drink, placed his cup on the table, and then, keeping his body equally upright, clasped his hands between his knees.

'You have trust issues with men.' It was a simple statement of fact rather than an accusation. 'One in particular or more. Either way, every man you meet has to field the blame.'

'That's…'

'True, Jemma.'

She stared at her collection of stones in a bowl on the table, accepting that he was right. She believed it was justified to protect her heart. He had no right to disparage what for her was a necessity.

She tamped down her irritation and, feigning a neutral expression, replied, 'I have good reason.'

His oblique nod showed that he understood—to a point.

'I don't doubt it. However, the best way for this collaboration to succeed will be for us to work closely together. And that requires your trusting me to treat you as an equal colleague. If—'

Her spine stiffened and her fingers scrunched the bottom hem of her cotton top as she cut in.

'Trust is a two-way street. Your initial greeting was superficial, at best, and you weren't exactly receptive to my having access to your novel.'

His eyes narrowed for a second or two, and then he stunned her by chuckling at her outburst. The realisation that she'd missed a sound she'd only heard a few times shook her. Unusual and gravelly, it was imprinted in her memory. *For ever.*

He leant back, his elbow on the sofa-arm, wiped his hand across his mouth and made no attempt to hide his amusement. 'We must be making progress, Jemma Harrison. You forgot to call me Mr Thornton.'

She really, *really* wanted to glare at him for sending her up, but her facial features and her body refused to co-operate. Her lips were mimicking his smile, her pulse was giving the impression she was running a relay, and a warm glow was firing up in her abdomen.

'I'll put a reminder in my calendar.'

Any bite she might have meant to give was negated by the suggestive breathy sound that came from her dry throat. A swallow of coffee didn't ease it at all—but then, the cause was right there, watching her with fascination.

'And I'll try not to warrant it.' He extended his hand over the table. 'Truce?'

She reached out to meet his gesture, and had to wriggle to the edge of the chair. 'Truce.' They both had much to gain by co-operation.

Wishing she didn't like the feel of his skin against hers so much, she sank back and curled her legs up onto the chair.

'So, will you be sending me the next chapters? Do we need some sort of written agreement? I have a back stock of paintings and can begin work any time from now.' She couldn't wait to read future instalments of *Trials of a Broken Man*.

'I'd rather not send them but, yes, that suits me—with provisos. I suggest we ring Brian tomorrow and find out the legal ramifications. Will you be free in the morning?'

She nodded, puzzled by his first answer and unable to speak.

'How obligated are you to your hours in the gift shop?'

'It's pretty flexible. There are two young mothers who don't want to be tied to regular shifts but are happy to go in for odd days or an occasional week.'

He nodded again, as if pleased with her answer, and then fell silent, his inscrutable gaze making her squirm and gulp the remainder of her drink. She almost choked when he spoke again, churning the words out without pause.

'We'll talk to Meg as well. The sooner we finish the

amendments the better. Emailing partials back and forth and waiting for each other to check them will take too long. Would you be prepared to come to Katoomba and stay with me until they're finished?'

'Stay with you?'

Idiot! Of all the phrases he used, that was the point you zero in on?

Her cheeks burned but she didn't dare look away, needing to see his reaction. She inhaled and exhaled in slow deliberation, her mind processing all he'd said. An elementary fact, an obvious problem and a logical solution. Practical and impassive. *So* him.

Every cell in Nate's body clamoured to go to her, take her in his arms and reassure her.

Yeah, a great way to prove you'll act like a gentleman and keep the relationship platonic.

He hadn't meant to shock her—to him it had been the best answer to a logistical problem. One which meant breaking his rule not to have any unrelated women staying in his home. Any liaisons were conducted in Sydney, in his apartment or at their homes.

This was the exception to break the rule. They'd need time with no distractions—somewhere they could take breaks, walk or run at will. Somewhere they could work, eat and sleep at odd hours as needed. That was the way he'd lived while typing most of those hundred-thousand-plus words. *And* all the ones he'd deleted or cut and saved.

Now he hoped to persuade Jemma—who probably only typed in her spare moments—to accept his way until they'd finished.

'It could take weeks.'

He started—had been so lost in thought he hadn't noticed she'd recovered from his startling proposition.

'There's no way of knowing. *You're* the one who emailed

to say that my characters' emotional relationship will affect every aspect of their lives. Being able to discuss any possible revisions and do them on the spot will speed up the process.'

'I get that. It's just the idea of leaving with no idea of a return date. That's asking a lot of my neighbours, who keep a watch on the house if I'm away. And I can't foist Milly on anyone for that long.'

'Bring her.'

Hell! That had shot out, bypassing any thought process. *Not* what he'd been thinking when he'd made his earlier decision, though having to buy bowls and a pet bed would strengthen his resolve to get a dog or cat of his own...

It suddenly struck him that expecting her to drop everything and come to his out-of-town house had been arrogant.

'I apologise, Jemma. I'm wound up and I want to get things rolling. Plus, I've lived solo for so long I've got used to making autocratic decisions. How about we allow a fortnight, to give us an idea of the timeframe we need? Then we can take a short break, or continue back here with me staying in the hotel.'

She didn't answer—just swung her feet to the floor, held out her hand for his now empty cup and, holding both, stared at the floor for a moment.

Then she sat down again. 'We're strangers. I've never lived with anyone but my parents.'

His heartbeat soared with an adrenaline rush he refused to attribute to her second statement, blaming it on her consideration of his offer.

'We both want success, so we'll agree on boundaries and work through any issues that come up. Compromising should get us through.'

Being surrounded by the house he'd designed as a refuge to keep him from ever again falling prey to romantic fallacies would be a constant reminder to him to stay objective and focus on the end result.

'Starting when?'

'Your decision. Whenever you can come.'

He heard a plaintive mew from behind him, and she looked past him to the doorway.

'Milly's hungry. I'll see my neighbours in the morning and phone Meg to arrange fill-ins. The takeaway menus are in the kitchen drawer.'

He waited until she'd gone before giving a short, triumphant fist-pump. This was no night for tinfoil cartons. They had a deal to celebrate—albeit a verbal one.

As he joined her in the kitchen, a phone number already punched into his mobile, Jemma closed a drawer of the dresser, turned and held out a handful of pamphlets.

'There's one from every takeaway in town. Pick what you fancy'

He might be in trouble if he did—and, anyway, for this evening he had an alternative plan.

'How long will it take you to get ready to go somewhere special for dinner?'

His muscles tightened, and his gut clenched at her enchanting reaction: cheeks colouring, lips parting in an O and beautiful eyes blinking. The sound she made was a delightful mixture of huff and laughter. He'd have to surprise her more often. *Or not.*

'To celebrate our agreement on collaboration. It's a milestone for both of us. Forty minutes, okay? That'll give me time to walk back for my car.'

At her audible intake of air and quick nod he pressed the already accessed number for the restaurant. A short conversation later he had a reservation for eight o'clock, with some leeway for the unfamiliar route.

'Where are we going?' She'd found her voice, and was eager for information. 'Casual dress?'

'Windy Point. My brother Sam's recommendation, and luckily they have a table. I've been staying with him for the last two days.'

If he'd thought he couldn't surprise her even more he'd been mistaken. Her eyes clouded for a millisecond, shuttered and then sparkled on reopening. 'It's back on my wish list. We were booked in a few years ago and had to cancel. The view is meant to be stunning—especially at night.'

'I'm glad you approve.' Her happiness lifted his spirits higher and gave the promise of an unforgettable evening. 'You did say it's quicker to town by road?'

'Yes—I'll let you out the front door.'

She squeezed against the wall of the narrow hallway, her perfume filling his nostrils as she passed, tempting him to press a light kiss on her lips.

Fingers held tight to his thighs, he crossed the threshold and told her he'd see her soon. With purpose in his stride, he pondered her *back on my wish list*. Why had it been crossed off? And who was the *we* she'd referred to?

Jemma leant against the closed door, shaking from head to foot, fighting to unscramble the sensations churning inside her.

She'd agreed to revise essential scenes in his manuscript. *In his home in New South Wales.* She would be taking time off from her part-time job, and wouldn't have time to paint while she was there. She was excited, overawed and nervous. And scared by how easily Nate had undermined her vows to stay detached.

She'd also agreed to go to a restaurant that not so long ago would have evoked dark emotions. The evening she and her ex were supposed to have had dinner there he'd rung to postpone, claiming an impromptu office meeting. They'd never rebooked, and a few weeks later she'd learned of his infidelity.

On the way to her bedroom she mused on the diverse changes in her life since that time. As she showered she vowed to embrace these latest ones and relish every moment, even while keeping her heart guarded and Nate at a distance.

Wrapped in a towel, she studied the selection of dresses in her wardrobe and chose two, holding them up in front of her to view in the mirror. They'd be eating in a popular venue with floor-to-ceiling glass windows, overlooking the city and the ocean, the sun setting on the horizon. Her aim was to be dressed appropriately and to appear stress-free while being escorted by Nate.

A quick calculation told her she had time to research the restaurant, and the images online helped her decide on a simply styled electric blue dress, with thin shoulder straps and a below-the-knee hem. Cloe's Christmas present to her—a similar-coloured, long-sleeved lacy knitted jacket—would be perfect when the temperature cooled. Comfy, medium-heeled shoes and silver jewellery completed the ensemble.

Well aware that she'd never challenge Vanessa's impeccable fashion sense, Jemma still found herself grinning as she nodded at her nice-but-nothing-special image in the mirror. Her sister would never write a book, let alone a good one—no riveting and satisfying emotional scenes worthy of being published.

Jemma's basic storyline *was* a problem, but she'd already decided not to hold Nate to his revision of a full story for her characters. It was too far out of his comfort zone. But she'd study his prose as she worked on it, talk to him and ask his advice. When his book was finished she'd enrol in writing courses and hopefully resolve her particular ineptitude.

Her phone, keys, tissues and emergency money fitted into her black clutch bag, and she left it on the hall stand while she checked on Milly. Finding her curled up asleep in her bed in the dining area, she shut the door to the hall so she wouldn't come out and hide while she was alone.

Waiting had never been a problem for her. She let her mind wander to plots and scenes, and never noticed time passing. Tonight was different. Her mind refused to co-operate, and would only dwell on her encounters with Nate.

She was grateful when the glare of his headlights in her driveway announced his arrival.

She went outside—and almost lost her footing stepping off the front porch as Nate came around the front of a silver sedan and stopped, taking his time to look her over.

Wow, he *really* scrubbed up well for a date. Not that this *was* one—it was a meal between two literary associates. All she had to do was ignore the pheromones bombarding her senses and stay calm and unaffected. Easy, right? *Like heck.*

Freshly shaved, and wearing a dark suit and a navy tie over a pale grey shirt, he'd draw *every* woman's attention. Her fingers itched to dishevel his neat, thick hair, which would make him even more desirable, and even more dangerous to her never-to-be-hurt-again plans for the future.

She dug one set of fingers into her palm and firmed the other on her bag.

'Hi, Jemma, you look…good.'

For an irrational moment she'd have given anything to know the word he'd caught back. But, sliding into the vehicle while he held the door open, giving her the full effect of newly applied cologne, she resolved not to care. If he wouldn't say it out loud, it wasn't worth hearing.

Buckled in, with the motor running, he turned to face her. 'Do you have any problem taking the winding route? The GPS offers that. Or do you want to go right down to the suburbs and up another way?'

'I'm lucky—never suffered from motion sickness.'

'Good.' He selected the setting and backed into the road.

CHAPTER SEVEN

A DISTURBING BATTLE raged in Nate's head. Taking Jemma—
whose appearance deserved a much more flattering word
than the one he'd stumbled over—to dinner being purely
business against the growing desire to be closer to her. To
hold and kiss her.

On the way to pick her up he'd reinforced every reason
he had for staying unattached and alone. His failure to dis-
tinguish the lies behind the sweet talking of a scheming
woman, which had taught him to be cautious. The suffer-
ing he'd seen which had left him sceptical of the façades
most people projected. He never took anyone at face value.

He'd believed he was in control until she'd stood there,
sweet and delectable, her blue dress and matching jacket
making the colour of her eyes appear darker and more alluring. He'd stopped dead, his throat had dried up, and his
pulse had rocketed. And he'd barely managed an inane remark not even worthy of a randy teenager.

Glancing at her composed profile, he saw her chin lift a
little, as if she'd sensed his action. *Was* she projecting a façade, like him? If he could see her eyes he might know. Unlike many of the sophisticated women he knew, she hadn't
learned the art of deception. For the sake of the man who'd
one day win her heart, he hoped she never would.

'You're very quiet, Jemma. Having doubts?'

'Over agreeing to come to Katoomba or to dinner? The
answer's no to both, Nate. You're driving a hired car on
a curving hilly road and the sun is beginning to set. You
need quiet to concentrate.'

He recalled places where there'd been the added dangers

of military conflict and gave a wry smile. 'Thank you for your consideration, but I prefer conversation over silence. How come you had to cancel your previous booking at Windy Point?'

Her barely audible intake of breath, and the hitch in her tone, told him more than her verbal answer.

'My date's sudden meeting—compulsory attendance.'

'Hmm. So we get to share the pleasure of a first visit here?'

She surprised him by laughing—a melodic sound he wished didn't stir him so easily.

'You've travelled around the world. You must have eaten in exotic and famous places I've only heard of or seen in magazines.'

'True. But I've also eaten meat and vegetables I wasn't game to ask the name of or to refuse. Consider every offer you're given, Jemma. Even bizarre memories are better than nights of wondering *what if?*'

'I've accepted yours.' She was resolute and firm.

'And I swear you'll never regret it. Make sure you pack warm tops; the evenings can be quite cool.'

'Like here?'

'Yeah, I guess it's pretty similar.'

'Except your winters are more severe and your snowfall higher. Do you ski?'

Jemma's question threw him for a moment. He hadn't skied since returning home—didn't want to revive memories of covert trips in wintertime Europe.

'Not for a long time. I've been otherwise occupied. Do you?'

'I've taken a few weekend trips with friends. Never got higher than the beginners' slopes but I had lots of fun.'

He pictured her in a fitted ski outfit, hair flying, cheeks flushed and radiant, eyes sparking with joy. Hands tight on the steering wheel, he sought for a diversion.

'I'm serious about bringing Milly. Write me a list of everything she'll need—or, better yet, email or text. Then I'll have it on my phone. I'll be shopping before you come.'

'She's not fussy...likes wet or dry food. Do you have a rug or old towel she can sleep on?'

'Not on your bed? That wouldn't worry me—our pets always did. Mum tried to dissuade them—and us. Eventually she accepted the inevitable.'

'I'd prefer she has a familiar setting—like a corner somewhere. I'll bring a couple of her toys.'

For the rest of the trip he told stories of the pets in his past, and Jemma loved listening to the escapades he, Sam and Alice had got up to, growing up in the suburbs.

She had a few dim memories of playing with Vanessa, but had rarely experienced sibling moments like her friends. Midway through her teens she'd realised the six-year gap between them wasn't the reason. Her sister had always been focussed on a modelling career and had had no time for games or any distraction such as a younger sister.

They arrived in the restaurant's car park earlier than expected, and Jemma felt pampered when Nate walked around to hold her door as she alighted.

'Can we go and watch the sunset?'

As a teenager, she'd often come here with friends—some of them dates, hoping for a kiss. Or more. She was glad her ex hadn't been one of them and her memories of this place were sweet.

'Fine by me. Looks like our timing is perfect.'

They walked down the path to a lookout, then further to a lower one at the edge of the hill, where the vista was partially blocked by trees. In the gaps there was a clear view, with the city sprawled from left to right from the lower tree line to the ocean's edge. Just below them cars negotiated the bend in the road, some with headlights already on.

Jemma sucked in a breath and blew out a long, *'Ohhh...'* How could she have forgotten how incredibly beautiful it was?

The sun hung like a glimmering yellow-and-gold UFO, appearing to be balanced on a wisp of dark grey cloud above the horizon. Its mirror image skimmed across the translucent blue sea towards them. Above and below, and spreading across their vision, the spectacular colours morphed into oranges and reds. Fascinating. Soul-warming.

As the lower curve of the sun dipped behind the cloud Jemma pulled out her mobile and snapped a few shots. She gasped with joy and clicked three or four times in succession as the dark shape of a plane, climbing after its take-off from the airport, flew across the split sun.

Glancing at Nate's face, seeing him moved by the experience too, made her feel light-headed.

'Different, isn't it?' Even though there was noise from the traffic below, she found herself whispering.

'Incomparable is a better word. A panorama of city and suburbs, with true blue gumtrees almost within reach, and the ocean and the sunset in the background. Indescribable.'

'Not for an aspiring author, surely?'

His brow furrowed, then cleared as he twigged that she was ribbing him. 'Is that a challenge, Jemma?'

'Not tonight.' She looked away from his too-knowing eyes. 'As the sun sinks lower those colours intensify, then fade, leaving the sea pitch-dark unless there's a boat passing. Shall we go in?'

Neither her dim memories of glimpses through the window nor the photos on her computer did justice to the dining area, with its curved glass windows ensuring a clear panoramic view for every table on each of the three levels. Jemma noted very few were unoccupied as they were led to a setting for two on the highest.

She had less than a minute to admire the crisp white of the linen, the soft glow of candles on each table and the comfortable upholstered chairs, before the roof began to open up, letting natural light in.

'Oh, someone told me that you dine under the stars, but I'd forgotten. It doesn't happen all year round, so our timing's perfect.'

'Sam mentioned a unique attraction and wouldn't clarify. Now I understand why.'

He stared upward for a moment, then scanned across the view and back. Jemma had already memorised it, and sensed he was doing the same.

'I remember thinking that at night-time, with all the different coloured streetlights and building lights, it looked like a true fairyland.'

A waitress brought them a carafe of water and asked if they would like to order drinks. She looked towards Nate, to ask if he wanted to share a bottle of wine, and felt her pulse hitch at the warmth of his direct gaze. It sped up at his words.

'Seeing as I'll have a special cargo on that winding drive home, I'll have one glass of wine and then stick to water.' His voice lowered to a conspiratorial tone as he added, 'We're in your territory, so you may choose a red to complement my Scotch fillet.

She'd happily comply if only she could find her voice after his compliments—the first more amazing than the second. Her reply sounded foreign, breathy and a little exotic, as she asked for two glasses of her favourite Shiraz, having already decided she would have the lamb dish from the online menu.

They chose Turkish bread to start, and Jemma declared she'd skip an entrée in favour of dessert if she wasn't too full.

Leaning forward, and keeping his voice low, Nate said, 'I've researched the selection and I'm betting you won't be able to resist.'

Outwardly she pretended to bristle, but inside she quivered at the intimacy of his soft yet edgy tone, her reaction heightened by the knowledge that he was probably right.

He requested medium rare for his fillet, and she shivered. He noticed, waiting until they were alone before asking, 'Not the way you like it?'

'It's a matter of taste. I prefer overcooked to under every time.'

'But don't let your parents know, huh?'

She joined in his laughter.

'They guessed when, aged around eight, I took some slices of roast beef back to the kitchen and grilled them.'

Their wine arrived, and he repeated the salute he'd given in Darling Harbour. This time she echoed his movement, and he nodded in response. After savouring the flavour, she set her glass down and traced her finger around the base. He'd seen her home, how she lived, but had only mentioned the location of his.

'Is your home old or new?'

'As modern as yours is colonial. It has everything I want and need and nothing I don't.'

'You designed it?' Of course he had—from the bricks to the door handles.

His shrug drew her gaze to the perfect fit of his tailormade jacket, and she had a sudden vision of his toned, sculpted torso, glistening in the sun as he stood poised on a diving board.

The clatter of cutlery from an adjoining table broke her reverie in time for her to catch his next words.

'With professional help. The location was paramount, and there was no problem with demolishing the seventies-style building in need of major repairs. My architect drafted the original plans from a rough sketch of mine and included everything I deemed essential. I now have the home I visualised.'

She'd bet her favourite paintbrush there'd been nothing 'rough' about his sketch. Every line would have been straight, and all the extras neatly depicted.

'I'm looking forward to seeing it.' She knew she'd learn more about his true character in a short stroll through his home than he'd revealed so far. 'Is it cat-proof?'

He smiled. 'Should be. Guess we'll have to keep an eye on her and find out. I'll add "research flight regulations" to tomorrow's list. How old are you?'

His out-of-the-blue question took a few seconds to register. Did it make a difference?

'Twenty-eight. Is that relevant to our agreement?'

'No—journalistic interest.'

He gave that almost-smile she was beginning to find endearing.

'I turned thirty-two the day before Brian told me how awful my one-on-one scenes were.'

She tried not to chuckle…didn't quite succeed. 'Happy birthday, huh? How does the view compare now?'

Apart from the discernible trees near the building, they were surrounded by a band of black. Its furthermost reaches were sprinkled with lights, their number and variety of colour and size increasing until they ended in a ragged edge of darkness to infinity, broken only by the rising moon and its reflection. Above them stars were beginning to emerge in the ebony sky.

Nate didn't say a word, and his enigmatic features hid whatever he was thinking.

Jemma sipped her drink, torn between intrigue over his reporting years abroad and the necessity not to become familiar with his history and personality. Agreeing to live with him for two weeks made the latter hard to maintain. But not impossible.

'I have to admit, Jemma, this is unique. Who'd have

thought Adelaide could compete with the sunset spectacles of the world?'

'Every true Adelaidean,' she declared with pride, and was rewarded with genuine laughter.

'Remind me to show you some photos while we're in Katoomba!'

Nate had expected his unease regarding having Jemma in his home for two weeks to grow stronger as his body responded to her enthusiasm for the sunset and the venue. Instead curiosity about the woman he'd aligned his literary aspirations with overrode any misgivings—though only at surface level. There was a line in the sand he'd sworn never to cross. If that danger surfaced he'd walk away—even if it meant breaking their deal.

Her skin glowed and her eyes sparkled at even the smallest event—like the timing of that plane moving through the sunset. She was bright and intelligent...an enchanting dinner companion. There had been no awkward silences as they ate their main courses, approving of the flavours and the choices they'd made. The discussion had progressed to sunsets around the world, and places she'd seen in movies and would love to visit in the future.

As he'd predicted, she was now poring over the dessert menu, seesawing between two items before selecting sorbet with fresh fruit and herbal tea. He ordered the same, with coffee.

'Doesn't drinking coffee this late keep you awake?' Jemma asked him.

'I guess I've grown immune to the effects over the years. There are places I've been where you couldn't rely on the quality of the water, or what the coffee grinds or tea leaves might actually consist of. Boiling hot coffee became the safest bet, and I caught the habit.'

Her eyes had widened as he spoke, and he pressed one

hand against his thigh and the other into the arm of his chair to prevent either from reaching for hers across the table. To prevent himself wrapping her fingers in his and caressing across her soft skin with his thumb.

Their desserts were served, their flavoursome tang enhanced by the complimentary handmade chocolates accompanying their hot drinks. An ideal ending for a memorable evening.

His only regret was the way it was going to end: saying goodnight at her front door with space between them. At this moment the idea of shaking hands and walking away didn't appeal at all.

Late the following Tuesday afternoon Jemma sank into her plane seat, worrying about Milly all alone in another part of the aircraft. Their visit to the vet for the required certificate for flying—luckily she was over the minimum age—had gone smoothly. The delay had been because this flight was the first available to have an allocation for pets.

Nate had arranged for a specialist firm to handle Milly's transportation in a regulation carrier from Hahndorf to Adelaide airport, and to collect and deliver her to them in the Sydney terminal. He'd also emailed chapters three to six of his book to her computer between phone calls on Thursday, while she'd prepared a ham and salad lunch. The final few pages needing her revision were in her satchel, to be worked on during the flight, along with a book and magazine.

On Saturday he'd asked her to send him her full romance, telling her he needed to read it all to assess the storyline. Their contract was for him to advise and help her, but she hadn't expected him to want it so soon. He'd flown out later that day, promising to be there to collect them when they landed, and she'd instantly both missed him and felt slight relief when he drove away.

Two full days of seeing his efficiency at work had left

her wondering what she'd agreed to. And whether she could stand up to his strong will if they had a conflict of opinion. She hadn't had a skerrick of unease for her physical safety—not for a second since they'd met. It was the underlying allure, the subtle dismantling of the rigid barriers she'd erected to protect her heart, that caused concern.

Well aware of her limited knowledge of legal matters, she'd let him and Brian do most of the talking during their call to the enthusiastic agent. As promised, he'd already sent the relevant information to them both.

Meg and her neighbours had accepted her excuse for going away: 'It's a personal matter.' And friends who'd wanted details, believing it was because of a man, had been stalled. They were right, but in a very different way from what they hoped for her future happiness.

Nate was an enigma. Polite and charming, with a definite soft spot for animals, and yet there were times when his eyes were veiled, hiding secrets she'd rather stayed that way.

Keep things professional, get his manuscript viable for publication, and on the way, learn, learn, learn.

The doors were sealed and the plane began to taxi along the runway. Instead of opening her satchel she closed her eyes and let her mind wander to an isolated farm and a tormented hero. She knew little of Outback Australia, but that was where the heroine in her next novel was going.

CHAPTER EIGHT

STRICT RESOLUTIONS TO stay impervious to Nate's charm dissolved into mush the second Jemma spotted him, standing apart from the waiting crowd. Wearing dark jeans, a black polo top and black sneakers, he depicted exactly the struggling man of her air-flight thoughts. Except with deliberate determination she'd given *him* green eyes, jet-black crew-cut hair and features as different from Nate's as possible. In addition, her hero's clothes and country boots were well worn from hours of hard physical labour.

'Hi, Jemma. Good flight?'

He reached to take her overnight bag, his fingers brushing lightly against hers. Tingles radiated from his touch. Mush got mushier.

It wasn't fair that he appeared immune as they walked towards baggage retrieval, his voice its normal tone. 'Milly's being collected and we'll pick her up by the luggage carousel. Do you have the bag you carry her in?'

'Yes, but…'

'I have a regular cat carrier in my vehicle. You look tense.'

Nate's chest tightened with a pang of guilt as he spoke. *Probably due to me.* He'd cajoled her into agreement, had told her nothing of his apartment, little of his home, and had avoided mentioning the intricacies of sharing. In fact he hadn't even mentioned they'd be staying in Sydney tonight.

'I'll be fine. The full reality of our co-writing agreement began to really sink in as I packed yesterday. I don't think it's going to be as simple as you made it sound, Nate.'

'My fault, Jemma. The prospect of finally having a

finished product made me push too fast and hard. Are you having regrets?'

'A few—all minor. Not enough to make me back out. It'll be a win for me too, remember?'

'From now on I promise to answer any questions you have with as much detail as you want.'

As long as they were literary, legal or general. Nothing personal. And he'd have to fudge any questions pertaining to how he'd gained the gritty basics of his story.

'Thank you.'

Suitcases and bags were already jostling around the turns of the conveyer belt, and passengers, two and three deep, nudged others in attempts to spot and retrieve theirs. Not being in a hurry, Nate and Jemma stayed away, leaving room for the impatient ones to succeed and leave.

'How many suitcases do you have?' Nate asked, glancing around for an available trolley.

'One. Bright blue, with purple and yellow ribbons tied on the handle.' She held her handbag, and the bag for Milly. The other two were on the ground between them.

'One? That's all? Plus this carry-on and the satchel? I'll admit your handbag's big, but for a two-week trip…'

Her shoulders relaxed, and she laughed. 'You *do* have a washing machine in your remote humpy, don't you, Nate? Unless you're planning for us to go dining and dancing every night, I have all I'll need.'

'There's all the amenities a lady requires,' he kidded, ignoring her jibe, glad to see her relax. 'And if we make good progress by the end of the week I'll drive you into town for a hamburger.'

Her smile widened. 'A true Aussie incentive.'

She twisted to allow a couple to pass, and glanced across the terminal.

'Looks like Milly's here.'

A man in a labelled uniform was walking towards them

holding a pet carrier. Milly's plaintive mews became audible as he grew nearer. Nate signed the form and retrieved the kitten, which tried to climb up his arm.

'Steady, little one—watch the skin.' He slipped her into the material bag now hanging over Jemma's shoulder, and moved over to join the few remaining people by the carousel. Within minutes they were exiting the lift on the fifth floor of the car park.

Nate stopped at the rear of his SUV, pulled his keys from the pocket of his jeans and activated the locks. He stowed Jemma's suitcase, turned, and then frowned at the sight of her perplexed expression.

'What?'

'It's an Outback monster for travelling and camping in the bush.'

'And that's a problem because…?'

It was perfect for him—it could go anywhere and carry any load required.

She made that huff-laugh mixture sound he liked as he tucked the other two pieces of luggage in safely.

'I assumed you'd have one of those sleek modern cars they advertise on television. I have no idea why. I guess it's the aura you emanate.'

He straightened up, throwing his head back and laughing out loud, causing the couple passing by to stare, and Milly to wriggle against Jemma's chest.

'I emanate an *aura*? Before I allow you anywhere near my friends or family I'll need a solemn vow you'll never repeat that remark to *anyone*, Jemma Harrison.'

He guided her to the front passenger seat, unable to contain his mirth. 'Mind you, I do like the way saying it has made you blush. Let me take Milly while you hop in. I've secured her carrier behind the driver's seat so she'll be able to see you.'

Cradling the kitten to his chest, he walked round and

put her into the brand-new carrier. She vocally made her dislike of being caged for a second time quite clear.

'Opinionated little devil, isn't she?' he said, backing out with care. 'Not surprising after today's new experiences.'

There was little talk as he drove through the heavy traffic. When it became apparent they were heading north across the Harbour Bridge he heard her sharp intake of breath.

'Did I mention we'll be staying here tonight and heading off in the morning? We'll get a better run through the traffic and it'll give Milly a break.'

'No, you didn't. But I agree. I'd like my first view of the mountains to be in daylight. I might even take a few photos.'

'For painting or writing? Have you started a new book, or are you still labouring on the current one?'

'I've typed up a rough synopsis and filled in character charts for my new hero and heroine. But they've been sidelined until yours is finished.'

'Do you want to discuss it?'

'No.' Sharp and abrupt. 'Sorry. One fictitious romance at a time for me.'

Convinced she'd suffered a painful break-up in the past, he bit back a quip about them being preferable to real life.

The scenes she'd revised had shown genuine anticipation of hope for a shared future between the man and woman. If she taught him how, he'd be able to go solo again. Perversely, instead of being motivational, he found the prospect disheartening.

With that disturbing thought running through his head he exited the highway.

'Not far to go. I've got a tossed salad in the fridge and steak ready to grill for dinner. I'd like to leave early tomorrow, and stop for breakfast when we're clear of the city.'

'Sounds good.' Jemma's answer was automatic, her mind focussed on the buildings they were passing. Each one was tall—multi-storeys tall—the iconic apartment blocks of all the pictures of the northern side of the harbour.

How far was 'not far'? How long until they reached more moderate dwellings? *Were* there any near the water in this area? If this was where he usually stayed... She raised her head, trying to count floor after floor heading skywards as he turned off the road and stopped to activate the gate leading into an underground car park.

'We're staying *here*?'

He flicked a glance at her. His chest rose and fell, and she knew without the slightest doubt that he was in a how-much-to-reveal? mindset. That capacity to blank all emotion from his features must have been an invaluable asset for a reporter. Add his knack of knowing when to hold back on giving information himself, and it was no mystery how he'd become a success.

She dismissed the girlfriend angle, and the chance of it being a friend's place, because he'd have mentioned either of those. It had to be family owned or his. Which meant...

He negotiated the downward curves to the second level as she mulled this over, and parked in an assigned spot.

'You're rich.'

It came out as a negative personal trait.

Switching off the engine, he unbuckled his safety belt and faced her.

'Yes, compared to some—minor league compared to others. Wealth is relative, Jemma.'

The blunt edge to his tone should have warned her not to stoke the fire, but completely out of character she continued.

'An apartment in this area puts the owner in the big league—especially if it's a second home, just for when you're in town.'

Add to that however many shares he owned, plus income from advising others on buying and selling... It explained his assured demeanour, and how he could take his time writing a lengthy stand-alone novel.

His guttural growl and narrowed eyes shook her from her reverie.

'What the hell difference does it make, Jemma? Does it mean you want to break our agreement?'

No! The word resonated in her head and contrition set in. Why had she raised the subject? She wanted to be the one to take his bad scenes apart, twist and tweak them and add magic to enchant the readers. More than she could ever remember wanting anything else in her life.

His economic status had nothing to do with their professional relationship. She had no idea why she was reacting this way—unless it was as a diversion from her responses to his smile, his voice. To the mere presence of him in her life. He'd awoken feelings she'd deliberately blocked since her betrayal, and she was in danger of having them torn apart again if she didn't regain control.

'No—and I apologise. Please forgive me.' She unfurled fingers pressed subconsciously into her palms and instinctively reached out to touch his arm, pulling back before making contact.

He moved quicker, clasping her hand in his with firm yet gentle pressure.

'I only take credit for what I've earned, and I concede that I'm doing okay. My siblings and I moved in here after my grandparents relocated to their house on the coast, which now belongs to my parents. The three of us inherited it seven years ago, after our grandfather died. He was the one with the foresight to invest in the building project and buy a unit off the plan.'

He released his hold and clicked her seat belt open.

'Let's go up. I think Milly's ready for a run-around.'

His tone decreed the subject closed.

They exited the lift into a small foyer. Nate turned left,

unlocked the door and allowed her to enter first. She walked in with confidence, believing that movies, television shows and her sister's mansion had prepared her for a luxurious sight.

But TV screens showed mere backdrops, and Vanessa's home was at ground level. This was high in the sky and had an almost touchable illusion. Jemma halted a few paces into a spacious kitchen with a marble-topped island, taking a slow panoramic scan of the open-plan design encompassing dining and living areas too, with a view of city lights at sundown. It ran the whole width of the apartment, with floor-to-ceiling windows on two sides.

It took a moment for her to refocus and acknowledge the quality of the dining and multi-piece entertaining settings. The light colour of the beech wood furniture complemented the bright blue shadings of the modular lounge, the two large deep-pile rugs and the open curtains. The scattering of mismatched bright multi-coloured cushions was the only aspect that didn't appear home-stylist-selected.

For her, it was too neat and clean—like a show home waiting to impress a buyer and lure them into a purchase contract. Or as if there was no permanent resident.

She looked at Nate, who was watching her with an amused expression. 'It's very impressive, Nate.'

'It's just an apartment, Jemma. One that isn't lived in much at the moment, but is regularly serviced by a cleaning firm. Let me release Milly, then I'll show you to the guest room.'

He placed the pet carrier on the sparkling clean mottled tiles and released the catch. Milly came out in a rush, stopped to look around, then began to explore her new surroundings with interest. Jemma empathised with her curiosity, and wished she felt as unperturbed.

Earned or inherited, Nate had fortune beyond anything she'd ever realise, and he accepted it as normal, his due right. Her ex had aspired to material possessions, and been willing to take a shortcut up the corporate ladder. Could she differentiate between the two?

'It's like a magazine picture, Nate. Like the luxury hotels I've researched. Like my sister Vanessa's new home in Melbourne, exclusive-decorator-furnished and ultra-modern, but…'

Her voice trailed away. She had to admit it would be a perfect setting for Vanessa, just as Nate fitted easily here.

'It's not your style? We did a full upgrade after we inherited—designed it to make a base for us when we are in Sydney, and a family place for visiting relatives and friends. Feel free to take photos or make notes for literary descriptive purposes.' He gestured towards the lounge area. 'This way.'

Carrying her big handbag, only used for travelling and shopping expeditions, and her laptop satchel, she followed him to a door in the wall that backed most of the open area. Opening it, he went in far enough to place her case and overnight bag on the floor, then stepped away.

If Jemma had been asked what she'd expected, the monster of a bed against the wall wouldn't have made the list, however long. She'd be lost in it alone.

Turning to ask if there was a smaller alternative, she was beaten by Nate's ready answer. 'They're *all* that big—and very comfortable. No chance of falling out when you roll over.'

The words were barely out when his expression changed. His lips firmed into a tight line, his throat convulsed and his eyes darkened. He seemed to have trouble speaking, and sounded huskier than he had a moment ago.

'En suite's through there. I'll be in the family room.'

He strode out, closing the door behind him, leaving her bewildered by the change. Trying to fathom its cause, she laid her suitcase flat and took out her toiletries bag.

There'd been nothing in his demeanour or tone as he'd described the bed's merits and glanced from her to it.

And then she was back on the words 'when you roll over.'

Had he imagined a similar scene to the one in her head as she'd stared at that great expanse of supportive mattress and the cosy light green quilt? *Not going to happen.* Bad move for them both. His novel was number one priority.

After freshening up in the immaculate, clean en suite, she listened for a moment at the open door, shy at the prospect of facing him, and afraid that her face would reveal her imagined scenario.

An intriguing jingling sound and the low hum of his laughter drew her out. Apart from those in front of the dining area the curtains had all been closed, making the large space seem homelier.

Nate was sitting cross-legged on one of the carpets, dangling a ball on a string, up and down, and chuckling as Milly tried to swat it. Both were apparently absorbed in the game. There was no trace of the emotion he'd displayed in the bedroom, though she noticed his shoulders flexed before he turned his head in her direction.

Scooping the kitten up and tickling her ears, Nate rose to his feet. Being physically occupied with a simple task, he'd tried to clear his head of visions of Jemma in that room and bolster his need to treat her as a working colleague. The amendments had to take precedence, and he needed to focus on her writing skills—her most important attribute as far as he should be concerned.

After his previous responses to her he'd steeled himself, and once again reinforced his defences on the drive to the airport. Outwardly he believed he'd succeeded, but inside his heightening reactions had him determining to… to *what*? Stay away from a house guest with whom he was

supposed to be collaborating? Go for long runs, leaving
her alone?

He'd known Jemma was near. The back of his neck had
tingled, he'd breathed in through his nostrils, seeking an
elusive aroma, and his pulse had quickened. He'd twisted
his head and seen her watching him, body stiff, eyes wary.

Her newly brushed hair flowed neatly down her back,
and he so wanted to muss it up a little, or have a few strands
lie across her shoulders, so he could lift them into place, or
run them through his fingers. Her short-sleeved loose top
with its yellow leaf pattern and her tan trousers were ideal
for travelling. But the image imprinted in his head was of
the blue dress she'd worn for their dinner date.

Not a date. A celebration of a business deal.

'Hi, take a seat while I start dinner. The TV remote's in
the drawer of the coffee table.' He bent to put Milly on the
floor. 'You stay out from under my feet, okay?'

The expected background noise didn't come as he activated the grill and took the bottle of white wine he'd
opened last night and the steaks from the fridge. Leaving
the meat on the benchtop, he turned towards the dining
table, already set for two, including two glasses in an ice
bucket at one end.

Jemma was standing by the uncovered window, staring at the twinkling view. He ought to pour their drinks.
Instead he walked up behind her, and knew she'd sensed
him by the hitch in her shoulders.

'Would you like to go outside?'

Spinning round, she nodded. 'Yes, please.'

'It'll be windy. You might need to wear something
warmer.'

She sped off to her room, and he went to put the steaks
on a slow grill, then unlocked the glass door leading out
onto the balcony. As Jemma returned, pulling on a navy

zip-up jacket, his firm intentions began to crumble. Her face was flushed and her eyes as bright as the city lights.

Images of numerous kisses, stolen with the excuse of protecting or keeping a girl warm, flooded his mind. The memories of fighting to control rampant teenage hormones had dimmed, and couldn't compare to the burning desire of a mature man coursing through his body.

He steeled his resolve, and made sure Milly was nowhere near before pushing the door open enough to allow them to slip through, shutting it behind him.

CHAPTER NINE

A LIGHT BREEZE caught her hair as she moved over to the glass and metal railing, lifting the ends to make them float behind her, tempting him to fulfil that secret wish. He followed, leaning on his arms by her side, the railing cold on his skin. She didn't seem to notice, her fingers gripping it as she peered over and swivelled her head to take in the full view.

'It's even better out here. I checked through the window of my room just now—it has a balcony, but no way onto it.'

'There's a sliding door on three sides, and the kitchen wall is the divider between the two apartments on this level.'

She walked towards the corner and he followed, knowing the wind might pick up there, ready to steady her if it did. She was occupied with the view and continued round, noting the rooms they passed after the lounge.

'This one's mine, and the corner one has windows on two sides *and* a door. Lucky devil.'

Nate tamped down the temptation to admit it was his room, and show her. She'd already invaded his nights; how much hotter would his dreams be if he had an image of her inside his bedroom?

She stopped at that corner, her features animated as she picked out buildings and landmarks. Her enthusiasm was contagious, making him feel as if he was seeing it all from a new and different perspective.

Unable to resist, he placed his hands on the railing either side of her, telling himself it was to protect her from the wind. Leaning in, he breathed in the fresh lemon scent of her hair as it blew across his face, and had to tighten his grip to prevent himself from running his fingers through the silken strands, all the way to the ends near her waist.

For Jemma, seeing the iconic view from pictures and movies was like living a dream. So incredible from this height, and such a vast array of lights in every conceivable colour, blinking and pulsing as if alive. A spectacle for her…a common scene for Nate.

She'd paused here to breathe in the aroma of the harbour. Instead her lungs were filled with Nate's special blend of vanilla, citrus and musk. Three scents that would haunt her for ever.

She glanced at his hands, firm and strong, one on each side of her, enclosing; protective. Heat flared in her core at the thought of those long, tanned fingers tangling in her hair, caressing her cheek and stroking her body until she melted against his. Crazy. Impossible. Taboo.

For a second she thought the low guttural sound of need she'd heard came from her. But it was Nate, his mouth close to her ear, his hot breath fanning her lobe. He surrounded her, yet there was no physical contact. Foolish to desire any.

Her heart beating as if she'd climbed the twenty-seven flights of stairs, she swung round, her breath catching in her throat at the fire in his storm-grey eyes as his head jerked back. They both froze. If an earthquake had struck she wouldn't have moved, wouldn't have been able to break the spell.

Nate leant in again, his intent obvious, and a flashback triggered in her brain, causing her to echo his recent movement away. He stopped, eyes narrowing and brow furrowing. His chest rose, and his breath was audible as it fell.

Stepping back, he allowed her room to leave the railing. 'We'd better go in. I need to check on the steaks.'

* * *

Jemma watched a quiz show while he served up dinner, taking little notice of the screen in front of her. Why would a man of Nate's status, with two homes and the means to support himself while he wrote a long novel—he'd mentioned how time-consuming his research and revisions had been—want to kiss *her*? She wasn't sophisticated, didn't do social chitchat, and hadn't the flair to host dinners or parties like Vanessa. She could never even begin to compete with her sister, had never wanted to.

All she had to offer was her talent to imagine and describe believable relationships between a man and a woman.

Her fingers balled into fists in her lap, and she bit her lip to prevent any sound escaping. Was that why he'd come so close? Had appeared to be going to kiss her? Did he intend to use charm to keep her sweet and willing to help him? Her ex had had no qualms on that score, and there was no doubting Nate had plenty to spare.

She knew nothing of his personal life. Maybe there was someone—a woman who didn't live with him—or perhaps they had a casual mutually satisfying relationship.

'Dinner's ready, Jemma.'

It took a moment for his words to penetrate as she suddenly realised he'd never asked *her* about any ties either. She clicked off the television, stood and walked over to the dining table. The overhead lights in the whole open-plan area went on and off automatically, leaving the dining area with a surprising sense of privacy as they faced each other. She refused to think intimacy.

'Are you okay having white wine? I opened the bottle for pasta last night, but we can take it with us if you'd prefer red with the steaks.'

'Purists would be shocked. But I don't mind.' She thanked him as he filled both glasses, waited until he'd taken his seat, then lifted her drink towards him in a gesture that was becoming a habit.

'Thank you for cooking dinner.'

He dipped his head, returned the salute, and after drinking began to eat.

Jemma's steak was tender, cooked exactly to her taste. The salad was crisp and the dressing tangy without being overpowering. She'd be happy to do all the cleaning and let him cook every meal if he kept up this standard.

'You enjoyed being outside? Great setting for a romance scene, huh?'

Looking up, she met a guarded expression. His tone didn't quite match the casual words. But if he wanted to ignore the episode outside she'd play along, and ensure she never found herself in the same situation again.

'One that's been used so many times, in so many locations around the world. The trick is in finding a new angle. How about for your rough and tumble scenes?'

His eyes softened and she sensed his shoulders relax, caught a hint of a smile.

'That was one of my grandmother's favourite sayings when Sam, our friends and I came into her kitchen, grubby from playing and wrestling. I've got a couple of fights on balconies, even guys falling off. If you feel any of those is a better place for any of the interactive scenes, go ahead and relocate them.'

She stared at him, and the hand holding her fork in front of her parted lips stilled. Less than three weeks ago he'd vehemently opposed her having any access to his manuscript, and since then they'd spent limited time together, spread over four days, before her flight this afternoon. Now he was saying he'd allow her to change a location?

Her hand dropped, the food left uneaten. He seemed oblivious to the enormity of his statement, and then his lips curled.

'I'm impressed with those scenes in your novel—and I do still have right of veto.'

He was teasing her, yet there'd been a serious undertone in his voice. Pushing it to the back of her mind for dwelling on later, she took a drink of the fruity wine as he changed the subject.

'I stocked up with enough fresh fruit and vegetables for a few days this morning. Any time you want anything I'll drive you into town, or you can take the SUV. I'm—'

'Whoa. Are you referring to that monster down below, or do you have another vehicle in the mountains? I've never driven anything that big, and I wouldn't feel comfortable trying it on unfamiliar country roads.'

Mouth agape, he blinked and his brow furrowed. Her stomach tensed and she wished she'd said nothing, just ensured the situation never arose. She assumed the women he associated with were competent in *all* fields of life, and she had many failings.

'I'm sorry, Jemma. I'm so used to it I didn't consider its size. Alice won't use it either—claims it's hard to park. I'll take you anywhere, any time, and if I'm not there you can call a cab from town.'

Grateful for his understanding, Jemma thanked him, and they finished their meal talking about the tourist attractions of Katoomba.

Nate insisted on cleaning up, grateful that there'd been no repercussions from his inexplicable behaviour earlier. Berating himself as he'd mixed the salad and turned the steaks, he hadn't been able to explain why he'd come so near to wrecking everything for a moment's pleasure in a moment's madness, caused by her scent and the soft sigh he'd swear he'd heard as he'd craved her lips under his.

The pain in her startled eyes as she'd pulled back had cleared his head and fired up his guilt. Her issues with men ran deep, and he had no intention of exacerbating them. He had enough personal issues of his own. And with her now on her guard, keeping control should be easier.

He went looking for her to suggest coffee, and found her in the hall between the bedrooms and the laundry. She was staring, transfixed, at the massive built-in bookcase that reached to the ceiling, every shelf filled with books of various sizes and piles of magazines.

There was no sense of order or filing system, no attempt to line up by height or writer's name. This was generations of his family, taking books out and putting them back, re-reading them and returning them to any available space.

He stood behind her and watched for a moment, empathising with her joy. As if mesmerised, she scanned the books, running her fingers over remembered titles and authors and sighing with happiness.

'We're all avid readers, and there's a lot of old favourites on those shelves. Wouldn't part with them for the world.'

She pivoted, and laughed, oblivious to the rapture evident on her face.

'Oh, I envy you. Children's books to science fiction, with every genre in between. For years I relied on libraries, and hated having to return those books I loved.'

'You now have quite a collection yourself.' He grinned. 'One of the first things I noticed in your lounge room. I've put the jug on if you want a hot drink.'

'What time do you want to leave in the morning?'

'Is six too early? I've learned it's the best time for getting clear of the city and avoiding multiple traffic hold-ups. No guarantees, but… And, like I said, I know the best places to stop for breakfast.'

'Six is fine. It's been a long day, so I'll put Milly in the laundry and go to bed. We'll have to shut her in, otherwise she might wander and hide.'

'Leave her to me. She can keep me company for a while.'

'Okay.' She crouched down to stroke the kitten, who'd

trotted over to join them, then stood up. 'I'm very grateful for the opportunity you're giving me, Nate.'

'Works both ways, Jemma. You have a good night's sleep and we'll talk on the way, once we hit the highway. Goodnight.'

Jemma didn't move—couldn't as Nate's grey eyes locked with hers, holding her entranced. His arms lay rigid at his sides, fingers curled, and she was acutely aware of his Adam's apple bobbing, and the steady movement of his chest in the rhythm of his breathing.

She licked dry lips, her heart pounded and she could swear the air shimmered between them.

Suddenly from nowhere the sharp pain of her ex's infidelity cut deep inside, breaking the spell.

She dropped her gaze, scrunched her eyes shut for a second to regain control and faced him again. 'Goodnight, Nate.' Only the slight tremor in her voice betrayed her.

'Goodnight, Jemma.'

He moved aside and she walked past him to her room.

Alone in the shower, she tried to compare the two men and failed. It seemed that over the years images of her ex had blurred, leaving behind only the deep-rooted anguish of betrayal, making her treat any handsome man with charm and aspirations of becoming wealthy as if they were in the same mould. It was because of his and her brother-in-law's social climbing endeavours that she avoided mixing with anyone she deemed prosperous or elite.

Nate fell into both of those categories, though she couldn't imagine him cheating for money. But his literary aspirations were different, strong, maybe even obsessional; he had a drive to prove he could achieve his goal. What would he do and who would he manipulate to have a copy of his published novel in his hand?

Some time later she vaguely heard music—soothing,

classical. Groggy with sleep, she turned over, snuggling deeper under the quilt.

Woken by her alarm in the morning, she was dressed and packing her suitcase when she heard a clatter through the adjacent wall. From the big corner bedroom. Where Nate must have slept.

Nate had hoped for a six o'clock getaway, would have settled for six-thirty, and was pleasantly surprised to be exiting the car park at ten to six—an hour or so before sunrise. Jemma looked relaxed and rested, which shouldn't have irked him but did, seeing as it was she who'd kept *him* awake for most of the night.

It had been one of those rare occasions when low music and the night sky view through open drapes had failed to lull him to sleep. Trying to equate the demure woman in the room through the wall behind his head and the sensual scenes she'd written had rattled his brain. Had they been penned from imagination or experience?

She used her pain as a shield, which was something he understood and emulated, along with his compelling desire to purge his own dark memories in his story. It never quite worked—merely pushed them a little further into the deep recesses of his mind.

Love scenes were different. Passionate and personal. He'd done with feelings and emotions, which explained his stilted written relationships. But was describing their sexual encounters cathartic for women?

In frustration, he'd turned the overhead light on and accessed her full manuscript, the relevant scenes highlighted in his tablet. He'd scrolled to each one, concentrating on the interaction, physical and verbal, and the varied ways she'd depicted loving gestures and emotions. Not his business, but his gut had tightened as he'd speculated on how she'd gained so much knowledge.

Waking from a restless sleep, he hadn't been able to remember his dreams, yet knew they'd been hot and steamy. Dressed, bed made and suitcase ready, he'd reached for his watch on the bedside cabinet—and knocked his clock radio onto the tiled floor.

Now, even with a meal break, they'd be at his property by mid-morning. Unless Jemma wanted to, there'd be no need to stop in the town.

'Do you mind if I listen to the news, Jemma?'

'No worries. Is keeping up to date with the news important for your writing? I assume you've started a second novel?'

'It's more for the effect current events might have on the share market. But, yes, I'm in the planning stage with different settings.' He gave her a quick smile and turned the radio on. 'I'll contact you for help when I get to a schmaltzy scene.'

'*Schmaltzy?* That, Mr Thornton, sells millions of books every year—print and digital.'

The chuckle he tried to hold back came out as a splutter. 'I surrender, Jemma. For now. One day we'll debate the pros and cons over a good bottle of wine.'

'And chocolates?'

The news began and Nate adjusted the volume. Jemma took a book from her handbag on the floor, wriggled a little until she was comfortable and began to read. Discussion followed the news, and as the traffic was building up Nate tuned to a more relaxing music station and gave his full concentration to the road.

Being in control of a reliable vehicle on good roads was a unique feeling—power with responsibility. Rattling along potholed dirt tracks in uninhabited areas overseas, wrestling with a clapped-out wreck and with no certainty of reaching your destination safely, was empowering—with the added pungency of danger.

Jemma was the perfect companion in peak traffic, occasionally looking up at the road or checking on Milly, otherwise absorbed in her reading. Nothing in her gentle demeanour even hinted at those torrid scenes he couldn't get out of his head. Even the milder ones raised his suspicions over where and how she'd researched them. And with whom.

CHAPTER TEN

THEY ATE IN a highway fast food outlet and shared a daily newspaper. Before setting off again he gave Milly a few minutes' freedom in a safe area behind the building.

The traffic was light now, and he was familiar with the road, and still those questions were drumming in his head. Having a fervent dislike of banal small talk, he broached the subject full-on—a habit from his reporting days.

'That him/her stuff you write, Jemma—how do you do it? Where does it come from?'

He sensed her eyes on him, figured he was getting the usual penetrating scrutiny, and surprisingly didn't mind at all.

'Define *"it,"* Nate.' Her voice was flat, with a hint of umbrage.

'You know darn well, Jemma. That intensity and inter-action with sensual undertones. That emotion and the dif-ferent ways you write it. The actual physical encounters. If there's a how-to-write book on *that* I'd like a copy.'

'I'll give you a list. If that's how you describe making love you'll need it. Reading well-written scenes you want to emulate is also a great teacher.'

'Plus practical learning?'

Her gasp coincided with his oath of regret, and he im-mediately tried to make amends.

'I'm sorry, Jemma, that was crass and uncalled-for. It sure didn't work for me.'

A quick glance at her pale face deepened his self-contrition. And his next remark would probably fuel the fire.

'I can't offer any excuse because there isn't one. I read

what you've written and I can't believe the variety of ways you describe the same actions and feelings. Can't help wondering how.'

He'd screwed up—virtually accused her of sleeping around—and wouldn't blame her if she told him to fix his inadequate scenes himself. What the hell had possessed him? Stupid question. She intrigued and bothered him.

The women he dated—which was hardly the correct description for mutual sexual satisfaction sometimes preceded by dinner or a function—were experienced. Jemma was a far cry from their determined-to-stay-independent and career-absorbed personalities. There was no explanation for his reactions towards her. He needed her brain, her description expertise, nothing more.

Yeah, that's why you can't stop thinking of her enticing blue eyes and her soft lips ripe for kissing. Why you take deep breaths to inhale her perfume. And why you pushed for this personal collaboration when your head argued for electronic contact only.

'Are you claiming actual participation in every aspect of your hero's covert operations, Nate?'

The biting tone of her challenge slammed him back to the present situation. The breath he hadn't realised he was holding whooshed from his lungs, and for a second his head spun.

Sucking more air in, he framed an answer he hoped would satisfy her without revealing the complete truth. 'I've met military personnel in a number of places, and worked with some to gain access to remote areas, normally inaccessible. Friendships with them and a few corporate employees working for international companies have been beneficial to my job. A lot can be learned from conversation over food or drinks if you're prepared to listen and be discreet.'

He hesitated, stared at the number plate of the camper van in front, and then inexplicably shared more.

'I've never betrayed nor had reason to regret any of those relationships. And being involved with a social group who meet in Sydney every month has aided my return to normal day-to-day life. The support they give is unconditional— never questioned and never denied.'

Jemma heard the words he spoke and filled in those he'd held back. Nate Thornton would refute any suggestion by others of being affected by his experiences, and yet she sensed he'd turned to these members for help at some time.

'If you're part of it, it's not just for ex-military?'

His eyes met hers for a brief moment, cool and confronting with an underlying warning.

No questions. I've said enough.

'Your business. Just keep in mind that any alterations I make in your characters' relationship will impact elsewhere.'

'As in…?'

'As in the friendlier they get, the more intimate details they'll learn, and the more likely it will be that they'll think of each other when apart…even at inappropriate times.'

Like I think of you, though you've never held me; we've never kissed.

'My amendments will influence how they react to each other in future scenes, Nate. They can't become involved without some changes in their behaviour.'

'Hmm…'

She gave him a moment to absorb what appeared to be a new concept for him, though he'd already accepted the few revisions she'd made outside her specified scenes. To continue, she needed to know about the couple's individual futures.

'It would be helpful if I could read the entire manuscript and get some idea of how often they'll be together and what happens to them. They had long breaks away from each other in the last four chapters I saw, but the action was so riveting it didn't matter.'

'In your story they seldom had a page apart.'

'Different genre. Different reader expectations.'

'You added music to mine too—something I hadn't considered. Even nailed the heavy rock band my hero listens to. The man I based his character on was a diehard fan.'

'Which means *you* nailed the character. Who, by the way, wouldn't appeal to *every* woman.'

'That was the furthest thought from my mind when I was writing.'

The atmosphere in the vehicle had changed—or maybe it was Jemma herself. Without being conscious of any deliberate action she'd accepted her irrational attraction to Nate, *and* the understandable apprehension of staying with a man she barely knew. On all but one level she trusted him. She no longer deemed him arrogant, but to her he was still the self-assured, I-can-handle-any-situation macho male she'd pegged in that foyer.

At her request, he switched radio channels to one playing contemporary hits. They discussed the merits, or lack of, in the music and performers, and agreed to disagree when their tastes didn't mesh.

The warmth of the sun through the windows and the steady purr of the engine combined with her early rising made her drowsy. She turned her face towards the window and slept.

Some time later she became aware of an almost familiar song as she drifted towards consciousness. Eyes shut, she tried to identify it and realised it was Nate, singing along with the radio. His voice wasn't bad at all, especially with the abrasive edge favoured by many hard rock fans.

The music finished and she didn't move, not wanting to embarrass him. As if *anything* could shake the man's composure. Opening her eyes, she saw tall trees flashing past, backed by blue sky, not the peaks and stunted tree-growth she'd pictured from television images of the Blue Mountains. They were different, though, and not as lush as those in Hahndorf.

Reminding herself they were at a much higher altitude, she stirred, straightened up and caught Nate's quick smile towards her.

'We're about fifteen minutes from Katoomba. We'll bypass it—unless you want to stop for a drink or anything?'

She checked her watch. It was twenty to nine. He'd mentioned living out of the town, but not how far.

'No, I'm all right. Shouldn't I be able to see the mountains now?'

He laughed. 'Not when you're driving along the top of them. Don't worry—you'll get plenty of photo opportunities in the next two weeks. I've got tourist brochures at home from when Dad and Mum stayed with me.'

'Will there be time for sightseeing?'

This time his glance included an eyebrow quirk.

'You agreed to come thinking I'd work you without any breaks, Jemma?'

His smile told her he was teasing, and she responded the same way.

'You said you wanted my input as soon as possible, Nate.'

'Ah, but even *I* take time out for pleasure.'

The phrase, *What kind?* formed on her lips, but thankfully didn't get spoken—although she was sure he'd give plausible answers. He ran to keep fit, and trained with the firefighting service. He had family and friends to socialise with. But he had given no indication of there being a regular woman in his life.

She'd been first to the dining area with her luggage this morning—not quite first, as Milly had been eating a small portion of dry food in her corner. Kneeling to stroke her, she'd heard the sound of Nate's suitcase wheels on the tiled floor, turned, and felt suddenly bereft of air and logical thought. Why was it no other man in jeans and a muscle-sculpting T-shirt had that power?

She'd love to ask if he'd had any requests to pose for those firefighter calendars like the one she'd bought for a friend's Christmas present last year. If Nate had been fea-tured she'd have that month on her wall permanently.

'Jemma? You've gone very quiet. It's a bit late to change your mind.'

'I'm not. I was wondering how far from town you live. You said it was too far to go by foot.'

'Ten-point-seven kilometres along the road—plus four hundred metres from the turn-off to my house. I *have* walked it on occasion. My normal routine is to leave the SUV in town with a friend if I catch the train to the city.'

'Are there other homes nearby?'

'No—that's part of the attraction for me. If you're wor-ried about safety it's textbook fire-and-storm-protected, and I clear any surrounding bush-growth every spring or when needed.'

She went quiet, noting the small number of turn-offs before he slowed down and drove into his which was un-marked and barely discernible, consisting of solid-packed dirt and weaving around a large tree for a few metres in, then veering off again.

'You don't have a mailbox?'

'Anything I can't get on email goes to a post office box in Katoomba. I cleared it last week.'

'And the house isn't visible from the road? Is all this land yours?' There were more trees than she'd expected, given his statement regarding safety and clearing land.

'Yes. Privacy is important to me. Anyone I invite here knows where it is.'

A final bend and they were in an open area with a view of a mountaintop across a valley. For Jemma, it was like seeing a picture from a classic architectural magazine for real. She couldn't conceive of a more perfect home in such a setting. Everything she'd imagined it might be flew out of her head.

Nate was justifiably proud of the house he'd helped design, with every eco-friendly device and technology available. Built on rising ground as a split level, with a solar-panelled sloping roof, the house's colours blended with its natural surroundings, and was fronted with a wide area of neutral-coloured pebbles. Beyond there was a variety of naturally growing, widely spaced low scrub bushes. The nearest trees wouldn't reach the building if felled by fire or man.

He drove around to the right, activated a remote control and stole a glance at Jemma as what appeared to be part of the side wall slid upwards into the ground-floor ceiling. Her wide-eyed response was all he'd hoped for, as it had been when family members and friends had first visited.

His parents had loved the comfort of cooling and heating, the views and the peaceful evenings. His brother-in-law and Sam had wanted to try every piece of gadgetry and know how they worked. Alice had been enthusiastic about everything, and had made playful fun of him for living there alone.

Reversing down the ramp, he experienced the same heightened anticipation as he had the first time he'd completed the manoeuvre. As if Jemma's opinion was significant.

If the smile on her face as she gazed around the illuminated garage and workshop was any indication, he'd earned her approval.

She was out of the vehicle and scanning his tool shadow board and built-in workbench and shelves before he had a chance to get around and open her door.

'Wow, are there any tools you *don't* have, Nate?'

'I bought these while we were building. Haven't had many yet, but I like to do my own repairs except when a licence is needed.' He pointed to the far corner. 'Laundry's over there—use it any time you need.'

Turning back to the vehicle, he went to the rear and began unloading their luggage, carrying it to a small lift near a set of stairs. She collected her handbag from the front seat, then unbuckled the cat carrier and took it over. Two more trips and everything was inside, ready to go up.

Nate caught her arm as she was about to enter and led her round the side. Between the lift and the ramp was a large back-up generator and an electricity switchboard. He gave her a quick rundown on the switches.

'Blackouts are rare, and the generator should cut in if one occurs. If I don't happen to be here, and it doesn't, you can do it manually. There's a torch and spare batteries in the bottom of your bedside cabinet, and in a kitchen drawer.'

'You've really covered everything, haven't you? Even putting in your own lift.'

He looked down into enchanting blue eyes, deep and alluring as the Mediterranean Sea, and the desire to dive into the tantalising depths was overwhelming. Only dredging up the memory of another pair of bewitching eyes kept him from dipping his head those few centimetres and claiming her lips with his.

A flash of wariness flickered in her eyes, but was gone as quickly as it came. Heeding its warning, he moved away.

'Useful when there are three storeys, and it cuts out arguing with Dad about him carrying suitcases up flights of stairs.'

Jemma went in first, standing sideways on to Nate in the small space left by the luggage, her eyes fixed on his chest as he closed the door and pressed the top button. The air she drew in was scented with his cologne, and it would take little effort for her to rise onto her toes and press her lips to his manly jaw.

Contrary emotions. A moment ago, she'd been afraid *he* was about to kiss *her*.

'We'll drop off the luggage, then go down to ground level,' he told her as they halted, stepping out to allow her to exit with her handbag, satchel and carry-on.

The wide corridor stretched the width of the house down to a picture window with shutters.

'You're in the first on the left, and the light switch is on the left by the door. I leave all the drapes closed and the blinds down when I'm away.'

Nate followed her with the two suitcases, set hers down near the bed and left with his. A good move for her, because she was incapable of speech, in awe of the suite she'd be occupying during her stay.

With her love of nature, this was her dream room. The soft green décor with traces of pale yellow, including a leaf motif on the enormous bedspread, pillow and an armchair, was soothing. She loved the way it was teamed with the light brown of the bedside cabinets, the desk table and chair in one corner, and the small round coffee table alongside the armchair by the window.

A double door which slid into the wall revealed a large walk-in wardrobe, with a dressing table and full-length mirror. She assumed every bedroom would be similarly furnished, with different designs. His? Or had he hired an interior decorator? She couldn't picture him flicking though swatches of fabric.

She'd begun to slide the single door open, catching a glimpse of a continuation of the colour scheme in the en suite bathroom, and heard him coming back. Whatever he'd been about to say was lost as she gave him a knowing smile, well aware that her eyes would be gleaming with mischief.

'That must have been quite a bulk deal you got on those beds, Nate.'

He chuckled, clearly appreciating her sense of humour. 'Nearly four years apart, but from the same dealer. You *did* find yours comfortable last night?'

'Very—I slept peacefully until my alarm. Seriously, Nate, I think this room's worthy of a five-star hotel.'

Nate was tempted to make a quip about twenty-four-hour room service but refrained, deeming.it might be miscon-strued.

'Thank you. Now, let's get Milly to the ground floor and free her before she starts objecting.'

Downstairs, he opened the shutters and green drapes, flooding the open area with light. Before releasing the kit-ten he latched the gates he'd installed across the stairs, up and down, preferring to keep her on one floor until she settled.

From the moment he'd driven onto his property his senses had been attuned to Jemma, trying to gauge her reaction to everything he'd designed, chosen, sourced and put in place. Although he'd valued his family's opinion, it hadn't impacted on him. It disturbed him that hers might. So far every reaction had been positive, lifting his spirits.

The similarities between here and the Sydney unit were deliberate, with ceiling-to-floor glass along one long wall, facing a panoramic view of the mountains across the gully. Here the colours were various shades of green, and the fur-niture teak. This was a subdued version, conducive to relax-ation, quiet evenings and a peaceful atmosphere for writing.

Partial glass on the side wall and front ensured plenty of natural light and a true living-in-the-country atmosphere. And behind the kitchen was a surprise he hoped she'd share with him.

CHAPTER ELEVEN

HE WATCHED HER walk the length of the open-plan area, her eyes focussed on the true-life mural through the glass, swivel for a slow scan of the décor inside, then turn to him with a bemused expression. Unable to gauge her reaction from where he stood, he moved closer.

'Sydney was awesome, Nate, and this is spectacular. What's your next project? A castle or a palace? Is it *all* your personal taste?'

'It took time, but everything here is exactly what I want, right down to the salt and pepper shakers, and it will suit me until I grow old.'

As he spoke he recalled selecting it all with a fierce determination that no one else would have any input, that his home would have only his stamp in every room.

Jemma was the first woman not related to him he'd invited here and he wanted her to approve, to feel relaxed and at home. *No!* He fisted his hands at this thought. Relaxed and comfortable for *writing*—not as if it were her home. She was a transient visitor, and on completion of the assignment she'd leave.

He switched topics. 'Where I write depends on my mood: in here, or outside—even in winter on occasion.' He flicked his hand towards a desk and chair in the far corner. 'Or over there, or in my study. You go wherever you feel comfiest.'

'Thank you. May I see the study?'

He led her to two doors in the lounge area, opposite the long veranda.

The first room was set up like an executive's office, with

top-notch furniture and equipment, and was showroom-neat and tidy. The bookshelf held a few photographs, and books that were all reference books.

Noting her frown at the latter, Nate quickly ushered her out and into the next room, standing to the side to watch her expression. He wasn't disappointed. She gasped, her lips parted and her eyes widened in ecstatic surprise.

Jemma coveted this room more than any other she'd seen in either home. Two full walls and the space under the window held replicas of the bookshelves in Sydney, even the random higgledy-piggledy stacking of reading material. In the centre was a comfy old armchair, with its footrest out and a coffee table alongside. She closed her eyes, envying his having both rooms, wishing that maybe one day…

'You approve, Jemma?'

Her heart blipped and her eyes flew open. She'd been so wrong at their first meeting. Forget romantic phrases—his soft tone against her ear would stir sensations even if he were reciting a dull repair manual. She swallowed, and managed to nod in agreement.

'I'll take that as a yes. Come with me. I think you'll like this too.'

He reached for her hand; she pulled away at the first touch—too late to stop the tingles shooting across her skin. He didn't appear affected.

She followed as he strode towards the front corner of the house by the kitchen, to a door with no handle in the side wall. He placed his right-hand fingers into a metal insert at his head height, she heard a click, and then it slid to his left, disappearing into the wall.

The humidity hit her and she knew what she was going to see apart from the weights and bench press in her immediate view. Past a screened change area and shower there was a lap pool, clear and inviting, extending nearly the width of the house. A lat pulldown machine stood in the furthest corner.

Her mind boggled, trying to take it all in: the actual building with its solar panels, the double-glazed floor-to-ceiling windows on almost every wall, and the underground area—what the heck would digging *that* out have cost? Add in the fixtures, fittings and furniture…

Her brain couldn't, *wouldn't* process the figure, had gone numb trying.

Her eyes met Nate's gaze. It was hopefully expectant—as if her opinion mattered, as if he really wanted her endorsement. But that was crazy thinking, and she countered it by voicing the silly thought that had flashed into her head.

'What? No spa?'

Instead of being insulted, he burst out laughing and raised his eyebrows.

Idiot, of course there was. Probably in *his* bathroom. No, probably in all of them. His approach upstairs had prevented her from looking right into hers.

As if he read her mind, he answered. 'How could I possibly enjoy my own spa if my guests had to settle for less? Apart from the colour scheme, and some difference in size, the bedroom suites are all the same. Did you pack bathing suits?'

She refocussed at his question. 'Yes, I checked out the nearby aquatic centre online, hoping to use it for exercise and an alternative to walking. This is amazing, Nate. You really are self-contained here, aren't you?'

She heard the envy in her own voice. He hadn't been joking when he'd said his home had everything he wanted. How she'd love to design her own home from scratch. How she'd love to have enough money even to consider it.

'As long as you're here, consider the pool yours as well. Do you want to unpack now, or go for a walk?'

'I'd love some fresh air and exercise, please.'

'Walk it is.'

* * *

Nate took two small water bottles from the fridge and they left via the front door, walked across a porch area and down two steps to the pebbles. The width of the path varied, constantly forcing the gap between them to widen and narrow. Each time they were close Nate flattened the fingers of his left hand to his thigh, fighting the desire to touch her and have her even closer to his side. Once or twice, when they were further apart, he became aware that his fingers were tapping, a sign of agitation he fought to control.

His solitary walks in the mountains would never be the same. They would now be imbued with the spirit of Jemma—her tranquillity as they strolled, her affinity with nature and the scent of her floral perfume.

He'd have to modify his lifestyle while she was here. He couldn't expect her to fit in with his erratic hours— sometimes he was up through the night and cat-napping in the day. It only happened here. Even if he was alone in the Sydney apartment he lived by regular business hours.

'Do you have a work schedule, or do you go with the creative flow?'

Grateful for the sudden question requiring him to refocus, he answered readily. 'I can write any time, anywhere. If you like, I'll rustle up some food while you unpack, then you can choose where you'd like to set up. We can sort out breaks as we go.'

'Sounds good to me.'

Jemma was enjoying the feel of the pebbles under her sneakers, loving the crunch of fallen leaves and undergrowth along the track even more. The filtered sun through the trees warmed her back, and the T-shirt and cotton pants she wore were perfect for the different activities of the day.

A slight breeze cooled her skin, and their footsteps were

the only sound apart from the occasional rustle of nature. It seemed they had the world all to themselves—or at any rate, this tiny part of it. She memorised the sights, sounds and smells, the latter a mingling of musk, vanilla and citrus. And the essence of Nate.

Their discussion on the return trip included aspects of living in the same house, morning rising and meal times, plus music and television show preferences. She admitted that her exercise consisted of walking to and from town as often as possible, spasmodic yoga classes and summer trips to the beach with friends. She kept quiet about her love of dancing whenever she was inspired by music…most often at home and alone.

Although she'd been at ease during the walk, Jemma's trepidation resurfaced as she mounted the stairs to her room, her fingers clenching and opening. Nate had a knack of disconcerting her with words, looks and limited touches. And an equal talent for bringing her back to equilibrium with the same.

Shutting her door was an unwarranted gesture. She was convinced he'd never enter uninvited. It was for her own benefit—a physical obstacle she needed because her emotions were rapidly dismantling her internal barricades.

The quick peek she'd given the bathroom confirmed its luxury, and now she pushed the door into its recess. It was as if he'd perused the same décor magazines and top hotel rooms she had in her research. She'd described it in her book and he'd built it. She'd fantasised about soaking in bubbles while he actually relaxed in them. Tonight, she'd be joining him.

No, no, *no*. Not together. Heat shot through her—head to toe, skin to core—as she tried to distance her imagination from her innocent thought process. Too late. And splashing cold water over her cheeks did little to diminish the colour or the burning.

Vowing to stick to showers, she left, shutting the door behind her, knowing that sooner rather than later she'd renege.

She knelt by her suitcase and began to unpack her everyday clothes in this room which deserved the kind of designer clothes her sister's closet held. Suitcase empty, she stowed it away and crossed to the window, overlooking the track they'd taken. Pushing the curtains further apart, she was thrilled to find a door leading onto a balcony. The beauty of the ancient peaks against a brilliant blue sky spurred her to capture this moment of nature's tranquillity, to have it as a permanent memento.

A few minutes later she had photographs taken from there, and others of the gully view from the corner of the house in her camera.

Shamed by her stubbornness in resisting her friends' pressure for so long, she stood for a moment, reinforcing to herself who she was and the reason Nate had invited her to his home.

You are here because you have an invaluable talent. Because Brian and Nate believe in your ability to enhance this novel. Because Nate trusts you. Because you are worthy of his trust.

He was also attracted to her, and she was vulnerable.

Only if you allow yourself to be.

She vowed to focus on the reason she was there, to complete her task as soon as possible, then return to Hahndorf, where she belonged, with no regrets.

Nate put the two covered plates of ham and salad in the fridge, wondering how long it took a woman to unpack one suitcase and a carry-on. He opened a bottle of beer and drank, leaning against the island. His fingers tapped on his thigh and he grunted, trying to understand why her approval of his home was so important.

Every moment spent with her tested his resolve to stay platonic, as he'd promised himself. She amused him, provoked him and stirred desires he'd sworn never to fall prey to again. When she'd decided where she wanted to work he'd pick another area, out of sight of her, where her evocative perfume didn't reach.

Huh, as if *that* would diminish how aware he was of her. Like right now, as the hairs on his nape stiffened, sensing she was near.

He squared his shoulders and sucked in his stomach. Twenty-five chapters to go—each with a minimum of one confrontational scene between his prime characters. In all, too many discussions with Jemma about feelings, emotions and sex.

He turned his head and smiled as she approached, looking cool and refreshed, while *he* was in definite need of a cold shower.

The rest of the day was spent as he hoped a fair portion of their time would be.

Jemma chose to work at the lounge room desk, with the full manuscript on her laptop and a printed copy she could make notes on. He took his computer, containing all the chapters she'd revised, his canvas folding recliner and a soft drink to his favourite spot on the ground-floor veranda.

They compromised on non-vocal music from classic movies in the background, and to limit distraction he pulled the middle blinds, blocking their view of each other.

That didn't stop him from being aware of the regular breaks she took to stretch or move around. But it was no fault of hers that he was as aware of her as he was of the words in front of him.

She went to the kitchen once, and twice brought a page

to him for clarification. Mid-afternoon they stopped for coffee and biscuits, and he called a halt at five, telling her he'd fix a chicken stir fry for dinner and she could cook tomorrow.

When Jemma yawned and said goodnight Nate stayed in the lounge, giving her time to fall asleep before he retired.

The tactic didn't work. He stared open-eyed at his ceiling, picturing her along the corridor, silken hair spread over her pillow, soft skin glowing in the moonlight through the window, her delectable lips curled as she dreamt of one of her heroes.

Hell, who needed sleep anyway?

Somewhere between two and three in the morning he gave up trying, and flung himself out of his crumpled bed. After showering and dressing in T-shirt and shorts he grabbed a sandwich and coffee, and stretched out on the long sofa. Milly, woken by the lights, came looking for attention, and he scooped her up onto his stomach.

'You're almost as distracting as your mistress, Scamp.' The name from his past came more easily than Milly. He tickled her ear, and she swatted his hand. 'The pair of you are getting under my skin, and that's not good.'

She curled up and closed her eyes, making him chuckle, and the movement of his stomach caused her to lift her head and blink at him. He stroked her and she settled.

Dragging his mind from an image of Jemma being in Milly's place, he tried and failed to mentally plot the opening scene of book number two as he ate and drank. Images of his encounters with her dominated, messing with his mind.

With an exasperated curse, he pushed upright and gently set the kitten down. If he couldn't sleep, he'd at least be productive.

He fetched his laptop and settled down with it on his lap, his feet on a padded footstool. After booting up, he created a new folder and file, blocked from his mind the figure asleep upstairs and typed.

SHADOWS OF A HAUNTED MAN
CHAPTER ONE

The only sound greeting Jemma when she descended the stairs at twenty past seven in the morning was the ball being patted across the tiles by Milly. She'd meant to ask Nate about a morning swim last night, but had been tired from the long day.

He wasn't in the pool. He must either be in his room or... He was running, according to the note attached to the coffee machine.

She brushed off irrational disappointment. Expecting to be included in an exercise she rarely participated in was selfish—as would be asking him to slow down to accommodate her leisurely pace.

She made coffee and toast, wandering as she ate, studying the photos attached to the few walls. It was easy to identify his family—his brother was so much like Nate, apart from a carefree look and shorter, trimmed hair. Had Nate's eyes been that clear and untroubled before he'd gone abroad? Or had being naturally sombre steered him towards the more thought-provoking stories he'd chased?

A movement outside caught her attention. Nate was moving fast and sure towards the house on a track opposite the one they'd walked yesterday. She drank in the power of his fluid motion, his feet pounding and arms pumping, eyes fixed straight ahead.

The desire to have that intensity focussed on *her*, that energy overriding her fears and that power sweeping her away to delights unknown swamped her, inciting tremors down her spine.

A second later, icy chills overrode all that.

There were stones and bits of broken branches on that uneven trail. How far did he run? What if he tripped and got injured? Couldn't make it back to the house? Did he take his mobile with him?

And why was she panicking about something that shouldn't concern her and might never happen?

His head jerked up as if he'd become aware of her presence, his eyes seeking her out through the window.

Please let him be too far away to see what I'm feeling.

Her prayer was answered with a light wave of his hand and, she thought, a smile. So if she couldn't see his mouth, then he couldn't see her expression. She began to deepbreathe, figuring she had roughly three minutes before he was in this room. Counting to ten with each inhale and exhale, she went to fetch her coffee.

His chest heaved with audible puffing as he came through the door, perspiration glistening on his skin and soaking the white tank top and black shorts, which left oodles of bare, tanned and toned muscle for her eyes to feast on. His eyes shone with exhilaration.

Clinging tightly to her hot mug, she prayed the internal waves of desire he created simply by standing in front of her, hands on hips, didn't show externally. His quick smile and back-arch reassured her that he hadn't noticed.

Both pieces of his clothing and his black and green running shoes looked worn and comfortable, but she didn't have to see their tags to know they'd be an international brand.

'I thought about waking you—wasn't sure what sort of reception I'd get after yesterday's early start.' He headed for the kitchen tap.

'A moan and the sight of me disappearing further under the blankets, if your appearance now means you've been gone for a while.'

He swallowed a glass of water in one gulp and leant on

the edge of the sink, grinning at her. How could a sweaty and dishevelled man look so gorgeous? He tugged at her heart strings and booted up her pulse to danger speed.

CHAPER TWELVE

JEMMA NEEDED A DIVERSION—something to distract him.

'Do you want coffee?'

Mundane but, with luck, effective. He shook his head.

'I was wide awake before dawn and left just as the sun rose. It's a great time to be out there. If you leave your drapes open the sun will substitute for an alarm. I'll take a shower and eat, then we'll get to it.' He walked towards her, arms outstretched, lips curved in a devilish grin. 'Wanna hug?'

Jemma's brain was trying to process 'get to it,' and her body was fighting the heat its connotations had fired up. He was within the required arm's length for the action before she reacted. She jumped back, and blushed even hotter at his roar of laughter as he gave her chin a gentle flick on his way past.

She mustn't… She wouldn't… She did. She twisted and watched him take the stairs two at a time, looking as hot and heady from the rear as he did face to face.

By the time he returned she was reading his script on the veranda, a glass of water and a bowl of mixed nuts by her side. It was the coolest place she could find, short of going into the basement.

'Hey, time for a break. D'you fancy a swim?'

Jemma started, blinked and dragged her mind from the ruins of the battered European town in his novel to the peaceful mountain scene in reality. Her laptop told her it was nearly two-thirty, and Nate was standing in the veranda doorway, watching her.

She'd chosen to remain outside after she'd returned from her solitary short walk after lunch. Declining his offer to accompany her, she'd claimed that solitude was preferable for forming mental images of the current scene. The crisp mountain air had been invigorating, and she'd begun to understand why people settled in the area, even with its cold, snowy winters.

'Sounds great.'

Clear water to refresh her mind and body after the stimulating scene she'd been working on, intensifying the characters' relationship, forcing the hero to admit to himself he might have feelings for the heroine.

Standing in front of the wardrobe mirror, she scrutinised her figure in the blue one-piece swimsuit, bought in the January sales. Cloe had often told her she'd look great in a bikini, but she couldn't shake her own negative comparison with Vanessa.

She swivelled in a circle and decided she didn't look too bad. The alternative was not to use the pool at all. Shoulders squared, she splayed her fingers at her image and left the room.

Keyed up with anticipation, and needing to expend nervous energy, Nate powered up and down the length of the pool, checking for Jemma at every end.

Her appearance was worth every second of the wait, and he was grateful for the distance of the pool between them, and for the fact that only his head and shoulders were above water as his body immediately reacted to the perfection of hers.

A shade lighter than her eyes, the blue swimsuit moulded her breasts and shaped her alluring curves, drawing his attention to enticing thighs and shapely legs. He trod water, fighting for breath, his heart jolting as she balanced on the pool's edge and raised her arms. *Lord, what he wouldn't do for a camera right now.*

Her smooth dive shook what little equilibrium he had left, and with each stroke bringing her nearer he wavered between catching her in his arms and striking out past her to the other end. In the end he kicked to the metal ladder, grabbed it and waited, fascinated by the coiled knot of her hair dipping into the water at each turn of her head.

She executed a faultless turn, then twisted to swim back and hold onto the edge, breathing evenly, her shining eyes and radiant smile directed at him.

'I am now officially envious of you. This would be a perfect way to start any day—or, like now, to ease muscles stiff from sitting and typing.'

He had another way in mind, but refrained from voicing it, not wanting to diminish the moment.

He dog-paddled over to her. 'A tiled hole full of water impresses you more than everything else?'

'I *have* almost everything else—in a more economical price range, of course. You have top-range. I'm enjoying every moment, and I aspire to the comforts, but this is extra-special. One lap and I feel refreshed and alive.'

That's how I feel watching you swim, looking at you now.

'You've had lessons? That was a spot-on turn.'

'In my early teens, with a friend. She made the team and I got toned and fit.'

'I noticed.' He couldn't hold back his grin as his eyes followed the rise of her blush from her cleavage to her forehead.

She retaliated to his teasing, taking him by surprise. Placing her hands on his shoulders and pushing herself upwards, she thrust him under the water before sprinting away. He came up sputtering and followed, passing her halfway along. An easy flip-turn and he surfaced in front of her, forcing her to stop or crash into him.

She saw him and backed away. Pity… He might have had an opportunity to hold her.

'You wanna play, Jemma?'

'No.' She feigned innocence. 'I want to keep fit. How many laps have you done so far?'

'Wasn't counting. How do you get all that hair into that small knot?'

'Practice. You're in my way, Nate.'

'My apologies, ma'am.'

He dipped his head and moved aside, liking the fact that she was more at ease with him than she'd ever been. If this was what it took, he was prepared to swim any time of the day.

Jemma slowed her pace, her movements automatic, her body acutely conscious of Nate whenever he swam past, her mind recalling the strength of his muscles under her palms. And the invitation in his eyes as he'd asked if she wanted to play. She couldn't believe she'd dared to dunk him.

She lost count of her laps and stopped at the far end for a moment, taking deep breaths. He flicked her a grin as he turned, the force of his leg-thrust sending him a fair way underwater before he surfaced. She counted three power-ful arm swings, then took off again.

As they passed his fingers brushed against her and she faltered, almost going under. Trying to ignore the tingles dancing over her skin, she turned at the end, wondering if it had been accidental or if he'd repeat the action.

Instead he caught her by the arm, pulling her to a halt, reactivating the sensation. His other arm slid around her waist, supporting her, holding her captive. She couldn't speak, couldn't find her breath, and he wasn't immune. His chest was heaving for the first time since she'd entered the pool. Desire darkened his grey eyes and a yearning to wrap her arms around his neck flared inside her.

With a sudden shake of his head he refocussed, his raspy tone betraying how much he'd been affected.

'I'm heading out at the end of this lap. Take as much time as you like.'

A gentle caress of her cheek and he swam away, leaving her to scramble for the poolside and hang on. She watched his progress to the ladder, and if she hadn't still had that hand grip as he stepped up she'd have sunk as mind and body went to mush.

From shoulders to calves he was sculpted like an athlete, his taut, trim and tanned image broken only by leaf-green swimming briefs. He was temptation plus, glistening with water sheen, drops flying around him like diamonds as he shook his head.

Her mouth gaped and then dried up. She couldn't breathe, and if her heart beat any faster she thought it might implode. As he began to turn towards her, hand raised to wave, she pushed off, ducking her face into the pool, not wanting him to see her gawking at him.

Three laps later she climbed out, wrapped herself in a towel from the nearby shelf and went to her room. She neither heard nor saw Nate on the way.

Showered and dressed, she went onto her balcony for a few quiet moments to prepare herself for another editing session. There was a light breeze through the treetops, and the distant hum of traffic on the road and an occasional bird call were the only sounds. *Heaven.* She leant her head against the pillar and blanked the rest of the world out.

'Next week at the earliest.'

Nate's voice floated up from the veranda, startling her into the present.

There was silence for a moment, then, 'Nothing that I wouldn't leave to come if you need me, Tess. You know that.'

Jemma backed slowly away from the rail into her room and shut the door, wishing she hadn't overheard.

Nothing he wouldn't leave? What about his declaration of 'the sooner we finish the amendments the better'?

It wasn't until she was in bed, mulling over the events of the day, that she recalled him mentioning a Tess once before, during his phone call at Circular Quay. From his tone, she had to be a friend... Not her business.

She fell asleep, waking early from muddled dreams of hot encounters in foreign places and tender caresses in cool oases.

On being awoken by the sun she went straight to the pool, and Nate joined her after his run. After that, apart from breaks—one of which Jemma spent walking—they worked solidly through the day.

Watching some recorded news after dinner, Jemma realised he always fast-forwarded through any items involving terrorist action or the military.

Did they trigger bad memories? How many of the scenes he'd written had he witnessed? He showed no sign of traumatic stress, but then he'd hardly share personal information like that with her.

Saturday was a repeat of Friday up until mid-afternoon, when Nate came out onto the veranda, where she was working, wearing grey trousers and a green polo shirt. Fashion-magazine-elegant. His mobile lay loose in his hand.

'We have an invite from my friend Grant for dinner tonight. He and his wife, Susie, own a hotel in town. If you want to go in now, we can have a stroll around first. There's a couple of great bookshops you might like.'

She knew—had seen the websites when she'd researched Katoomba and hoped for a chance to visit them. Without hesitation she logged off, stood up and began to collect her belongings.

'Leave that to me. You go freshen up and change. It's

casual and friendly.' He gave her a smile no red-blooded
woman could ignore. 'I'll give you fifteen minutes.'

His grey eyes twinkled, and if he'd been trying for se-
verity in his voice he'd failed. The words sounded cajol-
ing, seductive, as if he were suggesting more than a meal
with friends.

A sense of excitement accompanied her up the stairs.

Nate, after admiring the view, took her computer and other
paraphernalia inside and closed the drapes. He put food
and water out for the kitten, and talked to her as if she understood.

'Am I losing the plot, Scamp?' She rubbed against his
leg and he picked her up. 'Three weeks ago I was prepared
to work from dawn to dusk to get these rewrites done. And
I expected, or hoped, that she'd put in good hours too.'

Now he found himself thinking that they were going too
fast. At this rate they'd finish within his two-week stipu-
lation, and he'd have no excuse to go to Hahndorf. They'd
have a contract tie and, assuming Brian did a deal for them,
there'd be publisher's revisions to do. But she might not be
involved with them, and it wouldn't be the same as working together.

He determined to spend some extra time on the storyline he was writing for her romance, and then…

He hadn't heard a sound, and yet he knew she was there.
He spun round, clutching Milly to his chest, and recognised
the blue patterned top from their first meeting, now teamed
with blue trousers and black low-heeled shoes.

Her beauty caught his breath in his throat, and quickened his pulse as she turned from closing the stair gate to
face him, dark blue eyes sparkling and red lips begging
to be kissed.

Wishful thinking, Thornton. Cool down and get a grip.

'I've got two minutes to spare. Shall I go back up?'

The gentle taunt in her tone was rousing, causing his stomach to tighten.

'No.' It came out blunt and harsh, and she halted halfway across the space between them, eyes blinking in disbelief.

'Sorry. Let's settle Scamp and we'll head off.'

'Scamp?'

Eyes flashing, she took Milly from him, cradling the kitten to her body, sending his body into overdrive, and slapped her hand on his chest.

'Her name's *Milly*, Nate Thornton. Don't you *dare* teach her to answer to any other name or...'

'Or you'll revert to calling me Mr Thornton? Can't be having that, can we, Milly?' He tickled her ears and she purred. 'See—she likes my touch.'

He'd looked up at Jemma, and their eyes met as he spoke. If his had widened and darkened to the same awareness as hers they could be in trouble. Were they on the same wavelength? Imagining his hands caressing her body with gentle strokes?

Hell, now he was thinking the way *she* wrote. The sharp tug in his gut told him they'd better get out of here—now.

'Ready to go?' And he was sounding as raspy as she claimed his hero would when interacting with his heroine.

Unless he felt they were warranted, he didn't *do* explanations. With Jemma, he couldn't justify walking away unless she understood. By the end of their stint here she'd probably know his inner self better than Sam or his best mates. But not the deep stuff—not the dark side that kept him from bonding with women, the hard, frozen core preventing him truly trusting again.

He gave a self-justifying grunt as they approached the SUV and he activated the locks. She had personal issues not for sharing too.

Pausing for a moment with one hand on the driver's door,

he swiped the other across his mouth, then gave a wry grin. He was sliding on ice and had no inclination to jump off.

'Alice got a grey kitten for her sixth birthday and named her Rosebud...'

They were on the road to Katoomba and it was the first time either had spoken since her blunt 'okay' to his curt question.

The straightening of her body and her head-turn in his peripheral vision told him he had her interest.

'I mean, fair go—what did she expect from Sam and I? No way were we going to call *that* out when we went looking for her in the garden.'

He heard a stifled sound, suspiciously like a giggle, and glanced sideways to see one hand trying to smother her laugh and a sparkle in her eyes.

'So you dubbed her Scamp? I trust Alice got revenge.'

'Oh, yeah—with interest—a year or so later. He was an Alsatian Labrador cross, big and butch and a great guard dog. While we were out after school and on the weekends, she taught him to answer to Snookums.'

Her unrestrained laughter delighted him, and he took mock umbrage.

'Hey, do you have *any* idea how mortifying it is to have your mates see the dog you've built up as a fearsome protector race off in answer to such a sooky name?'

By the time he'd described how they'd bribed Alice, persuaded their friends not to tell, and reinstated Wolfhound as the only name the dog should respond to they were in town and entering the car park behind his mate's hotel.

He parked, glanced at the names on the two texts that had come through on the journey in, then put his phone into his pocket. He saw Grant was busy behind the bar, so he signalled that they'd be back and led Jemma onto the street.

* * *

Jemma usually loved browsing alone through bookshops, reading the blurbs on new or used novels of assorted genres, and also in second-hand emporiums, inspecting items for collector friends' birthdays or her own home. So why the hollow sensation in her stomach when Nate stopped at the corner, telling her he had to answer his messages?

'One's a client who wouldn't text unless he has genuine concerns, so I'm not sure how long it'll take. I'll catch up with you. Enjoy yourself—and remember we can pick up anything heavy or too big to carry later.'

He took advantage of a gap in the traffic and crossed the road.

She had no right or reason to complain—he'd told her where the bookshops were and given her freedom to wander at will. It was her own fault that she'd let herself look forward to his opinion on anything she might like.

With a sudden change of mind, she walked down a side street, intent on a different shopping trip.

An hour or so later, cheered up by her purchases, she was near the same corner, on the other side of the main street, debating whether to call Nate or stop for a drink alone. Her decision was made at the sight of him through a café window, still talking on his mobile.

His expression pulled her up short, and then had her racing past, praying he didn't look up and see her. That tender expression on his face had torn at her heart, reviving memories of her ex's ability for deception.

She circuited the block, disappointed at herself, and at the speed she'd judged him without justification. He was close to his parents and his siblings—it could be any one of those. Most likely his mother or sister. He owed *her* no emotional loyalty, and she had no right to expect any.

The café was not far ahead now, and she moved to the

kerb, ready to cross over and check from the other side. Her ringtone sounded as she looked to the left and she spotted him, phone to his ear, facing away from her.

She walked towards him, steeling herself to be cool and calm.

CHAPTER THIRTEEN

NATE SWIVELLED AS she came up behind him, his lips beginning to curl into a smile, then falling open as his gaze flitted from the bags in her hands to her face, and back. Twice.

'Someone having an irresistible "going out of business" sale? No sensible offer refused?'

There was genuine laughter in his tone, and her misgivings slid back to the deep, deep place they'd held for the last few years. She smiled, pleased there was no tension between them.

'I've written a novel—even if it's not publishable at the moment—and I have a contract to help revise yours to that status. I deserve to splurge on new clothes. So I did.'

He tucked his hands in the back pockets of his trousers, swaying on his heels, and his storm-grey eyes shone as if backlit by the sun. His quick appraisal of her from face to feet created in her a total body heatwave, and his wide smile sent her heartbeat into triple-time.

'Do I get a fashion parade when we get home?'

He arched his eyebrows like an old movie villain and laughter bubbled up inside her—followed by a sobering image of her sister on a catwalk. She'd never compete with her—wouldn't try—but the pain from this acknowledgment was less than usual.

'No, I'm not a model.'

'But you're beautiful, and every inch a woman. Let's put these bags in the car and have dinner. Maybe if I ply you with expensive wine you'll change your mind.'

Maybe it was his sincere compliment, or maybe she was happy with her new clothes. Or maybe it was purely the brush of his skin against hers as he took the bags from her that sent ripples of electricity across her skin.

One or all of them had her wishing with fervour that he'd take her hand and keep it in his as they strolled to his vehicle.

Jemma dozed on the way home, mentally tired from the day's revisions, her impulsive purchasing spree and staying up late talking to Grant and his wife, Susie. They and Nate shared the kind of close bond she had with Cloe and Mike, but they'd ensured she was included in the conversation.

Her sleepy thoughts churned through the comments Nate had made about his family, the group he belonged to in Sydney and his friends in the Blue Mountains. Did he keep them in isolated pockets of his life? Would they intermingle when he became a successful author? That he would had never been in doubt as far as she was concerned.

She would be an interlude for him. They'd finish the book, he'd help her with her basic storytelling and then learn to write his own personal scenes. She'd resume her solitary life in the Adelaide Hills.

She sighed, only realising it had been out loud when he spoke.

'Tired, Jemma?'

'Mmm. *Nice* tired.'

'Thank you for coming with me tonight.'

She was sinking into a haze of wanting something beyond her reach, so her weary brain must be imagining the emotion in his voice.

She woke at the gentle shaking of her shoulder, the husky sound of her name and hot breath tickling her earlobe. His features were as enticing blurred as they were when sharp and clear. And close enough to share a…

Her head jerked up, she blinked and her vision cleared— by which time he'd moved away.

Unbuckling her seat belt, she slid out and focussed.

'It's been quite a day. Thank you, Nate. I had a great time in town, and I like your friends.'

'The feeling was mutual. I've got your spoils from the trip.'

He held up both hands, clasping the labelled bags she decided she'd unpack in the morning.

'You go straight to bed. I'll see to Milly and meet you in the pool in the morning.'

Nate never bothered with lights on his way to bed, liking the peaceful aura of familiarity in the dark. Tonight, he paused outside Jemma's door, picturing her asleep. Did she curl into a ball, cuddle up to a pillow, or lie on her back? Whichever, her long silken hair would be splayed around her head, as he'd imagined before, and his fingers itched to thread their way through its strands.

She's a romantic lady. A true-love-for-ever lady. Be smart, Thornton, don't get involved.

But that didn't stop him having fantasies of her wearing whatever was in those five bags he'd carried in from the back of his SUV as he tossed and turned.

Whether it was yesterday's outing, dinner with Nate's friends or that morning's vigorous swim, something had energised Jemma. She set herself up on the veranda and lost herself in the intricacies of Nate's story. Breaks were taken at scene or chapter endings, and she found it easy to pick up the action on her return. It was enthralling.

She'd read the full manuscript again, and had reservations on his viewpoint over three of the relationship scenes. She debated whether to list and discuss them now, or deal with them as they were reached. Opting for the latter, she reasoned it would be clearer if the amendments had been done up to each point to be discussed.

Nate had settled inside, occasionally strolling round the house talking on the phone. On a quick trip to town he'd picked up newspapers, magazines and hamburger lunches. Neither of them had lingered over the meal, eager to get back to their individual pursuits.

The bubble burst mid-afternoon. She stared across the gully and huffed out a breath, her stomach churning. This encounter really didn't read true, and Nate wasn't going to like being told he'd got it so wrong. He'd accepted her critiquing and adaptations up to this point, though not without intense discussion. But this was major—a disagreement over his characterisation.

She reread his description of the moment his hero hitched a ride heading back to the capital. Going over it twice, even out loud, didn't alter her judgement. She'd promised him honesty, so that was what she'd have to deliver.

With a tight grip on the highlighted original, plus her revisions, she went inside, finding him sprawled in the lounge reading the financial news. A warm glow flared in his eyes and regret raked through her, anticipating their hardening at this criticism.

'Ready for a break…? Jemma, what's wrong?' He sat up, swinging his feet to the floor.

Her fingers tightened on the papers, and she struggled to swallow past her dry throat.

'This scene…their scene in her flat…'

His eyes darkened and narrowed, and the rest came out in a rush.

'It's *wrong*. He wouldn't cave in like that. Not him.'

Nate rose to his feet, fingers splayed at his sides, his chest puffed out. 'What the hell are you talking about?'

'He grabs her arm as they argue, she slams her hand on his shoulder and he *backs away*. Wouldn't happen, Nate. Not—'

He cut in, exasperation making the rough edge in his

voice hoarser. 'It happened before, in an earlier encounter, and you left it in. What's the difference?'

'*Them.*'

What kind of relationships did Nate have if he couldn't understand that continuing involvement meant more freedom of temperament—especially in tense or emotional situations?

'*Think* about it, Nate. He tried the he-man heavy tactics at their second meeting and she slapped him away. He backed off, as any decent man would. Right?'

Nate nodded with obvious reluctance, muscles tense.

'They've met quite a few times since, and had disagreements, but they can't stay away from each other. He's wound up after a traumatic night patrol, can't get her out of his mind, and he hitches a ride to her—not sure what to expect, but hoping she'll be eager to see him. She's not. Imagine how frustrated he'd be, knowing he only has limited time before reporting back.'

She could see Nate absorbing what she'd said, and instinctively moved closer.

'He'd take hold of her arm, probably more roughly than he intended, needing her to understand.'

Nate wrapped his fingers round her upper left arm, as if caught up in her narrative, drawing her body to his and causing her fingers to tighten on the printed sheets of paper. She struck his left shoulder, and in an instant play-acting ceased.

She was hauled against him and kissed with an ardency that scattered every coherent thought in her head. The papers fell from her hand as he released her arm, wrapping his arms around her and crushing their bodies together. Her fingers gripped his shoulders, then slid across his neck and into his thick, surprisingly soft hair.

Heat flowed through her veins as his heart pounded against her chest, and hers beat with a similar erratic rhythm. She answered the pressure of his lips with a passion that shook her to her core. Frightening. Exhilarating.

There was no day, no night—only this instance in time. And his low masculine growl mingling with her soft mews.

With a harsh gasp he broke the kiss and rested his cheek on her hair. Fighting for breath, she let her head fall to his shoulder, unable to speak, afraid that any words would diminish the moment.

'Jemma…' Her name had never sounded so special, so ethereal. So unique.

She looked up into dazed storm-grey eyes that mirrored her own bewilderment. The trembling of his fingers on her cheek and his rapid breathing were comforting—tangible indications that he was emotionally shaken too.

He kissed her forehead and eased away, holding her arms with a tenderness that allayed any feeling of loss. He swallowed, blew out air and then breathed in again, making a part-laugh, part-groan sound.

'Hell, that was… Jemma, I…I guess I just proved you were right.' He looked away, then into her eyes again, and gave her a wry smile. 'Let's go for a walk.'

She'd barely regained her composure and he'd shaken it again. Those last words were not what she'd expected to hear, yet they were entirely understandable.

A walk. Fresh air and open space. Room to think and process this—for her—emotionally traumatic happening. Room to recover from her tumultuous reaction to his touch and his kiss. Beyond that, she didn't dare anticipate.

'Yes. Let's.'

At first Nate fought the desire to lessen the gap between them as they walked, to take her hand and intertwine their fingers. He caved in before they reached the track through the trees, and the tight knot in his gut eased when she didn't resist.

His body hummed from the exhilaration of having her in his arms and that incredible kiss, like none he'd ever known. He'd been a hair's breadth from losing control, from sweeping her up and...

Don't go there.

For that blissful moment they'd been in tune—as one. He'd never believed it possible, deeming it a fantasy of fiction. Somehow he had to regain normality—though he feared he couldn't backtrack over the line he'd crossed. He had no idea how to explain his actions, and knew there was no way he could promise not to kiss her again. Hell, given the slightest encouragement he'd kiss her right now, and was well aware from her ardent response that she'd willingly kiss him back.

Or was she regretting her uninhibited reaction?

They had to set guidelines. He had to ensure she understood there'd be no rosy future, no wedding bells or settling down. For ten years he'd chosen women who accepted his terms and didn't ask for explanations. Jemma was different—she deserved the truth. Because it was he who'd broken the rules.

There was no pressure to begin a conversation, no urgency to bare his soul. He let himself live in the moment, surrounded by the sounds and smells of the bush and with Jemma's soothing presence by his side. She'd been as affected as he by their shared kiss, yet she now appeared calm. The tranquillity of this mountain area was once again weaving its magic.

He stopped by a group of gum trees, part of one split by lightning, leaning at an angle, its bare branches wedged solid in another. It had been like that for nearly two years, and he often leant against it while he took a break while running.

The undergrowth crunched beneath their feet as he led her over, let go of her hand and leant his back and elbows against the rough wood, its bark stripped away by the elements. Jemma stood on the down-sloping side, taking in the view, giving him the lead without pressure.

Staring straight ahead, he kept his voice level and radio-broadcaster-neutral.

'I'm assuming the reason for your move to Hahndorf was the result of a break-up? You'd have been twenty-five?'

She made no movement he could sense, and no sound, so he continued.

'When I'd just turned twenty-one, and had been requested to send in more reports for publishing, I thought I knew it all and could handle anything life threw at me. In truth I was *so* bloody green. I was an easy target for a woman whose only real interest was my family's money. I had a…a life-changing experience a few days after meeting her, and when she found me blind drunk in the bar of my hotel she was supportive and comforting. I was needy, immature and stupid.'

'Human—like us all.'

Looking sideways, he saw no condemnation in her eyes, only sympathy and understanding. Thankfully she didn't press for the details he'd buried with his shame. He turned towards her, fisting his fingers to prevent himself reaching out for contact. If she couldn't accept his proposition there'd be no touching, no kissing. No making love.

'I have my grandfather to thank for teaching me to always verify what I'm told, though I almost left it too late. Being fooled by her forced me to evaluate my future, who I really was. I stayed overseas, hopefully became wiser, and my perception of people and life altered. I know it's rarely black or white, more a murky shade of grey. I have family, who I love deeply, and friends I'd give my life for. Beyond them are colleagues and acquaintances I treat with courtesy but hold at a certain distance. I live a solitary life, and I intend to keep it that way.'

'For as long as you live?'

'Yes.'

Though he wasn't keen on her choice of wedding ceremony words, it meant she understood his resolve.

'And now? Are you involved with anyone?'

'If I was I wouldn't have kissed you, no matter how strong the temptation.'

Jemma heard the growl in his voice and sensed his resentment of her implication. Either the damage from that deception ran deeper than her own ex's betrayal, or there had been other disloyalties in his life.

Now was not the time to tell him or show him how mind-blowingly incredible his kiss had been. How it had felt as if they'd been alone in the universe and how she ached for more. Whatever the future held, that memory would be enhancing and uplifting.

She moved in front of him, placed her hands on his chest and looked him straight in the eyes. He didn't blink, and held eye contact warily.

There'd be no shared expectations of a happy home with children playing in the garden. There'd be no cheating, lying or broken hearts. Her only remorse would come if she declined what he was offering and never experienced the full pleasure of the passion he'd shown in that kiss.

'I want you to make love to me, Nate Thornton. No promises of for ever, no lies, no regrets.'

She went up on tiptoe, pressed her lips to his, and with a deep guttural groan he swept her into his arms. His hands caressed from her shoulders to her hips. Her hands wrapped around his neck, holding him to her, her sigh catching in her throat.

Her pulse shot into overdrive as he pressed her body tight to his. She trembled when he kissed a trail across her neck to her lips. He teased them with the tip of his tongue and they parted, allowing him entry to caress and savour until her head spun and there was nothing in her world but him.

Time had no meaning until the need for air broke them apart. He cradled her head to his chest, brushing his lips over her forehead, his rasping breath stirring her hair. Though there was no gap between them she wriggled to get closer and he groaned again, this time even more roughly.

'Jemma, darling, there's a limit for every man, and I've just about reached mine.' He cradled her face in his hands and gave her a quick tender kiss. 'Let's go home.'

CHAPTER FOURTEEN

JEMMA STIRRED, HER muscles languid and unwilling to move, and snuggled into the warm muscular body alongside hers, her head pillowed on a mat of thick, wiry chest hair. The slightest shift might shatter her dream, and this euphoria could be nothing else.

Gentle lips caressed her forehead and soothing fingers roamed her back. This was reality—and more spine-tingling, toe-curling and floating-to-the-moon wonderful than any dream *ever*. Cosseted and treasured, she wanted to stay right there, forget the past and let the future take care of itself.

'Jemma…'

She burrowed deeper against him, tightening her hold around his waist, loving the sensual touch of his skin against hers, loving the heady combination of musk, citrus, vanilla and *him* teasing her every breath.

His throaty chuckle reverberated through her, startling her into opening her eyes. Pushing up onto one arm, he stroked her cheek, gazing down at her with such a tender expression it melted her heart.

'For a supposedly good author, I'm stuck for words.' He kissed her with soft reverence. 'I've never…' He stopped and looked away, as if uncomfortable with the words forming in his head.

She understood. How could she not when her mind was blank too—and she'd *never* had problems describing passionate encounters?

'Nate, I understand.'

He grinned, and brushed his thumb across her mouth 'I guess we have to write a new love scene, huh?'

'Mmm…' Falling asleep in his arms was her preferred option, but… 'So, working instead of TV tonight?'

'We should.' He bent and blew gently in her ear, laughing as she quivered. 'Would he do that?'

'Not him.' She ran her fingernails over his chest, loving the way he sucked in air at her touch.

'How about this?' He nibbled her neck and she wriggled.

'You should know. You created him.'

'Hey, I penned a fighter, not a lover.' He pulled her tighter against him and she didn't resist. '*You're* the one who claims he'd want intimacy after sex. I visualised him getting up and leaving once the deed was done.'

He twirled strands of her hair around his fingers and dropped a kiss on the tip of her nose.

'But now I figure he'd stay longer. For this.'

He covered her mouth with his, soft at first, then hotter and harder.

She caressed a path up his chest and around his neck, anchoring his head. He parted her lips, allowing him to deepen the kiss as he pressed her into the large, firm mattress.

They'd be in complete agreement over his hero's next action.

Nate had never had trouble with after-sex talk, the non-emotional aspect of his encounters ensuring there were no expectations of romantic platitudes like those in the book Alice had given him and in Jemma's novel.

Today he'd found himself fighting not to say them, biting them back as quickly as they arose. Telling her how special making love to her had been, that she was different from the others, didn't seem right when he couldn't promise a lifetime commitment.

She'd said no promises, no regrets. Alone in the kitchen, he was already regretting letting her go to shower in her own en suite, instead of with him, and that he hadn't planted rose bushes in the garden so he could pick her a bouquet.

He made coffee, wishing it were champagne, and set out biscuits, wishing they were her favourite handmade chocolates—whatever brand they were. He'd have to find out, even if it meant telling her more about himself.

She hadn't mentioned his scars, but she must have seen them even though they'd faded over the years. The jagged pale lines ran over his left hip onto his stomach, and probably wouldn't have been noticeable in the pool. But naked on the bed...

He sucked in air as she came down the stairs, looking so fresh and beautiful she scrambled his vocabulary, leaving him with an inadequate, 'Hi.'

Her face lit up and he was across the kitchen, taking her into his arms even before her, 'Hi, yourself!' left her lips.

He covered them with a long, satisfying kiss he never wanted to end. It was Jemma who eased herself from his embrace and tapped him on the chest—right over his racing heart.

'We're supposed to be *revising* a scene, Nate Thornton, not acting it out.'

The dazzling smile she gave him and the teasing note in her voice blew his mind. For a moment he imagined a lifetime of friendly teasing and laughter and rosy cheeks. Then he tamped it down. Lifetimes were for others—not him. However satisfying it was now, their relationship wouldn't—*couldn't*—last.

He gestured at the neat pile of papers on the dining table. 'I read them as I picked them up. Couldn't fault a word. Or an action.'

He emphasised the final word, recalling her responses to his caresses, and her immediate blush proved she was too. He trailed a fingertip path down her cheek to her chin, cupped it, and pressed a light kiss on her lips.

'Hold that thought until tonight, Jemma.'

They slipped into a flexible routine based around a wake-up swim and walking, and taking quiet breaks between writing sessions. Jemma declined to join Nate in his gym workouts, letting him work off steam alone, and stayed home when he went to fire training.

Only two incidents marred the following four days for her…

On Monday her mobile bleeped as she was cooking her special scrambled eggs for lunch. Probably Cloe sending a promised recipe, she thought, smiling to herself. They chatted every few days, though Jemma hadn't yet revealed where she was, or why.

She called out to Nate, dished up the food, and then sat at the table opening the email. Just to check. Her smile faded and she lost her appetite as her stomach sank.

Vanessa. Her sister had sent her customary reminder for what was, as far as Jemma was concerned, an over-the-top annual charity event she'd conveniently semi forgotten. Her day-to-day life was good, and she'd learned to handle the now dwindling number of bouts of social inadequacy. But being at that particular glamorous function always rekindled her Cinderella complex.

'Bad news?' Nate's genuine concern was comforting.

'Only for me. An evening in a huge room of A-class notables I have nothing in common with and have problems talking to, battling a throbbing headache even if I take tablets before.'

'Don't go.'

'My sister and her husband are on the organising committee. As far as they and my parents are concerned my attendance is compulsory.'

Without shame, he leant over and read the businesslike message. He frowned. 'For a sister, she's not very personal.'

'We're not close.'

'From this I wouldn't be able to tell you were related.'

She bristled at his criticism, even if she did agree. Different personalities and a six-year gap had been insurmountable for them.

'Have your lunch before it gets cold.'

He ate in silence, brooding for a few minutes before persisting with the subject. 'Why the reminder?'

'I decided not to attend three years ago, and pretended I'd forgotten when my mother asked if I'd booked my flights.' She scrunched her nose. 'Hence the reminder missive.'

His husky chuckle brightened her up.

'You always attend solo?' he asked.

She ignored his inference that she couldn't get a date.

'That year only—and Vanessa partnered me with a widowed bank manager in his forties. Nice enough guy, but… I have a bachelor friend who's been willing to act as escort since. I'll ring him and confirm the date.'

She lifted a forkful of eggs to her mouth and chewed, contemplating the inevitability of her fate.

Becoming aware of a difference in the atmosphere, she looked up to meet dark storm-grey eyes studying her with an intensity that made her body pulsate.

'You've already asked him?'

'He knows the date, so…'

His eyebrows arched and her throat dried. Why was he…? He couldn't be suggesting… By then the manuscript would be with Brian or a publisher for assessment, and she'd be painting and tending shop in Hahndorf.

'I am corporate-dinner-trained, and can produce references if required.'

He was joking, yet his voice held an edge reminiscent of their original encounter. She was speechless.

* * *

Nate was acting on instinct, reacting to the cold clamp in his gut when she'd casually mentioned this friend. A male friend. Her tone had negated any romantic connection, so he had no reason to be jealous. That he'd even *think* the word rocked him, making his statement come out more roughly than intended.

He tried to atone. 'Jemma Harrison, would you please allow me the honour of escorting you to your sister's charity do in Melbourne?'

His heart flipped at the sight of her flustered face; cheeks rosy, eyes glistening and her pink tongue licking lips that strove to form words. The tight clench of his stomach proved how susceptible he was to that natural action.

'You might be already booked that weekend.' Breathy. Unsure.

'I'll make sure I'm free.'

Seeing her sudden dazzling smile was like watching the sun rise over the mountains or appear from behind the clouds as the rain stopped. The world was clearer, brighter. A better place to live.

As long as he lived in the moment and didn't plan ahead.

The second incident occurred as they arrived home from a walk on Thursday afternoon. Nate had answered his phone and the female voice at the other end sounded distraught, though Jemma couldn't make out the words.

'Hang on, Tess.' He shrugged and gave Jemma a wry grin. 'I have to take this. Wanna make coffee?'

He brushed his lips over hers and went out onto the veranda.

Tess again. None of her business if his friend needed help. Except he didn't mention it when he came in, just thanked her for the coffee and resumed revising. She brushed her qualms aside, but the seed of doubt had been sown. How often did the woman call when she wasn't there, and why bother Nate with her problems?

A wisp of hair soft as Milly's fur tickled Jemma's face, slowly rousing her from sleep. She sighed, flicked her hand, encountering only air, and buried her face deeper into the pillow. It happened again, this time accompanied by a musky aroma.

She blinked, saw a shadowy figure and opened her eyes. Nate was hunkered down by the bed, his fingers waving strands of her hair over her cheek. It was the most delicious way to wake up—the perfect face to see when she did. And even better when he pressed his lips to hers, reigniting the fires that still smouldered from the night before.

'Good morning, sweetheart. It's Friday morning, and you need to get up. Breakfast in fifteen minutes. Casual dress code today.'

Propping herself up onto one elbow, she double-blinked as the force of his energy swept away any waking lethargy.

'You're lively this morning. I know what day it is, and I thought we—'

He was dressed in a lightweight navy top and chinos, rather than the T-shirt and shorts he favoured at home.

'You're going out?'

'We are.' He slid his hand round her neck, and caressed her cheek with his thumb. 'Do you trust me, Jemma?'

The wariness in his eyes tempered his excitement, and the firm line of his mouth conjured up an image of a small boy not sure if his Mother's Day present would be well received, fervently hoping it would.

'What have you done, Nate Thornton?'

'What? No Mr?'

He smiled and kissed her softly, then harder as her arms wound around his neck. He finally pulled away, breathing rapidly, sat on the edge of the bed and took her hands in his.

'Temptress! I made a vow the day we met. Now I'm hoping to honour it. Shower and pack for two nights in Sydney. I've got the support meeting tomorrow night, so you might like to stay over with Cloe then and I'll pick you up Sunday morning.'

He stood up and strode to the door, looking back and winking before disappearing. She stared at the ceiling, wondering what he had planned. They had six full chapters and a few pages to go, and would have had no problems finishing by Monday—Tuesday at the latest. Probably wouldn't if they spent two days away.

Was he deliberately delaying her departure?

A quiver of delight vibrated along her spine at the thought. She had no illusions of a long-term romance—he'd been adamant on that score. There was, however, the possibility of a continuing professional relationship if she was needed. By email, as urgency wouldn't apply.

Springing from the bed, she gathered up her clothes and shoes and raced naked to her room. Warm weather was predicted, so she wore blue trousers and a new floral top. Remembering the sparkle in his eyes, she packed a new dress, guessing there'd be a restaurant meal included in his plans.

Nate tapped his fingers on the steering wheel, out of tune with the music, as they sped along the highway. Should he have told her before they left? If he told her now and his surprise upset her he wouldn't be able to pull over and reason with her.

'Is everything okay? You look worried and you're tapping.'

He flicked her a smile, liking the way she was concerned about him. He wasn't so sure about her growing insight into his character and what motivated him. Or why he was so determined to be with her in Melbourne and escort her to that function, three weeks in the future. When she would be back in Hahndorf.

'We'll talk in the unit.'

She didn't push the subject and he relaxed. He'd be disappointed if she refused, but it wouldn't be the end of the world.

They arrived at the unit about eleven, having stopped on the way to pick up sandwiches. Nate left Jemma to release Milly and make coffee while he took their suitcases to his room. On returning, he took two recliners and a low table onto the balcony, and set them up so they had a view of the city centre and the bridge.

Delaying his moment of revelation, he voiced the question he'd pondered since being told the name.

'Why Milly?'

Lord, she was gorgeous when she was surprised. Her wide-eyed reaction brought back memories of Alice on Christmas mornings, when his world had been safe and full of fun and laughter. He waited, his chest tightening with pride as he sensed the second she decided to trust him with a personal anecdote from her past.

'Milly was a favourite cartoon character from my early childhood. She was adventurous and feisty—everything I wanted to be at that age and never was. Best of all, she was funny-looking, with a button nose and frizzy hair. I've never forgotten the way she never let that impact on her zest for life, even if I'm not very good at emulating her.'

He dumped his mug on the table, moved across to sit beside her, did the same to her mug and gripped the sides of her seat with his hands, leaning over her.

'You've lost me. There's an implication there that you're neither pretty, courageous nor spirited.

She shrank away from him and he gave a huff of disbelief, took her hands in his.

'You are *beautiful*, Jemma Harrison. Exquisite and smart. You wrote a book, had the courage to send it to an agent and didn't give up when he gave you honest criticism. You put your own work aside and chanced coming here to help me achieve the goal you wanted for yourself.'

His heart blipped and his pulse raced as her fingers trembled in his, her chin lifted and her lips curled into a shy smile.

'Your book was so much closer to deserving publication.'

'You've shown sheer guts and generosity of spirit, darling. Now, can we harness that spirit for something special? I've booked us in for a walk over the top of the bridge.'

She gasped, and he bent his head to kiss her, smothering any protest. The softness of her lips, her unique Jemma aroma and the caressing touch of her fingers sliding around his neck shot every thought bar one from his head.

CHAPTER FIFTEEN

JEMMA COULDN'T SEEM to focus when he rested his forehead on hers, allowing her space to drag in short puffs of air. How could one man have the power to muddle her thinking and reduce her body to malleable clay?

The bridge? A climb? Reason rushed back and she pushed at his chest, forcing him to lean away, one hand settling by her thigh, the other arm lying across his.

'You think I'm too scared to do it? We're up high *now* and I don't have a problem.'

'Not with fear. Heck, I think you'd tackle a tiger if the need arose. You're a delightful mixture of self-assurance and insecurity, Jemma. You're confident of your ability to paint, to write about intense personal relationships and maintain long friendships. And yet...'

He flicked a hand towards her mobile on the dining table.

'All those photos on your phone—are any of you?'

'They're inspiration for my miniatures, and I'm the one taking them.'

No way can I compete with Vanessa, and nor do I want to be compared with her.

Yet she'd agreed to his escorting her to the Melbourne function.

'You don't like being in front of the camera. The bridge walk, a tandem skydive—they take photos as mementoes, and other participants take shots too. Come with me, Jemma. You don't have to pose, and we won't buy any copies of the photos if you don't want to. Please.'

She looked into the man's eyes seeing a boy's pleading

expectancy, and was overcome by a surge of regret for all the activities she'd denied herself because she'd judged herself inferior to her sister.

'I'm not agreeing with you, but I'll come to prove you wrong.'

With a triumphant, *'Yes!'* he kissed her again.

'You'll love it—and there's an extra surprise tonight.'

'I'm not abseiling down a building in the dark.'

His roar of laughter warmed her from head to toe. Their time together might be short, but she'd have a lifetime's store of precious memories.

Jemma's enthusiasm for the climb grew with each mandatory action—filling out forms, locking away all personal items and wriggling into blue overalls. She listened carefully to the safety talk, conscious of Nate watching her for any sign of nerves.

Every rung of the ladder and each long, flat step taking her higher was empowering. She wanted to surge ahead, race to the top and spread her arms in triumph. Whenever they stopped, she memorised the view, storing it for future moments of self-doubt.

Nate followed her, seemingly enjoying her reaction more than his own experience. Having already been up there, he pointed out the ferry route through The Heads to Manly, the location of the zoo and of his apartment. And he sneaked in a few kisses when she smiled at him.

He put his arm around her for the group photo on the way up, and at the very top joined in her triumphant gestures and laughter. His proud smile thrilled her as her pose leaning back against the sky was snapped for immortality. Together at the edge, he wrapped his arms around her for a single photo, then kissed her with a tenderness that had her melting against him.

The thumbs-up from their camera-clicking guide told

her it hadn't been a sudden whim. She didn't care. She was on top of the world, living out a fantasy she'd given scant thought to—if any. Even if she never did anything else extreme in her life, she'd proved she could and would.

That evening, she stood in front of the full-length mirror, her euphoria from the day's achievement undiminished. She looked good. No, dammit, she *glowed*, and she was stylish enough to compete with the women on the social pages of weekly magazines. Maybe…

Conceding that Nate had been one hundred per cent responsible for her buying this new dress, and for her taking extra time and care with her make-up, she twirled for effect. Staring at her unfamiliar reflection, she relished her new self-confidence—short-lived though it might be once he no longer needed her.

Not unless she let it.

Brushing the negativity away, she picked up her new evening bag from the bed and gave a final spin for luck, loving the way the box pleats flared.

Where *was* she? Nate paced the open-plan area, leant on the back of the modular couch for a moment, then made another circuit.

He glanced at his watch. No problem with time yet, and he *had* told her to dress up for dinner.

Where *was* she?

Her elation hadn't diminished one iota since her jubilant moment on top of the bridge. And on the way home she'd studied the photographs he'd purchased as if reliving her success.

She'd looked so incredibly beautiful, so full of joy, that he'd bought two copies of every one they were in, intending to frame some. And that was part of his dilemma. He didn't want to let her go, leaving him behind with only images of her on his walls.

She'd insisted on working, and they had finished another chapter before showering and changing. Was she eager to return to her solitary life in the Adelaide Hills? It didn't seem that way to him when they made love. Her responses were as passionate as any man could ever desire. And more. She—

She was here.

He pivoted. His chest tightened, his heart lodged in his throat, and a voice drummed in his head. *Keep her. Keep her.*

She was radiant—a glorious vision in red leaving him lost for words. She'd turn heads, and he wasn't sure he was happy with the concept that most of them would be male. How could she not realise how sexy she was in that dress, with the bodice hugging her delectable body and those pleats drawing his eyes to her lovely legs?

His own legs were none too steady as he stepped forward and took her hands in his, not sure whose fingers were trembling.

'You are *gorgeous*, Jemma.'

Her smile and the shimmer in her dark blue eyes made him regret his limited vocabulary in such a situation. He racked his brain for one of the phrases she'd attributed to his hero, felt like he was battling fog, and drew her against him instead.

It was a gentle kiss. Until her soft lips stirred his desire and he wrapped her into a tight embrace.

The sound of his ringtone broke them apart, earning a guttural objection from him. Their taxi had arrived downstairs.

He deliberately left a gap between them in the back seat, and pressed his fingers to his thighs to avoid pulling her to his side. He needed the space to regain control.

As they drove onto the bridge Jemma placed her hand on his arm, pointing upwards. 'I was up there, Nate, right on the top arch. Because of *you*.'

Her eyes sparkled and warmth spread from her touch. Would she now be receptive to other challenges?

'About those other extreme activities, Jemma…?'

She laughed, reminding him of a bubbling mountain stream, making him wish they were on the way home, not heading out for the evening.

'Uh-uh. I'm going to write my own list.'

'Do I get an invite to join you?'

'Do you want one?'

Her eyes, dark and teasing, were issuing a challenge no man could resist. He cradled her cheek in his hand and covered her sweet red lips with his, forcing himself to keep the kiss light and short. Later there'd be the ride home…to his big, welcoming bed.

Jemma thought she'd burst with happiness as Nate helped her from the cab. She craned her neck to stare at the high-in-the-sky restaurant she'd pointed to…was it only four weeks ago? It had been a life-changing month.

'You remembered, Nate!'

'Everything you've ever said to me, Jemma.'

Hand in hand, they walked inside to the allocated lift that sped them skywards in seconds, and she couldn't hold back her, 'Wow!' of joyful surprise.

Nate had booked window seats which were facing inland when they arrived. The circular room was packed, and the hum of happy patrons filled the air. The revolution was slow and hardly noticeable unless they watched the view changing outside. The city light show seemed to go on for ever, broken only by intermittent dark patches of undeveloped land.

Jemma was entranced, and didn't want to miss a single moment. 'It's fascinating. Utterly different to Windy Point.'

'Better?' Nate teased.

'I'd never try to compare them—or your views in Katoomba. And *you* must have seen some unforgettable sights abroad?'

She had a brief glimpse of something dark in his eyes as he swung his head towards the window. It had gone when he turned back to greet the drinks waitress.

Once she'd left they had a quick scan of the menu, then he sent her to the impressive array of serve-yourself food. She did a full circuit before making her selection.

'That's all you're having?' His eyebrows arched at the small portions on the plate she'd brought to the table.

'This time. There's so many nationalities—too many choices for one visit. Oh, what's that weird structure coming into view?'

They ate, talked and laughed. Nate's knowledge of buildings and landmarks was surprising, considering the years he'd spent overseas. And there were so many intriguing designs and shapes that Jemma would have happily drawn out the meal even longer, and vowed to come back with Mike and Cloe on a special occasion.

In the taxi on the return trip Nate drew Jemma close and cradled her head on his shoulder. She sighed, and nestled deeper into his side.

'Today was magic, Nate. A mere thank-you seems inadequate.'

He cupped her chin with gentle fingers, his eyes scanning her beguiling face and his body aching with anticipation of the night ahead. He couldn't repress his rough growl of contentment as his lips settled over hers.

Later, with Jemma asleep by his side, he lay awake staring at the night sky, dark memories clouding his mind, activated by her innocent remark. Some sights were better left forgotten. There'd been no reason for them to surface—

though his recent calls from Dave and Tess and thoughts of tomorrow's meeting, might have activated them.

Sunday afternoon's trip home was delayed by Mike and Cloe insisting Nate stay for coffee, rather than just taking off with Jemma. Knowing how fond they were of her, he didn't mind, but he was eager to return to Katoomba, to spend what time they had left together away from noise and other people.

He'd missed holding her last night, needing the comfort she gave him. He'd opened up more with the support group than he ever had before during the evening—another small step forward. However, he was still light years from believing that one day the damage he carried would lessen.

His spirits lifted with every kilometre they drove towards his home. Accepting that she'd be leaving within days, he determined to make every minute count. Morning swims, talks on a variety of subjects as they walked and watching television curled together on his roomy couch would be enjoyable preludes to having her warm and loving in his bed at night.

The downside would come with the progress they made on the manuscript. Every chapter, every page, every word he accepted as printable would bring her departure closer. And the Melbourne trip seemed too far away, like having to count the days down to Christmas as a child.

The following Sunday afternoon, he went out to the veranda where she was working, knowing that being out here alone would never feel the same as it had two weeks ago. He hunkered down by her recliner and kissed her, savouring the moment, exhilarating in the passion she returned. He had trouble controlling his breathing when he raised his head.

'How will I ever get any writing done without you?'

Her blue eyes clouded, intensifying his own regret that she'd be leaving soon.

'Easier, I guess, without distraction.' Brave words spoken with a tremble.

'The most engaging, welcome distraction a man could wish for.' He kissed her again, lifted her computer from her lap and placed it on the deck. 'I have something for you.'

He handed her a blue folder, labelled on the front with her name. Inside was a wad of printed pages, with her book title as the heading.

'I've expanded and hopefully improved your narrative. You can edit as you feed it in—I'll email a copy to you now I've given this to you.'

Her reaction was as illuminating as a sunburst on an autumn day, blue eyes shining, skin glowing and a beaming smile that sent his pulse soaring.

'How…? When did you manage…? I… Thank you, Nate.' She ran her fingers over the cover as if it were long-sought-after treasure.

Her delightful fluster made the time spent skim-reading the paperback romances he'd taken from Alice's collection in the Sydney apartment worth every tooth-grinding minute. Now, contrary to his own wishes, he had to bring them both down to earth.

'Have you phoned Meg?'

Her smile faded and he couldn't resist kissing her again—quick and light.

'I feel the same, Jemma. Does she need you?'

'She said she can manage, but…'

'We said two weeks only. As things are you'll be finished on Tuesday, and the only flight with pet allocation before the weekend is Wednesday morning. I don't w—'

She pressed her fingers to his lips.

'I know. You'd better book it before someone else takes the spot.'

He nodded, stood up, then hunkered down again.

This kiss was firmer, longer. Hungrier.

Jemma had always loved airports, with their sense of adventure, of jetting off to new and exciting places. Not today. Every muscle was taut with the effort not to break down, her eyes kept misting, threatening to flood with tears, and her heart hurt.

She refused to look at the clock—didn't want to know how little time she had with Nate, who had his arms around her. He'd hardly been out of her sight today, hardly said a word on the drive from Katoomba—but then neither had she. Even Milly had been quiet, as if sensing their mood.

'Jemma?' His voice had never sounded so husky, as if choking in his throat.

She looked up, and her heart squeezed at the sad expression in his storm-grey eyes.

'Hell, it's gonna be a long two weeks.'

An eternity. During heart-wrenching talks they'd agreed he'd come to Hahndorf on the Wednesday before the function, and that they'd fly to Melbourne on the Friday. In the meantime, he'd do a final read-through, send his novel to Brian and visit his parents on the New South Wales coast for a few days.

She'd serve in the shop, paint and begin merging his new text into hers.

There would still be too many empty hours.

The airline staff moved to the check-in point and the passengers began to line up.

Nate kissed her as if his life depended on holding her close, and didn't pull away even when her flight was called.

She was the very last person to board.

CHAPTER SIXTEEN

NATE HAD NEVER been so frustrated in his life. Dressed and ready to go to the charity event, he paced the floor of the suite Jemma had booked at the venue complex months ago. His query as to why she wasn't staying with her sister had received a succinct, 'My parents do. I don't.'

A week ago, he'd put her increasing edginess over the phone down to nerves due to the upcoming function. Now he was convinced of the fact. He'd gone to Hahndorf hoping to coax her into telling him what she feared. Instead she'd refused to discuss it, blaming her headaches on too much painting and typing.

Baloney—she *loved* creating her miniatures, had never had even a slight headache in the time they'd been together. But without knowing the exact problem he could only keep reassuring her that everything would be okay.

Brian's email on Thursday, telling them he was in negotiations with a publisher, had perked her up, and they'd celebrated at a local restaurant. In the morning her tension had resurfaced.

He checked his watch, brushed a non-existent hair from his cuff and tried not to picture her staying here, or at any other hotel, with her 'bachelor friend.'

Impatient to see her, he strode to the bedroom, pulling up short in the doorway.

His eyes focussed on the motionless figure by the window—the entrancing woman who'd somehow become part of his life. She'd teased and cajoled him into reframing so many scenes in his book, forcing him to re-evaluate the bad experiences he'd depicted. Making him a better author.

Stunning, so entrancingly feminine, she'd twined strands of her hair into a knot at the back of her head, but thankfully left the rest to flow down her spine, over the shimmer of silver blended with shades of blue and green moulding her slender form. The full-length gown had thin shoulder straps, and thankfully the only jewellery he could see was a watch on her left wrist.

His chest swelled with pride at being her chosen escort, his pulse raced at the prospect of holding her as they danced and his heart… His heart never wanted to let her go. His head still doubted his capacity to forget, forgive and fully trust.

'Jemma.'

He spoke softly, as steadily as his choked throat would allow, and held his breath as she turned toward him.

His world spun out of orbit, and not one of the thousands of words in his vocabulary came anywhere near to describing the emotion in that split second when their eyes met. That ticking of time when nothing was hidden and their souls were bared.

She blinked and it had gone, replaced by the insecurity that she denied was there. He walked across and caressed her cheek as lightly as he would a baby's.

'Enchanting. You leave me speechless, Jemma. I'll be the envy of every man in the room.'

She dropped her head to break eye contact, and spoke in a whisper. 'Not true, but thank you for the compliment.'

He growled in exasperation, tilted her chin up and stared into her dark blue eyes. They were wary and unsure. He knew nothing he said would change her mind-set at this moment. Instead he took the necklace and bracelet of interlaced gold strands from his pocket and held them up.

'I figured these would suit any colour you wore. A gift for all you've given me.'

* * *

Jemma tried to say thank you through her strangled throat. If only she could open up and explain how it felt to live in someone's shadow without sounding needy. She couldn't, and in a few moments, he'd be able to compare for himself when she introduced him to Vanessa.

'They're lovely. Thank you, Nate.'

Breathy and overwhelmed, she trembled at the touch of his fingers as he fitted the necklace and caressed her arms. His soft kiss on her bare shoulder increased her longing to close the door and stay here. Alone with him.

'Ready?'

She'd never be ready to walk into a roomful of elite society couples—especially tonight on Nate's arm. His height, sculpted build and striking features, along with the comfortable ease with which he wore his black suit and bow tie, were going to draw the eyes of any available woman. And many who weren't.

The reception area was ablaze with lights, reflecting the colours and sparking jewellery of the people queuing up to be greeted on their way in to the dining room. Jemma wished she could guide Nate to *any* line bar the one where her sister and brother-in-law held court. But better to get the introductions over now, when there was no time to stop and chat.

'This way. I have to say hello to Vanessa and Anthony.'

He looked ahead, stared for what seemed like an eon, then faced her with a stunned expression.

'You and she are *sisters*?'

Even though she'd believed herself ready for any comparison, she felt her world shatter. Over the years she'd become accustomed to similar remarks, but coming from him it cut deep. It took every ounce of fortitude she had not to flee the building, and to feign a smile and nod before taking a step nearer to the pain of introduction.

Jemma could never tell if Vanessa's greetings were genuine or part of her social persona. She smiled, returned her sister's hug and air-kiss, then clenched her stomach as she turned towards Nate.

'My friend Nate Thornton. Nate—my sister, Vanessa, and her husband, Anthony Bradshaw.'

She saw Vanessa's green eyes widen, and couldn't bear to see Nate's smile focussed on her, so moved quickly to greet Anthony. He was nice enough in his own way, but she believed both of them cared more about their social standing than the people they associated with in order to get there.

As the men shook hands the announcement for everyone to take their places at the dinner tables was made. Theirs was to the side and one row back, and the other eight guests were already seated. After an exchange of names Nate held her chair as she sat, brushing his fingertips down her arm before taking his place.

She smiled, joined in the conversation and ate the food placed in front of her, all the while wishing she'd never agreed to him coming, wishing she wasn't here. And vowing never, *ever* to come again.

Throughout the meal and the inevitable speeches Nate found reasons to touch her arm, nudge her knee with his or murmur compliments in her ear. An ideal date—if he hadn't also kept glancing with a puzzled frown towards Vanessa at the main table. That she understood. It was his tender attention to *her* that was puzzling. Unless he was maintaining a façade.

Tables emptied as the band began to play, and she half hoped, half dreaded his asking her to dance. He didn't—just took her hand and drew her to her feet, his eyes saying he'd brook no refusal.

Ignoring convention, he held their clasped hands on his chest over his heart, and brushed her forehead with his lips. Overwhelmed by his innate strength and power, she breathed in musky vanilla and Nate and let the world fade away until there was only them and the music.

If anything, Nate's exasperation had grown during the evening. He felt her tension dissipate as they danced, and berated himself for never making the time to dance before, but then relaxed and savoured the sheer joy of the way they fitted together and moved in harmony. He'd never been so in tune with anyone, and his avowed defences for protecting his heart were crumbling, leaving him exposed and vulnerable. And unable to regret it.

She took him to meet her parents and he liked them—though it was obvious within a few minutes that their world revolved around cooking and their restaurant.

Jemma had told him she always left as early as possible, so he was quite willing to go when she asked. The shadows round her eyes revealed her fatigue to him, though she'd sparkled for everyone else.

She left space between them on the way to their suite, and neither spoke, but as soon as he closed the door she turned to him, her features guarded.

'I'm very tired, Nate, and I'd like to sleep alone tonight.'

He reeled back as if he'd been punched in the stomach.

'Why? That's no reason to shun me, Jemma. You know I'd never ask for anything you're not willing to give.'

Her eyes flashed with anger, and if his own temper hadn't been rising he'd have found it stimulating. She'd never shown this spirited side—not even when he'd baited her in Brian's office.

'No, you were brutally honest, and I was never in doubt over the terms of our relationship. Your page-turning text and my emotional scenes complement each other. We've each gained what we wanted, and I don't regret a moment.'

'That's a damn lousy explanation, Jemma.'

He moved towards her and she backed away, breathing

hard and fast. He stopped, hands clenching and splaying at his sides. What the hell had he done? What the hell had changed?

'It's all I can give. You wanted no commitment, no ties. That's what you've got.'

She spun round and, before he could react, was in the bedroom with the door shut.

Pride stopped him from trying the handle and calling her name. Glaring at that barricade and raking his fingers through his hair didn't give him any explanation. Neither did taking a cold shower and going over every action of the day.

Nothing eased the pain of her rejection, and there was no one he could call to talk it out. He could only pray he'd be able to fix it in the morning.

Jemma changed and packed by the light on the bedside table, chiding herself for allowing herself to be so vulnerable and praising her strength in standing firm. Better the pain of a break-up now than the agonising anticipation of its coming.

He'd warned her, and she'd accepted the risk. No promises of for ever. No lies. No regrets. The defences she'd built to protect her heart had been successful until now because she'd never truly loved her ex, nor more than *liked* the other men she'd dated. But Nate had slipped past her barriers and she'd foolishly dared to dream of storybook endings.

Even if what he felt was only masculine admiration for her sister's beauty, she didn't want to live with the comparison. She was what she was, and would no longer settle for being an also-ran. He'd move on, and he still had this Tess to talk to. Whatever that relationship entailed. She didn't know because he'd never explained their connection.

She would... Hell, she had no idea *what* she'd do.

In the early hours of the morning she crept from the

suite, booked out and took a taxi to the airport. By late
morning she was home, picking up Milly from her neigh-
bour and ignoring her message bank.

She imagined Nate's brow furrowing, and his storm-
grey eyes darkening. Knew he'd be pacing as he waited for
her to answer. Knew it wasn't right to leave him dangling.

She sent a text.

Believe me, Nate. It's better this way. We can communicate through Brian on any writing issues.

Cradling Milly for support, she lay on her couch and
bit into the soft flesh at the base of her thumb to prevent
herself crying.

It didn't work. She sobbed until there were no more tears
to shed. Then, after taking a deep lung-filling breath, she
pushed herself to her feet, huffed it out and went to splash
her face with cold water.

Life didn't stop just because you'd been a fool.

Two afternoons later she wasn't so sure. Unsuccessful attempts to paint or write had left her restless, and
long meandering walks no longer soothed her soul. She
missed Nate—his gentle touches, his sombre expression
that morphed into a heart-stopping smile in an instant.
His ardent loving that took them to a world only they
could share.

Oh, how she ached to see that smile focussed on her just
once more. No, not once—a hundred thousand times more.
When she woke in the morning, over the breakfast table,
in the evening watching the sunset and in all the special
moments in between. And most of all as he cradled her to
sleep at night, watching her with tender storm-grey eyes.

It seemed like a lifetime since she'd last heard his
unique husky voice—except in her head as she relived

their conversations and the sexy teasing words he'd whispered in her ear as they lay in bed.

She'd begun to trust his word, and had sometimes thought, *Maybe this time...* It was the unspoken—those moments of silent contemplation and the times when his eyes had shuttered over a world he kept hidden—that had held her back. And the female voice of Tess and her sister's lovely face clouded her mind when she tried to think.

Her paintbrushes were dry, her keyboard silent and her inspiration absent and unattainable. Without closure she couldn't continue the revisions in her novel, couldn't move forward.

Catching up her phone, she walked outside and sat on the swing, scrolled through her contacts and pressed his name, then stared at the number she'd unknowingly memorised.

He hadn't called since she'd sent her text. Would he talk to her now? He'd wanted to talk on Saturday night, but she'd felt too raw and insecure, too unsure of his motives.

Oh, Nate, why did you hide what you went through from me? Why ask for my trust yet not give me yours? Why can't I tell if you love me?

She sucked in a deep breath, remembering her declaration about recognising love when she saw it. Had she subconsciously been so determined to avoid being hurt again that she hadn't recognised the pain in his eyes? Was he trapped in his past too?

A crazy idea, worthy of her most feisty heroine, shot into her head. Before she lost her nerve she went inside and booted up her computer, crossing her fingers for one piece of luck.

Hours later she slipped into bed, calmer and more optimistic than she'd ever been.

A lifetime of being non-confrontational, of quietly conforming while Vanessa bathed in the limelight and of accepting her ex's excuses and lies without question was over.

Tomorrow—against all the odds—she'd fight for a happy future. If it wasn't to be with Nate, at least she'd know she was strong enough to make it alone.

Nate was up before dawn, prowling from room to room, gut churning, fingers tapping on his thigh, for once oblivious to the scenic views. The plans he'd drawn and amended, the research into furniture and colours incorporating ideas from his global travels and the time and effort he'd put in all withered into insignificance.

His house, *his* home, had been built to suit a perceived lifestyle that no longer applied. Every room reminded him of Jemma. Every intake of air recalled her unique aroma, though it was no longer there. Every sound had him looking round in expectation of her presence. She was in his head…and in his heart.

He wanted her with him, here or anywhere in the world, every day for the rest of their lives. Running until his muscles burned hadn't helped tire him. Lying awake, yearning to feel her soft steady breathing against his chest, had left him antsy and short-tempered.

He'd been an idiot—so focussed on never being fooled again he hadn't seen the sweetest prize of all waiting in front of him. How could he have so totally misread the most important relationship of his life?

He stopped short at the sight of Milly's bed in the lounge area. Hell, he even missed that little fur ball. He'd bet she missed him too—she'd always loved him scratching behind her ears, or tickling her as she rolled onto her back. And Jemma? Did *she* miss his caresses, his kisses? Their making love?

It couldn't end like this.

Letting loose with a fervent curse, he stormed into his bedroom, accessing flight times on his mobile as he went. No suave persuasion or coercion this time. Like the hero he'd created, he'd fight for the woman he loved. Or at the least learn the reasons why.

As he packed he pictured her eyes. Big, blue and sparkling with exhilaration as she'd stood on the top of the Harbour Bridge. Soft and misty after they'd made love. And that was the image he clung to as he drove towards Sydney, towards the plane that would take him to her.

With time to spare at the airport he sat in the departure lounge and hooked one ankle over the other knee, forming a place to balance the clipboard and the sheet of paper he'd brought with him. With Jemma's image as inspiration he wrote from his heart, holding nothing back.

Reality hit home as he watched a woman trembling with anticipation as she scanned the passengers arriving in the lounge opposite, and then heard her cry of joy as she raced into a passionate embrace. Jemma hadn't been happy at his unannounced initial arrival in Hahndorf, and he had less reason to expect a welcome now.

Would she even be there?

His body taut as a drum, he walked while he accessed her number, holding his breath and willing her to answer. He almost buckled at the knees when she did. Tuning out the somehow familiar noise in the background, he heard only the sound he longed for.

'Nate?'

'Jemma, please. I need to see you. Are you at home?'

She didn't reply. His heart sank, but then picked up a little. At least she'd answered after seeing his ID.

'Jemma, please.'

A soft sound like a sigh came over the line, tripping his heart, then a hesitant voice. 'I'm on the Katoomba train.'

CHAPTER SEVENTEEN

'WHAT?'

The familiar noise. The train.

Nate's mind boggled at the irony of their timing.

'You're coming to me? Hell, Jemma. Of all the crazy... No, not you, darling. *I'm* the one who's been a fool.'

'I've been trying to decide when to call you, or whether to take a taxi and simply turn up.'

Just as he had. He was stunned by her actions after she'd broken all contact with him. Adrenaline spiked, followed by a cold chill of the knowledge that he might have lost her for ever. It was soon replaced by the primitive male urge to fight for his mate against any odds.

'Oh, Jemma, my angel. If I'd known I'd be waiting at the station now. As it is we have a slight problem.'

'You're not at home?'

She sounded disappointed and his hopes soared.

'That's what we get for not communicating, sweetheart. I'm waiting for my flight to Adelaide.'

'Oh.'

Picturing her sweet soft lips forming an O, and her lovely blue eyes widening in surprise, he ached to comfort her.

Jemma stared at the mountain scenery rushing by, seeing only Nate's magical smile, shaking with the intensity of the elation flooding her. The last skerrick of doubt that she loved him had dissipated. But whether they'd stay together depended on an honest, nothing-held-back discussion.

He was on his way to Hahndorf, expecting to surprise her as he had before. And a man who called her either 'darling,' 'my angel' or 'sweetheart,' in almost every sentence, even while agitated and under pressure, *had* to care. Could she dare to believe he loved her?

She let her head fall back onto the seat. Her heart was racing, she was smiling and her head was spinning in the nicest possible way.

'How far out are you, Jemma?'

'About an hour.'

'Okay, I'm heading for the check-in counter to ask them to unload my luggage. I'll call you in a few minutes. Don't go anywhere.'

'Hardly an option on a moving train. Except to Katoomba.'

'Except to there. Wait for me, darling.' He hung up.

Jemma ended the call with trembling fingers. So much for being calm and cool when they met. She'd become emotional even at the sound of his deep voice with that sexy hint of abrasion. Add his unique Nate aroma and enigmatic aura and she'd crumble at his feet.

'Well, Milly, still think this is a good idea?' She tickled the kitten's ears through the wires of the pet carrier she'd brought as extra baggage, and was rewarded with a contented purr. 'Of course, you do. He's putty in your paws. Maybe if *I* curled up on his lap and licked his fingers, huh?'

Delightful tingles shimmered up and down her spine as she remembered the last time they'd made love in Melbourne, before the gala function. Nate had made her feel she was beautiful, special, the only woman in his world. Then he'd seen Vanessa, and hadn't been able to hide his surprise that they were related or keep from looking at her, and Jemma's lifelong insecurities had crushed her euphoria.

'Good or bad, we're gonna sort this out,' she told the cat. 'Then you and I will either stay, or take another plane ride home.'

She was ready to answer his call before the first ring-tone finished.

'That was quick, darling. They're getting my case off the plane and I'll be on the road as soon as I've picked up the SUV from the apartment. Grant or one of his staff will meet you and take you to the hotel to wait for me. I'm a damn fool, Jemma. If I'd rung last night or this morning we'd be together now.'

'I'm guilty too.'

His light laugh tingled in her ear, heightening her pulse even more. 'We'll share the blame.'

In the pause that followed she heard a guttural sound, as if his throat had blocked.

'I've missed you, Jemma. I want to hold you, talk to you face to face, and convince you I've never lied to you and I never will.'

She couldn't hold back. That was why she was on this journey.

'Evasion *is* a form of lying, Nate, and you kept things from me.'

'Not long ago I'd have disputed that, Jemma. Now—'

He went silent as a male voice called out his surname. A moment later he was back.

'I've got my case and I'm on my way. I… No, that'll wait. I'll see you soon.'

'Soon' was over two hours away. She really hadn't thought this through, had she? Had *he*? If they were both riding on instinct—well, surely that was a truer gauge than the emotional baggage she'd let rule her life for years?

Nate went straight to his SUV on arriving at the apartment building, feeling rejuvenated and alert. This was the most important journey he'd ever take. Jemma was waiting for him, and all he had to do was release the past and embrace a life he'd denied wanting for too long.

Leaving his bags in the vehicle, he raced through the back door to the hotel's reception desk and prayed the couple there, booking in, were impatient to get to their room. It was hard to curb his impatience as they asked numerous questions.

'Nate, you made good time.'

He spun round to accept Grant's extended hand. 'I was lucky with the traffic. Thanks for looking after Jemma.'

'My pleasure. Jemma's in one of the rooms, resting, and the kitten's in my office.'

Nate froze. 'She brought Milly with her?' His elation peaked even higher than when she'd told him she was on the train. She'd come intending to stay a while.

'Friendly little thing. Can't have pets in the rooms, so...' He glanced over Nate's shoulder. 'Amend my previous statement.'

Nate swung round. His peripheral vision blurred, surrounding noise became muffled and his world narrowed to the elevator foyer. Jemma, adorable and enchanting, stood there, regarding him with the same tentative expression she'd worn the first time he'd seen her. And she was wearing the same blue patterned top and black tights.

His hopes clicked a notch higher.

Heart pounding, he moved with purposeful strides towards her, eyes locked with hers, mind racing to find the right words of greeting. She stepped into his open arms and he hugged her to his chest, then lifted his hand to caress her cheek.

'You brought Milly.'

Before he had time to berate himself for the inane greeting she sucked the air out of his lungs with a radiant smile that sent his head spinning. He kissed her as she deserved, with tenderness and reverence. Both of which threatened to morph into red-hot passion when her lips moved under his.

He pulled away, fighting for control, and saw the same battle in her eyes. Heard the same fight for breath and loved her even more.

* * *

The strong, rapid beat of Nate's heart pulsed under Jemma's palms, and the heat from his body matched her own, telling her she was where she belonged. Brilliant storm-grey eyes held hers captive, begging to steal her soul, and she willingly surrendered.

A deep chuckle from behind Nate sent him spinning, with her clasped in his embrace. Grant stood a few feet away, a broad grin on his face.

'You haven't forgotten you have a room upstairs?'

Heat flooded her cheeks, and a quick glance sideways showed Nate was blushing too. A scan of the area proved they were the only three around, and Nate recovered more quickly than she, or maybe covered it better.

'I guess we have.' He gazed down at her with something akin to awe in his eyes. 'Do you want to stay here for dinner?'

Her answer was forming before he'd finished asking.

'Take me home.'

'You only ever had to ask, darling. Let's get your luggage.'

He linked his fingers with hers and addressed his friend.

'We'll pick up Milly when we come down, Grant.'

'I'll be at the desk or in my office.' He was still smiling in the nicest I'm-happy-for-you way.

They rode the lift in silence, as if knowing a word or a glance might trigger the heat rush that simmered close to the surface. Her backpack and suitcase were ready inside the door, and her handbag lay on the barely disturbed bed where she'd lain, unsuccessfully trying to rest.

Nate's eyes flared as he studied the dent in the pillow, then he looked out of the window to the car park below.

'I was watching the cars come and go, and saw you arrive,' Jemma said.

'Ah, that explains your timely appearance downstairs,'

he said, grimacing at the bed as he reached for her luggage. 'And if we don't get out of here…'

His expression filled in the unsaid words. And they echoed in her heart.

They found Grant in his office, teasing Milly with a scrunched-up piece of paper. He put her into her carrier and took it to their vehicle.

'Thanks for your help and hospitality, Grant.' Jemma held out her hand but he ignored it, drawing her into a hug.

'Any time, Jemma. You two are always welcome.'

She wasn't sure what he said to Nate as the two men shook hands, but both were smiling as Grant stepped away and waved them off.

'He's a good friend.'

He nodded, giving her a quick smile. 'Yeah, one of the best.'

Now they were enclosed in a small space, his aura heightening all her senses, the need to sort out their issues was rapidly being overwhelmed by the desire to touch him and reassure herself this wasn't a dream.

She sat on her hands to prevent herself giving in to the impulse, allowing him to focus on his driving. Anything she asked might lead to a prolonged answer and, as he'd said on the phone, face to face was better.

When he pulled up to turn onto the track leading to his home she glanced across and met contemplative grey eyes. How often, especially in the early days of their relationship, had she seen that unfathomable scrutiny? Then he gave his special smile, and in the instant before he faced the wind-screen again she saw such an open look of adoration that she doubted her own sight.

Her head spun, heat engulfed her from head to feet and coherent thought vanished. She sat in a daze until he pulled up beside the house, leapt out and strode round to open her door.

'Jemma?'

Refocussing, she swung her legs out of the car. A second later she was lifted into the air, crushed against his muscled chest and kissed with a thoroughness that melted her bones. A much better use of his lips than forming words. She wrapped her arms around his neck and kissed him back with heartfelt longing.

'Welcome home, darling.' His eyes sparked and he jiggled her body against his. 'This time you'll stay until we resolve our problems—perceived or real.'

He nuzzled her neck, sending her hormones crazy.

She wriggled, and he growled against her skin, evoking a whimper of pleasure. Closely followed by a protest from Milly on the back seat.

'I think she recognises your home and wants out.'

Nate set her on her feet with slow reluctance.

'An impatient chaperone might be what we need. You bring your handbag and Milly. I'll get the rest.

Jemma released Milly from the carrier, and watched her totter straight for her two bowls. She had no problems adjusting to another move as long as she was fed and cared for.

For Jemma, life wasn't that basic. She'd lived with her ingrained insecurities for so long she accepted them as a natural part of her being. Now it was time to voice them out loud and deal with them.

By the time Nate had completed his second trip Jemma had pulled back the drapes, unlocked the glass door, and had coffee ready for him and a glass of iced water for herself.

Nate felt as if he was walking on mountain scree, not sure if the ground would slide away beneath his feet. He'd spent the drive home forcing himself to face the road for safety. Her feet had been in his peripheral vision, and her perfume had filled his lungs every time he breathed, and his own contentment had proved Jemma *was* there beside him.

Lifting her into his arms had been the natural act of a man taking care of his woman, and nothing else came near the feeling of rapture when she'd returned his kiss. But he hadn't dared pre-empt the future, and had left her luggage in the bedroom she'd had before.

Seeing her in his kitchen, and Milly crouched over her bowl, his world began to come together. To move forward he now had to make changes, open up to the people he cared for and no longer compartmentalise aspects of his life.

Anything that involved Jemma becoming a permanent fixture had priority. Since bringing her here every morning had begun with exhilarating expectation, and he didn't want—couldn't bear—to go back to being the loner he'd been.

As if sensing his presence, she turned, and her lovely face revealed her apprehension—along with her determination to see this through. He walked across to her, profoundly grateful for her bravery, enclosed her hands in his and relished the fulfilment the simple act gave him.

'I've missed you, Jemma, more than words can ever express.' He drew her into his arms, needing her warmth. 'It's not my first wish, but we do have to talk. Clear the air. And then…'

His pulse stuttered, then hammered under his skin as she studied his face. Oh, how he'd missed the way she seemed to read his soul. And yet, like a fool, he'd held back from sharing his true self, and the events that had made him who he was.

Never again.

'On the veranda.'

Her reply was low and husky. Unsure, yet resolute. He whooshed out the breath he'd been holding.

'I'll grab a couple of chairs—you bring the drinks.'

This was no time for recliners, so he took two of the dining chairs out to the corner protected by an extension of the inside wall, leaving the smallest space he deemed appropriate between them.

Was there a right place to start? Would Jemma consider professional or personal omissions worse?

He raised his mug to drink, trying to decide.

'What do you feel for my sister?'

He spluttered as hot liquid scalded his tongue, and stared at her for a moment before comprehending that the trepidation in her eyes was real. Her knuckles were white from her tight grip on her glass.

'What the hell kind of question is *that*?'

He dropped his mug onto the decking with a clunk, oblivious to the splattering, and leant forward. His gut tightened when her body backed away, then eased as she raised her chin in defiance. His admiration grew as tenacity replaced anxiety in her endearing features.

'I'm not stupid or blind. I saw the way you looked at her, and I understood exactly what you meant by your remark.'

'That's more than *I* do right now. All I said—'

'You *asked* as if it were unbelievable that we were related. Then you kept looking at her. I've always known I can't compete with her looks, but I thought I finally had my envy under control. I guess I'm not immune where you're concerned.'

'Oh, Jemma.'

He sank back, fisting his fingers, not daring to touch her—not while she harboured that crazy notion in her head. But her unintentional confession spurred him on.

'Of *course* I compared the two of you. Vanessa is the perfect example of a genetically attractive woman, pampered with every beauty product and procedure on the market, and showered with expensive clothes and jewels.'

Her body stiffened, her throat convulsed and her eyes

squeezed shut—then opened slowly as if by compulsion. Every movement strengthened his growing belief that she cared for him...cared enough to be jealous of her stereotypical sister.

'Take a photo of her and pin it on a board with a dozen or so other women and you'd be hard pressed to separate them. Yes, I *was* amazed that you're sisters. She'll hate growing older, fight it all the way, and it will show. *You*, my darling, are innately beautiful, and with your love of life and gentle spirit you will be as naturally lovely when you are ninety as you are now. And I'd like to be there to say, I told you so.'

She might not quite believe him now, but he intended to devote his life to convincing her. In Hahndorf, here or anywhere she wanted to be.

'You know there were other women in my life before we met. But there was never one I invited to my home— never one whose presence I wanted to feel or remember there—until you.'

Jemma scrutinised his face. Love, warm and encompassing, had turned storm-grey eyes into molten silver and all traces of reticence were gone—confirmation that she wasn't competing with Vanessa or any other woman. The depth of his unconcealed emotion shook her, had her gasping for breath.

'You're cold.' The words were rasped out. Protective. Caring.

'No. I've hidden behind an imaginary veil for too long. Maybe if there'd been fewer years between Vanessa and I we'd have been closer, more understanding of each other. But by the time I started school she'd already set her sights on a modelling career and was actively pursuing ways to achieve it. There's never been a middle ground for us.'

With a masculine grunt he dragged his chair across the

gap, took her drink and set it down with his, then wrapped his hands around hers.

'It's not too late to find one. Now, will you *please* tell me about the idiot who broke your heart so we can both wipe him from our minds?'

CHAPTER EIGHTEEN

JEMMA COULDN'T HELP laughing at his description of the self-centred man she'd believed she might marry. But she became serious as she remembered how near it had come to being fact.

'We dated for six months. He was handsome, charming and attentive, and said he loved me. He worked in an insurance office, was determined to climb the corporate ladder to high status and an impressive salary. Working extra hours impressed his superiors, and the extra pay was supposed to go towards the upmarket house he wanted.'

As she spoke Nate's expression grew darker, triggering a flush of happiness in her at his obvious jealousy. Though tempted to prolong it, she couldn't. She loved him too much to let him suffer.

'Or so he said. In fact, a lot of his late nights and special meetings were with a senior female colleague who'd promised to help fast-track promotion for him. I found out not long after he cancelled our dinner at Windy Point to be with her. Any feeling I had for him evaporated, and my trust was shattered.'

'Not just an idiot—one with bad taste too. But I commend his faults because they kept you free for me.'

'When I first met you, I saw the same type of good-looking, polite and—to me—arrogant man. The type I deliberately avoided. I allowed you and Brian to coerce me into that writing deal for the chance to be published. When I agreed to come here I had no reason to doubt my ability to resist your charm. In fact I never had a chance.'

He raised his hand to caress her cheek and she almost

melted into his palm. The memory of those phone calls held her firm.

'Tell me about Tess. She has a very distinctive voice.'

She hadn't meant to blurt it out, but now it couldn't be recalled. She bit her lip as his eyes widened and his brows arched. A twinge of guilt spiralled in her stomach at her act of shifting the confession obligation back to him, and then waned as she recalled that they'd both promised frank and open admissions.

Only when every skerrick of doubt for both of them had been voiced and banished for ever could they face a lifetime together.

'Tess…'

He seemed to be mulling over the words to explain, his Adam's apple bobbing, his eyes open and clear.

His chest rose and fell, twice. 'You can't have missed seeing the scars on my hip, yet you didn't mention them. I don't know how I would have responded if you had.'

He seemed to focus on the window behind her, but she knew he was in another time and place, reliving some horror.

His voice deepened with anguish as he continued. 'I was travelling with an army unit into disputed territory when we drove over a landmine and were then targeted by insurgents on a hill. The vehicle flipped, trapping me and two of the men. One of them was killed instantly. I…I watched the other die. I'd seen death before, but never that close. Never heard the awful sounds. Tess protected me as she and the others returned fire. She was shot twice before relief came and we were airlifted out. It's a debt of honour I can never repay.'

The last few sentences were rushed, as if he wanted them out and finished. Jemma covered his hand on her face with hers, wanting, needing to comfort him.

'She's a member of your support group?' She spoke in a hushed voice, with awe and respect for the woman she'd been jealous of for no reason. Jealousy that had blinded her to the obvious connection.

'They invited me to be a member before I came home. Any member can call any other, at any time, and he or she will be there, no questions asked. I still have bad dreams of incidents I can't forget, and still feel the helplessness of knowing there's nothing you can do to stop the carnage.'

'Except let the world know the truth.'

Nate huffed and tightened his fingers round hers on his knee, grateful for her understanding.

'Tess buried everything and tried to handle it alone. It's only in the last couple of years she's admitted to needing help. I'll never not take her call, nor refuse to go to her if talking on the phone isn't enough.'

'I'll never ask you to. She has my lifelong gratitude too.'

She squeezed his fingers, as if encouraging him to trust her. He gave a wry smile, lifted their joined hands and pressed his lips to her skin.

Staring across the valley, seeing visions he was glad she couldn't, he continued. 'I believed that keeping family and work, my overseas experiences and the group, and my writing as three separate aspects of my life would make them easier to manage. My obstinacy almost cost me the most precious jewel a man could have.'

He pulled her to her feet, then settled her onto his lap, cradling her tight, no longer ashamed to admit he needed the close contact. In the days, maybe weeks to come, he'd tell her more. Not now, and probably never everything of what he'd experienced. Instead he'd talk about the courage and fortitude of the other victims, and the compassion of those willing to risk their lives to help.

He cradled her head on his shoulder. One more admission and then he could move on to the good stuff, persuading Jemma to be his for ever.

'My last confession concerns the woman I told you about. Luckily for me I followed my grandfather's advice to never take anyone at face value, to always check. She already had a husband, and was counting on a pay-out to keep quiet about a bigamous marriage. Closing down emotion and treating women as colleagues only was my way of ensuring I didn't get duped again.'

Aware of her body stiffening and pulling away, he looked down, and his chest tightened at the sight of her now not-so-tender astonished expression.

'You *researched* me.'

It was stated with true indignation, and he longed to kiss her until her piqued expression became one of desire.

Delaying the inevitable for a moment, he answered honestly. 'I typed in your name, then deleted it. I didn't know why at the time. I just decided I wanted anything I learned about you to come from you or from being with you. It was one of my better decisions.'

Encouraged by the softening in her enticing blue eyes, he kissed her with the reverence she deserved, holding back the passion surging through his body. This was a time for making sure they were in tune and all suspicions allayed.

She couldn't be thinking the same, because she pressed closer, the tip of her tongue teasing his lips.

He pulled away, laughing down at her. 'Temptress. No more questions or fears, my darling.'

'No.'

Her eyes outshone the brightest stars he'd ever seen in the clear skies over the mountains, and it took all his willpower to resist kissing her again.

He stood and pulled her to her feet, and led her inside. 'Did you bring something special to wear?'

Jemma frowned, tilting her head as she stared at Nate, bewildered by his attitude. Why wasn't he carrying her to bed?

She wanted to be taking clothes *off*, not putting others on. And it was way too early to be going out to dinner.

'I have the dresses I wore to Windy Point and in Melbourne.'

'Go put on the silvery one and meet me here.'

He walked her over to the stairs and picked up a folded sheet of paper from the third step. Placing it into her hand, he brushed his lips over hers.

'This is for you. Take all the time you want. I'll be waiting.'

Her legs shook and her heart fluttered as she obeyed, her fingers holding the single sheet as if it were her lifeline. The door to the room she'd originally occupied was open, and her case was by the bed.

Should she read what he'd written now? She looked down at the outfit she wore, chosen because of their first meeting, then thought of the desire that had flared in his eyes on seeing her in the silver gown, and laid his letter on the bed.

After the quickest shower she'd ever had, she sprayed herself with perfume, brushed her hair to lie smooth down her back and slipped the dress over her head.

Curling into the comfy chair by the window, she began to read.

Nate waited in the lounge, wearing a royal blue shirt and black trousers, wishing he had a flower shop full of roses to give to Jemma. Instead he'd offered his heart, and a lifetime of love.

He'd closed his eyes for a brief moment, picturing her beautiful smile and sparkling eyes, and then had let his love flow from his heart through his hand onto the paper. Every expression came with a wish that she felt the same…every phrase held his desire to cherish her for ever.

He glanced at the ceiling, trying to imagine where she

was and how she was feeling. Did she understand that he'd
wanted her to change in order to make this special moment
even more memorable?

With a wry smile, he realised that he wasn't pacing as
he normally did when waiting. He had no right to be this
calm and confident, and yet his heart was as certain of her
love as he was of tonight's sunset.

A gentle swish of movement and she came into view,
taking his breath away and sending his pulse skyward.
Shimmers of colour framed a goddess, here within his
reach. An engaging mixture of gentle femininity, loveli-
ness and charm. An angel with an endearing sense of fun.

He waited for her to come to him, then took her hand
and led her onto the veranda. The sun was beginning to
sink towards the mountains across the valley—an ideal pic-
turesque backdrop. Turning to face her, he drew her close,
basking in the surge of macho power initiated by having
her in his arms.

Eyes sparkling, she gave him the most stunning smile
he'd ever seen. As he bent to cover her sweet lips with his
she stopped him with a fingertip touch.

'Thank you for the most beautiful and romantic prose
I've ever read, Nate. You make me feel precious and loved,
as if there's only you and I in our own paradise, and I'll
treasure every word for as long as I live. I love you—now
and for ever.'

If a heart could burst from a chest with happiness, his
would do it now. He tightened his hold, fitting her body to
his, rejoicing as she wriggled with pleasure.

'I love you, Jemma. My precious, adorable angel. My
own.'

He loved her.

Jemma had known the moment their eyes had met in
the hotel lobby. Had sensed it before, but been too timid to

accept it. Hearing him express his feelings in his unique abrasive voice released her from the bonds that had imprisoned her for so long.

She stretched up on her toes to kiss him, and he answered with a passion that made her quiver with ecstasy. He caressed in gentle strokes across her back and she responded, running her fingers up his neck, tangling them into his hair.

He trailed a path of kisses across her neck, nibbled her neck as she sighed with contentment, then kissed his way back, stopping with his lips a breath away from hers.

'I love you with all my heart, Jemma Harrison, and more than life. Will you marry me, help me to write romantic scenes, and to create babies as cute and courageous as their beautiful brave mother?'

'Yes, Nate Thornton. I'll marry you, have your babies *and* create novels with you. You are my love, my life, my hero.'

He kissed her for as long as their breath allowed, then swung her into his arms and carried her to his monster of a bed.

Later they celebrated with champagne, their arms around each other as they watched the sunset and planned their future. Here in the mountains, in Sydney and Hahndorf—anywhere life took them. With Milly, their babies and any other pets who joined them. A family together.

* * * * *

JOIN THE MILLS & BOON BOOKCLUB

* **FREE** delivery direct to your door

* **EXCLUSIVE** offers every month

* **EXCITING** rewards programme

50% OFF
YOUR FIRST
PARCEL

Join today at
Millsandboon.co.uk/Bookclub

MILLS & BOON

THE HEART OF ROMANCE

A ROMANCE FOR EVERY READER

MODERN
Prepare to be swept off your feet by sophisticated, sexy and seductive heroes, in some of the world's most glamourous and romantic locations, where power and passion collide.

ISTORICAL
Escape with historical heroes from time gone by. Whether your passion is for wicked Regency Rakes, muscled Vikings or rugged Highlanders, awaken the romance of the past.

MEDICAL
Set your pulse racing with dedicated, delectable doctors in the high-pressure world of medicine, where emotions run high and passion, comfort and love are the best medicine.

True Love
Celebrate true love with tender stories of heartfelt romance, from the rush of falling in love to the joy a new baby can bring, and a focus on the emotional heart of a relationship.

Desire
Indulge in secrets and scandal, intense drama and plenty of sizzling hot action with powerful and passionate heroes who have it all: wealth, status, good looks…everything but the right woman.

HEROES
Experience all the excitement of a gripping thriller, with an intense romance at its heart. Resourceful, true-to-life women and strong, fearless men face danger and desire - a killer combination!

To see which titles are coming soon, please visit

millsandboon.co.uk/nextmonth

JOIN US ON SOCIAL MEDIA!

Stay up to date with our latest releases, author news and gossip, special offers and discounts, and all the behind-the-scenes action from Mills & Boon...

 millsandboon

 millsandboonuk

 millsandboon

It might just be true love...

MILLS & BOON

MODERN

Power and Passion

Prepare to be swept off your feet by sophisticated, sexy and seductive heroes, in some of the world's most glamourous and romantic locations, where power and passion collide.

Eight Modern stories published every month, find them all at

millsandboon.co.uk/Modern

MILLS & BOON

Desire

Indulge in secrets and scandal, intense drama and plenty of sizzling hot action with powerful and passionate heroes who have it all: wealth, status, good looks…everything but the right woman.

MILLS & BOON
MEDICAL
Pulse-Racing Passion

Set your pulse racing with dedicated, delectable doctors in the high-pressure world of medicine, where emotions run high and passion, comfort and love are the best medicine.